Mr. Wright Now

MR. WRIGHT NOW

HEROES OF HENDERSON: BOOK 7

Liz Kelly

Published by Kelly Girl Productions
©Copyright 2019 Liz Kelly
Cover design by Tammy Kearly

ISBN: 978-1-7338604-0-6

For more information on the author and her works, please see
www.LizKellyBooks.com

For the real
Brenda and Billy Jones.

If you ever open a bed and breakfast,
everyone will want to stay there.

Who's Who in Henderson

Should you like a review, here is a reference to the
primary characters you've met in previous books.

Xavier Wright

Bossiest and oldest of the five Wright brothers. After a long stint in Arizona, he moved back in with his parents to help care for his sick mother. He quickly fell in love with his **Tweets** and took no time putting a ring on it.

Laidey Bartholomew, a.k.a. Tweets

Originally from Dallas, Texas, and favorite employee of Crain Carraway (whom she had a mega-crush on.) She now works for CC Henderson and has fallen hard for her very bossy, but very sweet, fiancé Xavier Wright.

Xander Wright

Twin brother of Xavier, he works in Charlotte, NC, and comes home rarely. Lately, he's been dating **McKenna Blakely**, Xavier's ex and the "daughter his parents never had."

Anna Beth Wright

Mother of Xavier, Xander, and the rest of the Wright brothers. She's currently recovering from an autoimmune disease that nearly killed her.

McKenna Blakely

Journalist for the Henderson Daily, she dated Xavier back in high school. The entire Wright family fell in love with her, including Xavier's twin, Xander, with whom she's recently reconnected.

Davis Williams, a.k.a. Pinks or the Ninja

Originally from Baltimore and a childhood friend of **Missy McReady's**, Pinks is now heavily involved in Henderson's economic recovery plan and E&E Investments. He's also heavily involved with **Red**, a.k.a. **Scarlett Langford**.

Scarlett Langford, a.k.a. Red

A Henderson native, Scarlett is now home after recently graduating from Ole Miss. She's jumped into the spirit of Team Henderson by working on opening up a wine shop and a restaurant, and producing a record starring singing sensation and baseball phenom Cal Johnson.

Hale Evans

Successful equity investor and Henderson's local multi-millionaire. Twenty years ago, his first wife left him devastated. Now he's been married for over a year to Lolly DuVal's mother, **Genevra** (pronounced Jen-ev-ra.) They now have a son named Beau. Hale owns E&E Investments with his thirty-year-old son **Vance** and is patriarch of Team Henderson. His mother, **Emelina Flores**, a.k.a. **the Big Em** is originally from Spain and lives with them.

Vance Evans (Bad Cop)

Part owner of E&E Investments and high school baseball coach, he's also the mayoral campaign manager for his best friend, **Brooks Bennett.** He married **Piper Beaumont**—defense attorney in Raleigh and his fourth-grade savior—over a year ago. Their son, Vance, Jr, is the same age as his Uncle Beau.

Cal Johnson

Orioles' rookie pitching phenom, whom Coach Cooper saved from drowning after Boston Red Sox fans tossed him into the harbor. He showed up in Henderson to give a pitching demonstration for the Opening Day Spectacular and became a YouTube sensation by singing with the band at the party that night. He's currently dating Scarlett Langford's college roommate, **Natalie Houser**, daughter of MLB Hall of Famer, Nate the Great.

Harry the Bartender

Mysterious young country club bartender with an uncanny knack for knowing your drink and reading your mind. His tequila shots have a way of bringing couples together.

Brooks Bennett (Good Cop)

Henderson's Golden Boy. He's determined to bring economic prosperity back to town and stop the mass exodus of the younger generation. He's running for mayor and is madly in love with **Lolly DuVal**, who is a couture dress designer and has recently set up shop in Henderson.

Missy McReady

Imported from Baltimore by Davis Williams to be Henderson High's girls lacrosse coach as well as the town's Marketing and Event-Planning guru. She is now considered the CEO of Team Henderson and is heavily involved with **Thurgood Watson.**

Thurgood Lewis Watson III, a.k.a. Thor

Former Army Ranger back home in Henderson and owner of a large plantation passed to him upon his father's untimely death. He's got a lot of plans for his land, and one of them involves marrying Missy McReady in the gazebo he's building.

Marnie Mitchell

Ten-year-old neighbor of **Thor—Marnie's** being raised by her grandparents. She's befriended **Xavier Wright,** who has offered to teach her how to ride a minibike.

See a complete list of characters at www.LizKellyBooks.com

CHAPTER ONE

This was not the way Jaxon Wright had planned to return to Henderson.

Far from it.

Jax had a dream. A big one. A *fast* vision for his life pursuing a career that had rooted itself early and so deep in his soul that his focus had been narrow and his education precise. And his hard work, all of the dues paying, the networking, the endless hours, and the filthy, dirty, calloused hands had all been about to pay off. He had it within his grasp.

And yet, here he sat with his head in his hands.

Hungover.

In his mother's kitchen.

For the third day in a row.

"Bro." Xavier's deep voice accompanied a steaming mug of coffee sliding into view. Jaxon was grateful for that. Not long ago, his oldest brother would have been more likely to deliver a slap upside his head with a hearty, "Buck up and deal." But these past couple of mornings, Xavier had said little while serving up a good, hot breakfast.

"Thanks," he mumbled. "I'll get my act together. Promise." He sipped gingerly at the aromatic brew.

"No hurry. Seriously, man. I get it. Life sucks right now."

It so does, Jax thought, unable to utter the words.

The brothers remained silent as Xavier started to whip up yet another breakfast. Their mother had apparently already eaten, returning to bed to continue healing from an autoimmune disease that had spent the last eighteen months kicking her ass. The family was breathing a sigh of relief now that, after undergoing a bone marrow transplant, the matriarch of the family appeared to be on the mend. That was reason enough for Jax to stop feeling sorry for himself.

Shoulda, woulda, coulda—*can't*. Can't was the only word Jax related to. *As in, I can't freaking believe I had the world in the palm of my hand for two weeks and now,* "Nothing."

"Hmm?"

"Na. Nothin'. Don't mind me. I'm ... just, ya know ... surly."

That got a smile out of Xavier as he set a plate piled with scrambled eggs and some kind of Arizona spiced up hash browns in front of him. There were thick slices of bacon on there too, and for some crazy reason that was the thing that sparked a little life from the pleasure center of his brain.

"Dang. I love bacon," he said.

"Bacon's good. But for me, it's always been potatoes. Or biscuits," Xavier said, sliding into the seat across from Jax. "I'd have made biscuits, but I'm no good at the damn things. No patience for 'em."

"Can't beat Lulu's biscuits," Jax said with his mouth full. "Don't even try."

"You need sugar? Something sweet? I can run over to Oxford and get some Krispy Kremes. Mom loves 'em. Happy to do it."

Jax stopped chewing and looked up at his brother who was nursing a mug of coffee. "Why are you being so nice?" He felt his face get all squinched up as he said it, because *yeah*—this was not the Xavier he knew and loved.

"Ma's sick, I feed her. You're sick, I feed you."

Jax pointed to himself. "Only I'm not sick."

"Your spirit's sick."

"My what?"

"You know, your spirit. Your life force. That thing that makes you, you."

"Dude." Jax collapsed back in his chair. "It's a damn good thing you've come back to North Carolina. Arizona has turned you all New Age and shit."

Xavier laughed. "Maybe."

"I mean it. Spirit? Life force?"

"Losing that sponsorship like you did? Last minute. Out of the blue. Hell, don't you tell me your spirit hasn't taken a beating. It's good *you* came home. Give yourself a chance to breathe and regroup. Plus, it'll do Ma good, once you ease up on being Mr. Surly and get back to being Skirt-Chasing Jax."

"Skirt-chasing? That's bullshit," Jax sputtered, sitting up to eat again. "I have never been a skirt chaser."

"Well, you're good with women," Xavier said, leaning over the table toward him. "Always have been. I'm good with exactly one woman. *My* woman. Tweets."

"Laidey." Jax stabbed his fork toward his brother. "Mom has given me strict instructions to address our soon-to-be sister-in-law by her name."

"Fine. Okay. Anyway, I need you to do something for me. And I'm thinkin' it may end up doing you some good in the long run."

"What's that?"

"There are two women over on Team Henderson who've got this insane idea that creating a beefcake calendar is the answer to this town's problems." Xavier leaned further in. "And these two babes are a force to be reckoned with, I'll tell you what. They have somehow managed to get Cal Johnson, the baseball star, to agree to be on the cover, and none of the pussy-whipped men in this town has had the balls to say no to Know-It-All Missy and her crazy friend Red. Not Hale, not Vance, not Brooks, nobody. They are all posing for this calendar. And because they need one more stooge, they have twisted my arm so tight I've agreed to do it. But I'm not going to. No way in hell."

"So, what? You want me to bail you out? Strip off my shirt, oil up my chest, and show off my empty pockets? Yeah, that'll send women everywhere into a frenzy."

"You probably will have to be shirtless. But they'll wanna get a pose of you doing your thing. You know, working on an engine that can go over two hundred miles an hour."

"Well, that was my thing. Up until Can'tGiveAFuck.com decided to pull their sponsorship." He grabbed his head and moaned. "I still can't believe this has happened. Do you have any idea how long it took Spits and me to pull together the perfect race team? We had it," he declared. "This was the dream team. Tremendous untapped potential. I know it. But now—thanks to some corporate-bullshit board of directors—we've all been scattered to the wind. Every last one of us unemployed in the middle of the season."

"Right. So ya know, somebody good at Photoshop could put your team's name on any car you were photographed in front of."

"A lot of good that'll do me."

"Now hold on here," Xavier said gently. "This might lead to nothing. But these two crazy women have a mind for publicity. They have big ideas about getting this calendar out to the general public all over the country. They keep talking about creating buzz. Ultimately, the calendar promotes Henderson, but I don't see a reason why it couldn't promote you and your race team as well."

Jax ran his napkin over his mouth, feeling less hungover now that he had a full stomach. "They willing to do the shoot in Charlotte? Kip Moore owes me a favor. Probably let me use his car if we Photoshopped out all the logos and shit."

Xavier shook his head. "Gotta be shot in Henderson. That's the point. Promoting Henderson."

"Oh, well, I'm sure there are several NASCAR or Formula One cars sitting in Henderson."

"You ever hear of a One-77?"

Jax cracked his head toward one shoulder and then another, trying to place the name. "Don't believe so."

"Hottest damn machine I've ever seen. Definitely gonna give a gearhead like you a hard-on."

"Who owns this One-77?"

"Hale Evans. But this Red I was talking about dates a guy named Pinks who drives it. She'll work it out."

Jax lifted a brow. "There's a girl named *Red,* who dates a guy named *Pinks?* Here? In Henderson?"

"A lot of shit's happened since you've been gone. Go on and hit the shower. I'm gonna make a call and see if I can set this up." Xavier got up and started clearing the table.

"It's not like I've got any damn thing better to do," Jax grumbled as he took his leave. But his thumb was pulling up the internet on his phone and googling One-77. When a picture came up, his eyes popped wide. "Damn sight better than bacon," he acknowledged and headed toward the shower.

Later that morning, Xavier dropped Jaxon off at what appeared to be a full-fledged movie set. The old corner Gas&Go was temporarily closed for business, both driveways blocked off by orange cones. The place had been polished up and shined like a new penny. The asphalt had been cleaned, and there wasn't a speck of dirt or a piece of trash to be found. The sign was new and frankly a bit disconcerting. For a guy who was comfortable with grease and grime and who'd spent the majority of his teen years hanging out over there in that exact garage, the unfamiliar glossy outer casing of this old gas station made him twitchy.

His fingers were twitchy too, because his brother had not lied. The exotic sports car being showcased under the abundance of photographer's lights did give him a hard-on, and he was just panting to slip his fingers under her hood.

"Jaxon?" He looked up to find a guy by the car motioning him over.

The kid could be his age. He was probably a little younger, but he was dressed for success in a pink business shirt and linen slacks, even though it was like a hundred and ten degrees. Jax probably didn't appear all that smarter as he was wearing his work jeans and boots. Still, his T-shirt was short-sleeved, white with a V-neck.

"Davis Williams," the guy said as Jax took his outstretched hand. "Everybody calls me Pinks."

"Right. Pinks." Curious nickname, but what the hell did he care? "And I hear you've got a girl named Red."

"Ahh. I've got a girl whose name is *Scarlett*," Pinks corrected. "*I* call her Red. Everybody else calls her Scarlett. She's the redhead standing with the photographer." Pinks pointed. "This calendar is her baby. So, she'll have some input for your photo shoot. My recommendation? Keep your mouth shut and go with it."

Jax's gaze drifted over to the redhead in question before he snapped out of his relaxed stance and into an abrupt, upright position. "No fuckin' way are *you* dating Scarlett Langford."

Pinks chuckled. "Same thing I say every time I look in the mirror."

"Dude. She's hot. I mean, she was hot in high school, but now?" Jax blew out a whistle. "She's smokin'. How the hell did you land Scarlett Langford and those bodacious legs?"

Pinks threw a thumb behind him. "I was driving this at the time."

Jax let out a breath shaking his head, and folding his arms over his chest. "Yeah–boy. A car like that'll get 'r done. Nice work," Jax said cheerfully. "Ya know, she and I went out."

"Once."

Jax chuckled. "Still." He looked over this Davis Williams of Scarlett Langford fame. "Doesn't bother you to know that she and I swapped spit?"

Pinks leaned back against the car—against the pearlized white, looks-like-it's-going-a-hundred-miles-an-hour-even-standing-still exterior with a price tag even Jax couldn't begin to guess—and he was the picture of cool, calm confidence. "Nope. Doesn't bother me at all. Because even with your reputation, I know for damn certain you did not give Scarlett an orgasm."

That got his back up. "My reputation? Who the hell's been talking to you about my reputation?"

"Vance Evans."

"Vance Evans? Well, if that's not the fucking pot calling the kettle black."

"Takes one to know one."

"Listen," Jax said, settling in next to Pinks to make sure he wouldn't be overheard. "Vance Evans was a great third baseman and probably the smartest guy to ever graduate Henderson High. But when it comes to women, he and I reside in entirely different categories. I *like* girls. As in, *friends.* Always have. Not saying I don't enjoy the feel of a woman's body or putting my mouth on one when they *ask* for it, which you know, now that I'm older, happens regularly." His shoulder jerked. "But in Henderson, nope. Back in high school, I dated a lot of girls *once.* Scarlett among them. Back then, I wanted to know what made girls tick. I'd buy a pizza or take them to a dance. We'd talk, have a few laughs, and then the night would end with a fairly chaste goodnight kiss. *Occasionally,* there may have been something more." He rubbed his jaw. "But trust me. I was no Vance Evans. No one was."

"Well, in case you've missed the news flash, Vance is now married and a father. And he's practically running this town, so you don't want to be talking trash about him."

"Dude. I'm just saying he and I were *never* in the same league. I don't know why he's even mentioned any of this to you."

"Because you've been at The Situation the past three nights and left with a different girl each time."

"Because they drove me home," Jax defended in earnest. "Look, I've been going through a rough patch. Beer is my way of self-medicating. Jeez," he grumbled, raking frustrated fingers through his hair. "I've forgotten how damn small this town really is."

"I hear ya." Pinks sighed.

"What could you possibly know about it?" Jax groused. "Aren't you some citified Yankee? Just a hired gun?"

"Trust me. Three different girls in three different nights is small potatoes compared to the trouble I got myself into. And there's no way you're not gonna hear about it. Look, we're good, man. It wasn't my intention to give you shit."

"No?"

"No."

"Because you totally did."

"My bad," Pinks apologized. "Just—you know—a word to the wise."

Oh. Well, there's the problem, Jax thought as a grinning Scarlett Langford sauntered up and hugged him up like the long-lost friend he was.

"Good to have you back, Jaxon. Now here are my thoughts on this photo shoot." As Scarlett doled out her very specific thoughts, Jax decided to take Pinks's advice.

He kept his mouth shut and rolled with it.

CHAPTER TWO

When the smoke started billowing from beneath the hood of his Maserati GranTurismo, Hale Evans knew his luck had run out. The engine light had come on five miles back, but instead of pulling over on the side of 85 North as he should have, he pushed it, wanting to make it back to Henderson.

Not happening.

For all his love of exotic cars, he knew he should be better about scheduled maintenance. Davis somehow managed to get the One-77 to the Aston Martin dealership in Raleigh regularly, and that kid was busier than a one-armed paperhanger. Still, Davis didn't have a new wife and baby to dote on in between meetings about everything from the coming sports academy to the dozen separate businesses Hale still owned across the country. But when smoke starts pouring out of your favorite car's engine, it's a telltale sign you've neglected a few things.

Only a mile from town, Hale pulled to the side of the two-lane highway leading into Henderson. Stepping out into the stifling July heat, he tapped the hood tentatively and, finding it not too hot, he fingered for the latch and managed to get the hood propped open, allowing the steam to rise into the afternoon air. Then he'd done what all good investment gurus did in this situation. He put his hands on his hips and stared at the engine.

Yep. That was just about all he was qualified to do.

He wasn't out of gas. That he knew. But why the engine light came on? Thirsty for oil? Water? What? He had no clue. Reaching into his back pocket for his phone he called Davis. Not that the kid had any more of an idea about how to fix his car than he did, but he was certain that if Davis didn't already know who to call, he'd find out. Pronto.

And Davis did. Of course, he did. Davis promised Jaxon Wright—tweaker of NASCAR engines—would be out to collect him ASAP. That was Davis for you. The not-so-little engine that could.

Too bad the engine he was staring at could not.

Hale stood there a few moments, feeling very out of his element, kicking himself for neglecting his fleet. Unable to do anything but fume in the hot sun, he walked toward the tall stand of trees at the back of the Maserati and found a shady place to wait. As luck would have it, his phone found a strong patch of cell service, giving him the chance to catch up on emails.

Engrossed in formulating a response to one email in particular, he paid little attention to the lone car that approached and then passed. He may have heard the car pull over in front of his, but it didn't really register. Not until he heard a car door shut.

He hurriedly finished his email and was stuffing his phone into his back pocket when he caught sight of a woman approaching. A young woman as fresh as a cool breeze on this hot summer day, flowing toward him in a full, ruffled white eyelet skirt. Her silky, red tank top and wide, matching belt gave her a polished air. The red heels she was tiptoeing through the gravel in were designer pricey. Hale knew at least that much about women's clothing. When his gaze landed on her long, side ponytail, a rich dark-chocolate brown, shiny and thick, hanging over her right shoulder, a heartbreaking alarm sounded in his brain. But it wasn't until he had a clear view of the heart-shaped face, the sparkling forest-green eyes, and the beautifully tanned skin and took note of her height and figure that he went into shock.

Catherine.

It was surreal. Hale stood there gaping. Astounded. Logically knowing she couldn't be who he thought she was. Couldn't be the woman he hadn't seen in twenty-plus years. Because this woman was far younger, yet she was the spitting image of …

"Do ya need some help?" Her sweet Virginia accent was enchanting. Almost as much as her bashful smile. Her long, delicate fingers slowly tucked a stray hair behind her ear as she continued. "I'd be happy to give you a ride."

Hale just stared. His jaw unhinged with shock from the sight before him. His entire worldview shifting into slow motion.

He watched how her brows dipped. "Sir? Are you unwell? May I be of assistance?"

"I'm a …" Hale shook his head, reaching for sanity in the face of … *who is this?* "I'm sorry," he said, working hard to produce moisture inside his mouth and gather his wits. "My car." He pointed. "Someone should be coming," he murmured, unable to stop staring at those familiar eyes, that pert nose, her mouth.

"All right," she said slowly, her gaze making a study of his own features. "Why don't I wait with you? Make sure someone shows up." After a moment, she asked, "Did you hit your head?"

"No. No. I'm just a little, um. May I ask your name?" It was all Hale could get out. And the only thing he could think about.

She nodded, hesitating only a moment before sticking out her hand. Her smile was filled with a cheerful self-confidence. "Jinx Davenport. At your service."

Instead of taking her hand, Hale stepped back, whispering, "Davenport."

"Sir? Are you sure you're all right?" She looked back toward her car. "Stay here in the shade a moment. I'm going to call 911. Get a medic here. Make sure you're not suffering from a concussion or heat stroke."

He blinked. Then held out a hand. "Wait. Please. I was wondering … I mean … are you from around here? Miss Davenport."

"I'm from Richmond. Virginia."

Hale rubbed a hand over his eyes in an effort to hide his anxiety. To hide all the questions swamping his brain. He brought his hand down over his mouth and studied the girl. Wondering.

She was going to call 911 if he didn't start acting normal. Since having to answer a medic's—or anyone else's—questions at the moment could bring about unknown consequences, he drew in a breath and forced out a smile. He offered his hand. "I'm Hale Evans." He put his name out there as a challenge, watching her closely.

She took hold of his hand slowly, as if in awe. "*The* Hale Evans? Owner of Evans & Evans Investments?"

That wasn't quite the reaction he'd anticipated.

She looked over at the Maserati. "Yes. Of course. I should have known. Wow. It's very nice to meet you."

"Should have known?"

She waved it off. "I've been doing research on the town of Henderson. I have an interview in"—she checked her watch—"forty-five minutes."

"An interview?"

"For the head position at the library."

Hale eyed the girl. Perhaps he was mistaken. "You don't look, ah, old enough to hold a master's in Library Science."

She smiled. A smile so hauntingly familiar it gutted him. "I am not old enough. But I am smart enough."

"So you ..."

"Skipped a few grades, earned several degrees simultaneously." *Holy hell.*

His attention was tugged away from studying the girl's face as a bulky silver pickup swung into a U-turn and pulled up behind them.

"Mr. Evans," Jaxon Wright hollered as he climbed down from the cab. The kid was in his later twenties, tall and athletic, with a thick head of dark-blond hair curling out from under a backward ratty-as-hell ball cap set over a cool pair of shades. He approached, wearing a fitted T-shirt and loose jeans, wiping his hands on a navy bandana. "Heard you could use some help." The men shook hands. "I'm Jaxon," he said, turning to Miss Davenport, offering her a smile instead of a hand, both of which he'd stuck in his back pockets.

"I'm Jinx." She beamed up at him in greeting.

Jaxon's smile broadened as he mumbled, "Bacon, a One-77, and now this."

"I'm sorry?" Jinx asked.

"Day just keeps getting better," Jaxon offered Jinx before shooting Hale a wink. He went back to reengage with Miss Davenport, but then his head swerved, laying a curious look on Hale. Jaxon's gaze began to alternate back and forth between him and Jinx.

All the while, Miss Davenport couldn't take her eyes off the boy. *Well, now.*

And now the boy was returning her stare, intently.

"Okay. Well." Hale grappled for words as his survival instincts kicked in.

"Yeah." Jaxon clapped his hands as he snapped his attention back to Hale. "Not every day I get to poke around a Maserati. Let's take a look at that engine."

With a pretty flush of her cheeks, Miss Davenport also appeared to come back online. "And now that you're in good hands," she said to Hale lightly, breathily, "I'll be on my way." She spun, as if forcing herself to take leave, but not before she shot another quick glance at Jax.

"Thanks for stopping," Hale managed to get out.

"Nice to meet you," Jaxon told her as all three of them walked toward the front of the Maserati. Jinx's fingers fluttered in a wave as she continued on to her car, looking back briefly as she opened the door before settling herself inside.

Both men watched her slide into the beautiful two-seater convertible. A blue Fiat 124 Spider.

"Pretty car," Jax commented.

"Gotta be brand new. Pretty sure that's the limited Prima Edizione," Hale told him.

Except for Jaxon tossing him another curious look, they both continued to stare as Miss Davenport's car started up with a sporty rev of its engine. They watched as she carefully pulled onto the road and accelerated toward town.

Jaxon finally turned his head to stare at Hale, who continued to watch the car disappear over the horizon. "I didn't know you had a daughter."

Hale took his time dragging his eyes from the empty road in front of him to meet Jaxon's probing gaze. "Neither did I."

CHAPTER THREE

Jinx Davenport found herself waiting in a small meeting room in the back corner of Henderson's Memorial Library. The space was fitted with interior glass windows, so she positioned herself on the far side of the conference table watching for the approach of her would-be interviewers.

They did not disappoint.

A very, very attractive fellow dressed in casual business attire was heading purposefully in her direction. His hair was dark, like hers, and he had quite the tan, like he spent a lot of time outdoors–maybe on the lake she'd recently read about. He was sexy in the way he moved, the way he wore his hair a little long in the back. He was fit, like a runner. His countenance appeared frisky as he stepped aside to guide an older woman in front of him.

She wore a playful smile, as if the two of them had just shared an off-color joke. In contrast, she wore an expensive summer-weight suit, one with ruffles and trim appropriate for a fancy ladies' lunch.

As the two neared, they caught her eye through the glass, both flashing her a smile. As she stood to greet her interviewers, she worried her attire didn't scream *librarian*. She'd donned a short, red cardigan over her silk tank wanting to look polished yet accessible. A call to the new era of librarians she hoped to bring to Henderson.

And now that the time had finally arrived, she was suddenly very nervous. To the point her hands felt clammy and her breathing hitched.

Lord, she *really* wanted this job.

"Miss Davenport, is it?" The handsome man held out his hand. "I'm Vance Evans and this is my grandmother, Emelina Flores."

Jinx shook Vance's hand and then offered hers to Mrs. Flores.

The woman's face went slack. Jinx was sure of it. In fact, she worried the woman might be suffering a stroke. Yet, it passed quickly, replaced by rapid blinking and a stiff smile. Regardless, the woman's features were unusually beautiful and elegantly made up. Her updo hinted at red, but a closer look brought the color to a mahogany brown. And although Jinx felt inexplicably drawn to her, she definitely wasn't getting a friendly vibe in return. In fact, Mrs. Flores threw a quick look toward her grandson before addressing them both in Spanish.

Jinx responded likewise, saying yes, though she wasn't exactly fluid in the woman's native tongue, she could understand and speak the language well enough. However, she added, she didn't trust her writing skills as much and, if being able to write well in Spanish was a requirement for this job, she would definitely need to brush up.

Mrs. Flores seemed surprised, then impressed, and then … subdued. As if Jinx's understanding of Spanish was presenting her with a problem. With the way the woman's eyes kept darting toward Vance, it certainly appeared Mrs. Flores wanted to share something else with her grandson. But following Vance's indication that the women should sit, Mrs. Flores did so, across from Jinx, folding her hands on top of the table and, *oh my,* staring daggers.

Jinx was shrewd enough to assimilate that for whatever reason— her outfit, her hair color, her ability to speak Spanish—she had already lost Mrs. Flores. So she turned her attention to Vance Evans and tossed off the well-worn shroud of insecurity that continuously nagged at her, more determined than ever to dazzle.

"Thank you for bringing me in for this interview. I know that although legally you are not able to ask my age, you can certainly make an educated guess from the dates on my résumé. And since on paper my age may appear a deterrent—"

"Deterrent?" Vance interrupted. "Not at all. Your age is the reason I asked to meet you."

"Really?" She grinned in relief, liking him immediately.

"Yep. Because either you're a sociopathic liar or your IQ is in the 135 to 155 range. We don't have many of either in Henderson." He grinned, his voice going silky. "So either way, I was curious."

"You don't get many sociopaths around here?" she quipped.

"Not applying for the library position, no."

"So you think I'm a genius?"

"Kinda betting on it." He stared her straight in the eye as he said that, his forest-green irises gleaming.

To Jinx, it felt like there was an actual meeting of minds. Like she saw into Vance and he could see into her. She tilted her head and asked curiously. "You too?"

He shrugged, but the smile remained, as if he was still reading her. "I used to be the smartest guy in the room. Then I used those smarts to hire somebody brighter than I am and things have worked out pretty well. I love this library. The books here taught me almost everything I know. My grandmother and I"—he indicated Mrs. Flores, who now wore a pinched expression—"are dedicated to keeping it state-of-the-art, especially with the new sports academy being built. We need this library to serve not only the citizens of Henderson, but the students of both high schools as well."

"I've read about the proposed academy," Jinx told him. "However, I don't know much about Henderson High, except as it relates to the baseball team."

Vance grinned. "You a baseball fan, Miss Davenport?"

"I am. Please call me Jinx."

"Is that your given name?" Vance asked, his eyes scrutinizing her application.

"It is."

When his head popped up, he sported a dubious grin. "Really? Your father *named* you Jinx?"

"My mother named me Jinx. My father thought it was cute and simply allowed it."

Vance nodded. "Well, he's right. It is cute." He looked over to Mrs. Flores. "Abuela, don't you think it's cute?"

Mrs. Flores didn't answer Vance, but remarked, "Your mother named you Jinx, you say? Whatever for?"

"I'm pretty sure I was a surprise. My half-sister Lisette was six when my parents married. We look nothing alike. Well, I guess she looks like him, and I look like—"

"Your mother," she guessed.

"Yes. I do."

"I see," she said with all the warmth of an evil queen.

Vance cleared his throat. "Abuela? Is everything all right?"

Jinx noted that one glance in his direction and Mrs. Flores's demeanor changed. The transformation from an old woman with a stick up her ass to a bright, easy spirit was immediate and, frankly, mystifying.

"Darling boy," she cooed in a lovely Spanish accent. "I do apologize. To you and Miss Davenport. As you said, she's surprisingly young." She looked at Jinx gifting her with a truly apologetic smile. "I promise not to hold it against you. Now, I'll let Vance proceed with the interview. I'll just sit here and … listen."

Jinx turned her attention back to Vance, assuming the next question would come from him. But Mrs. Flores held up a hand and said, "Although I am exceedingly curious. How is it you've found our little town?"

Jinx chewed her lip as her gaze slid between Vance's delighted green eyes and Emelina's foreboding brown stare. This was the moment of truth Jinx had been debating. Did she confess how she came to learn about Henderson and this job she thought was perfect for her? Or did she give them a more professional answer?

Jinx tilted her head, both hands nervously stroking the ends of her long, braided ponytail. She glanced down at her notebook briefly, licked her lips, and then confessed, "I'm a Cal Johnson fan. I have been since he started his pitching career with the Orioles. I saw the video of him singing. The one that went viral back in March? Since research and discovery come naturally to me, I investigated. Where he sang. Why he was singing. Who the girl was he was singing to." She laughed nervously. "I'm not stalking Cal," she tried to assure them. "I know he doesn't live in Henderson. However, because of Cal, I signed up for the *Henderson Happenings* e-newsletter. There's been a link to it at the bottom of every singing Cal Johnson video since."

"When I get home, I'm going to kiss my wife," Vance said. "She was the mastermind behind getting the videos out there and linking HH to it."

"HH? Oh, *Henderson Happenings*. Yes." Jinx couldn't help herself. She leaned over the table toward Vance and asked, "Who writes it? *Who* is the Henderson Hostess?" Jinx dearly wanted to know.

"I don't know," Vance chuckled. "It was started by Missy McReady in our offices at E&E Investments."

"Yes. That much I was able to discover."

"But she handed it off to a committee of writers. Top secret writers who have been sworn to never reveal themselves or each other." He looked pointedly at his grandmother. "No one wants to get sued for libel," he growled. "Or for ratting out their family members."

"Mrs. Flores?" Jinx wondered in surprise. "You?"

"No, darling. Not me," she assured. Although Jinx wasn't assured at all. "Shall we get on with the interview?"

"Ah, yes. Okay," Vance said, looking down at his papers. "So you were saying, you're a fan of Cal's, saw the video from the Opening Day Spectacular, and signed up to receive *Henderson Happenings*. Then what?"

"Well, I read the *Happenings* every Monday and Friday and"— really, was she going to tell them this?—"I would google for more information."

"More information?"

"About the town. About the people mentioned. About the events. I loved the way the *Happenings* was written, and obviously"—she indicated their library surroundings—"I love the written word. So I investigated whatever caught my fancy, never dreaming it would lead me to find an advertisement for this job."

"Which was not posted in *Henderson Happenings*," Mrs. Flores insisted.

"No, but I'm a librarian, right? I spent many of my afternoons as a youth inside libraries. Libraries are my *thing*, so of course, one of the first things I researched about Henderson was this library."

"And how did we look?" Vance asked, curious.

"Surprisingly new. I mean no offense. It's just I have come to thoroughly understand your town's struggle, so finding your public library as technically up-to-date as it is was surprising."

Vance nodded. "My grandmother and I love libraries too. We've been on the board of this one for years. However, now that our plates are full, we are looking for the person who can ..."

"Be your puppet?" Jinx said on an eager grin, looking between the two of them.

Vance chuckled, his green eyes sparkling with mirth. "Not exactly," he assured her. "Yes, my grandmother and I are control freaks. We may as well get that out on the table now. But we are only two members of the board."

"Two *prominent* members," Mrs. Flores added.

"Yes," Vance relented. "But, as I was saying, we have a lot on our plate. We've mapped out an agenda for the next four years in the hopes of elevating this place enough to brag about it in our sports academy marketing materials. We are looking for someone who is not only well qualified to handle the job *but* who is also as passionate as we are about the project."

There was no doubt in Jinx's mind that she was the person they were looking for. But first she needed to address the elephant in the room. "I'm only twenty-one and have never held a full-time library job. However, I've strategically educated myself with this exact job in mind. My father and his mother served on the Richmond Public Library's board just like the two of you. Thanks to them, I know and love libraries. My dad and I have spent much of our time together in many of them. I know how they should work. I know what they should offer inside their doors as well as in outreach programs to their communities. I understand the diversity of what people want when they set foot in a public library. From the ones who are desperate for help with research, to the ones who want a quiet place to work, to the ones who have nowhere else to go and are looking for solace. And I never forget the ones who are eager for the next juicy novel that takes them away from their lives for a just little while.

"Mr. Evans, Mrs. Flores, I started taking college courses at the age of thirteen. I graduated with a double major in English and Literature with"—she addressed Mrs. Flores—"a minor in Spanish.

Then I busted my butt for two master's degrees. Computer science, and library science. All this so I'd be well equipped to run a large library."

"But are you passionate?" Vance inquired, his tone full of teasing sarcasm.

She took a breath and sat back in her seat with a self-deprecating grin. "I'm sorry. Yes, as you can see, I am passionate." She sat up straight again. "And I want this job."

"Why?" Mrs. Flores asked. "Why here? Why Henderson?"

"Weren't you listening?" Vance chided his grandmother. "This is all about Cal Johnson."

Jinx squeaked. "No. No, I swear," she said aghast. "This is *not* about Cal Johnson. Not that I wouldn't enjoy meeting him in person someday. But he was simply the catalyst that brought Henderson to my awareness. I'm looking for a change. I was born and raised in Richmond. Entered the University of Richmond at the age of thirteen as a day student. Moved on campus as soon as they allowed me. I was enrolled both there and at Virginia Commonwealth University by the time I was eighteen. So I'm looking for change. For an opportunity to do real work and have it mean something. Knowing all that I know about Henderson and the people who are trying to make a difference here, this seemed like a job where I could roll up my sleeves and really get to work."

"So ... your parents?" Mrs. Flores asked. "No connection to Henderson?"

"My mother is originally from the D.C. area. My father is from Richmond."

"What did they say about your possible move to North Carolina?"

Jinx shut her mouth and sat back. This wasn't a question she was prepared to answer. "Is that relevant?"

Mrs. Flores said nothing but continued to stare at Jinx expectantly.

"Abuela?" Vance urged.

"May I ask your birthdate, Miss Davenport?" Mrs. Flores asked.

"Abuela," Vance scolded.

"It's quite all right," Jinx told him. "I offered up my age willingly because I want a chance to convince you it's not a liability. What do

I care that you know my birthday?" She told Mrs. Flores the month, day, and year and watched her write it down.

"All right. Vance, I'm going to let you continue this interview on your own. I have somewhere I need to be," Mrs. Flores said, gathering up Jinx's résumé and application. She stood. "This has been very interesting," she told Jinx pointedly.

Jinx nodded, standing.

"Sit. Sit," Vance told her. "I want to hear how you managed to start college at thirteen and finish two master's degrees by the age of twenty-one."

As Jinx watched Mrs. Flores go, she sat back down and tuned into Vance's charisma, matching it with her own. "Only if you're willing to tell me if all the mischief I've been reading about actually happens here."

Vance laughed, his sharp eyes studying her features. "You know I'm married, right?"

"To Piper, and your son's name is Vance, Jr. I read all about his birth in the *Happenings*."

"So when I go completely unprofessional and admit that you are one of the most striking girls I've ever met, you understand it's coming with a big-brother vibe, right? There's just something so—I don't know—*perfect* about you."

Jinx burst out with a laugh of utter disbelief. "No one's ever called anything about me perfect, that is for certain. But what's really funny? I was sort of thinking the same about you."

"Obviously, we're kindred spirits. Both passionate about libraries and Cal Johnson. You are the concrete evidence that the guy is helping us spread the word about Henderson. The fact that he's bringing in genius librarians? As far as I'm concerned, he's the gift that keeps on giving."

"What about sociopathic liars?" she joked.

Vance leaned in. "Seriously. Off the record. Not part of the interview so you don't have to answer. Between you and me and no one else *ever*." He pointed to himself. "148."

Jinx pointed to herself and shrugged. "147." It was a lie. She actually beat him by five points. And she'd tell him that. Just as soon as he hired her.

Vance sat back, all smug. "You'd fit in here, you know. We've got a lot of out-of-towners settling in Henderson, joining in with the locals seamlessly. After years of nobody doing anything to stop the bleeding in this town, now it seems everybody is on board. We are coming together as a community in a way we haven't in two generations. I have no doubt you'd be met with open arms. We need young people to move here and work."

Jinx leaned across the table. "Mrs. Buchanan. The librarian. I'm not sure she's thrilled I'm applying for this position."

"It's not you. It's the fact that we're looking for someone else to take up stewardship of the library as we move forward."

"Will whoever you hire be her boss?"

"Yes. But my grandmother has promised to handle Mrs. Buchanan. I trust she can get that done."

"Meaning?"

"You have nothing to worry about."

"Are you offering me the job?" Jinx teased.

"Not yet. No. First …" Vance said, getting serious. He picked up the folder in front of him. "Let's go through the short-term agenda we've developed for the library. I want you to ask all the questions you'll need answered in order to write up a proposal tonight."

"A proposal?"

"A proposal from your perspective on how best we should go about managing said agenda."

She grinned. Excited. Thrilled even. "Is this why you've set me up at a bed-and-breakfast? You had planned to give me homework?"

"Yes. This job is an important one, Jinx. We've seen several candidates already. All with experience and insight. What we have not seen is your passion. For libraries, for Cal Johnson, and for getting to the bottom of the Henderson Hostess's identity. All of which works for me. In my mind, the fact that you're tuned into Henderson from reading our e-newsletter gives you a leg up on your competition. But this is a big job. I need to know that you—all twenty-one and fresh out of school—can handle it."

"All twenty-one and fresh out of *grad* school. My age is not going to be a problem," she promised.

"No? You're going to have to manage personnel, all of whom will be older than you. The board members are fucking ancient. Pardon my language, but it's the damn truth. There will no doubt be subcontractors for upgrades and repairs. You'll be overseeing whoever has contact with the book dealers. We've got associates and members. You need to be able to handle all of it with authority. You won't have to be the bookkeeper, but you will have to be aware of spending, sticking to a budget, stretching what little assets we have to do the most it possibly can."

"I wrote my thesis on library cost analysis in the digital age."

That apparently hit the man right where it counted. "Do you happen to have a copy?"

She felt herself light up. Never had anyone outside of academia asked to see her work. "I do," she said, almost getting choked up at the thought of sharing it with *the* Vance Evans of E&E Investments. Which reminded her. "I met your father," she said while digging out the copy of her thesis and handing it to Vance. "Blue Maserati?"

"That's him," Vance said, flipping through the tome.

"He was broken down on the side of the road. I stopped to make sure he was all right."

"Broken down?" Vance looked up sharply.

"Yes. Steam coming out from under the hood. While I was there, someone named Jaxon arrived to help."

"Jaxon Wright?" Vance wondered.

Jinx shrugged, unsure. "On the tall side. Big. Blond."

Vance nodded. "I know his brother. In fact, Xavier is building out Piper's shop." Vance scowled briefly, like the thought of it gave him a headache. "The Wrights are a good, solid Henderson family. See," he said, passing her a folder. "Young people. Coming back. Applying for jobs. Bringing the median age of this town down, down, down. It's all good."

"So if you hired me, my age would actually be a huge help," she stressed as she opened the folder and took a cursory glance at Vince's short-term agenda for the library.

Vance shot her a crooked grin. "I'll be sure to keep that in mind. Come on, Einstein. Now let's see whatcha got."

CHAPTER FOUR

Jaxon stood at the threshold of what he had begun referring to as the Horsepower Stables, a.k.a. Hale Evans's garage.

Never the smartest guy in the room, Jax knew plenty about cars because, yeah, motors were his life. He also knew how to add, even the big numbers. Although he still had no freaking idea what that Aston Martin One-77 cost. That car was new to him, which was saying something.

Yep, he'd been a grease monkey since he could hold a screwdriver and ride a bike. Those popular newfangled bikes equipped with motors? He'd invented his own when he was twelve. Of course, his father wasn't happy that he'd disabled the family lawn mower to do it, but his dad had taken a spin on the bike and high-fived him at the end of it, so there was that.

Too bad neither he nor his dad had had the wherewithal to patent the idea and run with it back then. They both thought it was novel but hadn't imagined it was the *coming thing*. Of course, after that, Jax had graduated to minibikes and dirt bikes, which he started racing locally. He was an okay driver, but he was invaluable as a gearhead. There wasn't a motor he couldn't get running or make more productive if he put his mind to it.

Putting his mind to what was spread out before him now, Jax had to admit he was a little overwhelmed. "All of these are yours?" he asked Hale, who stood next to him, hands on hips.

"Yep. All mine. All my responsibility. Although as you know, Davis drives the One-77"—he pointed— "and Vance likes the

'Vette. My mother's car is out at the moment. That 1977 Trans Am barely sees the light of day. Lolly, my stepdaughter, drives that when Brooks Bennett isn't hauling her around in his truck. The two show pieces in the back have served well in a couple town parades over the past year." He indicated the rumble-seated Caddy and the old-school Rolls.

"So you drive the Maserati regularly?"

"I do. But now that we are dealing with car seats and babies, we've started pulling out the Rolls. So after you get the Maserati running, that's the first one I want you to service."

Jax licked his lips at the thought of getting his hands on that Rolls Royce. "Mr. Evans, I'm grateful for this opportunity. I am. But I can't be taking business away from Mr. Verlander down at the Gas&Go. I don't want to come back to town and start stepping on toes."

"Jaxon," Hale said, laying a hand on his shoulder and giving it a squeeze. "Verlander's a nice enough guy, but I don't let him anywhere near my cars. I drive them into Raleigh to be serviced, which is why the Maserati was choked by its own oil today. I don't know what your plans are now that you're back in town, but after coming to my rescue, talking cars, and hearing about your résumé, I feel certain that you are qualified to handle this fleet. Do you want the job?"

"Yes, sir. I am helping out my brother Xavier for the time being, placing orders and scheduling subcontractors, but if you don't mind me coming around on off hours, I'd be happy to see what I can do for you. I see you even have a lift."

"The intention was to store one car over another. Hadn't thought about it coming in handy for maintenance house calls."

"I've got plenty of tools, but if we need something I don't have, I've got access. Nothing in here is too computerized, so I'm pretty sure I can keep things running for you."

"I appreciate it. I can't tell you how guilty I feel running the Mas to the brink of its life. Fortunately for me, cars are not the love of my life anymore. Nor are they my babies, and today we saw how they are paying the price."

"I'm happy to foster-parent any and all of your vehicles. It'll be my pleasure."

"Good," Hale said. "That's real good." Then he stopped talking.

After several beats of silence, Jaxon tore his gaze off the orange 'Vette and met Mr. Evans's eyes.

Hale cleared his throat. "About Miss Davenport." He rubbed his chin.

Jaxon nodded. "Your secret is safe with me, sir. I mean"—Jax backpedaled—"not your secret. I didn't mean to imply that you have a secret. Just that, you know—"

Hale held up a hand. "If there's a secret, I've been unaware of it. Understand?"

Jaxon took one look in the man's eyes and saw nothing but heartache and anguish.

"You think she's yours," Jax stated.

"I think she looks very much like my ex-wife did the day she left me."

"Left you?"

Hale nodded.

Just then, the door to the farthest garage bay started to open. The two men watched as Emelina Flores, known to all of Jax's generation as the Big Em, parked her two-seater Mercedes.

"You want me to handle the Mercedes too?" Jax asked Hale.

"If you don't mind. Just check with my mother first. The woman has an aversion to driving any car but her own."

"She likes what she likes," Jax said, admiring the vehicle. "Can't blame her."

Not a moment after the car door slammed, Emelina called for Hale, her voice full of alarm. "Darling boy, I have something to tell you, and you're going to want to sit down."

Hale whispered to Jax, "Ten to one, she's met Miss Davenport."

Emelina pulled up sharp when she saw Jax standing there. "Oh, I'm so sorry. What am I interrupting?"

"Hello, Mrs. Flores." He stuck out his hand. "Jaxon Wright. We met at my mother's when you were there playing bridge last week."

"Of course, dear," she cooed as she took his hand. "I'm not one to forget a handsome face."

"Apparently Jaxon is more than a pretty face," Hale said. "He's going to use his superior automotive skills to keep this fleet of ours tuned to perfection."

Em looked from him to the fleet and back again. "Brilliant," she declared. Then she turned to her son. "Darling, when you and Jaxon are finished, I'd like a word."

"About Miss Davenport, I presume." At her stunned expression, Hale explained. "Jaxon and I had the pleasure of meeting the girl while I was stuck on the side of the road this afternoon. Miss Davenport stopped to offer rescue."

"You've met?" Emelina was aghast.

"Yes, Mother, and I'm sure my face looked exactly as yours does now. I was so stunned she assumed I'd hit my head and wanted to call 911."

"Of course, you were stunned. She looks exactly like—" Emelina snapped her lips shut with a scowl.

"Go ahead and say it, Madre. She looks exactly like *Catherine*."

"I refuse to say that woman's name."

"Whether you say it or not, a look-alike from *Richmond*, with the last name of *Davenport* is cause for speculation. In fact, Jaxon here immediately put two and two together and came up with three."

"Three what?"

Hale nodded for him to explain.

Jax rubbed his hands together and shuffled his feet. "I, ah, mentioned to Mr. Evans that I wasn't aware he had a daughter."

"No," Em whispered in horror.

"Yep," Hale confirmed.

Jax held up his hands. "Look. I haven't been around for a while. I came upon the two of them together. Same hair color. Same skin tone. Similar mannerisms. I just assumed. I'm not saying anyone else would make that connection. But to me, in that moment, it appeared they were father and daughter."

"Mannerisms?" Hale interrupted. "What do you mean, similar mannerisms?"

"Ah ... well," Jaxon thought back. "When you and I shook hands, you tilted your head slightly." Jax pointed to the right side of Hale's face indicating the direction of the tilt. "I only remembered that because when I introduced myself to Jinx, she did the same thing, and it made her dangly earring swing a little. The crystal at the end caught the sun, which sent sparkles all over her chest and shoulders. Also, her teeth are exactly like yours. I remember looking back and forth between the two of you double checking that."

"Our teeth?"

"Or your smiles. Maybe it's the smile, but it could have been the teeth," Jax said thoughtfully. "Either one. Maybe both. Not sure. Oh, and the way you both acted when the conversation stalled. You were silently snapping your fingers on your right hand. She tapped her middle finger to her thumb over and over. Also right hand."

"Dear God," Emelina breathed.

"Mother, I'm doing my best not to jump to conclusions here. These dire outbursts of yours are not helping."

"Under the circumstances, my dire outbursts are completely appropriate." She held up a set of papers. "*This* is the girl's birthdate. Less than *nine months* after I moved from Spain to Henderson."

Hale held out his hand. "May I?"

While he shifted through the papers, Jax wondered if maybe he should go ahead and excuse himself. He made a move to go, but Em stopped him with a hand to his arm, even though she spoke in an urgent fashion to Hale. "Why is your ex-wife's child applying for a job here in Henderson?"

"Once Miss Davenport mentioned she had an interview at the library, I was counting on you to figure that out."

"What about her birthdate?"

Hale shrugged a shoulder, but his facial features were tense. He looked up from the paperwork with a serious expression. "Since Catherine was having an affair with Mr. Davenport prior to her leaving me, I have to assume her daughter is his."

"But is it possible, given the date she departed and that birthdate, that the girl could be yours?"

The strain on the man's face was unmistakable. The answer was obvious to both Jaxon and Em. He twisted his lips a bit before saying, "It's possible. Yes. But improbable. Given these dates, if Catherine was pregnant when she left here, she may not have been aware of it."

"*Or* she left you *because* she was pregnant with another man's child. Are you sure you're remembering the date of her departure correctly?"

"Unfortunately, it's not something I've been able to forget."

Jax could feel the grief rolling off Mr. Evans as he stared at his mother. Mrs. Flores's eyes closed, as if standing witness to her son's sorrow swamped her. That's when the name *Vance* slipped from her lips.

"Was he there? For the interview?" Hale asked, his demeanor shifting from regret to concern.

"Yes. Of course, he was there," Em stated emphatically. "This was *his* candidate. The young genius he was so eager to meet."

"And?" Hale asked.

"Well, I was so taken aback by her looks that I immediately began shuffling through paperwork looking for parents' names, a hometown, anything. So I wasn't paying much attention to their interaction at first. By the time I looked up, Vance was animated. Enthralled. Smitten even."

"But did he *recognize* her?"

"No. He gave no indication."

Hale gave a sigh of relief. "Okay. Well, that's something then."

"But if Jaxon mistook her for your daughter, how long will it be before someone else does the same? Or realizes that she's Catherine's daughter?" Emelina's voice escalated as she said, "They look just alike. We must dismiss her as a candidate for the library and send her home. Immediately."

"Catherine had trouble making friends here. After twenty years, I'm not sure anyone will remember what she looked like."

"You can't take that chance. If Vance were to find out this girl is his half-sister, who knows how he'd react? When Catherine left, she took that boy's heart with her. She took *your* heart," Em stressed as something close to panic overtook her features. She let go of Jaxon and wrung her hands together. "I just got the boy back," she pleaded. "I just got *you* back. I can't bear the thought of losing either of you again."

"Madre," Hale said softly. "This girl could be *your* granddaughter."

Emelina stifled a gasp. As if the thought hadn't occurred to her.

"She could be *my* daughter," Hale went on. "I can't turn my back on this."

Jaxon's chest tightened as he witnessed the Big Em's eyes well with tears. Anguish was a flimsy word to describe what he was witnessing. Her lips trembled as she begged Hale. "You can't bring that horrible woman back into his life. She never once reached out to her baby, her own precious son. You can't do this to Vance. I won't let you."

Hale took a breath. "Madre," he whispered, stepping close to his mother, pulling her into an embrace. "There's no sense jumping to conclusions. In spite of heavy circumstantial evidence, nothing has actually been established. The three of us are aware of a possible situation, but for now"—he looked over to include Jax—"let's keep our heads about us. Jaxon, perhaps we could impose on you to escort Miss Davenport to dinner tonight? The two of you seemed rather intrigued by one another."

"Sir?"

"I'll call the club. You can take her on my dime. Let her question you on all things Henderson and … ah, perhaps you'd be willing to …"

"Find out what I can?" Jax offered.

"Would you mind?" he pleaded with a sheepish grin while Emelina wiped at her eyes. "I could call a private investigator, but you met the girl. I'm guessing that won't be necessary. Besides, you've demonstrated a keen eye for detail. I guess what I'm asking is for you to use it."

"What exactly do you want to know?" Jax asked.

Hale blinked a couple times, licked his lips, glanced at his mother and then back at Jax before he gave himself away. "Everything."

CHAPTER FIVE

Jax clapped his hands together and shouted from the living room of his parents' home. "Got a date tonight, Ma."

"Well, come on in here and tell me about it," his mother yelled back.

He grinned. He and his brothers had conspired over the last several weeks to do what they could to get their mother out of bed and moving. Since their father was of the mind to baby his beloved, Anna Beth Wright got away with playing Princess and the Pea. But no matter how regal she may look all tucked up in elegant sheets and lace, the doc said staying in bed was not doing her any favors.

"Nope. You want to hear about it, you need to get your ass out of bed. Now," he insisted. "Because I need to be in the shower in five minutes." He stared at his hands, hating the telltale black smudges under the tips of his nails. He knew no shower could get them completely clean, and he kept the damn things cut as short as he could in an effort to avoid the situation.

Still.

His mother appeared in a pair of black yoga pants and a pale pink, long-sleeved top. The outfit caused him to grin. "Where'd you get those, Ma?" he asked, delighted.

"McKenna bought them," she said, looking down at herself. "Are they too much for someone my age?"

"They're fantastic." Anything was better than seeing her in a nightgown and robe. "How do you feel?"

"Self-conscious."

He laughed, happy she'd completely missed his meaning. Feeling self-conscious was far better than feeling weak, dizzy, or exhausted, and a sure sign of continued healing. It wasn't but a couple of months ago Jax didn't think his mother was going to make it. Some rare autoimmune disease Jax couldn't pronounce nearly stolen her from him, his four brothers, and their father. And from McKenna. *The daughter his parents never had.* The girl who had dated his brother Xavier in high school and became a part of the family. Now, apparently, she was dating Xavier's *twin*, Xander, to his parents' utter delight.

Seriously, if Xander ever tried to dump McKenna, the family would be split over how to get rid of his body. His parents loved McKenna that much. And she totally deserved it.

"Ma, you look great," he assured her. "You wanna sit or are you good to stand for a bit?"

"I feel good," she said. "Now what's this about a date?"

"She's a pretty one, Ma." He knew his mother was going to love this, so he planned to build it up. Give her something juicy to chew on. "Long, dark braid, emerald eyes, an impish grin like she's been up to no good. Met her today as I was rescuing Mr. Evans and his Maserati. She was there with him when I pulled up in Xavier's truck."

"Who is she?"

"Her name is Jinx Davenport. She's from Richmond, Virginia, here interviewing for a position at the library. Mr. Evans asked me to take her to dinner tonight at the club. Show her a good time. Answer her questions about Henderson."

"Is she your age?"

"Younger. Twenty-one. It's not, you know, a real date, obviously. But I wouldn't mind it if it were." *Understatement of the year.* "Seems like a sweetheart. Smart apparently, since she's applying for the head job over there. So," he hedged, "I'm probably not *exactly* what she's looking for, but you know me, always happy to be Mr. Right Now."

His mother stared at him with a curious look. "I don't understand."

"You know. Not her, ah, *forever* Mr. Right. But good enough for now."

"Why would you even say that?"

"Oh. Well." He stopped and smiled, remembering Jinx eyeing him up. "I'm pretty sure I passed inspection," he allowed with a sly smile. "But," he went on jovially, "being as I'm not the sharpest tool in the shed, it probably won't be much of a match intellectually."

"Because you went to NASCAR Technical Institute and worked your butt off at all those other racing programs instead of college?"

"Because I work with my hands instead of my head. And I don't particularly like to *read* unless it's *Car and Driver*." He had an aversion to books. Always had.

"Sounds like the perfect match, if you ask me," she said blithely, sitting down on the edge of the sofa. "If she's spending all day in a library, she's not going to want to talk about books when she gets home."

Jax chuckled, loving his mother's renewed zest for matchmaking. "Ma, I think you've got your plate full right now with Xavier's upcoming wedding to a girl he literally just met. You go ahead and put your focus on that. Don't tax yourself worrying about me."

"I'm not worried about you. And I'm certainly not worried about Xavier *or* Xander. I'm"—she sank into the back of the couch—"ecstatic."

Jax grinned and went to sit next to her, cuddling her into his side. "You should be, Ma," he said, rubbing her shoulder. "Things are really looking up around here."

"They are. Xavier's moved home from Arizona. You're thinking of sticking around. Xander, well, McKenna's going to see that he moves back home. I've missed you all terribly," she confessed. "I'm absolutely delighted."

Jax had zero intention of staying in town, but why spoil his mother's bliss? "And you're getting better," he reminded her.

"So much better," she breathed. "I am so much better," she said sincerely. "I'm actually"—she shook her head—"beginning to believe I'm going to fully recover."

"You are. If your boys have anything to say about it, you definitely are."

"So, what are you wearing tonight?"

The change of subject threw him. "Oh. Ah. Hmm." He grimaced. "Not a suit, right? I'm taking her to the club. Sports jacket? Blue blazer?" *Shit*. He couldn't remember the last time he put on one of those. He used both hands to shove his hair back off his forehead and then entwined his fingers and rested his hands at the back of his head. "I'll find something. You got an idea how to deal with these?" He dropped his hands and held up his fingernails, showing off the motor oil.

"I googled that," she said proudly, holding up a finger. "Dish soap, because of its degreasing agent. Grab the bottle under the kitchen sink and take it in the shower with you. Use that nailbrush McKenna bought. See if that helps."

"Good googling, Ma." He kissed her cheek while standing to take his leave.

"Jaxon." She reached out and snagged his hand. "If you'd like to bring your date back here and introduce her to your parents, we'll wait up."

"Ma," Jax laughed. "I love ya bad, but there is no way in hell I'm bringing a girl home to meet my parents."

"Xavier brought Laidey home to play the piano for me."

"And look how that ended up. That sucker is *engaged*. No, thank you. You've got McKenna, and now you have Laidey. That's all the girls you're gettin' for now. Besides, being Mr. Wright *Now* works better for me." He gave his mother a quick wink and his patent wicked grin.

"Boy," she warned. "Do not let your daddy hear you've been disrespecting your dates. You know how he feels about that."

"Disrespect? Ma, you wound me." Jax clutched his gut as he feigned a grimace. "Never." He leaned down and kissed her other cheek. "Love you and your kind too much to ever do that," he promised.

"Hmm-hmmm," she chided.

"Seriously. I am no Casanova."

"Jaxon Alexander, you may be my baby, but I've been your momma for over twenty-seven years. Do not try to lie to me. I've heard things."

That stopped him cold. "You've heard what, exactly?"

"Things," she insisted, leaning toward him, a scowl marring her forehead. "At least Xavier came home knowing he needed to make amends for the wake of destruction he left in his path. You seem oblivious."

"Because I am," he yelled, throwing out his arms. "I have no idea what you've heard or what you're implying." He touched a finger to his chest. "I'm not out there sleeping with women willy-nilly, leaving them heartbroken."

"You're not?" she challenged.

Jax's brows drew together. "Where's this comin' from, Ma? Who says I am?"

"Evie Jackson, Darla Witherspoon's momma—"

"I did not lay a hand on Darla Witherspoon or her momma. That's all hearsay."

"Well, if people hear it said, they believe it."

"You?" he accused.

He watched as she blinked, softened, and apparently felt remorse. "I suppose I have." She looked at him then. Really looked into his eyes and asked, "I shouldn't?"

"No, Ma, you shouldn't. I mean," he said, sitting back down next to her, "I like women. Kissed the heck out of a whole lot of them. But beyond that here in Henderson? Trust me, I learned from my older brothers not to shit where I eat."

"That is a horrible expression." She shuddered.

"Yet it couldn't be more appropriate, yeah? You think I want some angry father—likely one of Dad's best friends—knockin' on my door? I may have dated a lot of different girls in high school, but that's because I didn't want to get tied up with any one of them and take things too far. And, truth be told, it's also why I'm not sure I actually want to move back here. Back then, my generation just had to deal with the good ole grapevine. Now, on top of social media, there's this *Henderson Happenings* bullshit. No way am I interested in having my love life bandied about in all of that."

"The *Henderson Happenings* is not interested in your love life."

"But you are, clearly. Evie Jackson is. Mrs. Witherspoon?"

"Darlin', forgive me if I've ruffled your feathers. It sounds to me like you have your reputation well in hand."

"Apparently not enough. Christ. You're actually the second person who has brought it up today. I really don't understand where this is all coming from."

"Sweetheart," she soothed. "People love to talk. Especially in a small town where everything's decaying around them. Coming back the way you have just now, you're fresh meat. The kind that everyone wants to sink their teeth into. So for just a little bit, you're going to be under some scrutiny. Old stories are gonna be retold. New ones with your name attached are going to be added. Everybody's going to want to know your business. That's just the way things go around here. But from now on, I promise. I'll simply refuse to believe anything salacious about my youngest boy that hits my ears."

"Good. That's good." He leaned over and kissed her cheek before he stood. "Unless you're in Chapel Hill. I've worked hard to earn my salacious reputation in Chapel Hill."

"What?" she breathed.

Same wink. Same wicked grin.

Only this time, he meant it.

CHAPTER SIX

"Hmm."

Jinx watched Vance study his phone. She'd found him far more gregarious than she'd anticipated. From all the *Henderson Happenings* she'd read about Vance Evans and Team Henderson and all the research she'd done on E&E Investments, she knew Vance was something of a force to be reckoned with. He'd been a ball player—a good one—in high school and college and, until recently, he'd served his community on the police force while coaching Henderson High's varsity baseball team through stellar winning seasons. She also knew he was hot for his wife, Piper, because they were not so subtly suggested as the couple who was seen entering and leaving local bed-and-breakfast establishments during the light of day.

She watched as he read a text message, his mouth twisting into something between a pained grimace and a wry smile.

On their tour around town, Jinx thought it was curious that Vance started with the baseball field. There, he'd explained, was where his friendship with Brooks Bennett, the soon-to-be mayor, had developed. The story, along with Vance's emphatic expressions of awe when he spoke about Brooks, tickled Jinx. She'd never been around a man who spoke with such admiration for another. She knew that if they happened to run into Brooks during their tour, she would need to make a very good impression. It was obvious Vance loved Brooks, and it was Brooks's agenda he was following when it came to Henderson.

While she and Vance had strolled down Main Street, she had to suppress just how much she already knew about the man's hometown. She let Vance go on and on, even though she was already aware of the coming Big Pie Plate Shop, CC Henderson and its connection to the infamous Crain Carraway, and the construction of *Reds*, the wine shop opening in conjunction with a wine-tasting bar—*Swirl*—and the farm-to-table restaurant—*Flights*.

There were other, older businesses on Main Street, but Vance's energy was focused on the new ventures. Like the *Sports Stop* that Vance admitted was going to be a gold mine in a few years, but forbade her from ever repeating he'd said so.

They were at the end of the street, looking back at the pretty sight Main Street was becoming. Not a cobweb had been allowed to form since the facades had been painted less than a year ago. She loved the quarter boards that hung sporadically down both sides. The huge pots of cascading flowers focused the eye, pulling attention away from scaffolding and building supplies that were piled up neatly here and there.

To Jinx, it was as if she'd stepped into a movie she'd been watching. Ever since March, she'd read and seen pictures of Henderson and what was happening here. Team Henderson's publicity department was good at its job, painting a bright future for the run-down town. She knew without a doubt she was standing in the brightest part of it all with one of its brightest stars. The moment could only get better if Cal Johnson walked into view.

"Hmm," Vance drew out again, the part grimace/part chuckle still present.

She tried her best not to inquire, but around Vance, she found her nature wasn't one of a shrinking violet. "Hmm?" she queried.

Vance looked up and twisted his lips before saying, "It seems my grandmother has set you up with a dinner companion."

She felt her eyes go big. "Me?" Thoughts of Cal Johnson danced through her head, even though she knew—*knew*—he was playing baseball on the West Coast for the next ten days.

"Jinx," Vance said. "My grandmother is a meddler. And she likes to be in on all the hottest gossip. She has more friends under the age of thirty than I do. So, *this* is something she does."

Jinx squinted at Vance in confusion. "Only she didn't seem too enamored with me."

"What?" Vance's attention came sharply away from his phone.

"I mean, she seemed rather"—Jinx struggled for just the right word—"flummoxed."

"Flummoxed?" Vance grinned.

"Perplexed. Greatly bewildered," she explained.

"I know what the word means, smarty pants. I'm just sure you're mistaken."

Jinx was pretty sure she wasn't.

"Em is a big personality," Vance explained as he stowed his phone in his back pocket. "I know she peppered you with personal questions, but that's a small town for you. And I'm suspicious she's one of the authors of *Henderson Happenings*. And if she is, she could have been digging for details to throw into that." He eyed Jinx. "You're gonna need a thick skin around here. Especially being a mover and shaker."

Jinx's smile went broad. "And you think the curator of the library is going to be a mover and shaker?"

"If it ends up being you. Which," he said, lowering his voice, "I'm hoping it will for a lot of reasons, your age and IQ being two of them. Because a hot babe running things at the library might inspire our male youth to visit the place more often. And I'm planning to recruit you into directing said youth into areas of interest that can benefit this town."

"How so?" She tilted her head, grinning like a fool.

Vance tilted his head in the opposite direction and grinned right back. "What's with the smile?"

"You."

"Me?"

"Yeah. You. I've known you for only a couple of hours, yet there is no way to miss that you are always thinking about Henderson."

"Of course." He straightened. "And, it's not in the job description, but … yeah, I want *you* thinking that way too. Look, Jinx, I'm just gonna lay it out here. The fact that you've already done some real research on our town, our people, and our cause speaks volumes. If I can get you to buy into what we are trying to do—get you to become part of the Ra-Ra Henderson propaganda and then dole it out over at the library—subtly, of course—that would be a bonus. And I think my grandmother thinks so too. Which is why she's got you set up with a date tonight."

"A date?"

"Well, she's not calling it that, of course. Sneaky Em is suggesting that having dinner with Jaxon Wright would give you a chance to ask questions outside of a formal interview."

"So this dinner isn't part of the interview?"

Vance shook his head. "No. Use it as your chance to do hands-on research while you're in town. Only..." his voice trailed off.

"What?"

He hesitated a moment. "Nothing. Jax is probably a standup-guy."

Jinx grinned. "Are you warning me off this non-date your *grandmother* has set up?"

"Hey." Vance held up his hands. "Lolly—she's my, ah, stepsister and is closer to your age—she says Jax had a reputation in high school. A one-and-done dating standard. Which to me means he's in it to hit it, but I'm the last person who should be throwing stones. Glass houses and all."

"So, you? In it to hit it?" She stared him up and down, starstruck. "I can absolutely imagine."

He pointed to himself. "Married and reformed. Still, yeah. Can't throw stones."

Jinx lifted her brows, dying of curiosity.

"Ah, moving on, Miss Davenport," Vance redirected, spinning her so her gaze was off him and focused down the street. "Em says he'll pick you up at the Jones's place—I mean B&B's B&B—at six thirty this evening. Come on, I want to show you the site of the sports academy before I drop you off."

Vance didn't simply drop Jinx off at the bed-and-breakfast. He walked her to the door, carried her bag inside, and introduced her to Brenda and Billy Jones like he had known them all his life. Which, she supposed, he had.

The size of Henderson was interesting, Jinx thought as she opened her suitcase and hung up the one outfit she'd packed. She looked down at her ensemble, the white eyelet skirt and the red silk tank, and figured if she put on the long necklace she'd brought for tomorrow's interview, she'd be dressed enough for dinner at any country club.

She'd seen this club. Vance had driven her through the parking lot to show her the tennis and golf facilities the sports academy would be using. The building was charming but not impressive. Not like the Richmond country club her folks belonged to. Since it was a Thursday, she figured she didn't have to be all that dressed up. As long as she stuck to the standard no-denim policy, she'd probably pass without drawing sideways glances.

The Joneses had graciously invited her to join them for either a sweet tea or stronger libation, as they'd put it, on their cozy front porch. So Jinx quickly touched up her makeup, figuring the more people who met her now, the better her odds might be for blending in if she was fortunate enough to land the job.

Then she smiled at her reflection because Vance hadn't hidden his exuberance about her "coming on board" as he termed it. Talking to her about Team Henderson and the sports academy as if she was going to play a pivotal role. In fact, when she casually asked him if he'd given the same tour to all of the other applicants, he stopped, stuttered, and then flat-out admitted, "No." He did go on to explain that the rest of the applicants were from the surrounding area, no one further away than Raleigh, and since she was from out of state, he thought it would be best to use the time she had here wisely.

She nodded, but noted his somewhat shy but mostly sly grin, which had given him away. Vance Evans liked her for this job. A lot. He'd mentioned her age several times, and though she had feared being twenty-one was going to be perceived as a detriment, apparently in this town, it was a plus.

She'd take the plus.

Mr. and Mrs. Jones greeted her with warmth and humor when she joined them on their front porch, informing her she was their only guest that evening.

"Our business is mostly weekenders," Billy Jones had told her, one hand in his pocket, the other indicating the rocking chair she should take. "We're packed to the gills Friday and Saturday nights."

"Because of the parties?" Jinx asked.

"You know about our parties?" Brenda wondered.

"I've been reading the *Henderson Happenings* since March. So I follow the social events here."

"Why on earth would a Richmond girl be interested in what's happening in this ol' town?"

"Cal Johnson," she said unabashedly. "I'm a fan. Henderson hit my radar when I saw the video where he sang at The Situation."

"Oh, that. My goodness, everyone put up such a fuss."

"Were you there?" Jinx asked excitedly. "Did you hear him sing?"

"Billy dragged me out for his pitching demonstration—"

"Which also would have made a great YouTube video," Mr. Jones added.

"But after we had our free taste of beer in the parking lot, we called it a day. That party went on until *three* in the morning. We weren't open as an official bed-and-breakfast yet, but we were housing the Harvin's children and their friends who'd come in for The Spectacular. That's how we got the idea to open the place up. People want to bring friends for the weekend, and we've got the room. Our four children live too far away to come home regularly."

Jinx discovered that the Jones's kids were not only dispersed around the country, but all around the world. All living interesting lives that Jinx found fascinating as they chatted, sipped, and rocked on the front porch of B&B's B&B. In fact, the three were so engrossed in a humorous story about China, dogs, and misinterpretation issues that Jinx didn't notice the huge silver pickup pull to the curb at the head of the Jones's long front lawn.

Jaxon Wright was halfway to the front porch when the group spotted him. Jinx spontaneously smiled at the sight of his height and broad shoulders, now convinced that she hadn't been seeing things when he'd hopped out of his truck that afternoon. He truly was as stunning as he'd first appeared. Although it did seem that some of those sexy rough edges that had caught her eye had been polished since her first inspection.

Earlier that afternoon, Jax had taken off his ball cap and run his fingers through golden locks, leaving it thoroughly tousled. Shorter on the sides, the hair on top was caught enticingly between curly and wavy. Right now, the ball cap was gone and his hair was tidy with enough product to out Jaxon for knowing what he was doing in the grooming department. He was definitely not your ordinary auto mechanic. She wondered if his grooming regimen included waxing his chest. Or … other things.

Jinx felt herself blush and imagined Emelina Flores somehow getting a hold of her inner thoughts and broadcasting them in the *Henderson Happenings*. *Yikes.* She shook that nightmare from her head and refocused on Jaxon.

His face was, well, gorgeous was the word that kept coming to mind. Tan, with a strong chin, straight nose, and icy blue eyes—the kind that were clear, like a summer day—under wonderfully thick and expressive brows. She remembered how the right one lifted independently as he'd scrutinized her this afternoon.

And he'd *definitely* scrutinized her. She hadn't remembered that little thrill until this minute, as he gave her the same notable once-over. And, like Vance, there was no way she could throw stones. Her greedy eyes were raking him up and down almost as boldly.

But isn't that what normal single people did?

This afternoon she had liked him. Right away. Before any words had been exchanged, she *liked* Jaxon Wright. She liked the way he held himself loose and casual. The way he'd greeted Mr. Evans with confident deference. The way he'd greeted her with a cute, easygoing grin before his curious head-to-toe once-over ended in a rather blatant smile of approval. One that set off sparklers deep down inside.

Yes. She definitely liked Jaxon Wright, so she was belatedly becoming a fan of Mrs. Flores too.

"Mrs. Jones." Jaxon greeted Brenda first with a big hug. "My momma said to tell you that your hot chicken salad hit the spot the other night, and she'd like your recipe. Mr. Jones," he said, shaking the man's hand. "How's that old hot rod of yours running? You need me to come over and give her a tune-up?"

"I might. You stayin' put?"

"I'm in town indefinitely. You give me a call over at Ma's if you'd like me to come over and work my magic."

"Will do. Now, I understand you've been given the duty of entertaining our lovely guest this evening."

That's when Jaxon turned toward Jinx and shined his gorgeous grin in her direction. "Kinda like I won the lottery, right?"

"Stop." Jinx waved him off, ducking her face as she felt it heat. "I sincerely hope this hasn't upset any of your plans."

"Pfft." Jaxon's brows furrowed before shooting high. "I palmed Mr. Evans a twenty hoping I could persuade him to give me your number. Not sure how I'm going to repay him for forcing you to go out with me."

"Oh?" Jinx tilted her head, curious. "I was under the impression this was Mrs. Flores's idea."

"Mrs. Flores is definitely the razzle part of Mr. Evans's dazzle, all conspiring so you'd have no choice but to join me for dinner without me having to ask."

"Since when have you ever been afraid to ask out a pretty girl?" Brenda teased.

"Well, I've never seen one quite this pretty. Have you?"

Brenda Jones, Billy Jones, and Jaxon Wright fixed their gazes on Jinx, who could feel her face heat *again*. "Stop." She twirled around. "All of you." She gave a short, nervous laugh as she swiped up her purse and sweater and then brushed between Mrs. Jones and Jaxon, moving toward the porch steps. "It's rude to tease the newcomer," she scolded in jest.

"Y'all have a good time, ya hear," Billy called from behind. She didn't wait for Jaxon, just waved a hand and kept moving. Her heart was beating too quickly to trust a response. Vance's words from earlier rang through her mind. *"You're gonna need a thick skin around here."*

She'd originally scoffed at that. She'd been the odd duck all her life. She'd imagined her skin was as thick as it could get. But it had always been her age or IQ that forced her into the center of speculation. The only comments ever made about her appearance were that she was the spitting image of her mother.

And Jinx thought her mother was rather hideous.

Perhaps the fact that gorgeous Jaxon Wright was the one paying her a compliment was the reason she was feeling so ... incandescent. She drew in a deep breath, tried to release nervous energy through the exhale, and then focused her attention straight ahead on Jaxon Wright's truck.

His rather oversized truck.

Well, the wheels were huge, that was for sure. She slowed her pace as she drew closer, wondering how she was ever going to get up in the thing.

"Hold on," Jaxon said as he jogged around her to open the door. "I'll give you a hand up."

"Up is right," she said, staring at the distance between the curb and the floorboards.

"This is my brother's," he said with a shoulder lift. "I'm sort of between rides at the moment, so I've been using the *Silver Hulk*. Probably should have thought to bring my mom's car."

"No. Ah..." she hedged, looking over the monstrosity. The name Silver Hulk definitely suited and somehow made the idea of riding around in it entertaining. "It's okay. I've never ridden in a truck with a name before. Maybe if I can just grab—*whoa.*"

Jaxon had taken matters into his own hands. Literally. While Jinx was busy reaching for the interior handle above the door, Jaxon had taken hold of both her hips and boosted her up into the seat. When she turned to him in shock, because, yeah, he'd just put his hands all over her ass, he whispered, "Wanted to give the Joneses something to talk about." Then he grinned like he'd just told a big, fat lie.

Ye-aah, this guy was smooth, Jinx thought as she watched him closely. Jaxon Wright was trouble. Trouble wrapped up in nearly irresistible packaging.

And—oh—how she totally needed to resist.

Because, she realized slowly, *this* was part of the interview. In fact, it was occurring to her that her entire stay in Henderson was part of the interview process. Of course, Vance Evans, as smart as he was, saw it that way too.

Yes, he probably did want her input on their four-year library plan, and she'd definitely be giving it to him. But knowing what she did about Vance and this town he was killing himself to save? He probably wanted to know if she would fit in and be more of a help than a hindrance to the overall cause.

Still, she was female and twenty-one, and therefore not immune to the thrill of being inside a ridiculously sized truck with a very good-looking guy. Jaxon and the Silver Hulk were giving her a head rush. And she was tempted to let it ride, just for the moment. After all, she was here—in *the* infamous Henderson—and if there was no chance of running into *the* infamous Cal Johnson, why not allow herself to be dazzled by Jaxon Wright and whoever else she may meet? Since this opportunity could turn out to be nothing but a bust, she figured she better gather as many memories as she could.

"Do you think the club will be crowded tonight?" she asked as Jaxon drove them away from the Joneses, who—by the way—were waving. *Seriously. Could this town be any friendlier?*

"I doubt it. Although lots of the old guard enjoy eating there regularly, so we won't be lonely."

"Any of your friends?"

He shook his head. "Few of them reside in Henderson."

"So what did you mean when you told Mr. Jones you were staying indefinitely?"

Jaxon drove with his left wrist casually draped over the steering wheel, but his focus was directed out the windshield. "Since my brother moved back from Arizona, he's fallen in love with a girl and his hometown. Now the pushy bastard is trying to wrangle me and all of my other brothers into moving back too. I'm his first employee."

"How many brothers?"

"There are five of us."

"Wow."

"Yeah. We're a handful." He glanced over and gave her a wink.

"So, you've moved back."

"I guess. Although I'm living with my parents, so that sucks," he said good-naturedly. "I have dibs on the badass bachelor pad over the garage once Chase moves out."

"Chase? One of your brothers?"

"No. No. He's, like, older than my dad. He was Xavier's employer in Arizona. The two of them are considering going into business together here. Architectural firm combined with land development."

"Oh. I just assumed you worked for an auto repair shop because you came to rescue Mr. Evans today."

"I'm good with my hands," he said, shooting a flirty grin in her direction while wiggling his fingers over the steering wheel. "Good with all sorts of tools. Though I'm particularly good with motors. When I heard Mr. Evans's Maserati broke down, I volunteered to go out and take a look." The smile that came at her now was conspiratorial. "The model he owns, that 2012 GranTurismo, was the last one built with a Ferrari engine." He looked over at her as he turned them into the country club parking lot. "Not ever gonna turn down a chance to get my hands on a Ferrari engine."

Not knowing anything about engines, Jinx couldn't help but smile at his enthusiasm. Then she noticed they'd parked between two other monster trucks. "Don't tell me," she said as he helped her down. "Your brothers are here."

Jaxon looked confused at first. Then he realized she was indicating the trucks. "No. As I understand it, *Big Red* belongs to an Army Ranger named Thor, and that one over there belongs to a Texas billionaire."

"Billionaire?" Jinx's eyes shot wide. "There are billionaires in Henderson?"

"Ah…" He scratched his head. "Probably not. I was just throwing that term out there to be descriptive. Probably should have just said a rich Texan."

"Crain Carraway?"

They'd been walking across the front porch, and Jaxon was grabbing for the door when he halted their progress, barring her way with a look of intense scrutiny. "And how is it you know about Carraway?"

Jinx shook her head, realizing she was probably going to be perceived as creepy if she kept spilling the knowledge she'd accumulated about Henderson's movers and shakers. "Vance gave me a tour of the area this afternoon. He described Mr. Carraway when he pointed out CC Henderson."

"Oh." Jaxon hesitated a moment more, searching her face as if he was trying to detect a lie. "Right," he said. But she got the feeling he wasn't certain everything was necessarily right.

Once inside and up the foyer steps, they were greeted by Harry.

Harry, the magical bartender Vance had described this afternoon. Harry the matchmaker, Vance had said. Harry, who Vance worried was in cahoots with his grandmother co-authoring the *Henderson Happenings* newsletters. Harry, whose dark hair and sparkling gold eyes were so welcoming Jinx had the urge to throw herself into his arms because of the joy she felt at the sight of him. There was something powerful emanating from Harry.

And boy, she wondered if Harry knew she could feel it. Because he just kept sparkling in her direction, looking her over as if he hadn't seen her in years and was very happy to have her in front of him now.

"Miss Davenport. Welcome to Henderson Country Club. I'm here to ensure your evening is an enjoyable experience."

"Back off, Harry," Jaxon joked. "You can swindle a date if she comes back to town. Tonight, she's mine."

Mine? Jinx wondered, all thoughts flying off Harry and onto Jaxon. Because—oooh—didn't the thrill of being *his* just shoot a tingle up her spine.

It was simply not possible to be in a better mood. To Jinx, it was like she'd landed in Hollywood and was running into all of the biggest stars. Harry led them to a table in the very center of the dining room. She looked around as he pulled out her chair. "This table certainly isn't inconspicuous."

"You need to be seen," Harry insisted as she sat. "People are curious about the new librarian."

"I haven't been offered the job yet," she countered.

"Nor has she accepted," Jaxon said, seating himself.

"Semantics," Harry assured both of them, placing napkins in their laps and handing each an open menu. Jinx noticed the prices were absent from her menu. "Mr. Evans requests you enjoy dinner on him. One of the perks of being the top applicant for the job." Harry departed.

"Wow," Jinx said, feeling giddy and biting her lip as she stared at Jaxon over her menu. "This definitely feels like the royal treatment."

Jax shot her a glance but immediately looked down at his menu. He cleared his throat. "The pasta dishes are mediocre, but everything else is outstanding." He folded his menu and set it aside. "At least it's far superior to the food served here when I was growing up." He leaned across the table conspiratorially and whispered. "New chef. Surprisingly good. I hope they can keep her. Her name's Regina. She's originally from Natchez, Mississippi, where there is scuttlebutt about her having a run-in with a rival garden club. She literally had to leave town."

"Are you a food critic?" she asked, as she looked over the menu items.

"Well, I can certainly tell a bland dish from a tasty one. I'll be curious if this fare holds up to what you're used to in Richmond. I've never been to Richmond proper, but I've spent some time at the raceway."

"NASCAR? You've been to the races?"

Again, he held up his hands and wiggled his fingers. "Worked on some engines."

Her eyes went wide. "Race car engines?" *Holy shit, she hoped her tongue wasn't hanging out of her mouth.*

He nodded. "Once as an apprentice and twice as a hired hand."

"Were you part of … what do they call it? The pit crew?" *Because—wow.*

"I wasn't one of the guys changing tires. No. I was the mechanic. Responsible for how the car functioned, for the engine tweaks and race strategy. Most everything I did happened during the week prior to the race. Pre and post-qualifying engine tweaks."

So much cooler.

"I've only witnessed auto racing on TV, but that sounds pretty heady."

"It is." Jax told her. Then he shook his head. "It was."

Harry arrived back at their table with an open bottle of red wine. "I'd be happy to bring you a cocktail," he said as he poured, "but Mrs. Flores has insisted you at least try her favorite varietal."

"Insisted?" Jinx's brows rose in curiosity as a distant alarm sounded in her brain.

"Insisted," Harry assured her with a wink.

CHAPTER SEVEN

"Where is everybody?" Vance approached a sleepy, blue-eyed Piper rocking a zonked-out Vance, Jr. in the mansion's blue bedroom. His heart swelled at the sight. For all the woman's lawyer-istic proclivities, right now, she looked as content as he'd ever seen her. Being a mother truly suited Piper. And having her here at home and happy to see him suited him just fine. Frankly, it was all he'd ever need. "I stopped by the house," he said quietly as he kissed her forehead, not wanting to disturb VJ. "They've dug the foundation."

Piper leaned her head back to look up at him, wetting her lips before she spoke. "It's a start."

Vance nodded. The house he was building Piper—the house they were building together—wasn't going to go up fast. It was large in scope, elaborate in technology, sleek in design, and being built with a large family and entertaining in mind. The architect and builder agreed it was a twelve-to eighteen-month project if all went well.

"We can look around. Rent something for the time being. I don't want to kick Pinks out of the pool house, and we'd need more space than that anyway."

Piper gave a soft laugh. "I'm in no hurry. Are you?"

He smiled and combed a hand over her hair. "I'm not the one living with my in-laws."

She shifted forward, handing Vance, Jr. over. "I love living here. Living with Genevra and Em is healing for me after the loss of my mother." She stood and indicated he should sit. "I think if they weren't here loving me and Vance, Jr., I'd be missing my mother terribly, so sad she hadn't lived to meet her first grandchild. The house is big enough for all of us. I'm in no rush to leave."

"I'm going to remind you of those words this time next year."

She nodded, curling up on the bed as Vance took her seat in the rocker.

"How's the kid?" he asked, looking down at his son. Dark hair, blue-green eyes, full cheeks, chubby arms and legs. He and Piper had only known him three months, yet he was their whole world.

"Good. Rolled over today."

"That's not new."

"No. He rolled over and over and over and then got himself stuck under a chair leg."

"When is he going to crawl?"

"He likes to roll. Might not crawl."

Vance gave his son a curious look. "All right." He looked up. "As long as he isn't rolling into kindergarten, I'm good. How are you?"

"Tired."

He nodded, hoping the stranglehold he was putting on the words dying to come out of his mouth didn't actually show.

"Molly and I had a teleconference with the firm who will be installing our manufacturing equipment at the end of the month. I did a walk-through with Xavier at the shop. Did you get a chance to stop in?"

He nodded, still struggling to keep his damn mouth shut.

When she didn't go on, he knew he had to comment.

"Baby, it's going to be a showplace," he admitted. "I…" he stumbled, looking down at Vance, Jr.

"Vance. I'm not leaving you or Vance, Jr. I'm going to be down the street from E&E, selling Henderson's Big Pie Plates."

"And cooking," he added, still looking at VJ. "In that shop. Not in our kitchen."

Piper sighed. "I love you."

Vance nodded. He knew she did. "I'm working on it," he said quietly.

"I know you are."

"Who took care of VJ?" he asked.

"When?"

"Today."

"I did."

He looked up. "During your conference call?"

She shrugged. "Sure."

"What if he started to cry? Or needed something?"

Piper blinked. "He did start to cry. So I nursed him."

"During the call?" Vance was startled.

"Yes."

"How?"

"What do you mean, how?"

"I mean, how did you conduct business while breastfeeding?"

"It was simple. Vance, Jr. did all the work."

"Piper."

"What?"

"You shouldn't have to breastfeed while you're in the middle of a conference call."

"No?"

"Of course not."

"Well, I could have given him a bottle, I suppose, but really, at this point, breastfeeding is pretty simple." She shot a sweet look at his baby. "The two of us are experts now."

"What I mean is, I'm not going to have a nervous breakdown if we hire a nanny so you can do what you need to do."

One of Piper's pretty eyebrows lifted in his direction.

"Don't look at me like that."

"Vance. Come on. This is an enormous shift in attitude."

"My attitude hasn't shifted one bit," he informed her. "But if you have the drive to build a pie plate empire, I'm not going to make it harder on you. We need a nanny. Hire one."

Piper blinked. "I'm not sure we do need a nanny."

This time it was Vance who raised his brows.

Piper sighed, sinking down onto the mattress.

"What?" he asked.

"Look. I hear what you're saying."

"Do you?"

She looked over at him. "I hear you saying that you love me enough to give me what I want, even if it kills you."

He barked out a laugh and then caught himself short, not wanting to wake his son. "Shit," he whispered and then grinned up at his wife. "That is pretty much exactly what I'm saying."

"I know." She smiled. "And I appreciate it. Thank you."

"Still doesn't mean my attitude has shifted."

"Duly noted."

"I'm just ... succumbing to reality. Trying to, you know, put on my big-boy pants."

"Vance, Jr. has a mother and a father who love him. He's got a great grandmother, grandparents, aunts, uncles—one even his own age who lives with him. He's got a lot of love. He's never going to feel that he's alone."

Vance swallowed, trying really hard not to cast his own insecurities onto his son. "I know." He nodded. "I know."

"I'm not going to leave him. I'm not going to leave you."

She must have said those words a thousand times, yet they never failed to soothe him.

"I'm trying, Pipes."

"Stop trying," she said softly. "Just let it lie. Let it be. I love you."

"Warts and all." He grimaced.

"Nah. You're perfect Vance Evans. I've loved you for as long as I can remember. To me—warts, scars, ill-gotten reputation—you're all I've ever wanted."

"Pipes, your standards are nothing to brag about."

She laughed. "Be that as it may, I'm yours, you're mine, and he's ours."

"When can we tangle up another one like him into this *Yours, Mine, and Ours* scenario?"

"Another baby?"

He nodded, locking eyes with her.

"For goodness sakes, he's just three months old."

"And we aren't getting any younger."

"I haven't even gotten my body back."

"Pfft. You're adorable."

"I mean it. And I want to enjoy this one with you—be a nice little *us*—before we go and add more."

"I always wanted brothers and sisters," Vance said, looking at his precious boy.

"And, now you've got Beau."

"Brody," he corrected. "And he's cool, but it'll be forever until he can do shooters with me at the bar."

"Is that what you think brothers do?"

"Sure. After they've competed in some sporting event."

Piper laughed. "What if the next one's a girl?"

Vance's gaze shot to Piper's. "We definitely have to have a girl, Pipes. Three boys and a girl. I'll leave the order up to you. Although having the boys first and all close together would be good. They could play on the same team. Hey, what's with Lolly not wanting to get engaged?"

Piper blinked, startled. "Where did that come from?"

"Brooks needs three boys too. And I want them similar in age to ours. Lolly needs to get with the program."

"Lolly is busy. You think I'm busy? She's crazy busy."

"It's not like she can't cook up a baby while she's busy designing fancy dresses."

"Yeah, but changing diapers on her drafting table might be an impediment."

"*She'll* have a nanny. Fucking Brooks is the one trying to talk me into it. You can be sure his kids are going to be dealing with the same shit."

"Same shit?"

"You know what I mean."

"Yes. Unfortunately, I do."

"Hold on. We're getting off track. We are talking about our boys and Brooks's boys playing ball together at Henderson High and bringing home state trophies year after year."

"Oh, is that what we're talking about?"

"Yeah. It's our dream. Can't happen until he knocks up Lolly though, so I want you to talk to her. Get her on board."

"You can't be serious."

"I'm perfectly serious."

"Vance. Look at your son."

He did. Totally made him smile. "Yeah?" he said, grinning down at the sleeping bundle.

"He's *three months* old," she insisted.

"And he was three minutes old just yesterday. Time flies, Pipes."

"And dreams change. For instance, Vance, Jr. will no doubt be enrolled in the new sports academy."

"Fuck," Vance spat.

"What?"

"Well, how's that gonna work?"

"What do you mean?"

"I went to Henderson High. Brooks went to Henderson High. We are the baseball coaches at Henderson High."

Piper blinked as if confused. "Yes, but you're building this sports academy. I just assumed …"

Vance's mouth hung open. Yeah, he'd assumed … what? He started rubbing his brows, his head beginning to hurt. Then it dawned on him. "This is what we're up against." He started to laugh. "This is why the town is divided on the academy."

"Ah–yeah," Piper proclaimed.

"Christ. I didn't see it before. Here I am, dedicated to Henderson High, yet I am creating another school, a *better* school right in its own backyard."

"Vance?"

"Shit."

"Vance!"

"What?"

"Take a breath."

He did. And it helped. At least it helped with the hot, tight, suffocating feeling in his chest, neck, and face. The pain in his head, not so much. "Jesus. Piper, I love this idea. This academy. The plans we have for this place—it's going to be *so* cool. But until this moment, it's been this conceptual dream. Something out there in the future. Sitting on a cloud with a heavenly light shining down on it. The Holy Grail, sitting on top of all the ideas everyone is putting into place to make Henderson a viable, healthy town again. I just didn't realize that I'd have to choose between my alma mater and the Holy Grail."

"You don't have to choose. Not today. Not right now."

Vance sighed, his heart sinking. "But I already have, haven't I?"

Piper shrugged. "If you've got enough love in your heart for three more kids, you no doubt have enough room for two schools." Piper proceeded to stretch and get up, moving into the en suite bathroom. "What you don't have to decide today is how to support them both."

"I suppose not," Vance said, getting lost in thought. For a smart guy, when it came to his personal life, he was still that kid whose mother left him and never looked back. Even though he now had everything he wanted—Piper, Vance, Jr., Brooks, Lolly, his dad, E&E Investments and Pinks, not to mention the satisfaction of seeing this town on the verge of revival—the brutality of his mother's betrayal haunted him. Deep down inside, he still held the fear of not being worthy of the people he loved.

That fear was what had made him loyal to a fault. No way would he ever up and leave a person, place, or thing that had stood by him in his past. So now he was feeling guilty about the new academy. Because it sure felt like that's exactly what he was doing to Henderson High.

And this nanny business? His adult self knew he simply needed to trust Piper on this. The woman unequivocally loved being a mother. She wasn't going to let Vance, Jr. go neglected. Hell, *he* wasn't going to let Vance, Jr. go neglected. He worked five minutes from home. He could get to his kid at any time. Check in regularly. His kid would grow up knowing he not only had two parents he could count on, but a whole community of support as well.

Along with two high schools to choose between.

Hell.

"So where is everybody?" he asked as Piper came out of the bathroom.

As if on cue, Pinks's voice called from below. "Anybody home?"

Vance carefully got out of the rocker holding VJ in his arms and headed for the bedroom door. "I'll see what's what," he said as he left Piper to fix herself up.

CHAPTER EIGHT

Jaxon watched as the exquisite Jinx Davenport licked her ruby lips, closed her long dark lashes, and savored the taste of Mrs. Flores's fine Spanish wine.

The girl was stunning.

And yet, most intriguing of all—other than that rich, thick, dark-chocolate braided mane of a ponytail cascading over her left shoulder (making him clench his fists to stop from reaching over and grabbing on to the thing, pulling her across the table to get a taste of those cherry-licious lips)—there seemed to be a consistent, delicate *glee* bubbling just underneath her surface.

He hadn't encountered anyone quite like Jinx Davenport. Childlike in her exuberant curiosity of all things Henderson, yet seemingly at ease being seated in the center of the room.

Jax sucked in a breath of deep satisfaction. After growing up in a household of males where grunts served as speech, farts and burps were emitted without remorse, and the stench of sweat and body odor prevailed, he *really* liked females. Tall, short, plump, thin, older, younger—it didn't matter to Jax. Topping the list of the many things he relished about females was the soft, sweet tone of their voices and their ability to converse. He was enthralled by the ones who rambled on, voicing every random thought. He was curious and amused by those who possessed the ability to change their minds, talking themselves into and out of things while he listened, nodding in rapt attention. Their ever-changing expressions and hand movements delighted him, and he was completely captivated by their laughter.

While most guys complained about females going on and on about one thing or another, Jaxon simply used that time to enjoy their gentle smiles, soft skin, and sweet, sweet scents.

Not unlike wine, he enjoyed the complexities of the fairer sex. The varying properties of color, body, and vibrancy. Unearthing each unique quality became his hobby. He liked delving below the superficial, searching for that something specific that made each woman rare and unique.

There was definitely something about this Jinx Davenport that was intriguing him more than most, though. A depth of intricacy he longed to unravel. Of course, his mission tonight was to uncover her parental heritage so his own agenda had to take a backseat. Which was a shame, really. Of all the girls Jax enjoyed spending time with, this one had a certain twinkle in her eye as if life still held a thrill.

Of course, she was young. Younger than him by six years. So how much real life had she had to deal with?

Since they'd set foot in the place, Jinx had been engaged with everything happening around her, almost giddy to be at the club she claimed to have read so much about. He watched her marvel over Harry and glance around from time to time, looking for someone she might recognize simply from the stories in the *Henderson Happenings*.

But not now.

Now her expression was morphing from enjoying-the-tasty-wine delight into a different emotion entirely. Jax couldn't tell if it was one of curiosity or … skepticism or—*wow*—incredulous speculation?

He wasn't sure.

But since she took a breath, looked right and left, and then leaned in, centering her focus on him, he figured he was about to find out.

"Is this a test?" she asked, pivoting her head so she was glancing at him sideways. Her dark brows were furrowed, and a mischievous grin played upon her lips.

Shit, she's cute.

His own brows rose. "A test?"

"Is it?" Her voice was crisp, but the sly expression on her face indicated she was mildly amused at the thought. "Were you sent to … seduce me?"

Jax fell back in his seat, gaping at her. Of all the things she could have said … "Was I sent here to seduce you?" A half laugh, half snort spouted out of him. "I *wish*," he insisted, picking up his wine glass and downing a big swallow.

She bubbled with laughter, the sound greeting him like jingle bells.

Seriously cute.

"Why in the world would you think I was sent to seduce you?" Then he leaned in, getting serious, and lowered his voice. "Would you *like* me to seduce you, Jinx?"

She blinked, stunned. And then backpedaled fast. "No. I mean, I don't think so. I mean, *of course* no. I just wondered—"

"*Of course* no?" he interrupted, making a good imitation of being completely offended.

"Jaxon." She glanced down, touching the silver of her place setting. "Please."

Jinx was blushing. He'd just made this uber-intelligent, beautiful girl blush.

Oh, Miss Davenport, you are so in for it now.

"All right," he said. "Since I need time to shore up my pride after that unadulterated, *No, Jax, I definitely don't want you to seduce me* comment, I'll listen to you explain yourself."

She gave him a withering look, proving she could quickly bounce back from his teasing. "During my interview, it was obvious Mrs. Flores was not a fan. In fact, she practically stormed out before the inquisition had hardly begun."

"Inquisition?" Jax widened his eyes over her terminology.

Jinx held up a finger. "Yet she arranged for you to take me to dinner and then sent a bottle of her favorite wine—which *is* rather full-bodied and delicious."

You're full-bodied and delicious.

"So, I'm just wondering—sort of putting puzzle pieces together here—if perhaps she has nefarious intentions."

"My seducing you would be nefarious?"

"If I allowed myself to fall under your spell—during an interview, no less—it may reflect poorly upon my character."

"So, I'm casting a spell." He smiled.

"Umm ..."

"Which you are fighting." He felt his smile turn into a grin. The wicked one. *Really. This was just too easy.*

"Stop it," Jinx begged, blushing all over again. "Obviously, I'm wrong. I apologize."

"No, no. I think we should definitely explore this seduction idea. Though I'm not usually one to work so quickly. I mean, we just met this afternoon. But hey, I'm a doer. A team player. If Mrs. Flores wants me to seduce you—if *you* want me to seduce you—I'm in. Lock, stock, and barrel."

"Okay. So this isn't a test," Jinx decided.

She held his gaze, even though that pretty blush of hers stayed put. The girl had grit.

"It is a test," he confessed. After all, he was here trolling for information on behalf of the woman who'd sent the wine. Jinx absolutely nailed that. Maybe he wasn't sent to seduce her, but Jinx wasn't all that far off the mark was she? "Obviously, the Big Em— Mrs. Flores—wants to loosen your lips with her pricey wine. She and her family are the lead benefactors of the library. And you're—" he looked her over, his brain scrambling for adjectives other than beautiful or captivating—"young. You can't blame her for wanting to know how you handle social situations. Sending you to dinner with me, a guy you barely know, where all eyes are on you and everyone is whispering 'Who is that?' Yeah, I'm pretty sure this is a test. But I'm guessing it's not designed to zero in on your moral fortitude."

"I apologize," she said contritely. "I didn't mean to offend you, or imply—"

"That just being in my presence leaves you spellbound? No offense taken."

Jinx sighed. "You're impossible."

"I'm going to let you in on a little secret." He leaned in and lowered his voice. "When it comes to strong moral fiber, the Big Em doesn't necessarily set the best example. So, you know. I don't think she'd throw stones."

Jinx settled back in her chair with her wine glass in hand and a big grin on her face. "That's the exact expression her grandson used today. When he was describing *you*."

"Vance?"

"Yes."

Shit. "How so?"

He watched as Jinx tilted her head, assessing him in that Hale Evans way he'd noticed earlier. "No. I've offended you enough. Please, forget I even mentioned it."

"You can't *offend* me, Jinx. I told you, I'm the youngest of five brothers. My skin is thicker than cowhide. Trust me, I'm immune to personal attacks on my character as much as I am to those on my body."

"Your brothers beat you up?"

"All the damn time," he stressed. "And if I wasn't the one stuck under the pig pile, I was the one being teased or goaded or simply slapped upside the head for existing."

"Yet, you're smiling."

"Oh, hell yeah." He sat back, crossing his arms. "I learned to give as good as I got. I'm the only one who had the balls to play football instead of that pansy-ass sport of baseball because I could take a hit. I could also run, dodge, and escape a tackle before I was ten. I was killer-good during my Pop Warner days. Held up darn well on the high school team too. I'm not the tallest brother, but I am the sturdiest, the fastest, and my mother loves me best, so ya know—"

"You're a momma's boy," she finished with a grin.

Shit. Seriously. She was getting under his skin fast. "Are you really sitting across from me right now jerking my chain? I'm her *favorite*," he insisted. "What the hell do you consider a momma's boy anyway?"

"I don't know," Jinx laughed as Harry brought their salad course. "I am jerking your chain, because you certainly don't remind me of a momma's boy. You're all"—she twirled her fork at him—"done."

"Done?" he asked, lifting his own fork.

"A grown man," she clarified. "Like you don't need a mother, or even *have* a mother. You're just—done."

He lifted one eyebrow. "And what about you? Are you done?"

"Actually, my mother was *done* with *me* early on," she said, cutting into her salad. So, I would say I'm"—she searched for a word—"half-baked."

He grinned. "You know that means—"

"Not fully thought through? Lacking a sound basis? Yes, I do."

"What are you? A walking dictionary?"

"I'm a librarian, so kinda, yeah. And I intended it to be a play on words, Mr. Brainiac. Indicating that I was forced to be *done* prematurely."

"How do you mean?" Jax felt a prick of guilt as he asked the question. The vulnerability he saw surfacing was palpable, and something Jinx had been decidedly without up until this moment. Still, he told himself, this is exactly what he'd been asked to find out. About her mother.

She breathed a heavy sigh that carried with it a simple, yet somehow defeated smile. "I, too, am the youngest. Yet, unlike you"—she managed a grin—"I'm not my mother's favorite. Ah–that is to say, my mother is her *own* favorite. And she's also my father's favorite."

"So you were, what? Left alone to raise yourself?"

"There was a nanny for a bit. Then there were all of the teachers and administrators that come with a prestigious girls boarding school. And there was my grandmother." She smiled, and this time her eyes lit up.

"Your grandmother?" he asked, thinking of how *Em* might also be her grandmother. The same woman who set her up on this sneaky date in order to swindle information out of her—which he was apparently doing.

"My grandmother liked me. Well," she corrected, "she at least took pity on me. When I was little, I would stay with her while my sister and parents went to New York. Paris. Australia," she said longingly. "I've always wanted to go to Australia."

"Your sister is older than you?"

"Lisette is my half-sister. Her mother passed away when she was an infant. She's seven years older than me. And she didn't beat up on me like your brothers did. She was kind, but she was distracted by her friends and her own life. She didn't have time for a younger sister."

"Jinx," he said without thinking. "You sound lonely."

"I was," she told him point blank. "I am," she said without any sort of bashfulness or unease. "You can tell the Evanses that if they ask you. Because I'll be dedicated to this job for a number of reasons, but loneliness is right there at the top of the list." Her eyes were wide, and with the moisture Jax detected gathering at the edges, his heart started to clench. "I was ... smart," she blurted. She dabbed a finger at the inside of one eye and then the other. "Too smart. Too smart for my parents, too smart for my school, too smart for my classmates, my ... teachers," she said. "I've been pushed to the next level over and over again, grade after grade, school after school. I attended two freaking colleges"—she said in exasperation—"*at the same time*. I'm as done as a twenty-one-year-old can be. Done with being pushed out. Moved ahead. And socially left behind," she sighed. Her eyes narrowed, and she gazed at him in earnest. "I'm hoping adulthood is going to be different."

He nodded. Felt himself nodding and nodding. Unable to do anything else to reassure her while words got tangled up in his throat.

"How old are you?" she asked.

"Twenty-seven." He gulped. It was as if she'd somehow transferred all of her vulnerabilities over to him.

"Done," she confirmed, looking down at her plate and then taking a bite of her salad. He followed her lead and started to eat. "Please tell me being an adult is different."

Jax cleared his throat. "Jinx. I'm the fifth child in a large family. I'm the *baby*. No one is ever going to consider me an adult. I don't even consider myself an adult."

"You don't?"

"No," he said honestly. "I don't. I don't have a real job. I don't have my own place to live. And no one I know seems to have a problem with that."

"Except you."

"What?"

Jinx held her cutlery still. "You obviously have a problem with that. Because you are an adult, and you want a real job and your own place to live."

He shrugged. *Did he? Did he want that?* "On my own terms," he said, surprising himself. "I want all that, yes. But I'm not interested in settling."

"No one should settle."

"No. They shouldn't. Would you mind explaining that to my mother?"

She glanced up from her plate, returning his grin, though hers seemed a little sad and a lot thoughtful. "Be grateful your mother cares," she suggested quietly. "Even if her caring irritates."

He nodded. "My mother is sick," he whispered, as if the fear that ensued grabbed him around the voice box. "Some autoimmune disease or two. Or three," he volunteered while looking at his plate. "I'm not a doctor, and when it comes to medical stuff, I'm better keeping my head in the sand. I just want her to be well. I want to believe she can recover. I don't want to hear about statistics and probabilities. Too depressing. So I picture her healthy. Like she was two years ago."

"There's something to that," Jinx assured him. "Focusing on what you want, instead of what you don't want. It's a thing. The Law of Attraction."

"Yeah?" he asked, his eyes brightening at the thought. "I just need to picture what I want, and what? I'll attract it?"

"Focus on how it's going to feel when your mother gets healthy."

In an attempt to get back to the task he'd been assigned by Mr. Evans, Jax responded with, "How about how it's going to feel when I get behind the wheel of that sweet Maserati we both stopped to rescue?"

"That is one beautiful car."

"You a car girl, Jinx?"

She shrugged. "I can't fix them. I don't even know much about them. But I sure like looking at exotic sports cars."

Like father, like daughter?

"Did you stop because you recognized Hale?" *And you're aware he's your father?*

"Recognized Hale?"

"Mr. Evans."

"Ah, no. No. I just stopped, you know, because."

"Because?"

Jinx blinked. "Because someone was broken down. I thought I could offer them a ride, I guess."

"Do you make a habit of that? Offering random people rides?"

"Oh." Jinx sat back, wiping the edges of her mouth with her napkin. "I see what you're asking. No. In fact, I never have before. But my GPS told me I was only a mile out from Henderson, and I already knew I'd have time to kill. The man was well dressed, and the car was expensive. I suppose a serial killer could drive a Maserati, but the odds seemed in my favor. Plus, I was sort of excited."

"About meeting Hale." He made a point to say it as a statement.

"About meeting *anybody* from Henderson." Her eyes were alight with mischief. "I didn't know who he was. Not until he introduced himself. But then I recognized his name immediately. Recalled the article about the birth of his son, Beau. It's funny. I've done a lot of research on E&E Investments and the sports academy they're building with CC Dallas. But his business credentials were not the first thing that came to mind when Mr. Evans told me his name. It was the juicy stuff I'd read in the *Henderson Happenings*."

Jaxon had to give it to her. Either she was the greatest con artist of all time or she was as genuine as she seemed. "I noticed you have your own sweet ride. That Fiat Spider is a pretty, little thing."

She beamed. "It's brand new. A graduation gift from my grandmother."

"I had no idea what it was, but Hale did. Mr. Evans. He knew exactly what you were driving. Even said it was some sort of limited edition."

"The color," she said pridefully. "The color is a limited edition. Well, it comes *on* the limited edition. I saw the color on the showroom floor and fell in love."

"So back to your folks," he ventured as Harry appeared.

"How's the wine?" Harry asked.

"Too good," Jinx told him pointedly. "I'm spilling family secrets."

"Then you're in the right place. Henderson loves a good secret." Harry poured more wine.

"Everyone loves a good secret as long as they're in on it." Jinx smiled.

"True that." Harry winked at Jax. "Your entrees will be out shortly."

Harry cleared their salad plates and then Jinx's eyes landed pointedly on Jax. "So you really weren't sent to seduce me?"

He shook his head. "No, Jinx," he said softly. "As much as I'd relish the job, I'm simply supposed to show you a good time. Answer any questions you have that you may be uncomfortable asking a future employer."

"Like what?" She sat up, eyes glistening in curious delight.

He shrugged. "I don't know. Where you should live? What we do for fun? How far to the nearest Starbucks?"

She scrunched up her nose. "Starbucks?" She shook her head. "I've got a French press in the trunk of my car, complete with an electric coffee grinder and Colombian beans."

"Then you don't care how far it is to the nearest Starbucks. Let me tell you, that's a plus."

"I want this job," she said, leaning in. "Tell me what the Evans family needs to hear from me in order to make that happen."

He leaned in too. "*Why* do you want this job?" he asked. "It's in *Henderson*."

"You don't like it here?"

"Of course, I like it here, but I grew up here. It's my home."

"Maybe I'm looking for that."

"A home?"

"A new place to call home."

Jax sat back, pondering what a pretty girl bright enough to be shoved from grade to grade and school to school could possibly find satisfying in Henderson. And then he remembered Hale Evans's face and the anguish in his eyes when he'd considered that he might have a daughter he never knew about.

"You'll like it here," he told her. "It's the perfect place to call home."

CHAPTER NINE

"Where is everybody?" Pinks stood at the base of the staircase and reached out for VJ as Vance descended.

"I'm good," Vance said, tucking his boy in closer. "Could use a beer though. And yeah, where the hell is everybody?"

The two men approached the unusually dark and quiet kitchen, Pinks flicking on the glass fixtures hanging over the tall countertop area, the cans over the huge center island, as well as the lighting underneath the vast display of cabinetry. He opened the beverage refrigerator underneath the standing bar and took out two longneck bottles. "Looks like it's just us guys," Pinks said, popping the top off two beers and handing one to Vance as he sat. "Wanna heat up some of Genevra's leftover lasagna?"

"Sure. Piper's gonna be down in a minute. There enough for her?"

"Think so." Pinks opened the fridge and pulled a note off the lasagna pan. Vance watched him read it. "Huh," Pinks said.

"Huh, what?"

Pinks set the pan on the counter. "They went to Oxford for dinner."

"Who's they?"

"Hale, Genevra, and Em. They dropped Beau off with Lolly. The note didn't say it, but I'm guessing Mr. Alexander is with them. Em seems pretty smitten with the guy."

"Smitten is putting it mildly," Vance muttered.

Pinks tossed him a wry grin as he preheated the oven. "Your grandmother is a flirt. And a looker. That combination doesn't stay single long."

"Nope. She goes through men like an ice cutter on Lake Michigan during a Polar Vortex. Leaving all kinds of churned up, crusted up havoc in her wake."

"You think she's, like, lookin' for a husband?"

"Lord only knows when it comes to Em. But I doubt it."

"Chase seems like an upstanding guy," Pinks pointed out.

Vance harrumphed. "Change of subject. I met a pretty young thing today who just may be smarter than you."

"Not possible." Pinks flashed a sarcastic grin while pulling out salad fixings from the fridge and then a loaf of Genevra's garlic bread from the freezer.

"Yeah, I wouldn't have thought so either—but you only earned your bachelor's and master's in five years. This chick attended two universities simultaneously and has accumulated two master's degrees at the age of twenty-one."

Pinks stopped all motion and blinked. "Impossible," he decreed, shaking his head.

"She's a certifiable genius. Started early. Says her IQ is a point below mine. I call bullshit on that. Pretty sure she's buttering me up because she wants the job."

"What job?"

"The library job."

"Other than knowing we want the academy students to use it, I've paid zero attention to what's happening with the library." Pinks started cutting tomatoes and throwing them on top of bib lettuce after oiling and seasoning a large wooden salad bowl.

"And there's no need for you to. Until—like everything else around here—it comes to fundraising. Em and I have started a search for someone who thinks like we do when it comes to this library but has the time and energy we simply don't. This girl has the energy for sure. And the passion. She doesn't look the part of an earnest librarian, but she talks a damn good game. I'm meeting with her again tomorrow to go over financials and get her thoughts on how best to add a full academic element to our already stellar public library. I want it to be utilized by both Henderson High and the sports academy." Vance studied his son, still asleep in his arms, as his thoughts churned with fresh ideas.

"Yeah," he finally said, looking back to where Pinks was making the salad. "I hadn't realized it until now, but the library needs to be the link—the catalyst—for forging a friendly relationship between the academy and our public schools."

Pinks shook his head. "It's definitely gonna take a couple of geniuses to figure out how to make that happen. Rural kids, most unable to afford private school. Suburban kids coming in wearing their designer jeans and driving pricey cars."

"No cars," Vance proclaimed.

"What?"

"We'll make that the first rule. No cars for academy students."

"Oh, so the Henderson High students can have cars but the academy students can't?" Pinks argued. "How is that fair? And this from a guy whose father owns a fleet of fancy cars. Look, there are going to be glaring differences between the two student populations. We can't hide that or fix that. We have to find a mutual need both sets of students have and bring them together through that."

Vance rolled his head. "This is why I like hiring people smarter than me."

"Damn right," Pinks muttered.

Vance smiled. "So, okay, Preppy McPrepster. What mutual needs do these very different student populations possess?"

"Well," Pinks mused, "community service credits for one. We can have those programs handled through the mayor's office for both schools. Get the kids working together on their service requirements."

"Cool. What else?"

"Extracurricular activities. Fun stuff."

"Like?" Vance asked.

"I'll have to think on it. But I do agree that being proactive about cultivating a sister-school mentality rather than an all-out rivalry is a worthy idea."

"Yeah. And with the idea of our library becoming the main link between the two campuses, maybe this Jinx Davenport could chair a committee on the subject."

"Jinx?"

"That's her name."

"Yeah?" Pinks laughed.

"Yeah, *Pinks*. That's her name. You got a problem with it?"

Pinks eyes flared. "Dude. Chill. It's an unusual name."

"Sorry. Yeah. It is. But it's cute and suits her. I uh …" Vance let his thoughts go unspoken.

"What?"

"Nothin'."

"Seriously?" Pinks prodded.

"Well, I was just going to say that I like her. I mean, it's … there's … something interesting there."

"Other than her two master's degrees?" Pinks joked.

"Yeah. Other than that. She seems … familiar."

"Who seems familiar?" Piper asked as she came into the kitchen, ignoring her husband and son but going straight to Pinks, kissing him on the cheek and relieving him of his salad-making duties. "I'll have a white wine spritzer, if you don't mind."

"Coming right up," Pinks said. "Lasagna is reheating."

"There's extra sauce in the refrigerator. Would you mind heating that up too?"

"Will do, boss."

Piper turned to Vance. "So who seems familiar?"

"This girl Em and I interviewed today. She's from Richmond. High IQ. Young. Wants the job, which seems odd, considering this *is* Henderson."

"A job's a job," Piper insisted.

"Yeah, but this girl could get a job anywhere. Oh, and that reminds me," he said, grinning at his wife. "The reason she even *knows* about this job is because of you."

"Me?"

"Yep. She's a Cal Johnson fan. Saw the YouTube video of him singing at The Situation and saw your link to the *Henderson Happenings* attached to it. She signed up and has been getting the e-newsletter ever since."

"Are you kidding?" Piper was astonished. "That worked?"

"Apparently. You've got to meet her, Pipes. She's sort of perfect, like you. You too, Pinks. You should both meet her. Tomorrow. What if we all did lunch here? Around noon?"

"You want to bring her here?" Piper asked. "Have lunch out by the pool?"

"Sure. That works." Vance turned to Pinks. "Can you fit it in?"

"I'll be here."

"Great. Great. It'll give us a chance to bring her in on the idea of fostering that sister-school mentality."

Piper's sweet voice reiterated, "It's going to be okay, Vance. You aren't going to have to choose sides."

"From your lips to God's ears," Vance breathed.

CHAPTER TEN

"Jaxon Wright. What do we have here?"

Jinx looked up from her hot fudge sundae into the faces of two eager brunettes. The gorgeous tall one was grinning from ear to ear. The super-cute petite one was far less demonstrative, though her eyes shone bright with blatant curiosity, which totally outed her as being intrigued to find Jaxon dining with a stranger.

Jaxon wiped his mouth on his napkin and stood before beginning introductions. "Jinx Davenport, may I introduce you to my—ah—my family's …" he trailed off as he looked at the taller brunette. "Well, she's sort of the sister I never had. However, it turns out she may eventually become my sister-in-law. I'm not sure of her exact status at the moment, but she means a lot to me and my family in general. This is McKenna Blakely."

Jinx exchanged smiles with the lovely, dark-haired ball of energy.

"Laidey Bartholomew is new to town." Jax indicated the curly-haired brunette. The one with the sympathetic, dark eyes. "And she actually *is* my future sister-in-law. She and my brother Xavier just recently became engaged."

"On the Fourth of July," McKenna said, holding out Laidey's hand to show off the mammoth engagement ring. "Xavier and I go way back, so I was in on the whole thing," she told Jinx proudly.

Laidey looked somewhat embarrassed that McKenna was showing off her ring. She pulled her hand away, asking sweetly, "Are you new to town?"

Jinx felt herself nod aggressively. "I'm being interviewed for a position at the library."

"Would you two like to sit?" Jaxon offered.

"Yes," McKenna said at the same time Laidey shook her head no.

"Yes," McKenna insisted with a meaningful glance at Laidey. "We'd love to get to know any potential Team Henderson members."

"You aren't even on Team Henderson," Laidey argued. "And we are interrupting their dinner."

"No. Please," Jinx insisted. "Join us. I'd love to hear more about y'all and what you do." She pulled her purse from the chair next to her, indicating they should sit.

"Perfect." McKenna nudged Laidey toward the chair before rounding the table to sit opposite her. "I write for the Henderson Daily, our local paper," she said, extending a hand to Jinx. "Would you mind if I mentioned your name and wrote a little bit about you and your application for the job?"

"McKenna," both Laidey and Jax scolded.

She threw up her hands. "It's my job."

"I promise I won't let her print anything," Jaxon assured Jinx.

Jinx eyed McKenna. "Should I start by saying this conversation is completely off the record?"

"Absolutely," McKenna insisted, holding up both hands. "My bad. It's just, well," she sighed, "there's so little news to report that I tend to go a bit overboard when there's even an inkling of something new brewing. You are applying for the *head* librarian position?"

Jinx smiled over at Jaxon, fairly certain her name was going to be in the local paper tomorrow and not sure how to stop it. As if reading her mind, Jax rolled his eyes and said, "She's like a freight train. There *is* no stopping her."

Jinx decided to take measures into her own hands and turned her attention to Laidey. "So, Jax said you're new to town?"

"I am. I work for CC Henderson. I've been here since March. I worked for CC Dallas for four years before I volunteered to come to Henderson."

"And how have you found Henderson?" Jinx asked.

"I find Henderson charming. I have since day one. But in the spirit of full disclosure, I should mention that my colleagues from

Dallas get a little itchy living so far from a city. They've made do by taking weekend trips to Raleigh."

"Why would they do that?" Jinx wondered. "I mean, from what I've read, there's a party a minute happening here."

"From what you've read?" McKenna asked.

"Jinx has been receiving the *Henderson Happenings* ever since Cal Johnson sang at The Situation," Jaxon explained.

"Oh?" McKenna questioned.

"That's how I found out about Henderson. I'm a Cal Johnson fan," Jinx confessed.

"He doesn't live here," McKenna warned.

"I know he doesn't live here. I'm not stalking the man. He's just the connection that led me to the library job. I recently graduated with my master's in Library Science. I know the job is a big one, especially for someone who has never actually been paid to be a librarian before. But I have a lot of experience."

"What sort of experience?" McKenna asked.

"I assist at both my college libraries."

"Both?"

Jinx waved her hands. "It's a long story. I'd so much rather hear about y'all."

"Hmm," McKenna said thoughtfully, looking Jinx over curiously. "Well, I've lived in Henderson all my life and have refused to leave." She shot a look at Jax. "Unlike Jaxon and all his brothers who headed off to college and never bothered to come back."

Jaxon appeared unmoved. "Cry me a river, McKenna."

"There are a bunch of girls my age who have stayed but not so many guys. Xavier is back, and now Jax, and hopefully Xander ..."

"Xavier and Xander? What's with the X's?" Jinx wondered.

"Says the pot to the kettle." Jax sent her a cute wink across the table. "Jinx is spelled with an X, correct?"

"It is. Which is probably why I picked up on the trend." She tossed a saucy smile back across the table.

"It gets worse," Laidey deadpanned. "Xavier and Xander are twins. *Identical* twins," she stressed. "And then there are two other brothers just like this one." She pointed to Jax.

Jinx didn't know if Laidey meant that there were two more gorgeous blond Adonises like Jax in the family, or just two more males with X's in their name.

She put her elbow on the table, her chin in her hand, and tossed him a smile. "What *was* your mother's fascination with X's?"

"Why in the world would your parents name you Jinx?" Jax countered with a flirtatious grin.

"Point taken. I really don't have a stone to throw here." She and Jax shared the private stone-throwing joke, but the warmth in his expression made her suddenly self-conscious. "So you're marrying …?" she asked Laidey.

"Xavier. When we first met, he claimed to be the oldest of the five brothers but never bothered to mention he is a twin. Which is why when I saw his *twin* kissing McKenna, I mistakenly thought it was Xavier. The two of them dated back in high school, so I assumed they'd gotten back together."

"Yeah," McKenna went on with the story, eyes shining in delight. "Xander—Xavier's twin—and I had kept our relationship quiet *because* I used to date Xavier. Although," she grumbled. "As it turns out, Xavier had never been interested in me at all. He was just trying to one-up his twin by asking me out because Xander didn't have the nerve."

Jaxon leaned in. "See what kind of messes we Hendersonians get ourselves into? I'd think long and hard before accepting that job and moving down to this crazy-ass town."

"It's not *Henderson*," McKenna claimed. "It's you crazy-ass Wright brothers."

Jax winked at Jinx. "You've been warned."

"Have you been offered the job?" Laidey asked.

Jinx had to reel herself in from the *holy-shit, he-just-winked-at-me* giddiness tickling her brain. "I have not. In fact, I'm in the middle of the interview."

"With Jaxon?" McKenna all but spat out laughter.

"What do you mean, with Jaxon?" he countered, looking offended.

"Well, you're not exactly library material."

"Library material?" Jax's eyes had settled into tiny squints directed at McKenna.

"Jaxon. When was the last time you set foot in a library?"

"Ahhhh. Never," he said firmly, grinning over at Jinx.

"Never?" Jinx was astounded.

"Nope. Never. I mean, as an adult. Never. As in never ever."

"So, what? You're an avid e-reader," Jinx surmised.

Both McKenna and Jax laughed. "Ah no. No e-reader, Jinx. I'm no kind of reader at all." He held up his hands. "Good with my hands, remember. Motors and the like."

Jinx leaned in. "So trade magazines, how-to manuals, that sort of thing?"

Jax sat back, thoughtful. "Okay. Yeah. I guess so. I read the stuff related to my job."

Jinx nodded. "All that can be found at the library."

Jax's eyes widened. Then blinked. "Owner's manuals? Do you think they'd have some vintage owner's manuals or engine design blueprints?"

"Probably not available in the Henderson library tomorrow, but the librarians there should be able to help you locate what you're looking for without too much of a problem."

"By locate, you mean what exactly?"

"Well, they'd find out where they were located. Electronically or in print. Then they could put in a request for whatever you're interested in seeing. Have it sent to the library here."

"They can?"

"Of course, they can."

"At the library. Here?" It sounded as if Jax didn't believe her.

"At any library, anywhere."

"Huh." Jax sat back, obviously thinking. Jinx tilted her head and watched him, wondering how he wasn't aware that almost any information was as close as his local library.

"So then, all of this would probably be online," he said after a moment.

"A lot of things are online. If you have the patience to scroll through all the advertising baloney that will come up in a search."

"You're right about that," Laidey inserted. "I can't tell you how annoying it is to google one thing and be thrown into advertisements for sites that have zero to do with what you really want."

"Sounds like Jinx might get you to venture through the doors of an actual library, Jaxon," McKenna teased.

"I'm certainly going to put her to the test," he claimed. "You get this job, Jinx, you are going to have to put your money where your mouth is."

"Looking forward to it," she promised.

It was after eleven when Jax helped Jinx into his truck, separating them from the small crowd that had walked out to the parking lot together. Once she was able to close her door after all the well wishes and great-to-meet-yous were done, she turned to Jaxon and said, "I'm not sure any of that helped with my interview, but it sure was fun. I'm going to have my work cut out for me." She checked her watch. "Luckily, Vance isn't meeting me until ten."

"You need your beauty rest?" he asked, driving them out of the parking lot.

"He's asked me to write up a proposal based on his plans for the library over the next four years."

"Jinx," Jax sounded startled. "Why didn't you say so? I could have had you back at the Jones's place long ago."

"I didn't want to leave. I enjoyed meeting your—what—almost sisters-in-law? And when we ran into Brooks Bennett at the bar? Well, that was a thrill. I've been reading about that man for months. I can certainly see why he's been deemed this town's Golden Boy, and why he's a shoo-in to be mayor." She gave a brief whistle. "The man would have my vote."

Jax laughed. "You already crushin' on Brooks?"

"No. I know he's mad for his Lolly."

"How in the world do you know about that?"

"Doesn't everybody?"

"Everybody who *lives* in Henderson."

She shrugged. "I'm a little like McKenna. An investigative reporter. I like research. Especially the undercover, not-right-there-staring-you-in-the-face kind."

"So you under-covered Brooks and Lolly, huh?"

"No," she laughed. "I asked Vance about Brooks during our tour today. *He* told me all about Lolly."

"Brooks and Lolly are Henderson's new power couple."

"Not Vance and Piper?"

Jax shook his head, grinning. "Xavier says that's a sore subject with Vance. We are building out Piper's Big Pie Plate shop, which is costing Vance top dollar. The shop is going to be tricked out. But even though Vance is paying for it and wants his wife to have whatever she wants, what he truly wants is for Piper to be home and in his kitchen. Not building some pie plate empire."

"Empire?"

Jax shrugged. "It could be big. At least according to my ma."

"Hmm. I'll have to do a little more investigating. Get my hands on this Big Pie Plate."

"You do that. Then share with me any and all results. I love pie."

"Ha. I'm no cook. Though I guess if I move here, or anywhere, that'll change. I can read a recipe and follow instructions. Shouldn't be too hard to whip up a pie." She looked over at Jax and smiled. "Here's the deal. Since you were so nice and took me out tonight, if I actually do get this job, once I'm all settled in, I'll make you pie."

"Oh, now I'm really going to put in a good word to Mrs. Flores," he teased.

Jinx shook her head. "I don't know what I did to make that woman take one look at me and wince, but boy oh boy, she does not like me."

"You don't know that, Jinx."

"It was obvious."

"She sent that wine for you tonight. Maybe it was an olive branch. An apology for running out on the interview."

"Or maybe loose lips sink ships, and she wanted to see how loose mine would get."

"Well, you didn't divulge any good secrets I'm aware of, so if that was her intent—mission thwarted."

"Seriously," Jinx said, getting quiet. She looked over at Jax thoughtfully before asking, "Are you supposed to report back?"

Jax pulled to the curb in front of the bed-and-breakfast and put the truck in park. He shut off the ignition and turned to Jinx, extending his right arm over the back of their seats and grasping her headrest. "I'm supposed to share any background information you gave me."

Jinx grinned, until she realized he wasn't joking. Her face fell, and she blinked. "You're serious."

He nodded slowly, his face cast in shadows. Then he shrugged. "This is a small town with big aspirations. Vance is obviously enamored with your brilliant brain and thinks you'd be a breath of fresh air, bringing that brain, your age, and your pretty face to our fair town. Hell, as far as I can tell, everything turns into a marketing campaign here, so I don't doubt he'd have your picture on the internet and printed in pamphlets or whatever. You fit the image Henderson is trying to create. Young, energetic hope for the future. Mrs. Flores just wants to be sure you've found your way here to Henderson for the library job not, ya know ..." his voice trailed off almost as if he was leading her to confess something.

"Not ... what?"

He shrugged, his index finger brushing up and down against her shoulder before it found its way back to the headrest. "I don't know. A Cal Johnson introduction, maybe? Some long-lost relative?"

Jinx rolled her eyes. "Ugh. I never should have mentioned Cal Johnson. Now she thinks I'm an insane groupie, applying for a job just for an opportunity to meet the man."

Jax gave her a little chuckle. "She's no doubt just playing devil's advocate to Vance's enthusiasm. Doesn't mean she doesn't like you."

She nodded. "All right. As much as I believe I can do this job if given a little wiggle room on the learning curve, I'm painfully aware I don't come with the experience Mrs. Flores is looking for."

"No, you don't. But no one ever does with their first job, do they? The Evanses will have to decide between your energetic passion and boring, old experience. My bet is that experience is going to take a backseat. After all, you will gain experience. Everything else you're bringing to the table is inherent. It can't be taught or acquired."

Jinx's smile grew big and broad. Her first instincts that afternoon had been correct. She really liked this Jaxon Wright. "You're awfully smart for having never set foot in a library."

He laughed. "Jinx, I am the furthest thing from smart. My brothers are smart. All of them. I'm just..." He shook his head.

"What?" She smiled, settling into her seat, admiring what she could see of his strong profile. "You're just what?" she asked softly.

He leaned over the center console, moving in close, he and his good looks just oozing all kinds of sex appeal as he whispered, "I'm just good with my hands."

CHAPTER ELEVEN

Yep.

He said it.

Just the way he'd intended.

I mean, come on. You don't sit in the dark with a pretty girl and not try to kiss her. Nope, Jaxon was well aware of where this was heading.

"I'm just good with my hands," he'd said.

Low.

Soft.

Meaningful.

His words heated the air in the Silver Hulk. The energy between them notching up from warm and friendly to something a bit more sultry. And with the way she was looking back at him, things were definitely heading to a nice, gentle simmer. He hadn't been sent to seduce Jinx Davenport, but that didn't mean he didn't think it was a damn fine idea.

The seduction of Jinx Davenport. Phase I: Ease Into A Goodnight Kiss and Leave Her Wanting More.

He watched her brow crinkle as she studied him, not exactly sure how to interpret what he'd said. He moved slowly, intentionally, leaning in. "Good with my lips, too," he promised. Hers parted in surprise, though she stayed put, watching him slide closer. Her tongue darted out, wetting her own lips, her breath coming faster. "Jinx, I know your name, your hometown, and that you made a mockery of most of your teachers. But what I want to know now is, do you kiss on the first date?"

Her adorable grin came on swift, her eyes twinkling. "Is this a first date?"

He nodded once, mirroring her grin, loving how all of that exuberant curiosity was now focused solely on him. "So you think it'd be all right if I gave you a goodnight kiss?" he whispered. "Off the record."

She nodded. Her red, ripe lips notched open, her body remaining perfectly still, but she'd nodded her acquiescence and *that* stirred his dick.

Jinx Davenport, you are so mine.

With one hand on the headrest, he leaned his upper body over the console to place his mouth against her cheek, his tongue grazing just the sweetest little corner of her lips. He felt the soft butterfly kiss of her eyelashes against his cheek as her eyes closed. He shifted his mouth to her chin, gently nuzzling the edge of her jaw. Then to the other cheek, intentionally teasing her skin with light, sweet, soft sensations that lingered against his own lips and tongue. Each spot fascinated him. Called to him. Stirred him. Her bottom lip summoned him, and he answered, first licking at the crease where her lips came together. Then running his tongue lightly over her plump bottom lip from edge to edge before he gently sucked at the middle of it.

He felt her fingers at the side of his face, returning the same tentative treatment. Wanting more, he leaned into her touch as he tilted his head, finally connecting the full of his lips to hers. Top lips. Bottom lips. Tender. Plush. He relished the smell of her perfume, allowed himself to be caught up in the caress of her hand and the gratifying feel of her lips against his own. The awakening of desire wasn't necessarily surprising as much as it was satisfying. To realize what he'd suspected from the first time he'd laid eyes on her that afternoon. That, yeah, she did it for him. Not just on paper, but in practice. In this simple kiss. In the touch of her hand.

He wanted to take the kiss deeper, give her his tongue. Experience the sensation of hers. He wanted to ravish her mouth, put both hands in her hair …

Reel it in, Jax.

He slowly pulled back, licking her taste from his lips, centering himself before opening his eyes.

She was batting her eyelashes, which ended in a smile as bashful as all get out.

Yeah. Take that, Jinx.

"Probably oughta see you to the door."

She nodded and then reached for her purse on the floor before turning to open the door. Jax jumped out and came around, catching her hand as she took that big hop to the ground. As she started to stumble, he stepped into her path, blocking her from a fall. Their bodies collided awkwardly, his awareness zeroing in on the most sensitive spots. His dick jammed into her hip. His arm brushing across her breasts. His hand grabbing at her waist, steadying her against him.

"Sweet Jinx," he whispered, pulling her around so their bodies lined up in a much more pleasant scenario. "If you want me to continue to sweep you off your feet, just say so."

"What?" Her head snapped up, eyes bright with embarrassed horror. She began to squirm against him, pulling away.

"I'm kidding," he laughed, tangling her up in his arms and settling her against him. She really was the perfect height. With her head tilted up in question, he looked down and let his gaze drift over her green eyes, the heightened color in her cheeks, her narrow chin, her lips.

Her *parted* lips.

"I'm teasing," he whispered. Wanting to kiss her again. Pretty sure she wouldn't push him away if he tried.

Leave her longing for more.

"And that's your fault, you know. You *daring me* to seduce you."

Her features grew alarmed. "I didn't—"

"You put it in my head," he told her. "You're a librarian. You know the power of words. You can't be flipping a word like seduction around and be surprised when the Law of Attraction delivers it to you."

"Jaxon." She laughed while pulling out of his embrace and starting toward the front door. "You're incorrigible."

He fell into step with her. "Maybe. But I'd still like you to encourage me. Invite me in for a nightcap."

"A nightcap?"

"The Joneses leave port out for their guests. Invite me in for a snort."

"A snort?"

"A short pour," he explained.

Jinx stopped halfway to the door. "How do you know the Joneses leave port for their guests?"

"Heard it said."

Her brows were quirked in a way that said she wasn't exactly sure what to do with him. "Jax," she said, as if reaching a conclusion. "Thank you for escorting me to dinner. I really enjoyed it."

"Good. I did too," he said honestly.

"Now, I'm going to go in and get a good night's sleep so I can get up early and have something ready for Vance at ten."

"So … no nightcap then."

"No. No nightcap."

He nodded, kinda liking she was holding him off.

"You come back, and we'll do this again," he said.

She chuckled softly. "*If* I come back, I will have already been offered the job, and Mrs. Flores will have no need for you to seduce me."

He leaned in. "Yeah, but over dinner I compiled a long list of my own reasons."

"Your own reasons?"

"To seduce you."

She grinned in amusement.

"You think I'm kidding, Jinx? I'm a Wright brother. We don't kid when it comes to seducing women. Ask the crazy twins."

"Good night, Jax," she said, turning to leave him where he was standing. "And thank you for introducing me to Henderson."

"Come back, Jinx," he called as he watched her take the steps to the Jones's front porch. "Job or no, you and I have unfinished business."

She waved her hand over her head, and Jax stared after her, a goofy grin plastered on his face. This girl from Richmond was squeezing his heart in such a good way it lit him up on the inside. It felt good.

He glanced up and gave a salute to nosy Mrs. Jones before she let her bedroom curtain fall back into place. And that's when he noticed the strands of Jinx's hair stuck in the links of his watchband.

The Joneses had kept the light on for her. And yes, Jaxon was right. They'd left a folded note on the round table in the living room with two glasses and a bottle of port. She rubbed the note over her tender lips, reminiscing about the feel of Jaxon Wright's mouth against hers.

The kiss had been so delicate. So sweet. Yet dangerously intoxicating. She held the decanter of port to her nose and took in a heady breath. Yes, Jaxon's kiss was a lot like this. A whiff of pleasure with the promise of something darker. Something rich and satisfying. Something worthy of sipping slowly.

He'd been teasing her, of course. Jaxon Wright was by all determining factors a gentleman. Yet his simple, sweet, barely-there kiss had proven very potent. Like lethal venom—just a drop and the victim would succumb.

Had all the girls he'd kissed felt that way? Or was she overly susceptible to the curious lips of Mr. Wright?

CHAPTER TWELVE

"Come in, come in," Hale beckoned as he stood up from behind his desk early Friday morning.

"Mr. Evans," Jaxon said, stepping into the expanse of Hale's richly appointed home office and closing the double doors behind him.

"Please, call me Hale. I appreciate you stopping by the house. I generally work from home. Old habits and all."

"Old habits?" Jax asked as he shook the man's hand.

"I used to be sole owner of the company. So I'm used to working by myself. Used to the quiet."

"I understand."

"Please sit." Hale indicated a leather chair.

"Sure," Jax said, feeling a little anxious for the man.

"How was your dinner with Miss Davenport?" Hale asked, coming around to lean a hip on the front of his desk. He folded his arms across his chest as if he was ready to listen to a good story.

"Fine. Good." Jaxon couldn't hide a smile and wondered why he was even bothering to try. "Jinx threw me a curve ball as soon as we sat down to dinner. She flat-out asked me if I was sent to seduce her."

"Sent to seduce her?" Hale was appalled.

"I know." Jax chuckled. "I set her straight."

"Why in the world would I send you to seduce her?"

"Em. She thought the Big Em had sent me. She's convinced that Mrs. Flores isn't keen on hiring her. She wondered if our dinner was a test of her moral fortitude."

"Good Lord."

"As I said, I set her straight. But I have to admit, I had some fun doing it."

"All right. Good. Now, what did you find out?"

"Well, obviously I'm not a private detective, but I'm about as convinced as I can be that Jinx Davenport has no idea that her mother was ever married to you. In fact, it appears she could be entirely unaware that her mother was ever married prior to her union with Mr. Davenport. And, sir, when she mentioned her mother, it was not in the most becoming light."

"Oh? How so?"

"Well, during our conversation, I mentioned that I was not only the baby of the family, but I was also my mother's favorite. She responded by saying that although she too was the baby of her family, she was decidedly not her mother's favorite. She went on to say that her mother was her *own* favorite, and her father's favorite as well."

Hale's arms fell to his sides, and he gripped the edge of the desk with both fists.

"Her parents and older sister traveled often, leaving Jinx in the care of her grandmother."

"Marguerite?"

"She didn't give me a name."

Hale nodded. "Go on."

"Well, sir, just like you saw yesterday, she seems very well adjusted. But the tale of her childhood seemed rather lonely. Nannies and her parents' travels being part of it. But it sounded like that was compounded by the fact that she's academically gifted and was continually pushed ahead of her age group. She started college when she was thirteen."

Hale's jaw tightened a moment before he rubbed a hand over his face.

"She ended up attending both the University of Richmond and Virginia Commonwealth University simultaneously because they were in proximity to her home. Eventually, she moved on campus—I don't know which one—and now holds two master's degrees."

When Hale didn't say anything, Jax went on.

"You think she looks like your ex-wife, I think she looks like you. She has similar mannerisms. She's lonely, and in her words, she's looking for a new place to call home." Jax presented the baggie in which he had placed his watch and the strands of Jinx's hair he'd captured with it. "I don't know anything about DNA tests. But I thought I'd at least offer you the opportunity to find out if this could help."

Hale leaned forward and took the baggie from Jax's hand.

"I, ah, kissed her goodnight," he confessed. "Must have gotten my watch caught in her hair."

Hale stared at him before examining the contents of the see-through bag. "You think she's my daughter?"

"I think you should find out."

"You think I should speak to her first? Get her permission to test her hair?"

"That depends. Are you prepared to live the rest of your life without knowing the truth if she doesn't consent?"

The two men stared at each other.

"Sometimes it's better to ask for forgiveness instead of permission. *If* it turns out she's your daughter. If she's not?" Jax shrugged one shoulder.

"But based on physical appearance and her mother's name alone, we do know she is, at the very least, Vance's half-sister."

"Yes."

Hale started to pace, apparently thinking things over. Jax figured his work here was done and he should leave the man to it. "I'll head down to the garage and see about the Rolls. You need me for anything, you've got my cell."

"Thank you, Jaxon," Hale said. "I appreciate all you've done."

"You can count on my continued discretion, sir."

"I appreciate that most of all. I have no idea what I'm going to do."

Jax tilted his head and eyed him thoroughly before shooting him a meaningful grin. "Sure you do."

CHAPTER THIRTEEN

"Well, that went well," Jinx thought aloud as she shut herself inside her car. Vance had been blown away by her budget analysis and suggestions for tackling the library's update one step at a time. So instead of getting on the road and heading back to Richmond, she'd been invited to lunch—at the Evans estate.

Seriously?

Vance wanted her to meet his wife, Piper, and Davis Williams a.k.a. Pinks of E&E Investments. She wasn't exactly sure how meeting these two worked into her interview for the library position, but it sure worked into her curiosity about Henderson. That very first *Henderson Happenings* newsletter was all about Pinks and somebody named Scarlett and somebody named Red. It was full of innuendo—didn't come right out and say what apparently everybody who had been in town that weekend knew. If Jinx remembered correctly, there was a sister factor, but the story definitely hadn't read like a newspaper but rather a gossip column with a lot of insinuations, leaving some room for speculation to fill in the blanks.

She drove her Fiat from the library, following behind Vance in his vintage orange convertible. Vance had struck her as such a family man that the Corvette seemed out of character. Until she remembered that his father was Hale Evans of the broken-down Maserati fame. The love of cool sports cars must run in the family.

"Well, I hit that nail on the head," she murmured, following Vance down a long stretch circling behind the house to a stable area. Only it was obvious that the horses here were counted in horsepower as four of the eight bays were open and all kinds of glorious machines were tucked inside. Outside was a light blue car—*what? Is that a Rolls Royce?*—with the hood propped up. And—*whoa*—leaning over the engine was a fine-looking, denim-covered butt that had her heartbeat spiking. Something about those blue jeans ... Yep. When he stood up, wiping his hands on a crisp, white towel was the man who'd kept her up half the night reliving the kiss he'd laid on her in his brother's enormous truck. Which, she quickly ascertained, was nowhere to be seen.

Jaxon Wright had on the same ball cap that had turned her head yesterday and the same grin he'd teased her with at the end of their date last night. She dragged her gaze off him long enough to shift into reverse and ease her car to the side of the drive so she wouldn't block others from coming or going. She grabbed her satchel, not knowing if she was going to be doling out more resumes, lifted her sunglasses as she took a quick glance in the mirror to make sure her makeup hadn't drooped, and then set her glasses back in place before exiting the car. By the time she turned toward Jaxon, he'd propped that fine backside of his against the Rolls and was folding his arms over his chest.

"So we meet again," he called as she approached. "Couldn't get enough of me last night, you had to track me down before you left town?"

He was *such* a flirt.

"Something like that." She gave him her sassiest grin.

Vance walked out of the garage and Jaxon turned his head briefly toward him. "You gonna hire this know-it-all?"

"Know-it-all?" Jinx took offense.

"She does seem to know it all," Vance fired back. His gaze drifted from one to the other. "The two of you hit it off at dinner, I take it."

"She didn't fill you in?"

"Fill me in on what?"

"How the ol' Seduce the Librarian scheme went down."

"Seduce the what now?" Vance shot severely arched brows toward Jinx.

"Jaxon Wright, you are no gentleman." Jinx played into his antics by scolding him and putting her nose in the air. "You promised you wouldn't kiss and tell."

"Kiss? You kissed her?" Vance's eyes widened.

"Kissed her, hell. I did better than that. I got her to promise she'd bake me a pie if she gets this job of yours. So, please, for the sake of starving auto mechanics everywhere, hire the lady and do it fast."

Vance looked between the two of them. "Huh. Well, from the hungry way you're lookin' at her, you definitely appear to be starving."

"Jaxon was a gentleman," Jinx assured Vance.

"Until she challenged me to try to seduce her then all bets were off."

"I did no such thing."

"Fine, she grilled me about whether your *grandmother* had sent me to seduce her."

Vance's brows furrowed at Jinx. "Where the hell would you get an idea like that?"

Jinx blushed. "Well, she sent a bottle of wine. A very *good* bottle of wine. And since she took one look at me and ran off during the interview, I wondered if she might be trying to sabotage my application for the job by getting me sloppy drunk so I'd make a fool of myself. It was the wine and *you*, warning me about Jax. For a moment, I thought maybe I was being set up."

Jaxon's brows raised as he slowly turned a disbelieving look at Vance. "*You* warned her? About *me*?"

"Seen you with a lot of women since you've been back in town."

"Seriously, dude?" Jaxon was stunned. "What happened to the Bro Code?"

"We aren't bros," Vance told him.

"I like the company of women," Jax defended. "Doesn't mean I'm sleeping around."

"Doesn't mean you aren't."

"Are you kidding me, here? Come on, man."

"Did he try to seduce you?" Vance asked Jinx point blank.

Jinx blinked. Then she turned her face toward Jax, catching his eyes with hers. She couldn't help but smile. "No," she said softly. "He was the perfect gentleman."

"Okay." Vance nodded. "All right. Good." He started to pull away, saying, "I'll let you two catch up while I go rally Piper and Pinks. See you up by the pool in say"—he checked his watch—"five minutes?"

"Five minutes," Jaxon said without taking his eyes from hers. Those lips of his were pretty much killing her at the moment. The way they moved when he spoke. The way they twitched right before he pulled them back into a grin. Jinx sighed internally, thinking of how those lips had made her feel last night. How he seemed to fit— his lips to hers—so easily. She took a step closer to him as Vance made his way toward the house. Jaxon reached out and with one curved finger, he latched on to the belt at her waist and pulled her even closer. He spread his legs out as he leaned back against the car, pulling her in between, leaving a mere twelve inches of space between their bodies.

"You don't have to fight my battles," he said quietly.

"Just wanted to set the record straight."

"That I didn't seduce you?"

"That you didn't *try* to seduce me."

He licked his lips, his gaze taking in her entire face. "Jinx. You come back to Henderson, I will definitely try to seduce you."

She blushed softly, both her hands reaching up to stroke the long braid at her shoulder. "Is that a threat or a promise?" she whispered going up on her toes.

"Simple truth," he said. "I didn't get enough of your lips last night."

"Ahh, yes. You did want a nightcap as I recall."

"And you refused me."

"Yet your ego seems unscathed."

"Last night, you were worried your future employer sent me to seduce you. You get this job, you don't have to worry about anyone else. You'll know that when I make my move, I'm doing it because I find you ... luscious."

"Luscious?" She tested the word, dropping her heels to the ground, her eyelashes fluttering. "No one's ever described me as luscious."

"No?"

She shook her head slowly.

"Hmm. Well, after round one of true confessions, I'm pretty certain that's because you've developed this Smart-Girl bravado you hide behind in order to survive in your overachieving world. But what lies underneath your IQ? *Luscious.*"

Smart-Girl bravado? Damn. Jinx felt her lashes flutter. And flutter. And continue to flutter. The reaction apparently trying to mask the quickening of her breath and the lump of embarrassed angst in the center of her chest. *My gosh.* She felt as though she was going to cry. *Jaxon. Wright.*

She shook off her reaction to his brutally accurate summarization, pulling from his grasp and taking a giant step back. She sniffed, dropping the so-called Smart-Girl bravado into place with a dazzling yet artificial smile. "Well, Jaxon Wright. Aren't you clever, coming up with that very succinct description?" she said in a heavy Virginia accent. "May I return the favor by saying you are *startlingly obsequious.*"

"Obsequious?" Jaxon squinted, pushed off the Rolls, and crossed his arms over his chest.

"Attentive to an excessive degree," she primly explained.

"Oh. Am I not supposed to know that word? Right. Because I'm just an auto mechanic and you're a human dictionary," he accused, coming to loom over her. "Which, if that were at all true, means you could have laid the word *intuitive* on me, yet you basically went with a synonym for *ass-kisser.* Fine, then." He shot an arm in the direction Vance had headed. "Since it seems this session of the Seduction of Jinx Davenport has come to a bitter and disappointing end, I'll do as the bossman directed and escort you to your next meeting."

"The Seduction of Jinx Davenport?"

He nodded sharply, with no humor about him at all. His eyes were downcast, his neck bent, and his arm remained pointing away. As if he couldn't stand the sight of her any longer.

She stepped into his personal space, forcing him to lift his gaze and see her. "Jaxon," she whispered. "I didn't mean to offend."

"You sure about that?" His words were curt. His face drawn and taut.

She'd hurt him. The first person who actually saw her clearly enough to stick a label on her … her … what did he call it? Bravado? Clearly, she knew the truth when she heard it, but it was quite obvious she couldn't handle the truth because she'd immediately lashed out while drowning in her own insecurities. "Jax." Her voice was a faint whisper, struggling to get out of the tightness in her chest and through the bottleneck in her throat. "I'm sorry," she offered. "You hit a soft spot, and I reacted badly."

"It's okay Jinx."

"It's not okay. I hurt your feelings."

"No," he corrected. "I meant it's okay to have soft spots. We *all* have soft spots."

When she couldn't speak for fear of bursting into tears—because sweet baby Jesus, was he ever stomping all over her soft spots—he went on. Quietly.

"I'll be careful of yours, if you be careful of mine."

Did a man like him have soft spots? Well, she guessed so, since proclaiming him to be *startlingly obsequious* had set him off.

"Deal," she murmured.

"You can fix this with a kiss," he coaxed, teasing her out of wanting to boo-hoo into his chest.

"Ha!" She stepped away. "You'd like that wouldn't you?"

He pulled her back to him. "I would. I'd like that a lot."

"Right here? Where anyone could see us? I am technically on a job interview, you know."

"Got news for you, *Webster*. The cover of darkness didn't do us much good last night. Mrs. Jones had her nose pressed to the upstairs window."

"Webster?"

"Yeah. As in the dictionary."

"Oh. Right. You're not a fan."

"Kiss me, and I'll get over it."

"I'm not going to kiss you."

"Fine." He stepped forward, wrapped his solid arms around her, cupped the back of her head, and dipped her into a blatant, obvious, no-discretion-at-all kiss. The energy was aggressive, yet he didn't smash their lips together and plunder. He fitted his top lip between both of hers and stroked his tongue over her bottom lip until she opened up to once again experience the thrill that was Jaxon Wright.

Way too soon, a whistle cracked the air, bringing their kiss to an abrupt end with both their heads turning in the direction of the piercing sound.

"You two wanna stop dickin' around?" Vance shouted. Then he pointed an irritated finger at Jaxon. "You are not sticking to my good side."

"What's that supposed to mean?" Jaxon shouted as he brought Jinx upright, where she wrestled herself out of his arms. She pulled her satchel over her shoulder and sheepishly started up the hill toward Vance.

Embarrassed wasn't quite covering how she felt. Humiliated might be a tad strong, but only a tad. Yeah, actually *humiliated* was pretty darn accurate she thought as she made her way up the hill, still unable to look Vance in the eye or turn her head back to sigh over Jax. By the time she arrived at Vance's side, she'd scraped together a modicum of courage and was able to raise her gaze and greet the scowl directed at her.

She shrugged. "He's a great kisser."

"Probably does a lot of things great," Vance griped, turning and falling in beside her. "Doesn't mean you should be testing the waters."

For some reason that struck her funny. "No?" she teased.

"No," he said firmly.

"And you're telling me this as my employer, Mr. Evans, or as the self-proclaimed bad-boy who shouldn't be throwing stones?"

"You want the job, you've got it. You want Jaxon, that's up to you."

"Then why are you grouchy? And by the way, yes, I want the job."

"Don't take it because of Jax. Heaven knows where he's gonna be by the time you get back."

"I'm taking the job because I'm perfect for it. Jax is just a fringe benefit."

"From what I understand, those Wright brothers are all about fringe benefits," Vance groused.

"The fact that you two are already bickering like siblings is only slightly less disconcerting than the fact that you actually look like twins."

Jinx's head popped up to find a guy standing a few feet away, legs spread in a solid stance with his arms crossed over his chest. He had fabulous hair and wore killer shades. He pointed at Vance. "I'm not sure this is the way to woo your top candidate for the job."

"I've already accepted." Jinx grinned, holding out a hand. "Davis Williams, I presume?" Jinx took off her shades to make the introduction more personal, but when Davis's jaw dropped, she wondered what had gone wrong.

"Seriously," Davis stammered, shaking her hand slowly before taking off his own sunglasses and staring between her and Vance. "You've got the same color eyes and everything. You two could absolutely be twins if, you know"—he pointed to Vance—"you weren't so damn old." He turned to Jinx. "He's got to have at least ten years on you."

"You think we look alike?" Jinx shined a playful smile at Vance, using this opportunity to kid him out of his grouchy mood. "You did tell me I was one of the most striking girls you'd ever seen. Maybe you just like what you see in the mirror, and I remind you of that." She bumped him with her elbow.

But Vance didn't kid her back as anticipated. No quips. No cute comebacks. In fact, he stood there, extraordinarily still. Actually, ramrod stiff might be a more accurate description. Such a startling contrast to what she'd expected that the moment became awkward.

When he finally spoke, his words came out quiet and decisive. "Excuse me a moment." He didn't turn his face toward her or Davis. He simply sidestepped between the two of them and strode off on his own toward the palatial home beyond the pool.

CHAPTER FOURTEEN

Vance managed to find his way to the door of his father's study without encountering anyone. That worked for him because as off balance as he felt right now, Vance figured it was registered all over his face. No way could he hide it. And this was not something he wanted to discuss with Piper or Genevra.

No.

The dread that gripped him after Pinks uttered the words "ten years younger" while comparing Jinx's striking looks to his own was immediate and it was fierce. Curious bits and pieces of information over the past twenty-four hours lined up and fused themselves together so sharply the clarity cut right through him.

The familiarity he felt every time he looked at Jinx.

His grandmother's immediate plunge into Spanish the moment she met her.

Em's unsettled demeanor and quick exit from the interview.

Jinx's IQ, for fuck sake.

This Jinx must be what? His truant mother's love child? *Dear God.* The thought landed like a puncture wound to the chest. He rubbed at the center of his ribcage as he faced the closed door where his father labored inside. This Jinx literally was the sociopathic liar he'd accused her of being. An enemy intruder breaching their camp just as things were going so well. How was he ever going to tell his father?

Only ...

Not encountering Hale over a span of twenty-four hours while residing in the same house? Unusual. Yet Vance had thought nothing of it until this moment. Maybe he wasn't as observant as Davis, but his intellect was starting to sort shit out fast.

His father. Em. *They both already knew.*

With a hand on the doorknob and no knock to announce him, Vance dragged in a deep breath and held it as he entered his father's sanctuary, turning to close the door behind him with a final, quiet click.

"Hey." He heard the soothing sound of his father's voice coming from behind him, causing him to squeeze his eyes shut against the sudden surge of emotion. He stood with his back turned on the only person who knew his heartache. "How's my number-one son?" Hale asked.

With his voice lost in the hurricane blowing through his mind, Vance could only imagine what he must look like as he faced his father, his heart falling into tatters all over again.

"Hey," Hale said, his voice laced with a healthy dose of empathy as he stood, clueing in real fast something was up. "What's going on?"

So befuddled by this cataclysmic turn of events, Vance sank into the closest chair, right by the door, his lips parted in disbelief, his eyes shimmering with unshed tears.

I'm a grown man, he thought. I'm bigger than this.

He tried to lift a hand. Eventually he managed to get it to his mouth, his thumb and index finger smoothing over his lips as he tried to reconcile what he knew to be true.

"This, ah, Jinx—" Vance started and then stopped. He dropped his hand and shifted his gaze around the room, unable to come out with the words. He jiggled his head, trying to shake loose the anguish engulfing him. Finally, he settled his eyes back on his father.

Hale's entire countenance reflected pain so acutely familiar neither of them moved. They just shared it in silence.

How were the two of them going to get through this?

Eventually, Vance moistened his lips and found voice enough to speak. "Catherine Davenport? Is that her name now? Davenport?"

Hale nodded.

"I'm assuming this is why you were scarce? Last night? Again this morning?"

"Look, son—"

Vance held up a hand. He didn't need his father to apologize because of this bullshit. "And this is why Abuela bolted from the interview. Because she recognized what is immediately apparent to everyone but me. That Jinx is what? My fucking *sister?*"

"Vance—"

"How is this even possible?" The anger he felt was suffocating. "Did you know? About her?"

"No." Hale spread his hands in defeat, looking every bit as off center and out of control as Vance felt. "But from the moment I saw her yesterday ..." he trailed off.

"What? From the moment you saw her yesterday, what?" Vance demanded.

"I knew she was Catherine's."

Vance squeezed his eyes shut, unable to stop the pain pulsing through his bloodstream. Waves of sorrow and heartache broke free of the barrier Piper's love had built. The dam burst with anger, and torment flowed. The grief over his mother's abandonment hit him as fresh as the moment he discovered she was gone all those years ago. And he was stuck reliving it—all of it—because of Jinx Davenport.

"What does she want?" Vance asked through gritted teeth.

"Who?"

"This ... Jinx. Why is she here? What does she want?"

"Vance." His father shook his head. "There's no evidence Jinx is aware of anything. Of you or me or—"

"Oh, come on," Vance shouted, shoving himself out of the chair, advancing on his father. "That's complete and utter bullshit, and you know it. Jinx Davenport from fucking Richmond, Virginia? Whose mother's name happens to be *Catherine*, shows up here in goddamn Henderson asking for a job? No way."

"That's why I had Jaxon take her to dinner last night. He recognized her as my daughter the moment he saw the two of us together."

Vance reared back. "Your daughter? I thought she was *his* daughter. How can she be your daughter?"

"I don't know that she is. But her date of birth seems to hold the possibility. I think she looks like Catherine. Jaxon thinks she looks like me."

"I didn't pick up on the resemblance at all, but Pinks took one look at the two of us standing side by side and declared us twins."

The room settled into silence as the men stood staring at one another.

"What are we going to do about this?" Vance seethed. "Because I was planning on having you go out there and tell that little gold digger that the offer for the library job has been rescinded, and we'd appreciate it if she didn't venture below the Virginia border ever again."

Hale tilted his head and sighed. "Is that really what you want?"

"Hell yeah, that's what I want. What do you want?"

"I want to know if she's my daughter."

"Really? You do? Then what? You gonna add her to your will? Hand over the family fortune and say thanks for coming down and rocking our world just as things are finally looking up? Fuck that, Dad. That girl is the enemy."

"How is she the enemy?"

"She's your *ex-wife's* love child."

"Maybe. But at the very least, she's *your* half-sister. Which makes her family. Your family."

"Bullshit."

Hale held up his hands. "Fine. Look. You're my top priority. You don't want to open this wound, we don't open it. Like you said, things for you and me are finally looking up. Between Genevra and Piper, Beau and Vance, Jr. we're solid." Hale reached for his phone.

"Who are you calling?"

"Jaxon. I'll have him make our excuses to Miss Davenport."

"Jax? Why Jax? The way the two of them were going at it down by the garage just now, he's probably in on it."

"In on it?"

"Her scheme," Vance shouted. "To bilk us out of our millions."

"If there's a scheme, Jaxon's not in on it." Hale halted dialing. "I had him take Miss Davenport to dinner last night on a fact-finding mission."

"Fact-finding? You mean Jax has been acting as your spy?" Somehow, within all his inner turmoil, that didn't sit well with Vance.

"Jaxon offered to do some digging. Find out how much she knows about her relationship to the Evans family."

"And?"

"According to Jaxon, she's oblivious. Jinx told him her mother was from the D.C. area, which is correct. She didn't mention that her mother was divorced before marrying Mr. Davenport. Jaxon said she seemed oblivious not only to that, but also to the fact that Catherine once resided in Henderson."

"How hard did Jax press?"

Hale eyed his son. "Hard enough to find out Jinx isn't a fan of her mother." He paused a moment to let that sink in. "And, he brought me this." Hale reached into a desk drawer and pulled out a Ziploc bag holding a man's watch. He set it down on his desk between them. The band was made of metal, linked, and had a solid clasp.

"What the hell does that have to do with anything?"

Hale pushed the bag closer. "Those hairs caught in the end of clasp? Miss Davenport's. Jaxon thought it might be enough to have a paternity test done."

"Fuck, no." Vance grabbed his head and spun. "She left us. She left you," he insisted as he came around and dropped his hands flat on his father's desk and looked him in the eye.

"You're talking about Catherine. Not Jinx."

"Yeah, I'm talking about *Catherine.*" He spit the name. "She left you. She left me. She never once came back to see me, *her firstborn,* and this whole thing is bullshit."

Hale pointed toward the door. "That young woman out there is *not* your mother. And she had nothing to do with your mother leaving."

"Seriously?" Vance's hands flew up. "She's *the reason* my mother left me."

"You don't know that."

"Of course, I do," Vance shouted. "I wasn't good enough. So she had another kid and decided to actually raise that one." Vance planted his hands back on the desk and leaned toward his father. "I *hate* my mother for leaving me. For leaving us. Do you think I'm going to hate that … *Jinx,*" he spat, "any less? I hate her *more.* As far as I'm concerned, she's the reason my mother left me and never came back. And you know what?" Vance pushed off the desk. "This is actually a good thing. Because for years, I've wondered what the hell kept her away. And now I know. It was Jinx. That girl out there is the reason *I* grew up without a mother."

Hale sat down in his chair, defeated.

"What?" Vance shouted.

Hale spread his hands. "I'm not going to try to defend Miss Davenport. You're right. We have no idea why she's here. And"—he hung his head, shaking it—"what your mother did to you is indefensible."

"But?" Vance pressed.

Hale looked at his son and shook his head. "No buts."

Vance let out a breath and scrubbed his hands over his face. His eyes peered out even though he held his fingers over his mouth. He spoke through them. "You're gonna test those hairs anyway."

The corner of Hale's mouth twitched.

"Goddamnit, Dad." Vance sat down in the chair across from his father.

"I don't know what I'm going to do," Hale said quietly, leaning forward. "But I'm pretty sure that until I have proof one way or another, I'm not going to be able to sleep at night."

There was a timid knock on the door. "Yeah?" Hale responded sharply.

Piper poked her head inside the office, the gurgles from Vance, Jr. coming in with her. Vance turned abruptly, raising himself from the chair to walk over and take VJ out of his mother's arms. "Something's come up," he told Piper without meeting her eyes. He kept his focus on Vance, Jr as he nuzzled his son's head. "If you wouldn't mind leaving VJ with me and handling our lunch guests, I'd appreciate it."

"Everything okay?"

Vance didn't allow his gaze to stray from his son, nestling him in the crook of his elbow. "I've got our boy in my arms. What could be wrong?"

Piper smoothed a hand over her baby's head. She leaned in to kiss him, and then she pecked her husband on the cheek. "You're a good dad. I'll take care of your interviewee. I've invited Jaxon Wright to join us. Have you noticed the way he looks at this Jinx?"

Vance simply lifted a shoulder in a noncommittal response.

"Well, I'm telling you. There is something going on there. Maybe I'll get Em to join us too. She's good at ferreting out that stuff."

"No," both Hale and Vance said at once.

"Ah, Em's busy," Hale said. "Important stuff."

"She's down in the basement searching for Mardi Gras souvenirs for Missy's next party," Piper protested.

"Look," Vance said doggedly, finally taking his attention off his son and putting it on his wife. "Just do me a favor. Leave Em alone and move all our lunch guests to the club or wherever you want to go. Just … get everyone off campus, please."

"O-kay," Piper hesitated.

Vance leaned over and kissed her quick on the cheek. "Dad and I just need a little time to work through a few things. 'Kay?"

"Okay. I'll, um …" Vance pushed Piper through the door and then closed it before turning back to his father.

"Do the test."

"What?"

"The paternity test. Do it. You need to know if she's your daughter."

Hale's gaze drifted back and forth between his son and his grandson. "Do I have VJ to thank for this?"

"Yep."

"And what are you going to do in the meantime?"

Vance kissed the side of VJ's head. "Play with my son in the baby pool his grandfather had installed for Vance, Jr.'s uncle." At the mention of his half-brother Beau, Vance's eyes shot to his father. "All this time, I thought I was an only child. Now it appears VJ has an uncle and an aunt."

Hale cleared his throat. "Are you, ah, softening to the idea of a sister?"

"No. I'm not. But if Vance, Jr. ever needs a kidney or a bone marrow transplant, I figure it'd be good to know if this *Jinx* is a relative or not."

"All right. We'll do it for the sake of Vance, Jr. And Beau."

"Get Brody and meet your grandson and me by the pool. I'm declaring E&E shut down for the rest of the day. Life's too fuckin' short to let ourselves get tangled up in bullshit."

"I like your attitude." Hale rose from his desk and dropped his pen.

"I'm banking my attitude until those test results come back. Then my attitude is calling in lawyers. Good ones. And a shaman."

"A shaman?'

"Yeah, a shaman. Or whoever the hell knows how to get rid of a jinx."

CHAPTER FIFTEEN

If Jinx thought the two-day interview with Vance had been stringent, she'd have to classify the lunch with Pinks and Piper as harsh. Well, not that Pinks and Piper were harsh—no—they were welcoming smiles and generous compliments. But their questions concerning her abilities to take over and run the library transformation were hardcore, in depth, and pulled no punches.

Although she definitely had to take her time and think things through to formulate her responses, she surprised herself by knocking the answers out of the park. She was the perfect person for the position she realized. Not just because she liked the idea of library ownership—because, let's face it, nobody was going to have time to police her on this project, which was why choosing the right person was so very critical. No, she was the perfect person for this job because she had all the right answers. She understood libraries, and she understood the needs of Henderson and the two schools the library would link as well as any outsider could.

That is until Jaxon threw in his two cents.

He'd cleared his throat, and for the first time since the grilling had started, he interjected a concern of his own. "You know," he said, addressing the table. "Y'all are lawyers"—he pointed to Piper—"and smart business people"—he pointed to Pinks—"and dictionaries"—he pointed to Jinx. "But that is not representative of the majority of this town. I'm not saying the majority of our citizens aren't savvy or smart, but I think you're neglecting guys like me with all this state-of-the-art research baloney. If bringing the kids who attend Henderson

High and the sports academy together is a goal, and from what I'm gathering, it's a big one, you're going to need the library to offer more than just books."

The three of them blinked. Then Jinx said, "There are movies, audiobooks, magazines ..." She trailed off as Jax held up a hand.

"*Fun.* You're going to need to offer kids who aren't bookworms a way to see the library as fun."

"Fun? At a library?" Piper asked.

"Sure. At a library." Jaxon nodded.

"Like what kind of fun would be library appropriate?" Pinks wondered.

Jax spread his hands. "Any kind of fun can be library appropriate." He sat up, raised one finger and said, "How about this? I'm a race car guy, right? Libraries not so much. But what if the library sponsored something like a soapbox derby? I mean, I would have been all over that as a kid. No motors to worry with, but plenty of design work. It would encourage the kids to do some research—*at the library*—to build one. You could have a guest speaker come in to talk about the building process or aerodynamics. Stuff that they can't find on Google or YouTube. There could be weekly meetings where adults would help the kids with their build-outs. Then have it all lead up to a big race day. Block off that hill coming down from the Foresters' place and let 'em run their soapboxes right onto Main Street. Have a big banner for them to bust through and give out a trophy. Make it a real family affair. Maybe even raise money for the library by selling food and such. I mean, I'd be more than happy to lend a hand with that."

Despite her personal reservations about turning the library into some sort of vehicle assembly plant, Jinx couldn't help her grin. Imagining Jaxon Wright perking up her day by sauntering into the library with all his auto-mechanic sexy going on was enough to at least get her to consider the idea of library-sponsored "fun."

"Isn't this what y'all do?" Jinx turned her attention from Jaxon to Piper and Pinks. "Here in Henderson. Throw crazy themed parties and parades for Opening Day?"

Both Pinks and Piper grinned, their eyes twinkling. "It is," they agreed.

"Well, it has been since Missy McReady came to town and put on The Spectacular," Pinks clarified. "Anything that is going to draw folks to Henderson and find a way to pay for itself is welcome. I hadn't given much thought to the library, but hell. Jax is right. Why wouldn't the same principles apply? Our parties and events cater to the Hendersonians who have jumped ship. We're trying to entice them to come back on weekends and eventually consider moving back home. Library-sponsored events enticing the student population of both schools to come together and mingle isn't a bad idea."

"And there's room," Jinx added. "The library has several good-sized meeting rooms in which to host guest speakers and specialty classes. I really like this idea, Jax. Although I will admit, that of everything we've talked about concerning the library, this is the one thing I have the least amount of confidence in."

"What do you mean? You don't think the idea will go over?"

"I don't mean the idea is bad. I think it's good. I just mean, personally I'm a little fun-challenged. My brain has been focused on learning, studying, test-taking, researching, writing, and the like for so long"—she laughed—"I don't know the first thing about fun."

"That's ridiculous," Jaxon insisted. "Last night was fun."

"Last night was conversation over dinner. And yeah, it was fun. But it wasn't like, think-it-up-and-manufacture-it fun. I'm going to need help getting into the Henderson groove. The fun groove. Thinking things up like that soapbox derby. I don't have a mind for that."

Jax grinned in disbelief. "Well, thank God we mere mortals can help all you brainiacs with something around here." He pointed to his chest. "I'm fun. My brothers are fun. There are a whole lot of non-Mensa folks around here who can form ourselves a think tank and come up with fun."

Piper laughed. "We are putting you in charge of that Jaxon. My mind is overloaded with Henderson's Big Pie Plate Fun."

"And all I've got time for these days is promoting Henderson and building the sports academy fun," Pinks joked.

"And I'm going to have a lot of fun updating the library's technology platforms and raising funds to get the job done," Jinx added. "It looks like the library fun will be left up to you."

"Consider it done," he said. "When do we start?"

All eyes turned toward Jinx.

She blinked, startled. Because Vance had indeed offered her the job, and she had greedily accepted. But no specifics had been set in stone. No start date. No salary agreement. "Vance didn't say."

"Well," Pinks asked. "When *can* you start?"

With adrenaline rolling and her heart full of enthusiasm, she blurted, "Monday?"

"Monday it is," Pinks declared. "We're fast tracking as much as we can around here. Don't wait for the academy to open its doors to start the library fun. It'd be good to get the Henderson High kids on board so they start seeing the library as an additional source of entertainment. Hey, you know what? We need to focus on our senior population too. We also want them engaged in the community."

"Oh, yes," Piper chimed in. "And on that note, here's a tip. Em has been moaning about line-dance classes. She wants to take them but isn't interested in driving to the YMCA in Oxford to do it. She's been on me to find someone to teach them here in town, and I've said I would, but you know …"

"You don't have time for line-dance fun," Jinx offered. "Well, I need a way to impress Mrs. Flores, so please don't tell her you mentioned it to me. Finding a line-dance teacher who will come teach at the library will be on the top of my To-Do list once I start. Monday." She glanced at Pinks. "You sure?"

"Can you? Go home, get packed up, and be back ready to work on Monday?" Pinks encouraged.

Jinx's mind was a whirlwind of chaos. It was Friday afternoon. Could she get back here by Monday? Her parents had no idea she was even interviewing for a job. But, since they were in Europe—*again*—were they even going to care? By the time they got home a month from now, she'd be settled into her new …

"I need a place to stay," Jinx said. "Do you think the Joneses would put me up at their bed-and-breakfast for a while until I find something permanent?"

"I don't see why not," Pinks said.

"If they would work with me on a price for the month maybe, I can be back and ready on Monday. I won't worry about furniture or stuff like that until I figure out where I'm going to live."

"I'll talk to them on your behalf," Jax said. "See if they'll give you a deal. Maybe they'll just charge you for the weekends since that's their busy time."

"Whatever you work out will be fine," Jinx told him. "I appreciate it."

"Though …" Jax stalled. "Maybe you should take some time and discuss this job offer with your parents before you promise you'll be back here on Monday."

"And tell them what? I don't have any details." Jinx suddenly felt like she was jumping the gun. "You know what? We're getting ahead of ourselves. What happened with Vance?" she asked Piper. "I mean, he offered me the job, tossed it out there, saying it was mine if I wanted it. But I don't want to count my chickens until I have an offer in writing."

"The way he was talking about you last night, I'm pretty sure he meant that offer." Pinks looked to Piper for confirmation. "Right?"

"Absolutely," Piper agreed. "And I'm sorry he isn't here. Something serious must have come up, because things between him and Hale looked tense when I interrupted."

Pinks checked his watch and stood. "I'll head back. See if they need me for anything. Jinx, it was great to meet you. Jaxon, you'll take care of getting Jinx sorted with the Joneses, and I'll tell Vance to email her a formal offer by tomorrow if he wants her here on Monday."

"You will?" Jinx asked, feeling a little shocked about Davis taking over.

"Sure. We out-of-towners have to stick together. Trust me, this town can use all the new blood it can get. You'll be an asset, for sure."

"I just hope the current head librarian thinks so."

"Oh hell," Jaxon said. "Mrs. Buchanan is a pill."

Piper smirked as Pinks left them and headed toward the door. "She's … stuffy. But Em says she has a lot to offer. I suggest you leave Em the task of getting her on board. Now, Jinx, is there anything you want to ask me before we send you home to pack?"

"Ask you?" Jinx wondered.

"About anything."

"Here, hand us your phone," Jaxon suggested.

"My phone?" Jinx dug it out of her purse.

"Let Piper put in her contact information, and I'll do the same. If any—ah—*issues* arise, or—ah—you end up having any questions you don't want to run through Vance, you'll have two other people who aren't Evans family originals to run things by."

Jinx wasn't sure what to make of that. She leaned forward as Piper typed on her phone. "What's wrong with the Evans family?"

Piper snorted. "Nothing." She looked up, grinning. "Except that they're intense. And busy."

"And you're not intense or busy?"

"Ah, I am busy, yes, and my intensity level increases or decreases depending on whether I'm dealing with my husband's issues over my Big Pie Plate business or simply cooking in the Evans family kitchen."

"You and Pinks are close, I noticed."

"Pinks is the permanent mediator in my marriage. Vance can't do without him at E&E, and I can't do without him on the home front. The best way I can describe Pinks is to say … he knows where all the bodies are buried."

Jinx's brows shot up. "Really?"

"He's the best of us. Less intense. Like Genevra."

"Who?"

"Hale's wife, Genevra. She's not intense at all. She's just"—Piper shook her head—"sweetness and common sense. And love. She brought the love into the Evans family when it really needed it."

"Em's intense," Jaxon countered.

"Yes," Piper agreed. "Em is … competitive, opinionated, and has the potty mouth of a truck driver."

"What?" Jinx tried to cover her glee.

"Oh, yeah," Piper assured her.

"She's also sleeping with a guy a good ten years younger than her," Jax added.

"Are you sure?" Piper turned to Jaxon, delightedly curious.

"Ah, yeah, I'm sure. She spends a whole lot of time in the man cave Xavier built over my parents' garage."

"She's sleeping with your brother?" Jinx was horrified.

Piper snorted a laugh. "No. No. Mr. Alexander is Xavier's boss. Or mentor. Maybe business partner. I don't know—his something. Anyway, he's living over the Wright's garage until he decides if he's staying in Henderson or heading back to Phoenix." Piper leaned in toward Jinx. "He's a *very* attractive gentleman."

"He must be if he caught Mrs. Flores's eye. She's stunning."

"She is," Piper agreed. "I don't know if she's chasing her youth or just still living it. I do know I want to emulate her exuberance as I age."

"I may need some help with Mrs. Flores," Jinx admitted. "She seems to be very concerned about *my* age and abilities."

"I'll do my best to champion you whenever she's around. Now, I'm going to leave the two of you here and run back to the house and check on Vance, Jr. Jinx, it was a pleasure meeting you, and I look forward to working with you on Team Henderson."

"And Jinx is looking forward to purchasing one of your Big Pie Plates." Jaxon rubbed his stomach. "She's promised me a pie upon her return to Henderson."

"Are you a baker?" Piper asked, looking at Jinx like she was a newly discovered treasure.

"No." Jinx's moan was forlorn. "I hate to disappoint you, but I'm no cook at all. But now that I'll be living on my own, I figure it's time to learn."

"Genevra and I *love* to cook. You have any questions, just ask. We also love to talk shop."

"I appreciate it."

Piper waved and headed toward the door.

Jaxon watched her leave and then turned his face back to Jinx, scooting his chair in as if he were getting ready to interrogate her. "So. You got the job."

"Almost," she said. Smiling because while looking at Jaxon Wright, it was hard not to.

"Have you told your parents yet?"

"Jaxon, I just got the job an hour ago. So, no. In fact, they don't even know I'm here."

"What do you mean?"

"They are vacationing in the south of France for the month. It's their annual trek. They took off moments after my graduation."

"You didn't want to join them?"

"I wasn't invited."

Jaxon's face dropped. "Oh."

Jinx waved her hand, "Don't cry for me, Jaxon Wright. I'm not a poor, little rich girl. I mean, at least not anymore."

"So, they don't know about this interview. About you being in Henderson?"

"They don't care," she insisted. "Which is why I'm willing to drive home today, pack up over the weekend, and be ready to work on Monday. No one is going to miss me. I'm only part-time at the university libraries, and my best friend, LiLi, is moving to D.C. in a few weeks. She's going to be working on the Hill. I'll go visit her after she gets settled. Maybe she'll come down here for one of Henderson's theme parties before she moves."

"What about your sister?"

"What about her?"

"She in Richmond?"

"Nope. She's in New York."

"Working?"

"Yes. She's actually found a real niche. She's a lawyer for a real estate investment firm, and by all accounts doing very well. And, like Mrs. Flores, she's dating a younger man."

"How much younger?"

Jinx lifted a brow. "Four years."

"Really?"

"Mmm hmm."

Jaxon pursed his lips. "What aren't you telling me?"

"Oooh. Aren't you the perceptive one." She leaned in toward Jaxon. "I've had two"—she held up two fingers—"boyfriends. *He* was my first."

"Wait. Your sister is dating your first boyfriend?"

"Yep."

"And how'd that happen?"

"I introduced them at a tailgate before a University of Richmond football game."

"And?"

"You know the expression, behind my back?"

Jaxon nodded.

"Monday after the game, a professor of mine showed me a picture he'd snapped from his vantage point in the stadium. It was of my sister sitting next to me, holding hands with Andre who was seated on the other side of me. Their hands were literally clasped behind my back."

Jaxon let out a long, low whistle. Then his eyes squinted. "Wait a minute. That professor had his eye on you."

She nodded. "Two weeks later, he became boyfriend number two."

Jaxon's head snapped back. "Jinx."

"I know." She laughed.

"He *totally* took advantage."

"Maybe. But it soothed the sting of being traded in for an upgrade."

"How old was this professor?"

"Old."

"Like, real old?"

"Like thirty-two. Attractive in a buttoned-up-professor way." *Definitely not in a ball-cap-and-monster-truck way,* she mused.

"Please tell me you were of age."

"He asked to see my driver's license. I showed him my fake ID."

"Stop."

"I was curious," she confessed with a shrug. "I missed prom and dates and had crap for a social life, being shoved so far ahead of my contemporaries academically. I had little dating experience, so when my one and only boyfriend managed to find my sister more to his liking, yeah, I was vulnerable."

"Of course, you were. And your jackass professor took complete advantage." Jaxon pulled out his phone. "What's his name? Next time I'm in Richmond, I'm looking the asshole up."

Jinx grinned. A really big grin.

Jaxon wasn't grinning. He was irritated. Angry. Upset on her behalf. He looked up from his phone, expecting her to give him a name. She gave him her heart instead.

"No one has ever, *ever* stood up for me the way you are right now."

"Your father would have if he'd have known about this lowlife."

She nodded. "Yes. He would have. He's a good one. A good man. But obviously that wasn't something I shared with him. The professor or the fact that Andre dumped me for my sister Lisette."

"And Lisette? How did she handle the situation?"

"She apologized. Both she and Andre apologized. It was such a terribly awkward conversation that I let them both off the hook fast."

"And then hooked up with this professor," he deadpanned.

"I was young," she claimed.

"You're still young," he grumbled.

"Are you saying I'm *too* young?" she said all flirty-like trying to pull Jaxon out of his antagonistic mood. "For you?"

"I don't know, Jinx," he said seriously. "Maybe."

Their eyes linked as Jinx stared at him in baffled silence.

Wow.

Not ten seconds ago, she'd handed him her heart, and he'd just gone ahead and handed it back. Maybe Vance Evans really was the smartest guy in Henderson, and she should have heeded his warning about Jaxon Wright.

She reached for her purse, ready to leave. Jaxon put a hand on top, stopping her. "Friends?" he asked.

Friends? Seriously?

She pulled her purse out from under his hand and spat his own word back at him. "Maybe."

"Jinx." Jaxon scrambled after her, but she didn't stop, just headed straight into the parking lot even though she'd planned to use the ladies room before her three-hour drive home. "Jinx!"

She whirled as she arrived at her car door. "Do you know I've never told *anyone* about that." She marched back toward Jaxon wanting to smack him with her purse. "Never. Because it was the one thing I did in my whole life that was *unseemly*. The one thing I worried people would judge me for. And you, well, you just proved

me right. So"—she threw her arms out at him—"thanks for that."
She twirled and moved to yank open her car door, throwing her
purse inside.

"Jinx. I'm sorry."

She slammed the door and turned on him again. "For what,
exactly? For shaming me? For implying that I'm not worthy of your
affection now that you know my dirty, little secret? Or are you
apologizing for doing what neither Andre or my professor was able
to manage? Break my heart in less than"—she checked her watch—
"twenty-four hours?"

She hit her mark. Left him speechless. Whirled around and got
in her car, not caring if she hit him as she backed out or when she
threw it in Drive. And she wasn't sure how it happened, but she
figured that of all people, Jaxon Wright would appreciate the message
she sent as she burned rubber out of the parking lot.

That was the last he was ever gonna see of Jinx Davenport.

CHAPTER SIXTEEN

Well, don't I just feel like shit?

And the fact that Jinx knew how to peel out of here like a rock star made it all that much worse. Who the hell was he to throw stones? Or act like an overprotective jackass around a woman who was not his? *Yet.*

Now, not ever.

Probably.

Fuck.

For a man who thought women were awesome, he just got himself ejected from the #MeToo movement.

Tell me your secrets, Jinx, and let me piss all over them. He'd never acted like such a fucking jackass. He pulled out his phone, intent on doing damage control. He texted Vance. *Just pissed off your top candidate for the library job.*

Vance texted back. *Works for me.*

What? *Seriously. I'm pretty sure this is going to be a problem.* He'd work at it from this end, because he stupidly didn't get her number.

Nah. We're good. Don't lose any sleep. Plenty more librarians in the sea and all that.

Oh. *You talk to your dad?*

Vance did not respond.

So here Jaxon stood, in the middle of something that wasn't going well for anybody, wondering what the hell he could do to get it all back on track. For lack of a better idea, he decided to head back to the Evans estate and at least do what he'd been hired for and put their cars in working order.

CHAPTER SEVENTEEN

Three months later...

Genevra DuVal rang the doorbell of the beautiful antebellum home situated in the heart of one of Richmond's most posh neighborhoods. Dressed in a stylish suit with her dark brown hair in its traditional updo, she drew in a deep breath and forced a smile, willing herself to relax and trust that her intentions would lead her to say what needed to be said. She only hoped her words would not fall on deaf ears.

The door was answered by an attractive woman several years her senior, and Genevra surmised, with more ease than she'd anticipated, that this was the original Mrs. Hale Evans.

"Catherine Davenport," she inquired, giving the woman a soft smile. "My name is Genevra DuVal *Evans,* and I've driven up from Henderson, North Carolina, in hopes that you and I may speak."

"Genevra Evans," Catherine repeated slowly. "So, you're ..."

"Hale's wife." Genevra nodded.

"I see."

The women stared for a moment, assessing each other gently. There were no harsh looks. No suggestion of ill feelings.

Catherine stepped back. "Please come in."

"Thank you," Genevra said, and meant it.

"Perhaps a glass of wine? On the terrace?"

"Yes," Genevra smiled. "That would be lovely."

Catherine nodded. The woman was far from what Genevra had expected. She was dressed in designer jeans and a flowing floral top.

She didn't bare fangs nor did she ride a broomstick. She had Hale's coloring, and it was easy to see how she and Hale had made gorgeous children together. Genevra followed her into a spacious kitchen and glanced at the traditional surroundings as Catherine retrieved a bottle of white from the subzero refrigerator. She took two glasses hanging from a rack and motioned for Genevra to follow her out a back door. She led the way to a small sitting area in the shade. Although it was early October, the weather was heavenly.

"Please make yourself comfortable," Catherine said, setting the glasses down on a low table and making moves to pour the wine. "I assume I know why you're here."

That surprised Genevra. "You do?"

"My daughter?" Catherine raised her gaze to Genevra as she poured.

"Not your son?" Genevra asked in response.

Catherine stopped pouring and glanced up at Genevra for a brief moment before shaking her head and resuming her task.

"He's a wonderful man, you know," Genevra told her.

"Hale or … our son?"

Genevra clasped her hands in her lap. "Both. Hale, of course. But Vance, he's …" she stumbled, searching for words. "He's resilient."

Catherine blanched slightly as she handed Genevra her wine. Then she turned away and settled herself onto a loveseat across the small expanse. "*Are* you here about Vance?"

"No. Not really. But of course, I'm curious."

"As to why I left him."

"Hale or Vance?" Genevra questioned.

"I left Hale because I needed more attention than he was willing to give me. I left Vance because Hale needed him. For all Hale's flying around the country, he was still a family man. I was already taking enough from him. I didn't want to take his son from him as well."

"So you left Vance?" Genevra's voice went up in accusation. "With a father who worked out of town five days a week?" She immediately cut herself off and tried to take back the words. "I'm sorry. I did not come here to discuss Vance. I apologize."

Catherine sat back and crossed her legs, holding her wine in front of her. "I was having an affair while Hale was off making his fortune. When I became pregnant, I was forced to make a decision. I decided I needed a husband who was willing to dote on me. However, I didn't have it in me to potentially take both of Hale's children away from him."

"Both?"

"I was unclear as to who the father was. I didn't want to bring more upset into Hale's life. Vance adored his father, he loved his friends, and he was a happy child. I didn't want to take that away from him either. So I left. Leaving the two of them together. I cut all ties so as not to muddy the waters once my new baby was born."

"You didn't want Hale to know he might have another child."

"My current husband was very much under the impression the baby was his, and I did nothing to discourage his thinking."

Genevra leaned forward. "I appreciate your candor. I have to say it's a bit ... surprising."

"Yet it's the reason you've driven all this way to see me."

"It is." Genevra sat back. "Are you aware that your daughter Jinx applied for a job in Henderson a few months ago?"

"I am, but only because I found a gas receipt from her trip. And a bed-and-breakfast brochure. When I asked her about them, figuring she'd somehow found out about my past—Jinx's research is as good as any detective's—she surprised me by mentioning the library position. When she refused to tell me more, I did my own research, hoping the Evans name was not associated with the library there. But of course, it is. Since you've shown up on my doorstep, I assume Jinx's visit did not go unnoticed."

"She looks like Hale. She looks like Vance, too. But to hear Hale tell it, she's the spitting image of you. On the day of Jinx's interview, Hale's car broke down just off the highway on the road heading into Henderson. Jinx stopped to offer him assistance."

Catherine spouted a choked laugh of disbelief. "Of all people."

"Hale recognized her as your daughter. His mother Emelina was conducting the library interview and recognized her too. She asked for Jinx's birthdate. A friend provided strands of Jinx's hair. Hale submitted those for a DNA test."

"And?"

"She's his."

Catherine sighed heavily. The expulsion of air left her looking physically depleted. She sat in silence for a brief moment, sliding her fingers around the bowl of her wine glass. "What are you going to do?" she finally asked, lifting her gaze toward Genevra.

"I'm here to plead my husband's case. He, of course, wants Jinx to know the truth. He wants the opportunity to build a relationship with his daughter. However, he believes it best that you be the one to explain it to her. Give her your side of the story."

Another laugh of disbelief. "Hale. I'm surprised he doesn't want to use this against me. Send an anonymous report to my husband and let the chips fall where they may."

Genevra gave her a gentle smile. "He simply wants to know his daughter."

When the silence dragged out, Genevra pulled her phone from her clutch. "Hale and I have a son together." She pulled up a picture of Beau on her phone and moved to the seat beside Catherine. He's six months old now."

Catherine looked at the photo solemnly.

"And, if I may, you have a grandson the same age. Vance, Jr." Genevra swiped her phone a few strokes and showed off not just a picture of Vance, Jr. but one of Vance holding his child.

"May I?" Catherine whispered. She took the phone from Genevra, enlarging the photo to study the faces. Her finger drifted over the image.

"Swipe to the right. That's Piper, Vance's wife."

"They appear very happy," Catherine whispered.

"They are. We all are. They—Hale and Vance—were not for a very long time, but everybody is happy now. Only since the test result has come back, my husband can't stop thinking about Jinx."

Catherine nodded. "*My* husband is going to be heartbroken. And Jinx loves her father. She truly does."

"Hale would respect their relationship. In fact, that's one of the reasons he hasn't contacted Jinx."

"Yet he sent you."

"No, no. I'm here on my own. On his behalf."

Catherine looked Genevra over, considering. "You must love him very much."

Genevra smiled broadly. "That, Mrs. Davenport, is an understatement."

CHAPTER EIGHTEEN

Jinx wasn't exactly sure how she'd managed to arrive on E&E's doorstep. The drive had been a blur, her head so tangled up in holy-shits and you've-got-to-be-fucking-kidding-me's. Her mother—*her mother*—had booked an impromptu cruise, and when she called to alert Jinx about it, she casually mentioned she was leaving something important for her on the foyer table. She asked her to please come by first thing in the morning and pick it up.

It was a letter explaining that her mother had once been *married* to Hale Evans, and that there was a distinct possibility she could be his daughter.

Yep. The holy-shit, you've-got-to-be-fucking-kidding-me that started it all.

She tried to reach both of her parents by phone, but neither of them picked up. Unable to comprehend what her mother's note implied, she booted up the family's computer and easily verified that almost eleven years before she was born, her mother, had indeed, married Mr. Evans. She stared at the picture posted in the Henderson Daily announcing their union.

No wonder the man had seemed concussed the day they'd met on the side of that road. She looked exactly as her mother had on their wedding day.

Again. The holy-shits and what-the-hells kept on coming. How was she not privy to this information? Why didn't her parents tell her? Why was this all such a freaking secret?

And then it occurred to her. Just as she was about to enter E&E Investments, she understood. Her dad *didn't know*. He didn't know he may not be her biological father. Which was why her mother had whisked him away on a cruise, dropping this bombshell on Jinx to deal with on her own.

Well, right. And wasn't that the biggest what-the-fuck imaginable? *Seriously.*

"Jinx?" The voice, rich in timbre, came from behind her as she stood on the sidewalk facing the door to E&E. She whirled and came up blinking at the one person she had not anticipated seeing today. The one person she hadn't considered when it came to this what-the-hell nightmare.

Jaxon Wright.

After running on adrenaline the entire length of the drive, her head swimming with the question of her ancestral DNA, she didn't have the stamina to thwart the effects of his gorgeous hair and handsome face effectively. Her entire body sighed at the sight of him. Her first thought was that his shoulders looked like a great place to lean into and cry. She held up a hand, planning to let him know that she couldn't deal with him and the sexy way he wore his ball cap at the moment. But she didn't get the chance.

"Jinx?" Another masculine voice came from behind her. This one gentle and uncertain. She turned to find Hale Evans holding open the door to his business, his eyes beseeching her. "Come in," he motioned. "Please. Come in."

She looked back and forth between the two men. "Go on," Jaxon coaxed. "We can catch up later."

Jinx nodded, because what else could she do? She turned and, after a brief nod to Hale, she watched the ground in front of her as she headed into the offices of her ... father?

Possibly.

And her ... brother? Oh, dear Lord.

Seriously, Mom. What-the-ever-living-hell?

"I'm sorry to have arrived on your doorstep like this," she began. "If you need me to make an appointment, I can do that. I can come back if this isn't a good time," she rambled.

"Jinx." Hale settled her. "I'm happy you're here. Anytime you show up is a perfect time."

She nodded, unable to hold his gaze. So she glanced around the small foyer, using her tongue to wet her dry lips. "My, ah, mother," she started.

"Catherine." Hale nodded, his hands in his pockets, standing there, watching her. Classically handsome. Calm. Beautifully dressed. Her mother's first husband.

Jinx reached into her bag and pulled out the note. "She left this for me and then fled the country. I opened it early this morning."

Hale took it and read. His hand came up to his forehead as if he were in pain, then he shook that off and appeared to be reading the note again. Finally, he folded it up, his eyes glancing from the stationery to her. "Perhaps you'd like to join me in my office." His arm indicated the way down the hall. "First door on the right."

Jinx nodded and headed in that direction. She stood next to the chair situated in front of his desk and was grateful when Hale closed the door, securing their privacy. She assumed he wasn't interested in having an audience for this conversation, and neither was she. The fewer people who knew about this the better.

"I'm not here to upset your life," Jinx promised. "Just the opposite. I drove here to make it clear that when we first met, I was unaware that you'd been married to my mother. "

"Jinx—"

"And also"—she went on quickly—"to get some answers, since it's obvious my mother isn't interested in discussing this with me."

"Please, take a seat. I'm open to anything you want to talk about."

She looked at the chair beside her and moved to sit down. "Research indicates that what her note says is true. That the two of you were married."

"That is correct."

"And, is Vance … *her* son?"

"Yes. Vance is our son."

Jinx tilted her head, hardly able to comprehend that answer. "I don't understand."

Hale sat down in the chair next to her. "What don't you understand?" he asked softly.

"Why didn't I know any of this? Why hadn't I met Vance before?" *How is it possible you could be my father?*

"Jinx. When your mother left, she didn't look back. Not once."

She rubbed her forehead, not really getting it. "Why? How could she do that?"

Hale held up the note, and for the first time, Jinx heard anger in his voice. "How could she leave you this note instead of sitting you down and discussing this with you?"

"I don't know." Jinx's hands started to shake with rage as her eyes filled with evidence of her distress. "She won't answer her phone. I tried to call her *and* my father, and they both aren't—" Just at that moment, her phone started to ring. She pulled it out and said with a huge sigh of relief, "My father." She held the face out to show Hale.

He nodded, getting up out of the chair. "I'll leave you the office. Take as long as you want. I'll be here when you're done."

She bobbed her head quickly, her heart racing just as fast as she watched him leave. She wanted so badly for her father to be the one to end this nightmare.

"Dad," she began to cry, all the pent up frustration and upset pouring out of her. She tried to sniff it back, but the dam had been breached.

"Baby girl, I am so sorry," her father said. "Your mother. She just told me. And I'm on a sketchy offshore line in the middle of the ocean. I'm not certain we won't be cut off, but I had to try to contact you. Sweetheart, I love you. You know I do. I'm your father. I was there the day you were born, and I'm not going anywhere now. I don't need proof. I don't want proof. I just want you to know that I'm your dad, and you're my daughter. Do you hear me, darlin'?"

Jinx nodded, using a tissue she found at the bottom of her bag to blot her face. "I hear you. I do. I'm just a little emotional hearing your voice."

"Baby, this ... I'm so sorry your mother chose to handle it this way. I wouldn't have left you alone. You know that, right? If I had any idea, we would have talked. In person. Right? I'm working on flying out of here as soon as they can line it up. I'm not a medical emergency, so I've got to wait until we get to our first port. Then I'll book transportation home."

"What?"

"I'm flying home. As soon as I'm able."

"Why? Dad, don't do that. It's not necessary."

"Of course, it's necessary. You're my daughter, and I'm not letting anybody take you away from me. I'm coming home."

"Dad. No one is taking me away from you. I love you. And Mom will freak if you leave her to her own devices."

"Your mother is a grown woman who is going to have to deal with this grenade she just launched into our lives. For the first time, your mother is not my top priority. You are."

Jinx sniffed and smiled. "I appreciate that, Dad. I really do. But I'm good on my own. You know that. You raised me to be okay on my own. Mom? Not so much, yeah? So you stay and milk this for all it's worth. You've catered to her for a long time now. It's time she does a little kowtowing to you."

"Jinx. Honey. I don't want you to be alone right now. And I need to lay eyes on you. To know you're all right."

"FaceTime me when you get to port. We'll talk some more. I appreciate you wanting to come home, but … ah, I think I'm going to take a little time for myself. Maybe take a little trip of my own."

There was silence on the other end of the phone.

"Dad? You still there?"

He cleared his voice. "Yeah, darlin' I'm here."

"I'm okay. Really."

"You planning to go to Henderson?"

She looked around Hale Evan's office, the apprehension in her father's voice registering. "I'm … thinking about it."

More silence.

"Dad?"

"I'd rather you not, honey. Not until I get home, and we can talk about all this."

"It's okay. I'm okay. I'm not running away or anything."

"You sure about that? Your mother leaves you a note telling you I may not be your father and you don't feel the urge to run away?"

"No. No, just the urge to clarify things. To get answers."

"Answers?"

"Yeah. Maybe. Answers."

"Darlin'."

Jinx sat there in silence, sorrow crashing back into her. She sniffed. "It's okay, Dad. We're going to be okay."

"Honey. Jinxy. Please. I don't need answers. You're my baby girl. I'm your dad. I'd like to leave it at that."

She couldn't respond. Didn't know what to say.

"But, hey." She heard him take a deep breath. "I'm not gonna make this about me. I love ya, sugar. You need answers, I'll do whatever you need me to do to help you get them. I know that your mother likes to drag me all over the European continent, but metaphorically, I'm right there with you. By your side. And if you need me physically, I'll be there as fast as I can get there, ya hear?"

"I hear," she said. "Thank you. I love you. You know that, right?"

"I do, sweetheart. I surely do."

"Thank you for calling me. Don't make plans to abandon ship. I'll let you know if I need you to come home early."

"All right, darlin'. If you're sure."

"I'm sure."

"Still want to FaceTime you when we get to port, all right? Need to see your face. Make sure you're okay."

"All right. I'll look forward to seeing your face too."

"Bye, baby."

"Bye. Thanks for calling."

"Love you, girl."

"Love you too."

The call ended.

Jinx sat there feeling stunned. Overwhelmed. Exhausted. Grateful her father was man enough to face the things head on her mother didn't seem able to. She shook her head. Her mother. What the hell was her problem?

This was all so baffling.

There was a knock on the door before Vance Evans blew in with his head down, looking at a pile of papers in his hand. "Good news from the stadium engineering crew," he started in. "We've lucked out." When his head popped up, Vance stopped short. "Jinx?"

"Hey," she said meekly, tucking her phone into her bag. Then she sat there, blinking at Vance ... her brother ... Vance.

"What's going on?" Vance said warily, apparently looking around the room for his father. "What are you doing here?"

She tilted her head and looked at him, wondering if he didn't know what she knew. If his father hadn't mentioned the fact that she looked just like his mother.

"You don't know?"

"Oh." Vance stood very still, staring at her. Finally, "Did Dad call you?"

"No, I didn't," Hale said as he entered the room behind Vance. "Jinx just arrived a few minutes ago. We were just starting to have a chat when her phone rang. I gave her the room for some privacy."

"Oh. All right, then. I'll leave you to it."

"Would you like to stay?" Hale offered.

"Nope," Vance said decisively and turned to leave like he couldn't get out of the room fast enough. He pulled the door solidly shut behind him.

Jinx turned a stunned look toward Hale. "O-kay. So I see my father is not the only civilian casualty."

Hale held up both palms. "First. How was your conversation with your father?"

"She told him. My mother"—she flittered her fingers toward Hale—"Catherine, told him I may not be his biological daughter. He offered to come home immediately. I told him not to bother. The two of us are going to have a longer chat when they arrive in port."

Hale nodded, moving behind his desk to take a seat. "I recognized you right away. I mean, you look so much like your mother."

Jinx pulled out the picture she'd printed of their photo in the Henderson Daily and slid it across the table. "I look just like she did when the two of you were married."

Hale swallowed as he picked up the picture and gazed at it. He put it down and cleared his throat. "I loved your mother," he stated. "To distraction. We were happy. Well, I was happy. I think, for a while, she was happy too. But I had ambition and I got lucky in the business world. I'd equate it to a gambler hitting it big, time after time, where it then becomes addictive. You don't want to stop because things are going so well. So I spent a lot of time buying up and investing in new companies across the country and ended up spending more and more time away from home while I worked to help them grow. Catherine enjoyed the money I was making and didn't complain. I'm not sure whether she ever complained, but if she did, I was too caught up in my success to hear it. I came home one day, and she'd left a note." He tossed his hand at the note her mother had left her. "I was devastated. To say I didn't see it coming is an understatement. I begged her to come back. I promised her the world. I told her Vance and I couldn't—" And then he stopped himself, his palms coming up again. "None of that concerns you. I'm sorry. It's ancient history, and she's your mother. I promise, I won't go down that path."

Jinx blew out a laugh. A laugh followed by tears. "Why not? I thought I knew how terrible a parent she was, but apparently, I had no idea. I mean, yeah, she loves me—*now that I'm grown*. I may not have seen her much while I was growing up because she wanted to be in France more than at home, but I had no idea she had *another child* whom she *never* saw." She wiped her eyes. "Don't censor yourself on my account. Frankly, right now, I need someone I can trust to tell me how it is. To tell me the truth."

"Okay," Hale said, nodding his head. "I can be that for you. As long as you know it's my version of the truth. Eventually, you'll want to coax your mother into giving you her version."

Jinx bobbed her head, continuing to wipe her eyes. "Is it true? You could be my father?"

Hale nodded back at her. "It's true. Given your appearance, given your birthdate, I *absolutely* … ah, could be your father. Which is why I'm so relieved you're here." His voice dropped to a quieter, more intimate tone. "The guilt I feel over not knowing about you—"

"I don't want a paternity test." The words flew out of her mouth before she considered how they'd land. "I'm sorry," she said to his taken-aback expression. "I just … I want to know." She nodded her head. "I do. I want to know the truth," she assured him. "But my father doesn't. He doesn't. He said he doesn't want to know."

"Jinx, I understand that your father and his feelings are important to you. I promise to respect that. No matter what a paternity test reveals, I get that he's the man who raised you. He's the one you call dad. I simply want to get to know you."

"Why?"

"Why?" Hale blinked, and then his eyes started to water. "You're my"—he stopped himself abruptly—"you could be my daughter."

Jinx swallowed.

Hale sat back, unlocking their gazes by looking down at his desk. He cleared his throat. "Let's table the paternity issue for the moment." He looked up at her. "You've been given a lot of information to absorb. I will simply state for the record that if I knew Catherine was pregnant when she left me, you can be sure I would have followed up to find out if you were mine, Jinx. I would not have let her keep my daughter from me. It was her choice not to see Vance. I never stopped her. And believe me, that—" he stopped himself, holding his hands up again.

"What?" Jinx implored.

"Not relevant. What is relevant is that you're here, in Henderson, and I'd like you to stick around. You and Vance share a mother. For that alone, I think we all should get to know each other."

"So Vance does know about me," she confirmed.

"He figured it out when Davis suggested the two of you looked so much alike you could be twins."

Jinx didn't remember. "When was that?"

"Just before you left town. Vance came to me in a state of shock. Asked me about your mother. His mother."

"So he's fully aware."

"He is."

Jinx thought back to no follow-up interview call and Vance's face when he found her in his father's office just now. "He doesn't like me."

"He doesn't like the situation. As I recall, he liked you very much."

Jinx gave a short, sorrowful laugh. "Before he realized we're related."

"You have to understand, Jinx. He was abandoned by Catherine when he was ten. For a long time, he hoped she'd come back."

Jinx fell back into her chair as understanding dawned. "Oh."

"So, you see. This isn't about you."

"No. I do see. In a way, it is all about me. Right? He thinks I stole his mother."

"Mr. Davenport stole his mother while I wasn't paying enough attention. I'm the culprit here."

"You? You just said you didn't stand in the way of Catherine seeing Vance. How can you be the culprit?"

"I should have been around more. Taken better care of my wife. Secured the family unit."

Jinx leaned across the desk and leveled Hale Evans with a serious stare. "No one could possibly pay enough attention to my mother to make her happy. My father is blessed with an inheritance that allows him to cater to her every whim. I love him, but he was an absentee father because she demanded all his time and energy and wanted to be overseas as much as possible. No way can you blame yourself. She and I have a relationship because I lived in her household. If I was living in a different state?" She shook her head. "She probably wouldn't have bothered."

"I'm sorry, Jinx."

"For what?"

"For you having to suffer like that."

She shrugged a shoulder. "I got used to it. It is what it is."

"Well, it's not how the Evans family does things. At least now."

"Now?"

"Ah, have you met my wife, Genevra?"

"No."

"So, you'll probably understand when you meet her. She's changed the way the Evans family operates. She, along with Vance's wife, Piper."

"I have met Piper."

"The two of them have brought a lot of warmth into our home. Into our hearts. Vance and I were, ah, wounded warriors, you could say, driven to define ourselves by our success before we were lucky enough to find Genevra and Piper. My mother—you met Emelina—was supporting us with food and managing the household, but once I met Genevra, everything changed. You'll like her."

"Does Emelina know? About me?"

"She took one look at you and had a fit. She knew you were Catherine's right away. And I'll apologize for her conduct. It is an understatement to say she wasn't a big fan of your mom."

"So she's not a fan of mine?"

"Once she realized you could be her granddaughter, she softened."

"Softened?"

"Stood down. Stopped worrying."

"Worrying? About what?"

It was the hesitation from Hale that lit up her brainwaves. "Oh! Oh, my God." Jinx felt chills go up the side of her head. "You all thought I knew, didn't you? You thought I knew about you and my mother. You thought I came to Henderson because ... because ..."

"Jinx, we *thought* you came here for the library job."

"I did. I swear I did. I had no idea." She took a deep breath and sat back. "But they don't believe that do they? Vance. Mrs. Flores. *You?*" She sat up wondering. "What did you think?"

He shook his head. "I admit I was overwhelmed. I knew who you were immediately. And when my mother recognized who you were, her only concern was Vance. She didn't want you bringing your mother back into his life. So she ..."

"Didn't want me to have the job." Jinx nodded.

"Jinx. You understand this is very complicated."

"Yeah. It is." Suddenly, she was angry. At everyone. For making her life so damn complicated.

"I want you to work with me to uncomplicate it," Hale requested.

"How about I leave town and promise never to come back?" She grabbed at her bag and started to stand. Hale stood, reaching out a hand.

"That won't do. Don't you see? If nothing else, you have a brother and a nephew. It's ... likely I'm your father and Emelina is your grandmother. I can't let go of any of that. Can you?"

Jinx collapsed back into the chair and willed herself not to cry. "I came for the job," she told him. "I just wanted the job."

CHAPTER NINETEEN

Jaxon paced in the alley behind E&E Investments. It wasn't like he didn't have a shit-ton to do, but until he apologized to Jinx, he wasn't going to be able to focus on anything else. It had been three months since he'd pissed her off. Three months of thinking about her as soon as his head hit the pillow each night, and three months of her being the first thing he thought of in the morning.

Jinx Davenport.

The stolen daughter of Hale Evans.

He owed her an apology, yeah, but more than that, he wanted to know how she was taking the news.

"What the hell are you doing out here?"

Jaxon's head whipped around to find Vance coming out the back door looking like someone kicked his dog. "Hey," he said. "What's up? Jinx in there? She all right?"

Vance busted by him, pulling open the passenger door of his orange 'Vette and dumping a bunch of heavy folders into the seat. "Don't know, don't care."

"What?"

Vance turned on Jax. "I don't know how *Jinx* is doing. And I don't care." He slammed the door.

"Come on, man. Sure you do. She's your sister." Jax tailed Vance to the other side of his car.

Vance spun on him. "*That* is not common knowledge."

"Yet," Jax assured him. "Not common knowledge, *yet*. But she's here, in town. I assume your father's going to tell her. Or has already. I don't know. I thought you'd know."

"All I know is like a bad penny, she keeps turning up."

"Whatever, man. So now what?"

"What do you mean, now what?"

"You gonna hire her now?"

"No, I'm not going to hire her. I'm hoping I don't have to talk to her, ever."

"Dude. I seriously don't get it. What are you so worried about? It's not like she's come to lay claim to your inheritance."

"It's not?"

"No, man. She's got her own money. No doubt you checked into that, thoroughly."

"I'm not discussing this with you," Vance said, trying to duck Jaxon and get in his car. Jax put a hand on his shoulder, stopping him.

"You liked her. Before. She's perfect for the job. You haven't hired anyone else. And now she's family. So there's that."

"Yeah, there's that. And if she weren't family I would have hired her months ago. Step aside, Jax. And get lost, will ya? I didn't like you sniffing around her when she wasn't my sister. I'm certainly not going to feel any differently about it now."

"What? Fuck you."

"Seriously. I don't know where the hell this is all ending up, but you, man, are not going to be a part of it."

"I'm already a part of it."

"Then *bow out*," Vance ordered. "I've got enough to deal with."

"Look. I'm no threat here. But I do need to apologize to Jinx before I do anything else."

"Apologize?" Vance whipped off his sunglasses. "What the hell did you do that you have to apologize for?" Vance butted his chest up against Jax's.

"None of your business," Jaxon said, holding his ground. "And may I point out that at the moment, you seem overly concerned about someone you don't want to claim as a sister."

The two men stared each other down. "My reasons for not claiming, not hiring, or not *liking* Jinx Davenport are my own. Doesn't mean I have any intention of letting her be pawed by the likes of you."

"What is your problem? Seriously? You don't even know me."

"I know your reputation."

"Which doesn't hold a candle to yours."

Vance's brow lifted.

"So that's it? You don't want a guy like *you* messing with your sister."

"You said it."

"Then let me put your mind at ease. I'm *nothing* like you used to be."

"I've seen you in action, Jax. That's bullshit."

"*This* is bullshit." Jax stepped back, waving a hand between them. "You've got issues. We *all* know that. Whatever you're dealing with, don't toss that shit on me. I like women. I treat women with respect. I hurt Jinx's feelings right before she left town, and now I'm going to apologize for it."

"You're nothin' to her, Jax. Don't waste your time."

"I'm nothin' to her? I may not be her *brother,* but I'm pretty sure I'm the reason she never followed up after that interview."

"*I* never followed up after the interview."

"Then you have something to apologize for as well."

Vance's phone pinged. He looked down and grimaced. Then he looked at Jax and started talking as he ducked inside his car. "I'm already gone, ya hear. You want to speak to Jinx, now's your chance." He motioned his head toward the back door. "But I'm gone. Clear?"

"Sure. Clear." Jax stepped back and watched Vance's 'Vette slink out of the alley. "Coward." He turned his sights on E&E's back door, gathering his own courage. He'd done this over a hundred times in his head during the past three months. He wasn't going to slink away like Vance. Nope. He was going to man up and get 'r done.

He opened the back door and started walking down the hall like a man on death row, in no big hurry to get where he was going. In his head—his fantasies—he'd been able to smooth things over with

Jinx. In reality, the verdict was still out, about to be delivered one way or the other.

He stuck his head in the first open door he came to.

"Hey, Davis."

"Hey, Jaxon. You need me?"

"Nope. Looking for Jinx. Wanted, ah, a word."

"Jinx? The librarian?" Davis squinted. "Is she finally here?" He got up, moving toward Jax. "Vance told me he wanted to handle all negotiations with Jinx personally. I've been wondering what the hell's been holding it all up." Davis moved out into the hall in front of Jax and then stopped and knocked on a closed office door.

"Come in," Hale called.

Davis opened the door and looked around. "Jinx!" he said, straightening, leaving Jaxon to look over his shoulder. "Finally."

"Davis. Good to see you." The tone of Jinx's voice was engaging. Like she was smiling at Davis. Happy to see him. Jaxon couldn't see her until she came over and gave Davis a hug.

"I didn't even know you were here." Davis threw a thumb over his shoulder. "Jaxon told me."

Jax pressed his lips together and nodded. "I hoped you'd give me a minute. When you have time."

Her smile faltered. "I don't ..."

"We were expecting Vance," Hale said.

"Oh. Yeah," Jax acknowledged Mr. Evans. "I saw him head out a while ago. Had a meeting. Something."

"All right. Later then," Hale said to Jinx.

There was an awkward pause. All four of them standing there, silent. Jaxon looked longingly at Jinx, wanting to put her and himself out of this misery. "Jinx. Have you eaten? May I take you to lunch?"

"Perfect," Hale insisted. "Jaxon can take you to lunch, and I'm sure Vance will be back to discuss the status of the library job by the time you're through."

"You okay with that?" Jaxon asked Jinx, figuring he'd better offer her an out. Not that she'd take it. The awkward factor was crazy high.

Her response was a lackluster, "Sure." What else was the girl going to do?

Still, he wasn't looking a gift horse in the mouth. He was going to take advantage of getting her alone.

"I'll come too," Davis chimed in, until Jaxon shot him a glare. "Or not?" It didn't take Davis long. "Right. Can't eat. Too busy," he said as he bustled by him to get out the door.

"Jinx?" Jaxon said as he held out his arm, indicating the front door.

"I've got my car," she said. "I'll follow you."

Once Jax was outside and it was just the two of them, he didn't waste any time. "I would have called to apologize, but I didn't have your number. Nor would Vance give it to me. Mr. Evans didn't have your number either, and I didn't have the balls to ask the Big Em. I called your parents' home, but whoever answered refused to give it to me. Which, you know, in general is a good thing, I guess. Still"— he pulled off his ball cap and stroked a hand through his hair—"I wanted to apologize." He replaced his hat.

"You're forgiven," she said curtly, opening her car door. "So lunch is no longer necessary."

Bullshit, it's not. Jaxon pulled open the passenger door of her cute, little Fiat and quickly folded the length of his body inside.

"What are you doing?"

"You aren't blowing me off, Jinx. We're going to talk. We need to clear the air."

"Jaxon," she sighed, drawing out his name. "I've got *way* bigger fish to fry."

"I don't doubt that. Still, I've done nothin' but imagine this conversation for the past three months, so we're having it."

"I'm not going to be able to eat anything. My stomach is a wreck."

"Okay," he softened, putting himself in her shoes. "Just drive. I'll give you directions to the lake. We can sit there and … I can, you know, grovel."

"You don't have to grovel," she said, starting the car.

"Pretty sure I do. Take a right at the end of the road. Now just follow this until it dead ends. Then take a left."

She followed his directions, not saying anything.

He looked around her car, clean as a whistle and still looking brand spanking new. It even had that new-car smell, but he caught a whiff of something floral too. It was subtle, but it was there. It reminded him of the brief moment he'd stuck his nose in her neck at the end of their date all those months ago.

Tamping down the urge to stare at her profile or touch her, he allowed his gaze to travel down her navy blue slacks to her shoes—matching heels with a pointed toe. Her dark hair was styled just like it had been the day they'd met. A side braid, thick and long, laid against her crisp sleeveless blouse over the swell of her breast, the tiny white ribbon at the base landing at her waist. Noticing the finer points of her figure caused him to recall their kiss. Their *several* kisses. Reminding him how easily they'd fallen into that. And then his phone buzzed against his ass. He moved to pull it out, finding a text from Hale.

She doesn't know I ran the test. Please hold my confidence.

He texted back a quick *10-4*

So then, why was she here? If Hale hadn't informed her about the paternity test, what was going on?

"Take the left up ahead," he indicated. "You like boats?"

She hitched a noncommittal shoulder.

"Our Indian summer is not going to last forever. Pull into the marina up ahead." She did and followed his directions toward the dock where the Old Dog sat. "It'll be quiet down here, being as it's a Monday."

"Good," she snapped as she put her car in park. She turned and looked at him full on. "You'll be able to grovel without witnesses."

Jax opened his door murmuring, "True that."

After Jaxon encouraged her to exit the vehicle, Jinx followed him down the pier, pulling out her sunglasses and covering those brilliant green eyes. Her arms were crossed over her chest and tucked in tight with her slouchy bag hanging at the crook. She took off her heels and held them in her hand while he took the cover off the back of the boat, rolled it up, and tossed it into the storage cabinet. "You know how to swim?" he asked as he held out his hand, helping her down into the boat.

"Yes."

"Mind if we take a short spin, then?"

"You *really* don't want people to see you grovel."

He gave her a brief nod and pointed to the seats spanning the length of the back. When she sat down, he opened the engine hatch and sniffed for fumes. Then he turned the key and started the ignition. He let the boat idle while he hopped off and untied the bow. He untied the stern and jumped back on board, shutting up the engine hatch before backing out of the slip. He pointed to the cooler near Jinx as he spun the Old Dog around. "Might find something still cool in there. We were out on her yesterday."

Jinx moved to open the cooler. "You want something?" she called.

"Beer?"

She nodded. Next thing Jax knew, she was at his side, handing him an opened can. She had a Coke in her own.

"You on the wagon?" he asked.

"Need the caffeine," she said. "Mind if I sit up here?" She motioned to the seat next to him.

"Not at all."

"Where are we going?"

"No place."

Jinx simply nodded as she sat.

She didn't look at him. Her gaze was directed out over the water in front of her. Out toward the cliffs in the distance. He studied her feminine profile, noticed how the wind whipped tendrils of her hair from her braid as she sipped on her Coke, seemingly content for the moment. He was itching to know what was going on in her mind. Curious about what had brought her back to Henderson. Curious about what she knew and how she knew it.

When she'd driven off all those months ago, he'd assumed she'd be back seventy-two hours later. Yeah, she was pissed at him, and Vance was cagey about the library job, but he didn't think that shit was going to stick. He'd gone straight to the Joneses and worked out a deal for her to stay at B&B's B&B for as long as she needed. Then he'd phoned Vance to tell him as much and to get her number. Vance told him then that the library job had been put on hold and didn't say more. It was Mr. Evans who'd explained the situation: that Vance had figured out Jinx was his sister, and he didn't like it.

At the time, Hale didn't know what he was going to do about Jinx, and Jaxon hadn't felt he could badger the man about it as time wore on. So when it came to Jinx Davenport, Jaxon found himself dead in the water.

But now … here she was. The two of them in the same boat, literally.

He pulled the throttle back and brought the boat to a slow, easy forward motion. If he was being given this opportunity, no sense wasting time. No sense trying to be heard over the wind, either.

"You back for the library job?" he asked.

Jinx didn't look over at him. She just shook her head. Sipped her Coke.

He cut the engine.

"Jinx. What's going on?"

She turned her pretty face toward him, those dark-green eyes still hiding behind her shades. He hated that they prevented him from getting a fix on her emotional state. "A lot," she said succinctly. "None of it having anything to do with you."

Ouch.

"Okay. Well. I appreciate your candor … I think." Jax clapped his hands and rubbed them together. He sat sideways in his seat, his focus on her for the most part, one hand on the wheel. "The last time I saw you, you gave me a severe verbal thrashing and then made an impressive exit by burning rubber out of the country club's parking lot. I've had a lot of time to contemplate how things that had been going so well ended up in the crapper so fast."

Jinx turned her attention to the water in front of them.

Jaxon went on. "You and I hit it off pretty good. So good that you shared a piece of yourself you'd never given anybody."

She flinched.

"And because I'd gotten a little tangled up in you, I reacted like an overprotective SOB. Jinx, you told me I made you feel ashamed. But that was not my intention. I was angry at your professor. I was looking at the situation like a jealous boyfriend. I didn't bother to take your feelings for the guy into consideration. And who am I to judge, anyway? Hell, he could have been your soulmate for all I know. I just … to me—from the outside looking in—it looked like he took advantage of you and the situation with your sister and your—*her*—boyfriend. I reacted to that. And dumped it on you. I'm sorry. I truly am. I was one hundred percent in the wrong."

He watched as she took a breath. Watched her sigh it out, her posture collapsing from stiff and rigid to defeated. "You're not one hundred percent wrong," she grumbled.

"I'm not?" *Hell. He'd take any inch he could get here.*

"No," she said into the wind. "He wasn't my soulmate. He probably did take advantage of me. But, Jaxon, I let him. I mean, I wasn't socially inept. Even back then, I could read a room. I knew I was vulnerable." She looked over at Jax. "At the time, I just didn't care."

Jax felt a pang in his solar plexus, but he covered it up with a nonchalant shrug. "Then no harm, no foul."

"Oh, please. The guy should be shot. I was half his age and still a minor. And my fake ID looked exactly that. Fake."

Jaxon pursed his lips. "So, it's okay I acted like a dick on your behalf?"

"Yes. But it's not okay that you let it change the way you thought of me."

"What?"

"It's not okay to *judge* me for my past. Especially since I've been warned about yours."

"Jinx, I was mad at your professor, not you."

"Jaxon Wright, you suggested we be *friends*," she claimed with air quotes. "Went to shake my hand and everything."

"I did?"

"Yes! You did …" She may not have actually spoke the word *asshole*, but it was definitely implied. "After making out with me the night before and then dipping me into a kiss that very afternoon—in front of my future boss no less—you then told me, none too gently, you just wanted to be *friends*." She spat out the word.

"God, Jinx. I'm an ass. I'm sorry. I don't know what got a hold of me during that conversation, but clearly, I wasn't in my right mind."

"But you were. Of course, you were. Those were absolutely your true feelings. After hearing my story, you wanted nothing more to do with me. Which, as it turns out, completely justified my worst fear."

"How?" Jaxon wondered. But then he answered his own question as he worked it all out. "Because you trusted me. You felt comfortable enough to share a part of yourself, and I made you feel ashamed."

"Yep." Jinx sipped her Coke and looked back toward the horizon. "You did that."

Fuck.

CHAPTER TWENTY

Yeah. He'd done that. He'd made her feel ashamed.

But the truth was she was already ashamed of falling into that nonsense with her professor. It was stupid to get involved with him. She'd known it at the time, but yeah, Professor Smooth's attention went a long way to soothe her pride over her sister stealing her one and only boyfriend.

At the time, Jinx was pissed. And not just at her sister, but at the entire world. Dating him was her way of flipping the bird at life. Her social life sucked because she was in class with people a whole lot older who were interested in things she shouldn't be—sex, drugs, rock and roll—not to mention they looked at her like she was some kind of freak because she was really into the academics and didn't mind losing herself for hours at a time in the work. (Library much?) Watching friends and lovers interact while she was stuck inside a snow globe, so to speak, became lonely. When she started dating Andre, things began looking up. And then—bam!

Entering into a liaison with someone forbidden, who shared her passion for academia seemed like a good way to get back at the world. And her family. But being someone's secret didn't exactly provide the boost her ego needed. Neither had it been all that satisfying. She ended it once she realized she was only hurting herself.

She should really let Jaxon off the hook. And she would. It just … well, his rejection still smarted now that they were back in close proximity.

Friends. She'd been friend-zoned.

Man, she'd really liked him from the moment she'd laid eyes on him. Was so attracted to the blond hunk of glorious testosterone with his wicked grin that she didn't just drop her guard, she leapt over it. In her peripheral vision, she could see him staring at her. Felt his mood radiate as he sat there, knowing he'd made her feel ashamed and feeling sufficiently contrite because of it.

Why is he even bothering with me? She looked out over the lake to her left. *Why is he bothering to go out of his way to apologize to a girl he'd only known for a day?* The fact that he was working so hard to understand why she was angry and then make amends just made her like him all over again.

Yep, she really should let him off the hook. Because clearly, he was one of the good ones. All this show of angst over her feelings was making her heart beat in his direction. And that was a problem.

He was tricky, this Jaxon Wright. On the surface, he was a truck-driving good ol' boy whose passion was NASCAR and all things auto mechanical. He wasn't interested in libraries or books, yet she'd found him compelling. He'd been kind to her. Took her to dinner and been an attentive listener as she spoke about her childhood. Not only that, he'd been empathetic. Sincerely empathetic, which—you know—she'd never been able to get enough of.

And, today he'd managed to get her alone on a boat while she was still severely pissed off. Go figure.

Another compelling thing about Jaxon was his ability to create fun. And man, she'd been craving fun ever since she'd left town. Even now, with the tension so ripe between them, she'd be hard-pressed to deny that being on this runabout with a guy who wore his ball cap backward was the most fun she'd had in ages. Because in her world, fun consisted of Words With Friends, hours spent geeking out hip-deep in research, deeply emotional literary works, and the occasional glass of wine shared during one of the three book clubs she'd joined in Richmond.

The *Henderson Happenings* spouted the kind of fun she was craving. Jaxon Wright embodied that kind of fun and more. And he wasn't just the let's-go-out-on-a-boat kind of fun. He was also the kind of stimulus her body couldn't resist. Yeah, he was *that* kind of fun. He was magnetic attraction. A chemical reaction. The steal-a-kiss and make-me-swoon kind of fun any red-blooded American girl in her twenties would be drawn to. Even those whose aspirations were to be librarians.

She let out a laugh.

"What?" Jaxon asked, surprised.

She shook her head. "I just realized how truly boring I must sound."

"Boring?"

Turning her head, she leveled Jaxon with a deadpan glare. "My *goal* in life is to a *librarian*. Could anything sound more boring than that? I mean, accountants don't get as bad a rap. And I, I actually want—*sincerely* want—to be a librarian."

"Jinx. You're far from boring."

"Your dream is to be on a NASCAR race team. Do you know how un-boring that sounds? That's like swimming with sharks or climbing Mount Everest. That's as far from boring as you can get. As a librarian, I *read* about those kind of things. Help others research those kinds of things. I don't actually *do* them."

"Tell me what's exciting about being a librarian?" Jax asked with all sincerity. "You certainly aren't boring, so there's got to be something about what you do that excites you. You wouldn't be so passionate about it otherwise."

Jinx felt herself lick her lips as she turned her attention to the horizon. What did she find so enthralling? She started speaking, surprising herself with the force of her conviction. "It's the complexity of providing a high level of community service. Giving the public access to a place to read, learn, and investigate the world. I mean, how does that happen? And how does a library stay relevant when today, most everyone can hold the world in the palm of their hand. We can get books, research, music, news, how-to videos, all sorts of entertainment, and we can even meet the love of our lives for heaven's sake, all through the computers we call cellphones. I've grown up in an interesting age. Spent a lot of time in libraries because I was curious about the world. Because my father read two books a week and taught me to love the written word. Because when you aren't enjoying what's going on in your life, being sucked into research or a good book can take you away for a short time. Like a drug. Only, in most cases, safer."

"In most cases?" Jaxon laughed.

"I don't know. Anything in excess can be dangerous."

"Reading? Reading can be dangerous?"

"Reading can separate you from those around you. If you always have your nose in a book, what kind of life are you actually living?"

"Well, you get to visit places in your imagination. Have grand adventures in your head, right? Just like watching a movie. I imagine a good book can get your adrenaline running pretty good, make you feel things."

"Exactly. That's why I love books. I do. But libraries are changing. They *need* to change to keep up with the times. Henderson is lucky they have a devoted library board, and this new sports academy will give their public library new life."

"Do you still want the job, Jinx?"

"Of all the library jobs in all the land, that one would *not* be boring."

"Because you'd be in charge. Of all of it."

She sighed. "If only it were that simple."

They shared a moment of silence.

Jinx looked back toward the horizon. "I suppose Vance gave the job to another applicant."

Jax shook his head. "Not that I'm aware."

Jinx blinked, her forehead creasing in confusion. "I just assumed …"

"You know what they say about assuming."

"Yeah, but they were ready to hire someone. Wanted someone on the job fast."

"As I recall, you agreed to start work that next Monday."

She gave him a quick glance. No need to blow up his ego by telling him he was the reason she didn't pack up and race back to Henderson. That because he'd been able to break her heart within a mere one day's time, she realized she needed to curb her enthusiasm for all things Henderson and slow herself way, way, way down.

Not that she'd allow Jaxon Wright to dictate whether she'd take the job or not, but she had decided to wait for the formal offer to come in. She had planned to take her time, look it over, and negotiate the terms if she felt it necessary. She knew she was the right person to carry out Henderson's library aspirations, and she knew that Vance knew it too.

But no offer came. No phone call. No email.

Nothing.

That's when she began to mourn not only the brief flirtation with Jaxon but the idea of being a part of Henderson as well. And the job. Of course, the job.

"I never received a formal offer."

"Even so, Vance had offered you the job, and you had accepted."

"Verbally. No salary offered. I jumped the gun by committing to return so quickly."

"So?"

"So?"

"Jinx. Why are you here, if not for the job?"

"I'm not sure I can say."

Jaxon huffed. Removed his cap and ran fingers through his hair and then replaced it before he got up and headed back to the cooler and grabbed two beers. He came back, holding one out to her.

"It's the middle of a weekday," she said, staring at the can like it was going to explode.

"Come on, Webster. Live a little." He jiggled the beer in front of her.

Well if that didn't just hit her where it hurt. She snatched the can out of his hand and popped the top, her eyes shooting daggers.

"Good," he said, apparently unimpressed with her scowl. "Considering you don't know many people in this town, and most of the ones you do know have the last name of Evans, I'm going to do you a solid."

"A solid?"

"Be a friend."

"Hmm." *The friend zone. Ugh.*

"I'm going to promise that starting right now, I will do my best to not judge anything you tell me. Trust me, three months of sleepless nights has taught me a thing or two."

"Sleepless nights?"

"I'm not the heartless asshole you have categorized me to be. I feel things. And the pain I caused you caught me right here in the gut." He pointed to his solar plexus. "Same place I felt it when my mother had her latest setback."

"Your mother had a setback?"

"A while ago. She's good now. Focus, Webster. I'm trying to tell you something."

"Fine." Jinx slid her legs to the side of her seat so her whole body faced Jaxon. "You have my full attention."

Jax nodded, chugged a good portion of his beer, wiped his sensual lips with the back of his hand, and then stepped into her personal space. "The day we met?"

"Ah-uh." *He really does have sensual lips.*

He put his free hand on the windshield in front of her seat and leaned in close, whispering, "I took one look at you, one look at Mr. Evans, and mistook you for his daughter."

Her mouth dropped open under his penetrating blue stare.

"Now, I know you're pissed at me, but you might wanna get over that because I'm pretty sure I know why you're back in town. And like I said, not knowing a whole lot of folks without the last name of Evans, I'm guessing you could use a sounding board. A friend."

Yep. She could definitely use a friend, she thought as she licked her lips. But not one quite so yummy. God, his lips were mesmerizing. His mouth perfectly proportioned with his wide jaw. The scruff he sported barely showed because the hair on his face matched that caramel blond of his hair and made him look so delicious she wanted to stick her tongue out and lick him.

Wait. *What did he just say?*

She shook her head to surface from the erotic fog created by being this close to Jaxon.

"Step back." She reached out and pressed her palm against his chest, pushing his solid mass back a step so she could breathe. Or think. Yeah, breathe. Well, both of those. "Okay, wait. *You* thought I was Mr. Evans's daughter? Why?"

"You look just like him."

"I look like my mother."

He nodded. "Right, annnd ..." he drew out, as if coaxing her to finish the sentence.

"Annnd what?"

"Come on, Jinx," Jaxon said exasperated. "I've been in on this mystery from the beginning. Right after we met, you drove off in that sporty, little roadster of yours, and I turned to Mr. Evans and said, 'I didn't know you had a daughter.' And you know what he said?"

She shook her head while her mouth continued to hang open.

"He said, 'I didn't either.'"

"What?" she whispered.

Jaxon stepped back in, leaned down, and counted on his fingers. "You two have the same skin color, the same hair color, the same teeth and smiles, but what really gave it away? You both have the same nervous tells."

"Nervous tells? I don't have a tell," she said, as if this was the actual topic of conversation and she'd been offended by the suggestion.

"You do. You both tilt your head exactly the same way, and while Mr. Evans snaps his fingers silently when he's becoming impatient, you simply tap your thumb and middle finger together."

"Seriously? Anybody could do that."

"Yeah, but you *both* did it. Oh, and then there's the fact he thought you were an apparition of his ex-wife."

"He *told* you that?"

"Yeah, Jinx, he did. He told me that because the man was in shock. In addition, I was standing right there when the Big Em cruised in, all flipped out because you were in town. *She* knew immediately who you were."

"Who was I?"

"At the very least, Mr. Evans's ex-wife's daughter."

"*You* knew all this? Back then?"

"Yep. Right place at the right time. So, you gonna spill? Tell me what you're doing here in Henderson so I can assist you in whatever way you need?"

"Jaxon. *I* didn't know any of this back then," she said, scrambling to get out of her seat and out of the cage he'd formed with his arms. She paced toward the back of the boat and then side to side. "I came here for a job interview. I had no idea my mother had history in Henderson."

"But you know now, right? Did Mr. Evans call you?"

"No. My mother left me a note telling me they were once married and, oh yeah, the possibility exists that I could be his daughter."

Jaxon squinted. "She told you this in a note?"

Jinx nodded.

"Oh my God. Well, how do you feel about *that*?"

"How do I feel about her turning my world upside down in a note?" she yelled. "How do you think I feel?"

"Blindsided."

She stopped pacing abruptly and gave a curt nod of her head.

"Confused," Jaxon went on.

"You can say that again." She resumed pacing.

"Angry. Upset. Frantic."

She pointed at him as she continued to pace. "Frantic. Yes. Good word."

"What about … curious?"

She slowed her pace.

"Or intrigued?"

She took in a breath, breaking stride. "I don't know. I'm definitely curious about my mother and Mr. Evans's relationship. Less so about my parentage." She lifted her gaze to Jaxon. "Is that odd?"

He shrugged. "You already have a dad. It's not like you're looking to replace him."

She blew out a long breath, resuming her pacing. "No, no, I'm not. Definitely not."

"And then there's Vance."

She snapped her head around. "What about Vance?"

"Well." Jaxon made a *like, duh* face. "He's your brother, right? The two of you share a mother."

"Ye-ah, he's made it pretty obvious he's not down with that."

"With what?"

"Me. He's … ah, keeping a wide berth."

"Well, you get why, don't you?"

She shook her head. "I'm an interloper?"

"No Jinx. You have an all-access pass to *his* mother."

"So … he's pissed at *me*?"

"That'd be my guess. He's also pissed at me, so as far as I'm concerned, you're in good company."

"Why is he pissed at you?"

"For taking your side. Oh, and for what he called *pawing you*." When she raised a brow, he shrugged. "He saw us kiss, remember?"

"Ah, yeah. Thanks for that, by the way. Probably why I didn't get hired."

Jax choked out a laugh. "Oh yeah, and you turning up as the sister-he-didn't-know-he-had had nothing to do with it."

Jinx stopped pacing and faced Jaxon, digesting all this information. "Well, I guess it does make a little more sense now. Him blowing me off like that, after we'd gotten along so well."

"You going to talk to him?"

"About the job?"

"About sharing a mom. Jeez! You know, for a genius, you're being rather obtuse."

"Another good word. However, I'd like to remind you that you've had three months to digest this information, and I've had"— she looked at her watch—"six hours."

"Jesus, Jinx. You mean you just found out? Today?"

"Yup. Today. So, ya know, you might want to cut me some slack."

"Man." Jaxon sat down on the seat behind him. "You're doing pretty well for just finding out."

"I'm in shock."

"Right. Of course, you are."

"Once the shock wears off, I'll probably freak."

Jaxon threw out his arms and slapped his thighs. "I'm here if you do."

That caused her to smile, a small chuckle creeping out.

"What?" Jaxon asked.

"You're a good guy, Jaxon," she relented. "Not many guys wanna be around a girl when she freaks."

"I'm not like other guys. Usually," he said, holding up a finger. "Usually I'm okay with the emotional stuff girls put themselves through."

"Put themselves through?"

"Sure. A guy's gonna hit something. The culprit. A wall. A bottle. We handle stuff like morons. Women? You might delve way into your crap and wallow around for a time, but I get it. You gotta, you know"—his two hands flailed around his head—"think it to death."

"Think it to death?"

"Yeah, but whatever. Guys don't usually think about crap at all."

"You do."

"Yeah. I do. That's why I get it. For the most part."

"You get that I came to Henderson for a job interview having no idea I had blood relations here?"

"I do."

"Well, you're the only one who is going to believe that."

"So what? What difference would it make if you knew about your connection to the Evanses? Who would blame you for wanting to meet them?"

"But I didn't *know*," she said emphatically. "This was all about Cal Johnson, the *Henderson Happenings*, and the library job."

"So I'll help you with your problem," he said with finality. "I'll help you with Vance."

CHAPTER TWENTY-ONE

Jaxon wanted to help Jinx with her problem, he really did. But now he had his own problem.

He wanted to touch her.

He not only wanted to touch her, he wanted to strip her out of that sexy business getup she had on, find out if she fancied little, tiny undies, and then bend her over the seat where he was sitting and do her doggy style out here on the lake in broad daylight.

Fuck, she made him horny.

The way her body moved, the way her clothes fit that body, and—*goddamn*—those juicy lips she liked to twist up when she was thinking, all of it made him tight in the jeans.

He snorted up a lung's worth of air to shake himself loose from the lust driving his thoughts. "You need to stay." The tone he used left no room for discussion. "In Henderson. Figure this—all of this—out with Vance and Mr. Evans. Get your dream job back and just, let the dust settle."

He stood, pulling his cell out of his pocket. "I'll work out finding you a place." He already knew the Joneses were out of town, and their B&B was locked up tight for the week. Which was all to his advantage, because now that she was back, he wasn't interested in letting her out of his sight.

"You gonna call the Joneses on my behalf?" she inquired.

"Something like that," he said, texting away. "I've got a couple ideas."

Engrossed in his texting, his thoughts, and his concern that his boner was uber-obvious even though his jeans were loose fitting, he let the silence between them drag out. When he finally glanced up, she had taken off her sunglasses and was giving him the once-over.

Perfect. Great opportunity to toss her his never-been-turned-down grin. "Like what you see?"

She blushed. Sweet and pretty. Then rolled her eyes. She turned her head to look over her left shoulder, the boat rocking gently beneath them. "Who do you think knows about Vance and me?"

"I imagine the whole clan. All the Evanses and Pinks. Whoever lives on the estate."

She squinted. "How many people live on the estate?"

Jax lifted a shoulder. "Em, Mr. and Mrs. Evans, Vance and Piper, two kids, and Pinks. Scarlett Langford spends most nights in the pool house, but that's not common knowledge. Still, she may know as well."

"Scarlett? The one building the wine shop and restaurant?"

Jaxon moved over to sit beside her. "You still reading the *Henderson Happenings*?"

She shook her head lamely. "After, ah, you and I had our falling out, and Vance never followed through with an offer, *and* I didn't hear from him even after I followed up with an email, I stopped."

"What? Just went cold turkey on Henderson?" he teased.

"Yep. Cold turkey."

"So you have no idea what's happening tomorrow."

"Tomorrow?"

"Election Day. Tomorrow, the good citizens of Henderson will finally come together and officially vote Brooks Bennett into office." He leaned to the side and nudged her shoulder. "Even someone trying to go cold turkey is going to have a problem saying no to that."

Jinx's eyebrows lifted. "Wow. So tomorrow is a big deal."

"It is. The Evans family is preparing for an *impromptu* celebration. So impromptu they've had the caterer lined up for weeks."

"Oh. So, I've truly arrived at the proverbial inopportune moment."

"No, Jinx. I'm certain that's not what Mr. Evans is thinking."

"Maybe not. But as far as Vance is concerned ..."

"This could actually be the perfect time for you and Vance to talk this out. I mean, not tomorrow, obviously. But with the town all atwitter over its Golden Boy finally becoming mayor, you aren't going to be the center of attention you could be on any other given day."

"What do you mean?"

"Being that you're"—Jax chose his words carefully—"new to town and ... beautiful, your presence will not go unnoticed."

"You mean, because I look like Vance's sister."

"Gossip is one of Henderson's predominant pastimes. You won't go unnoticed for long. And if someone remembers your mother and wonders at how much you resemble her ... well, having the election take place and the celebration that will follow is a really good distraction until you and Vance have a chance to speak."

"All right. Okay."

When Jinx went quiet, he pressed. "Tell me what you're thinking?"

"I'm thinking that I should have thought all this through a bit more. That I probably shouldn't have barreled into their office today looking for answers."

"You deserve answers. You have family you've known nothing about who has known nothing about you. And all of a sudden, bam. Here you all are."

"Bam is right," she said, getting up to stand as she rubbed her forehead.

"Hey," he said, standing along with her, taking a finger and brushing it lightly over her temple. "You all right?"

"A headache. Probably from the tension."

"Who wouldn't have a headache?" He couldn't help himself. He added a few more fingers and gently grazed the skin of her cheek as he settled them under her chin, lifting her face toward his. "I've got a first aid kit with some ibuprofen. Let's get a couple of those in you. Then I'll pilot the boat around quietly and let you just sit here and ... breathe. Relax. Absolutely nothing needs to be untangled today."

She cast her eyes toward their shoes and rubbed her forehead again. "I think Mr. Evans is expecting me back. He'd hoped Vance would join us to talk."

"I'll text him. Let him know we're on the boat and you're getting some fresh air. He'll understand."

She nodded as he helped her to the seat she'd occupied earlier. Then he managed to find the ibuprofen and retrieved a bottle of water from the cooler, offering her both. "I think I'm going to head home," she blurted.

"To Richmond?" That was not happening. For so many reasons Jaxon couldn't let that happen.

"I'm not prepared to deal with this. My parents are overseas, and I should really talk with them at length before I insert myself into Henderson and the Evans family."

"Jinx," he said quietly. "The cat is out of the bag. What good can come from delaying any of it? If your mom were going to give you answers, she'd have done it by now. Stay," he implored. "Take control of the situation and figure this out. I'll help you."

"Why?"

"Why?"

"Why are you going to help me? You don't even *like* me."

"Jinx." He let his voice drop low and drip with meaning. "I *like* you. I *very much* like you. Trust me, I wanted to bite my tongue off after the last time we were together. And I really want to make that bullshit up to you. Let me help guide you through the landscape of Henderson and be your support as you navigate the Evans minefield. I promise. Everything's gonna be all right."

"You can't promise that."

"I just did."

She gave him her twisted smile, and he felt it deep in his balls.

"Seriously, how *bad* can this turn out? Besides, you're the best candidate for that library position, and you still want it. You're just going to need a little patience when it comes to Vance. I'm pretty sure if you stick around for a bit and he gets used to seeing you— gets used to the idea of having a sister—he'll work through whatever issues he has and eventually be okay with it. With you."

"He liked me," she moaned in dismay. "And I really liked him. Like, a lot. The whole thing couldn't have been more perfect."

"Yeah. The two of you have a lot in common. Almost like you're siblings," he joked.

"Half-siblings."

Hmm.

Jaxon took his time before he quietly said, "You sure about that, Jinx? You don't think there's a good chance you might be Mr. Evans's daughter?"

"Yeah," she said, looking him dead in the eye, daring him to challenge her. "I'm sure."

CHAPTER TWENTY-TWO

Jinx didn't recognize the route she was driving as she followed Jaxon to the Jones's bed-and-breakfast. Nothing looked particularly familiar, but maybe she'd blocked out all the landmarks after the disappointment of being friend-zoned by Jaxon and not landing her dream job.

Of course, the friend-zoned bit should somehow pale in comparison to the reason behind her job offer being rescinded. Vance didn't want to work with his secret half-sister. Lord, her life had turned into a soap opera overnight. But at least now she understood why she'd been dropped as a candidate for the job.

However, with all this Evans hoopla saturating her brain, she realized she had no ability to keep Jaxon Wright at a distance. As much as history dictated that she couldn't trust him with her heart or her most vulnerable emotions, he *did* look awful sturdy. Like she could hand over all her present troubles and he'd pile them on his back, bearing them when she needed a moment of peace. And since he'd become aware of her unusual relationship with the Evans family almost immediately, who else could she rely on?

She was stuck with Jaxon.

Not that she minded looking at him, because—*whoa*—the man was still as delicious as he'd appeared the first time she'd seen his uber-fit body hopping out of that enormous truck. She just knew better now. Knew to stop her heart when it wanted to beat in his direction. Knew to stop her imagination when he looked her up and down and licked his lips. Knew to stop her hands from reaching out and her fingers from drifting up his bulging ... bicep. Right, *bicep.*

She so needed a legit boyfriend.

The dirty thoughts inspired by Jaxon were wreaking havoc on her ability to deal with the bomb that had exploded her world. *That* was what she should be concerned with. Worried about. Not whether she'd let Jaxon kiss her again if he ever tried.

Because yeah, that was a slippery slope.

And yet her mind continued to drift to their time on his boat. When he'd allowed her simply to sit while he drove them around. When he'd put his hat on backward to keep his rich, vanilla-colored curls from drifting into his eyes as he stood looking over the windshield, manning the helm. He was so attractive, looking at him made her nervous. She'd been mesmerized by how his rust-colored T-shirt rippled with the wind against his torso, outlining many of his hidden assets. His muscular chest. His flat stomach. Those arms, taut while gripping the wheel, were sculpted art as well. His hips were narrow, his butt filled out his jeans—real jeans a guy could actually work in. His feet were bare since he'd kicked off his work boots and left them on the pier and were ghostly pale in contrast to the golden tan flaunted by the rest of his exposed skin.

Andre, her ex-boyfriend, had been athletically built and on the shorter side, dark-haired and preppy. Professor Smooth had been slight of stature, with all of his appendages matching that description. Jaxon, by comparison, was the magnificent antithesis of everything she'd known before. And now that she'd gotten a glimpse of the bulge at his fly, she suspected that his *package* was one most girls would want delivered to their door.

Yeah, allowing Jaxon Wright to be her friend was the equivalent of playing with fire. Because talk about vulnerable? She was feeling that and more. One look from Jaxon—one wink in her direction— and she'd fall into his arms seeking solace. Just thinking about it made her want to. Made her *hope* that he'd up the ante on the friend zone and put her in his friends-with-benefits zone. She could totally use the distraction, even if it did make her pathetic.

You don't want to be pathetic, she insisted, sitting up straighter behind the wheel, giving herself a pep talk.

Nope. But I sorta do want Jaxon, her ego conceded.

Who wouldn't want Jaxon?

Right? My point, exactly. So, would you really be all that pathetic if you what? Jumped his bones?

Not if he jumps mine first, she countered.

Right. If he jumps yours first, then … whatever.

Whatever?

Yeah. Whatever.

The dialogue in her head came to a screeching halt as she realized she'd just driven into someone's private drive. Because she absolutely did remember that the Joneses did not have a circular drive. This was definitely not the Jones's.

She parked behind Jaxon's truck and exited quickly. "Where are we?" Jinx asked, pulling her bag out with her.

"My parents'," Jaxon said. "We've got an extra couple of guest rooms, and my mother is thrilled you've agreed to stay."

"What? I haven't agreed—what? This is your *parents'* place?"

"Come on." He grazed a hand over her shoulder as he passed by, leaving tingles that dripped down the rest of her body. "They're all dying to meet you."

"All? Who is all?" She swung her bag over her shoulder and caught up to him. "What's going on?"

Jaxon pushed open the front door of a two-and-a-half story, sprawling red brick home. "She's here," he yelled into the expansive foyer as he stepped aside to let her lead the way.

Piano music halted.

"The librarian?" a gruff voice rang out.

Jaxon grinned at Jinx. "Your reputation precedes you," he said quietly. He motioned for her to drop her bag at the base of the staircase and then led her into the living room.

"Everyone," Jaxon addressed the room while rubbing his hands together. "This is Jinx Davenport from Richmond, Virginia. Jinx, that is my mother over there on the couch wearing yoga pants. The woman does not actually do yoga but apparently wants to look the part."

"Oh, stop," his mother insisted as Jaxon carried on.

"This idiot with his mouth hanging open is my brother, Xavier."

"That is no librarian," the tall, dark-haired guy insisted with a scowl.

"And the musical genius sitting on the piano stool is his fiancée, who you may remember from the last time you were here. Laidey Bartholomew."

Laidey stood and gave Jinx a shy smile. "Good to see you again, Jinx. Are you finally taking the library job?"

Before Jinx could answer, Jaxon replied, "She's back for a second interview."

"Oh, with Vance?" Laidey wondered.

"Yes, with Vance," Jaxon replied. "The two of them have to negotiate a few things. It might take a while, but I'm hopeful Jinx will be taking charge of the library before too long. In the meantime, or at least while the Joneses are on vacation, she needs a place to stay. I figured she could stay with us since we've got two open bedrooms at the moment."

"Wonderful," his mother said, making an effort to get off the couch as Xavier moved to help her. "Jaxon why don't you get Miss Davenport settled upstairs and then we can all meet in the kitchen for a cocktail. Xavier's got a roast in the oven big enough to feed everyone. Your father will be home shortly, and Laidey, if you'll stay for dinner, it'll be like a party. I could use a party."

Jinx was immediately sucked in by the effusive welcome and tickled over how a small impromptu party sounded very Henderson-like. Very fun. "Sounds good to me," she stated, forgetting how uncomfortable she was at the thought of staying in the Wright's home until she was halfway up the stairs. "Jaxon," she whispered. "I'm imposing."

"You heard my ma, right? Saw her pick her ass up off that old sofa because you walked in the room? We need her to do that. To move. Her energy level is shit, but the doctor says she needs to push herself in order for it to come back. I was hopeful that bringing you here would encourage her enthusiasm. She's always putting on a brighter face when Laidey is in the house."

"So, I'm here to encourage your mother?"

"Yep. And because you need a place to stay."

"But I've read in the *Happenings* that there are other bed-and-breakfasts in the area."

"None better than this one," he assured her. "My brother Xavier may look like a gorilla, but he learned to feed himself while he lived in Arizona. Feed himself well. He's the one doing the cooking around here now. He's so good at it, I almost don't mind living at home."

Jaxon motioned for her to enter the bedroom to the left at the top of the stairs. It was decidedly masculine with a plaid comforter and four bed pillows stacked in twos against the nautical headboard. She dropped her tote by the foot of the bed. "Is the man cave over the garage still occupied by Big Em's boy toy?"

Jaxon's smile grew broad. "You remembered that?"

"I was only here for twenty-four hours, Jaxon. There isn't much I don't remember."

"Well, then," he said quietly, stepping in close, smoothing calloused fingertips over her cheeks. "Do you remember this?" His fingers drifted into her hair, sending goosebumps across her scalp. She felt his other hand wrap around her braid, his knuckles skimming her breast as he clasped the ribbon at its end. His lips tickled the right edge of her mouth before she understood where this was heading. She pulled back with a small, "Oh," of surprise.

Jaxon gently tugged at her braid, urging her back toward him. Once again, he lowered those sensuous lips to her mouth and spent a long ten seconds reminding her of their chemical combustibility while seducing her with soft, tantalizing, *exquisite* kisses. He sucked on the bow of her top lip and then licked the fleshy part of her bottom lip, using stealthy, titillating, *artful* kisses to set fire to the end of a long, luxurious fuse. Her body melted beneath his tender caresses. Her skin ticklish, her insides quivering. The pace and pressure of his kisses were remarkably sweet, but the feels they ignited were insanely erotic. All of it just a meager taste of what she craved.

When Jaxon pulled back, her breasts ached and her body longed for his. His pupils had dilated, the icy blue of his eyes appearing darker in hue. Spellbound by their color, she watched Jaxon's gaze drift lazily over her features before settling back on her eyes.

"Did you remember that, Jinx?"

She wet her lips in response. Realized her fingers were caught up in the soft fabric of his T-shirt.

"Because I did. Every night, I remembered our kiss."

A loud clearing of a throat filtered into the haze—*the spell*—Jinx had fallen under. Jaxon stepped back, dropping his hand from her face. "Yeah," he called out.

"Ah, sorry," Xavier said, pushing the door wider as he looked cautiously between them. "Ma wants the two of us to share the bathroom at the other end of the hall so Jinx can have this one to herself. I'll move my stuff out and give it a once-over. McKenna just arrived, said you called her. Something about clothes for Jinx."

"Oh, yeah?" Jaxon seemed pleased.

"Hmm?" Jinx wondered, her mind still adrift in the sensual pool he'd created.

"You bring enough clothes for a week or more?" Jaxon asked, looking at her tote. "Thought maybe you could use a hand in that department seeing as Henderson doesn't have a Macy's or even a Target where you could easily pick up a few things."

"So it's okay to send McKenna up?" Xavier asked.

"Yeah, send her up." Once they were alone again, Jaxon got serious. "You need to stick around. Eventually work all this out with Vance. I'm trying to think of ways to make it easier for you."

Jinx's mind was still back on the part where he'd had his lips on hers. "Uh-huh," she said inanely.

"You met McKenna before, remember? She was with Laidey that night at the club. Sat down and made herself at home at our table. Tried to interview you for the paper."

"Uh-huh."

"Might wanna remember that." Jaxon let his voice go quiet. "She catches wind you're Vance's sister, it'll be too juicy of a story not to print. Or at the very least, hound you about."

"Uh-huh."

"Jinx?" Jaxon questioned, taking her face between both his hands. "You all right?" He was grinning and licking his lips like he was all kinds of proud of himself.

"I'm fine," she insisted, irritated she had to come back to her senses. She pulled out of his hands and turned her back on him.

"Stop laughing at me," she ordered, but then she cracked a smile, because really, that grin of his was just too cute.

"You like me," Jaxon whispered stepping in behind her.

She tucked her chin hoping he wouldn't see her smile while she fluttered her hand over her shoulder like he was a fly she wanted to swat away. "That's your ego talking."

He put his chin on her shoulder and wrapped both arms around her middle, pressing the entire length of her back into his chest. "I like you too, Jinx," he whispered, his breath warm and soothing against her ear. Chills ran down her neck, gathering in the exact spot he then bent to kiss.

"Jaxon." She stepped away from him, spinning out of his arms before she gave into the urge to tip her head and give him further access.

"Come on," he complained. "Admit it. You like me."

She rolled her eyes, feigning exasperation. "I don't have a choice, do I? You're like my, my Henderson therapist. You know all my secrets. You knew my secrets before *I* knew my secrets."

"What secrets?" McKenna inquired as she burst through the half-opened door carrying a large shopping bag in each hand. "Hi, Jinx," she said, proceeding across the room to place the bags on the bed. Then she snorted. "High jinks. Get it?" She put her hands on her hips and twisted her head from Jaxon to Jinx and back to Jaxon again. "And ... from the looks of things, I'm guessing I've caught the two of you in the middle of a little high jinks."

"McKenna," Jaxon scolded. "Don't let your imagination run away with you." He winked at Jinx. "I'm simply Jinx's ... ah, tour guide while she's in Henderson."

"Yeah, right." She looked over at Jinx. "Jaxon's a great guy. I mean a *really* great guy. But he's no tour guide. You want a tour guide, come to me. I'll give you the ins and outs on everything happening in Henderson."

"I'd actually like that," Jinx said, realizing she needed to cultivate another friend. One she didn't want to kiss. "Though I bet tomorrow's going to be a big day for you."

"Oh, tomorrow is going to be epic. I'm stationing myself outside of the polling booths all day long, getting exit interviews."

"Are you concerned Brooks may lose?" Jinx inquired.

"No. But, as we've seen, you can't count your chickens until they hatch. Marcie Watts hasn't been spotted in months, but who knows if she's been working behind the scenes."

"Marcie Watts? I wasn't aware a woman was running against Brooks."

"Long story," Jaxon said. "I wasn't around for most of it—"

"No, you weren't around, so why even bother to open your mouth?" McKenna scoffed. "Like I said," she addressed Jinx. "If you want a real tour guide, one that can fill you in on *all* the pertinent history around here, I'm your girl."

"I'll keep that in mind."

"Good. Now, I've brought you some items from a boutique in Oxford I just love. Nothing too special, just a few things Jaxon worried you might not have thought to pack."

"All right." Jinx wasn't sure exactly what was happening, but heck, she'd bite. "You want to show me?"

"First"—McKenna dug into one bag and pulled out—"A bathing suit."

Jinx took one look at the skimpy teal-blue bikini and turned a disbelieving eye on Jaxon. "I need a swimsuit? It's October."

"It's still warm. And the Evanses have a hot tub."

"So?" she challenged.

"I get to use it since I'm taking care of their cars. I hang with Davis and Scarlett a lot. And Missy. You'll like Missy."

"Yes, you'll like Missy," McKenna agreed. "She's the party planner. We all like Missy."

"They do a lot of planning while in the hot tub," Jaxon added. "I just figured if you're gonna be here, you don't want to miss out if the opportunity arises."

"To get in the Evans's hot tub," she deadpanned.

"McKenna?" Jaxon asked, clapping his hands together. "What else you got?"

"A cover-up." She pulled out a filmy floral wrap in muted jewel tones that Jinx truly adored.

"Mmm," she said. "Nice."

"I have some other things in here too," McKenna said while looking deep into the bag. "Things you may want to look over once Jaxon gets his nose out of this. Oh!" She reached for the other bag and started pulling items out. "Jeans, two casual tops, a pullover sweater, a pair of shorts because like Jaxon said, it's still hot, and a dress." She held up a short-sleeved dress. "Black. It'll take you anywhere. To whatever comes up. I own several pairs of black heels in a couple different sizes. I'll bring a few over for you to try on."

"McKenna, thank you. I may have packed a little more thoroughly than Jaxon is giving me credit for, but I definitely didn't bring a bathing suit, and there is nothing in this pile that I'm not happy to have on hand." She walked over inspecting the items. "How did you know me so well?"

"I'm a reporter. I made notes about what you wore when we met. Your height and body shape too, hoping to write a piece on the new librarian who doesn't look like any librarian this town has ever seen."

"Right?" Xavier bellowed, coming back into the room. "That's what I said. No offense, Jinx, but you're way too young and far too hot to be a librarian. Except for maybe the type that shows up in a porno flick."

Jinx blinked. "Ah, that's definitely not the image I'm trying to fit into."

"What *are* you trying to fit into?" McKenna asked this as if she had her reporter's tablet out with pen poised, ready to take notes.

"Fit into?" Jinx questioned, flashing a look at Jaxon. Did McKenna know about her relationship with the Evanses? From the brown-eyed scrutiny she suddenly found herself under, Jinx was certain McKenna knew something. "Hey," she said, addressing the men in the room. "How about you guys let me have a moment with McKenna. A little girl time."

"Girl time?" Xavier looked disgusted. "What the hell is girl time?"

"Does it matter?" Jax asked doggedly, physically turning his brother toward the door. "Seriously, dude, it's shocking Laidey has agreed to date you, much less marry you."

"I just asked a question," Xavier said as Jaxon pushed him from the room. "Sue me."

The door closed securely, leaving Jinx and McKenna alone inside. The quiet settled around them as they took measure of one another.

"You know my secret." Jinx laid it out there as a fact.

"I know a woman named Catherine Alfonso married Hale Evans on June nineteenth thirty-two years ago and that her picture looks a lot like you."

"She's my mother."

"I also know that she and Mr. Evans divorced twenty-one years ago."

"And?"

McKenna gave a quick head bob. "I was hoping you'd fill me in on the rest."

"What rest?"

"Why you're here? Now?" McKenna sat on the bed, crossing one knee over the other, leaning back onto one arm. "Your library credentials check out. So do your degrees. Did you get that Mensa magic from your mother or your father?"

"McKenna," Jinx breathed, taking a seat next to her newest tormentor.

"Does Jaxon know about all this? Or are you simply stringing him along? Using him as a cover as you spy on the Evans family?"

"Is that what you think I'm doing?" Jinx popped back up to a standing position. "Spying on the Evans family?"

"Did your mother send you? Does she need money?"

"Oh my gosh, McKenna, stop," Jinx insisted. "Your imagination is running away with you."

"Is it?"

"Yes," she said emphatically.

"Then stop it. Stop my imagination from coming up with ideas about why Vance was so keen to hire you until he absolutely wasn't."

"You've spoken to Vance?"

"I called him the day after I met you, hoping he'd give me a quote for a story I was doing on the new faces in Henderson. I assumed hiring you was a no-brainer and wanted his input. He shut that conversation down hard and fast."

"Yes, well, up until a few hours ago I, too, was surprised that he shut the hiring process down hard and fast. You may not believe

this"—she let out a big sigh, sitting back down beside McKenna—
"hell, nobody is going to believe this, but I had no idea my mother
and Vance's father were ever married. No idea! Can you imagine?"
Jinx fell back on the bed, exhausted from dealing with it.

McKenna twisted to scowl at her. "Seriously?"

"Seriously."

After studying Jinx for a moment, McKenna relented, "I believe
you."

"No, you don't."

"I think I do."

"Well, I wouldn't if I were you."

McKenna chuckled. "It's a story. The best ones are always hard
to believe … and true."

"This one is apparently true, and yet even I'm having a hard time
believing it."

"So … Vance is your brother," McKenna deduced.

"My half-brother. And from his reaction, he doesn't like the idea
of that one little bit."

"Just a half-brother?"

Jinx rolled her head in McKenna's direction. "Don't ask me that.
Off the record, I don't have the answer. And since my father doesn't
want to know the answer, I'm not going to be finding out the answer.
So for the record, yes, he's my half-brother."

"People are going to wonder."

I'm wondering. "Not if the party line is I'm Hale's first wife's
daughter from her second marriage. They'll accept that as fact."

"Unless they dig up the dates. Your birthdate. Their separation
date …"

"McKenna. The average citizen isn't going to care about dates.
You are the only one who cares about dates. I'm asking you, please be
part of the solution here."

"And what solution is that?"

Jinx blinked a couple times and then twisted her mouth and bit
down on both lips. She let them loose with a pop. "I don't know."
She sat up. "I should just leave." She looked to McKenna. "I should
probably leave, right?"

"No," McKenna said emphatically. "Absolutely not. This is the best story we've had in months. Maybe years. Maybe since Vance and his father had back-to-back shotgun weddings. What is it with the Evans family?" McKenna wondered. "So many secrets lurking about."

"I'm guessing that's exactly how Vance sees me. He's probably afraid I'm going to expose our relationship to the good citizens of Henderson from the top of the nearest soapbox."

"Why would he be afraid of that? A lot of people have half-siblings."

Jinx shrugged a shoulder. "Not sure exactly. Except Mr. Evans— and this is strictly *off* the record. Do I have to keep saying that to you? Do your friends always have to say that to make sure their business is kept out of the local gossip column?"

"I write news. Not gossip."

"Still."

"No. My friends do not have to keep saying this or that is off the record. We've agreed that if I want to write about something they've shared, I ask for their permission."

"So, what's it going to take for you and I to become friends? Temporarily."

"Why temporarily?"

"It's likely I'm not staying in Henderson."

"Oh, Jinx. Stop." McKenna had to purse her lips to stifle a laugh. "You're the most perfect thing for Henderson there could ever be. You're young, you're smart, and you're Vance Evans's super-secret baby sister. *You* are going to be able to ride that wave of notoriety for years. Whatever story you put out there—truth or fiction—it will become legend. On top of that, the library needs you. I understand things are in chaos over there. And since Vance oversees the library, he should be begging you to stay. I'll talk to him. He'll see the light."

"No. Absolutely not. Do not talk to him about me, ever. Promise. I plan to talk to him myself. But with the election tomorrow, I'll probably let it lie a few days. Then I'll see if Hale will arrange a meeting."

"Well, that's one way to go."

"You have a better idea?"

"Sure. Show up at the celebration tomorrow night as Jaxon's date. Let him introduce you to other Hendersonians. Get people used to seeing you around before your true identity breaks. I mean, what's Vance so worried about anyway?"

"I don't think he's worried about anything. I just don't think he likes me."

"Well, why?"

"I remind him of our mother?" Jinx asked as if she truly wasn't sure.

"Hmm."

"I'm putting a lot of faith in you, you know. Speaking freely like this."

"I thought we decided we're friends," McKenna said.

"Did we?" Jinx scowled. "Let's clarify that right now. I want assurance. In fact, I want *insurance*. I want you to tell me one of *your* secrets. Something no one else knows. That way I'll have leverage. I'm a great secret keeper by the way."

McKenna snickered. "You're no dummy, that's for sure." Then McKenna puffed up her cheeks and blew out a breath. "I do have a secret. Maybe. I'm … well, I'm hoping it's going to be resolved soon, but …"

Jinx sat back down on the bed. "Oooh, please let it be something ripe with scandal so I can stop thinking about my own story for a few minutes."

"It is scandalous. Well, not all *that* scandalous, but I'm dating Jaxon's brother Xander, Xavier's identical twin. The fact is I dated *Xavier* in high school, until he left for college and then"—she lowered her voice—"I hooked up with Xander."

"And by hooked up, you mean?"

"Slept with."

"Oh!"

"Hold on, that's not exactly the scandalous part. I mean, yeah it is, but that was a long time ago, so whatever. The present scandal— wait a minute." McKenna got up, went to the door, opened it, and stuck her head out, looking up and down the hall before closing it again. She came back and situated herself on top of the bed with her legs crossed and folded. "No one in this house can know this. So yeah, if I tell you, we're friends. Like, big-time friends. Like, we've-taken-a-blood-oath kind of friends. Because no one in the Wright family can know that Xander is not only dating me, but he's got another girlfriend as well."

"Say what?"

McKenna sighed. "I know." Her shoulders slouched. "They're going to kill him if they find out."

"*They* are? Why aren't *you* going to kill him?"

"I'm not going to kill him because I'm the *other woman*."

"Excuse me?"

"Yep. I'm the other woman in this scenario. He's been dating this Becca chick for a good while now, and I hadn't seen Xander in a long time, so I had no idea. He'd been keeping the relationship from his parents so they had no idea either, and yeah, they still have no idea. His parents, who love and trust me, think that the two of us are dating exclusively and are expecting us to become engaged, just like Xavier and Laidey. I keep telling Anna Beth she needs to focus on Xavier's wedding and stop worrying about me, but now *I'm* starting to worry about me."

"Wait. What? You've got to start at the beginning. I'm coming in cold, remember?"

"Okay, yeah. See what happened is—"

A knock on the door intruded. "Y'all done with girl time?" Xavier called from beyond the door? "Because Ma has changed into some decent clothes and is *expecting* you both to join her for cocktail hour. How about you bring girl time downstairs?"

"We're coming," McKenna hollered. "Another minute and we'll be right there."

"No more minutes," Xavier shouted. "You're hogging the new blood all to yourself. Jinx, get your ass out here. Come out and properly meet the Wrights."

"All right," she called. "Man, he's bossy," she said as she got off the bed.

"I heard that," Xavier shouted. "And if you think this is bossy, stick around," he growled. "Come on. I need help in the kitchen."

McKenna went and opened the door. "Where is Laidey?"

"Where do you think? She had to go back to work and finish up some stuff."

"Oh. No wonder you're grouchy."

"And I'm going to keep being grouchy until you both get your asses down the stairs and join Ma for cocktails. Come on. The lady is excited Jaxon has brought home a girl." He looked over McKenna's head to Jinx. "Just, humor her, okay?"

"Humor her?" Jinx asked as she tucked into her heels and ran fingers through her hair.

"You know, act like you're into Jaxon. It's the woman's dying wish to see all her sons happy."

"Stop that." McKenna swatted at Xavier's bicep. "She's not dying."

"Thank the good Lord, no. But it is her wish. And I'm being smothered since I'm the sole groom in this house. I need Jinx here to step up and take some of the focus off Laidey and me. Please," he pleaded in Jinx's direction.

Jaxon's brother was a tall, strong-willed, intimidating force of nature. The fact that he was marrying a woman with such a delicate demeanor was almost comical. "I'll see what I can do," she said grinning, moving toward the door.

"I mean, I know it's going to take a lot of acting to pretend you have any interest in Jaxon at all. The kid is unqualified to set foot in a library. Much less *date* a librarian."

"What about a porn star?" she asked as she passed him to follow McKenna down the steps.

"Porn star. Pfft. You look like a damn prom queen. Just how old are you anyway?" Xavier was fast on Jinx's heels.

"Twenty-one. How old are you?"

"Thirty-two. You're a damn baby."

"You're just jealous because you're old."

"Smack talk. I like it."

"Oh, Lord. Now you've done it, Jinx," McKenna said as she led the way down the main hallway and into the kitchen. "You've engaged with Xavier, King of the Practical Joke. Proceed at your own peril."

Jinx looked over her shoulder. "You don't scare me," she said—not really feeling it, but putting on her smug face anyway.

Xavier just grinned at her as he brought up the rear. On second glance, she wasn't exactly sure if it was a grin or him baring his teeth before he devoured her. When she turned into the kitchen and found Jaxon stuffing lime wedges into Corona bottles, she felt relieved and went right to him. "Thanks," she said as she took the bottle out of his hands. "How did you know this was just what I needed?"

"Beer, Jinx?" Xavier teased from behind her. "Jaxon, you might want to card the prom queen. I don't believe she's twenty-one."

"She's twenty-one," McKenna confirmed, taking a seat next to Mrs. Wright at the round table.

"And how do you know, Pushy?" Xavier asked. "Never mind. I forgot who I was talking to."

"Research queen," McKenna said, pointing to herself.

"Generally, I'm considered the research geek," Jinx said sitting down on the other side of Mrs. Wright. "So I'm delighted by this prom queen nickname. No one's ever mistaken me for a prom queen."

"Seriously?" Xavier asked, accepting a beer from his brother. "I totally pegged you for a prom queen." He looked from Jinx to Jaxon. "What's that movie where the prom queen falls for the grease monkey?" He pointed his beer at Jaxon and then Jinx. "That's you two."

"We're not a couple," Jinx said. "Jaxon has simply rescued me from homelessness, for which I'm grateful.

"Yeah, but we kiss. So we're sort of a couple," Jaxon supplied.

"I knew it," Xavier said, as McKenna spilled a sip of beer down the front of her shirt.

"Wait," McKenna said. "You two kiss? Oh, do tell."

"We don't *kiss*," Jinx protested.

"Jinx, my mother is sitting right there. Please don't perjure yourself," Jaxon said.

Jinx's eyes went wide as she looked at Mrs. Wright. "Are you a judge?"

"No. Ah. No," Mrs. Wright said to Jinx. "Jaxon, stop teasing the poor girl. And don't kiss her if she doesn't want you to."

"She *totally* wants me to," Jax said, grinning.

"Oh my gosh," Jinx moaned. "Jaxon."

"Yes?"

"Stop. Just …"

"Stop being an idiot," Xavier told him. "Now, Jinx," he said as he took a seat beside McKenna. "When exactly did all this kissing go down? Before they crowned you prom queen or after?"

"I'm guessing it was after their date at the club," McKenna interjected.

"Their date at the club?" Mrs. Wright asked.

"Three months ago," McKenna supplied. "Laidey and I were there. We met Jinx then."

An enlightened look crossed Mrs. Wright's features. "You're the girl from Richmond. The one Jaxon took to dinner."

"I am. He was kind enough to show me around Henderson when I was here for a job interview."

"I remember," his mother said. "Jaxon was worried about getting his nails clean for his big date."

"Ma!" Jaxon scolded.

Xavier began laughing his ass off.

"What? Was that a secret?" Their mother glanced around innocently.

"Ah, what a man does to get ready for a date is a secret, yeah. You think I want Jinx knowing I waxed my chest, my ass, and my balls before I took her out?"

Xavier spit beer out on a hoot, McKenna howled a belly laugh, and even Jinx cracked up.

"Oh, Jaxon, stop." His mother covered her mirth. "Jinx is going to think we're just awful."

Jaxon caught Jinx's gaze and winked. "She's a librarian. What do we care what she thinks?"

"A librarian is important," Mrs. Wright started in. Jaxon pointed his beer in his mother's direction as he smiled over at Jinx. "That's a fine profession," she told Jinx as if she had to apologize for his barb.

"Indeed it is," Jaxon said. "I just meant that she's not likely to see Dad or any of your offspring spending time in the place." He leaned into the table and looked at Jinx. "We aren't library people."

"No?" Jinx teased back, her gaze dodging between Jaxon and Xavier. "I had the Wright brothers pegged as bookworms."

"Don't bring me into this," Xavier said. "I *love* books."

"So you visit the library regularly?" McKenna asked sweetly.

"Ah, no. Never."

"Never?" Jinx was aghast.

"She did that same thing to me," Jaxon told Xavier. "On our first date. The one where I cleaned my nails and shaved my balls."

"Jaxon!" his mother threatened. "No more balls talk, please."

"I mean testicles. The date where I shaved my testicles. Is that better, Ma?"

"Oh my goodness, no." But she giggled and then burst out laughing, putting a hand on Jinx's thigh. "Forgive us. I'm sure he doesn't shave his testicles. He's just sayin' all this for my benefit."

"I *do* shave," Jaxon insisted as Jinx started to tear up from laughing. To hear his mother repeat the word testicles—it was really too much.

Too funny.

Too *fun*.

"The real question is if Jinx here has firsthand knowledge of whether you're tellin' the truth?" Xavier teased.

"I do not," Jinx said, holding up her hands. "Yes, we have kissed, but I haven't inspected his fingernails or anything else. Scout's honor."

Xavier let out a disgruntled snort. "Prom queens. Never live up to the billing."

"What do we have here?" A tall man with gray shot through his thick head of dark hair entered the kitchen dressed in a shirt and tie, holding a jacket and his briefcase.

"Darling," Mrs. Wright said at the same time Xavier stood and said, "Dad, we're having a house party. Come on in." He moved aside and offered his father his chair. Mr. Wright put his briefcase in it and folded his coat over the back.

"A whole lot of caterwauling hit my ears the moment I came in the door. And who is this?" He nodded toward Jinx.

"Jinx Davenport, meet my father, Maxwell Wright. Dad, this is Jinx. She's the one who interviewed for the library job," Jax said by way of introduction.

"Welcome." Mr. Wright nodded his head and grinned. Then he walked around to his wife and leaned down to kiss her on the cheek. "How's my girl doin'?" he asked.

"Fine. Just fine," Anna Beth said.

"And my other girl?" Mr. Wright asked, bending to kiss McKenna on her cheek as well. "We gonna have the pleasure of your company over dinner tonight? Is Xander coming to town?" he questioned.

"Tomorrow," McKenna assured him. "He's coming tomorrow. His license still lists this address, so he's able to vote in the election. He promised not to miss it. He definitely wants to help make Brooks mayor and celebrate his victory."

"Good. Good."

"Jinx is staying with us for a few nights," Anna Beth told her husband as he helped himself to the bottle of bourbon Jaxon had left on the counter. "Is that right?" He looked over at Jinx. "To what do we owe the pleasure?"

Jinx shrugged, not exactly sure what to say. Jaxon spoke up. "Last time she was here, she stayed at the Joneses' B&B. But they're out of town this week, so I figured we could put her up."

"You give her a good rate?" his father teased.

Jaxon shot her a wink. "I've given her the friends-and-family discount."

"So, Xander will be here tomorrow?" Mr. Wright questioned McKenna again.

"Yep. I'm pushing him to stay the week," she said. "Work from here and stay through the weekend."

"Good. That's good. You stay on top of him, ya hear?"

"I bet you're good at that," Xavier smirked.

His father smacked him on the back of his head.

"What?" he implored. "You should have been here when Jaxon was talking about his balls."

"I'm going to change," his father told the room at large. "Join you in a minute. Ladies," he said as he grabbed up his briefcase and jacket and left the room.

Jaxon immediately imitated his father by smacking Xavier on the back of his head.

"Quit it, dickhead."

"Boys," their mother scolded. "I swear," she said to Jinx, "it never ends. You'd think they were twelve."

"Wait until all the brothers are under one roof," McKenna shared. "If they're not singing with their arms around each other, they're tangled up like idiots, wrestling on the floor."

"Y'all sing?" Jinx questioned. "What, like the von Trapp family?"

"Yes," Xavier deadpanned. "Exactly like the von Trapp family."

"Don't be mean," his mother scolded, shaking her head and looking to Jinx. "They sing for their own pleasure."

"No. We sing for her pleasure." Jaxon pointed to his mother. "Though we might break out into song for our own ... *amusement* every now and then."

"Like what?" Jinx wondered. "Do you rap or are you more of a barbershop quartet?"

"Well, since there are five of us, that's a big no on the quartet," Xavier scoffed. "And we just kind of join in with whoever starts something."

"Has Laidey ever seen this?" McKenna asked.

"No," Jaxon laughed. "Xavier doesn't want Laidey to see the true Wright brothers in action until she's given him her vow of 'until death do they part.'"

"Damn right. The woman has enough to deal with looking down the barrel at marrying me. I'm not adding any of our spontaneous bro-shit to it."

"I bet she'd like it," Jinx said. "I wanna see."

"Not until you share some of the Davenport Family insanity with us," Xavier demanded. "I need a fair trade."

"Oh. Well. My family's insanity is not so entertaining, I assure you."

"What? No singing? No acting? No rumbles in the living room?" McKenna joked. "I don't have any brothers or sisters. It's just my mom and me, so we're boring."

"Hell, you're the daughter my parents never had," Xavier said. "And we could use a soprano. So next time, just jump on in."

"I can't sing a note," McKenna huffed. "No way am I joining in."

"I remember. You sound like a cross between a screeching cat and a bullfrog. On second thought, keep quiet. In fact, you can start practicing being quiet while you join me in mashing the potatoes."

Jinx popped up. "Can I watch?"

"Watch?" Xavier questioned. "We're not doing kinky shit, Prom Queen, we're just mashing potatoes."

"I need to learn how to mash potatoes. I'm teaching myself to cook now that I'm living alone."

"Which reminds me," Jaxon said, getting up from the table. "You owe me a pie."

"She does?" his momma asked, curious.

"She does indeed," he said, moving to pull an apron off a hook and handing it to Jinx. "She said she'd bake me a pie in one of those Henderson Big Pie Plates."

He spun Jinx around and took the ties out of her hand, tying the apron around her back. "I've got this," he said to Xavier as he guided Jinx to the counter.

"Oh, you've got this?" Xavier questioned, dumping the steaming water out of the pot of potatoes. "Since when do you know how to cook?"

"Since Ma taught me after y'all left for college."

"Is this true?" Xavier turned to his mother. "The low man on our totem pole knows how to cook?"

"He does," she confirmed.

"And all this time, I've been the one stuck in the kitchen like a damn scullery maid?"

"Hey, bro. I said I can cook. I never said I was any good at it. However, I'm pretty sure Jinx and I can handle the potatoes."

"Make sure you do them with cream. Lots of salt and pepper and butter. Don't chintz out on the butter. We need to fatten Ma up, and she loves her potatoes."

"We'll be fine." Jaxon waved him away. "We'll let you taste test."

"All right then." Xavier handed his mother a bowl of sugar snap peas. "Ma, snip the ends off will ya? McKenna, how about you mix up that dressing you wowed us with the last time Xander was in town. What's with the two of you anyway?"

Jinx looked back at McKenna to see her shrug off Xavier's question. "We're good."

"Really?" Xavier questioned.

"Why do you ask?"

"I don't know, just seems he's not racing home as much as he ought to be."

"He's busy," Mrs. Wright defended. "He's working his way back home," she said with a smile toward McKenna. "Now that he has something to come home for."

"Hmph," Xavier said, studying McKenna.

"He'll be here tomorrow," McKenna told him. "Now, where have you hidden the avocado oil?"

Jinx turned her attention to Jaxon as he used a strangely shaped device to smash the potatoes. "What's the name of that thing?" she asked.

"Potato masher."

"Makes sense."

"You want to try?" He handed her the masher.

"Oh. Not as easy as it looks," Jinx commented.

"I'll start tossing in the butter. Just keep doing what you're doing."

Eventually, after butter, cream, salt, and pepper were added, a big hand mixer was brought in. "Do you have one of these?" Jaxon asked.

"No, but I do know what it is," she quipped.

"You living on your own now, Jinx?" Jaxon asked quietly over her shoulder.

"Not exactly. I moved into a condominium owned by my grandmother. She's not living there any longer, so I've got my own space at the moment."

"Cooking for yourself?"

"Ah, no. My grandmother had staff she didn't want to let go. So they take care of me now."

"Your grandmother had staff?"

Jinx gave a weary chuckle. "Yes."

"So, now *you* have staff."

"I have access to her staff."

"And what do they do for you? Cook, clean?"

"Wipe your ass?" Xavier chimed in.

Both Jinx and Jaxon's heads whipped around.

"Y'all don't have your heads together as close as you think. And I've got great hearing." He pointed to his ears. "Plus, I'm curious about our resident prom queen. Sue me."

"Butt out," Jaxon threatened.

Xavier gave a chin lift. "How are the potatoes coming?"

"Just whipping them up."

"Put them in this and then keep them warm in the oven." Xavier looked at Jinx. "That's the rectangular box situated underneath the stove. It heats food, in case you were wondering."

"Ha. Ha." Jinx said. Then she grinned back at Jaxon. "Your brother is hilarious."

"If I had a dime for every time I heard that," Xavier said, moving away to check on the salad he had McKenna creating.

Jinx chuckled. "He's cute."

"Cute? He's an idiot," Jaxon defended. "I mean, he's smart— smart as shit—and don't let that library comment fool you. He's spent plenty of time in libraries for his undergraduate and graduate degrees. He's an architect who likes to get his hands dirty."

"Hands dirty?"

"He likes to build."

"Well, hello," came a low-pitched voice. When Jinx turned toward the kitchen entrance, she saw an attractive older man sauntering in wearing jeans and a dress shirt. "We thought we'd come in to say hello. See how Anna Beth was faring today." Following him came a shock to Jinx's solar plexus.

Vance's grandmother entered the room with a bright smile in an orange and green flowing ensemble. Her hair was beautifully coiffed, gathered on the back of her head, and her shoes were absolutely to-die-for. They were Roger Vivier, green heels with a gold buckle. A visit to that particular Paris designer was on Jinx's bucket list.

Jinx knew she should be concerned about Emelina's reaction to her being in the Wright's kitchen, but she was so enthralled with the woman's shoes, she couldn't pull her gaze from them.

"Anna Beth, how are you, dear?" she heard Emelina ask. "McKenna, is your darling Xander in town? Oh!"

That had Jinx looking up.

"Jinx?"

The room fell quiet. Completely quiet. Jinx heard her own heartbeat echoing through her chest. "Mrs. Flores," she finally managed after having to surf her brain for the woman's last name. All she kept hearing in her head was the Big Em, the Big Em.

"You two have met?" Xavier asked, curious.

"Of course," Emelina said before Jinx could further untie her tongue. "Jinx is the top candidate for our library head. Though I didn't realize you were in town. Did Vance finally call you?"

"Call me? No." She shook her head. "Vance didn't call me. Was he supposed to?"

It did not escape Jinx's notice that everyone else in the kitchen had stopped moving and was playing close attention to the interaction.

"Yes. I asked him to call you."

"About the job?"

Em licked her lips, her eyes darting to the spectators. "Of course. The job."

"Oh," was all Jinx could say to that.

"Is Jinx getting the job?" McKenna asked.

"I'm not at liberty to say," Mrs. Flores said, her Spanish accent becoming more prominent. "Nothing has been settled. In any case"—Emelina looked at Jinx—"it's a pleasure to see you again. I hope you'll consider coming to Brooks's victory party tomorrow night. That is, if he wins, of course."

That broke the silence, as everyone started talking at once. Jaxon pulled Jinx around to get her to focus on the potatoes they were making. "You okay, Webster?"

Jinx nodded. She was a bit more than okay. She was actually feeling hopeful. "What do you think all that was about?" she whispered. "Sounds like Vance was supposed to call me."

"Yeah. It does."

"About the library job or the other thing, you think?"

"Don't know Jinx, but you just got an official invitation back on campus, and I definitely think you should take it."

"McKenna thinks so too. She thinks Vance needs to get used to seeing me around."

"You told McKenna?"

Jinx rolled her eyes at Jaxon. "McKenna already knew. She figured it out like the day after we met. She researched the shit out of me, and it led her straight back to Henderson via my mother."

"Whoa."

"Yeah. But she and I have declared ourselves friends. She's keeping my secret, and I'm keeping hers."

"As if McKenna has any secrets," Jaxon joked. "When I say she's like a sister, I mean, she's *exactly* like a sister. The fact that she's sleeping with Xander is almost obscene."

"*Are* they sleeping together?" Jinx asked. "I mean, are you sure?"

"Well, kinda sure. When he's in town, they are certainly touchy-feely."

"You don't approve?"

"No. I do. Totally do. I'm just saying to the rest of us, she's like a sister. Clearly not to Xander. And she doesn't have any secrets. She's never left town, as far as I can recall. She loves it here. So, ya know, she's basically an open book."

"Mmm. If you say so."

CHAPTER TWENTY-THREE

Jaxon felt a strong sense of relief when Chase and the Big Em declined to join them for dinner. Xavier had been right. There was plenty of food to go around. But Jaxon had intended for the Wright household to be a safe haven for Jinx, giving her a place to take her mind off the Evans situation. He was concerned about the kind of trouble that might ensue with Emelina and Jinx at the same table.

Laidey had returned to the house during the dessert course, McKenna had gone home as soon as the dishes were done, and his parents had retired early to their room on the first floor. Now, with Xavier making things uncomfortable by planting kisses on Laidey's shoulder at shorter and shorter intervals as they sat together at the piano, Jaxon figured he'd better take himself and Jinx elsewhere. So he pulled her off the couch and led her outside.

They stood on the edge of the covered patio, enjoying the night air, looking past the roof over their heads into the sky. "Pretty clear," he said, taking her hand and walking her out into the grass, looking around the heavens. "Wait here."

He went and flicked the patio lights off as well as the landscape lighting in the backyard. "Let your eyes adjust for a moment," he said, coming back to her. "Then the stars will begin to reveal themselves."

Jinx nodded once before doing the sexiest thing. She gripped his forearm to steady herself as she slid those rich-girl heels off, stepping down into the cool grass and wiggling her bare toes.

Jeez. He had it bad.

He stepped out of his flip-flops and joined her.

They stood side by side, her arms crossed over her chest, staring up at the stars. "What's the ladder for?" she asked.

"Ladder?"

Jax turned his head toward where she pointed. Damn if there wasn't a ladder, fully extended and lodged under Xavier's bedroom window. "You gotta be kidding me."

"What?"

"He's sneaking Laidey in through the window? I thought I heard some freaky shit going on the other night."

"Why sneak her in through the window?"

"Must be some sort of fantasy role playing. The guy's a pervert. "

Jinx laughed. "You're not into role playing?"

"Are you?" he asked, curious.

"Ah, just that whole naughty student–cheeky professor thing," she teased.

"Don't remind me," he grumbled, looking back at the stars. But he did wonder and couldn't help but finally ask. "*Did* he fulfill your fantasies, Jinx?"

She hesitated and then shook her head. "He just showed me the ropes, so to speak."

"So there *were* ropes," he teased.

"No." She chuckled. "No ropes. No props of any kind. Just … normal stuff."

"Except you were half his age."

"Except for that."

"I'm sorry I freaked out about all that. Forgive me?"

"Sure." But she wasn't looking at him when she said it. She was looking at the stars.

Jaxon returned his attention to the stars too. "So you did all right on the potatoes tonight. You gonna make good on your promise and bake me a pie?"

"If I get the job."

"Then I have an incentive to do what I said I'd do. Help you with Vance."

"I need all the help I can get."

Jaxon fought the urge to take her hand as they stood in the dark, remembering every bit of the last time the two of them were surrounded by the night, locked up tight, lip to lip, in his brother's truck. He'd decided then he was going to do what Jinx had accused him of earlier that same evening. He decided he was going to seduce her.

Yeah, that hasn't changed.

Only now, he felt protective of Jinx, keenly aware of her unique vulnerabilities. He didn't want to pounce on her when she was contemplating a secret brother, and he sure didn't want her mixing him up with thoughts of that jackass professor. He noted the piano music had halted soon after they'd stepped outside, so he turned to Jinx and asked, "You up for some fun?"

"What kind of fun?"

"Serious, sneaky fun."

"Serious, sneaky fun?" she questioned, but her eyes lit up with excitement.

"How stable are you on a ladder?"

"Can't remember the last time I climbed a ladder, but I should be okay."

His chin lifted in the direction of Xavier's room. "Put on your shoes. Let's climb the ladder and see what we find."

She chuckled and followed him, but as Jaxon started to climb, she whispered, "What if Xavier doesn't think this is funny?" She grabbed on to his leg to halt his progress. "I don't want to be on his shit list."

Jaxon leaned down and spoke quietly. "He definitely won't think this is funny. But it's about time someone served him a heaping plate of his own horseshit. If you and I pull this off, we'll have bragging rights forever."

"You think he's going to push the ladder over while we're on it?"

"He's big, but he's not that big."

"He doesn't own a gun, does he?"

"Nope."

"Does your dad?"

"Nope."

"Okay. Proceed."

Jaxon climbed to the top and peered into Xavier's window. He saw exactly nothing. No lights and nobody in the room as far as he could tell. He pushed the window up slowly, as quietly as he could, before leaning his head inside. "They're not here," he said, turning to look back down at Jinx. "Whoa." She was right behind him. "You librarians sure are quiet."

"You said to be stealthy."

"Come on. May as well crawl inside." He leaned in, using the desk under the sill to maneuver himself through the window. "Here." He reached back to help Jinx climb carefully through the tight space while still wearing her fancy-girl clothes. "That's it. Good. Did McKenna bring you any play clothes?" He helped her down off the desk.

"These are my play clothes." Jinx looked around the dark room. "Why two beds?"

"This is Xavier and Xander's room. The twins."

"Oh. It must be cool to be a twin."

"They're close. Real close."

Jinx sat down on one bed, testing its bounciness, both feet on the floor. "You ever feel like odd man out?"

"Nah. The rest of us brothers outnumber them, so no." He closed the window then joined Jinx on the bed, sitting to her right.

"What's Xander like? Is he as demanding as Xavier? As loud?"

Jaxon grinned his amusement. "He can be. But when he does it, he's putting on a show. With Xavier, it's his natural state."

"So Xander is ...?"

"Easier. Easier to be around. Much more subtle than Xavier. In every way. Except they look exactly alike. No one can tell them apart."

"Not you?"

"Yeah. I can. I mean, they're my brothers. We grew up in the same house, so I can. And once they open their mouths, it's obvious. So, if Xander wants someone to be unclear, he just starts talking like Xavier. But Xavier can't pull it off in the other direction. Although he did come back from Arizona far more Zen than I'd ever imagined him. But since he's been home, his mellow seems to be wearing off. So tomorrow," he said, taking her hand up in his, because hell, they were sitting in the dark and he couldn't keep himself from touching her any longer. "You wanna do as McKenna suggested? Be my date to Brooks's victory party at the Evans estate?"

"Ahh–" Jinx didn't look at him. She simply stared straight ahead and let her response die right there.

He swallowed, wondering what it was going to take to get the two of them back to what had been brewing so nicely before he'd turned stupid and chased her out of town. But then he felt her squeeze his hand, pushing it into the bed between them as his name was whispered in panic. "Jax." Jinx turned toward him, bending her right knee up on the bed so her body faced his directly. "My sister." It came out in a hushed gasp.

He moved to mirror her, his right foot still on the floor. "Your sister?"

"Are we related at all?" she wondered, stricken. "I don't know who my father is." That last part came out so full of emotion he just knew her eyes were tearing up. Her breath hitched, and she started fanning herself with both hands. Sounds of hyperventilation tore at him.

"Jinx," he said, looking her over in the dark, caressing her arms, wanting so much to soothe her but not knowing how. "Breathe." His hand caught up her heavy braid and tugged gently to get her attention. "You grew up in the same household. The same family unit. The two of you call the same people Mom and Dad. That's what makes you sisters, regardless of biology."

She nodded while a sniffle and a long-drawn breath met his ears.

His fingers rubbed against the silky weave of her hair. "Not to change the subject, but this braid of yours continually reminds me of the story of Rapunzel," he told her quietly. "I keep wondering what'll happen if I convince you to let down your hair."

"Jaxon," she whispered on a broken laugh, her fingers coming up to caress the hand holding her braid. "Thank you." She collapsed toward him, her forehead coming to rest against his chest just under his chin. Her hand curved over his around her braid. It felt natural to wrap his free arm around her and stroke her back.

"For what?" he whispered over her head.

She rocked her head a little, moving it from side to side but not out from underneath him. "Just letting me hang on to you in moments like this," she breathed.

"My pleasure." No truer words, he thought. "I'm in this with you, Jinx." He slid his chin to the side so he could put a chaste kiss on the top of her head before righting himself, content to let her lean on him for as long as she needed.

The hell she must be in, realizing that all she thought was true was nothing but a house of cards. He debated whether to just tell her. Tell her that Hale Evans was her biological father and was desperate to have her in his life. That Vance was her full-fledged brother and that despite the fact that Vance had issues with Jaxon, being a part of the Evans family wasn't something to be afraid of.

Of course, if your brother didn't want to claim you publicly, the situation probably wasn't going to be a picnic.

But from what Jaxon recalled of Jinx's lonely, isolated childhood, and how on that first night she had professed the hope of finding a new home in Henderson … well, he was torn.

Ah, hell. I'm damned if I do and damned if I don't. The truth had a way of coming out. No doubt Jinx would eventually learn it. Mr. Evans didn't seem like the kind of man who'd play this game for long. He had a grown daughter who'd been kept from him for twenty-one years.

And Vance just needed a good ass kicking for him to realize that having your genius sister turn up to run your damn library wasn't the worst thing that could happen. He didn't get where Vance was coming from. He really didn't.

But with Jinx's soft breath falling against his chest, the floral scent of her perfume surrounding him in the dark, and his grip on that braid that liked to drive him crazy, he was willing to put all the Evans bullshit on the back burner and distract Jinx into doing it as well.

He nudged her head to the side as he leaned down and put his mouth to her ear. "No need to bother with the victory party tomorrow night when I can think of so many better things we can do with our time." Then he pressed his lips against her neck.

"Mmm," she murmured, lifting her head from his chest slowly, sleepily. "Jaxon Wright, are you planning to seduce me?"

"What if I am?" he whispered, wishing they were in his room, on his bed, but afraid to ruin the vibe they now had going. So his fingers worked at the end of her braid. Loosening the ribbon there. "Rapunzel," he whispered as his fingers delved into the end of her braid. "Rapunzel," he whispered again as he worked to pull the mass apart, the backs of his fingers skimming against her breast as he did so. "Let down your hair."

Jinx's chest expanded on a shuddering breath, her bare arms sprouting goosebumps. "No need to be nervous, Webster," his voice came out husky as he kissed her neck while continuing to unravel her braid. "I'm planning to take things real"—*kiss*—"slow"—*kiss*. "At any point you want to stop"—*kiss*—"we stop"—*kiss*. "Simple as that," he promised against her cheek.

CHAPTER TWENTY-FOUR

There was nothing simple about what was happening. The chaos Jaxon was creating within Jinx's heart, her mind and—holy-wow—her body was far from simple.

Oh. My.

Jaxon Wright has just upped his game.

Sitting on a bed with him hovering so deliciously close in the dark, Jinx's senses were heightened. Her nipples had pebbled as the backs of his fingers skimmed her breasts while he took his time pulling apart her braid. And now his hands were shoved into the back of her hair, loosening the strands, massaging her scalp, as he placed slow, seductive kisses along her neck and chin.

The quiet room had magnified the effect of his hushed words. His voice—low yet still rich and demanding against her ear, reciting her favorite fairy tale—had caused goosebumps to break out along her flesh and sent internal chills throughout her mind. Her brain molded itself around the idea of Jaxon and his physical touch. So when he teased his fingers over her breast, when he tugged at her hair, when he laid a smattering of kisses along her jaw and neck, she wasn't just ready for them, she desired them. Craved them.

Wanted all of Jaxon Wright and more.

So she turned her face so that his next kiss landed on her lips.

"Lie back," he urged, his mouth against hers, his seductive tongue coaxing its way between her lips. His body pressed and his hands guided her down so her back was flat against the comforter, her head on a pillow, and her right side was tucked beneath his hips and chest. Her right hand was caught under him but the other palmed his cheek while they continued to make out.

Her body sank decadently into the plush mattress as Jaxon's mouth and tongue created a visceral delight. There was absolutely nowhere else she wanted to be right now. His mouth on hers was so intoxicating her mind just settled. Under the comfort of Jaxon's weight and attention, she didn't have a care in the world.

He looked down and watched as his big hand splayed possessively over her stomach, his fingers bunching up the fabric, tugging the hem of her blouse from her slacks. "Wanna touch you," he whispered, looking back into her eyes, easing his hand underneath the crisp cotton. She wanted that too, and his calloused, strong, tool-savvy fingers did not disappoint. She licked her lips and lifted her mouth to his, reengaging their kiss because she hadn't had enough. He leaned back in, giving her what she wanted, while his hand skimmed her body from hip to beneath her breasts. She pulled her hand from underneath him, her fingers finding their way under the back of his T-shirt. With a low, grinding hum, he rolled more of his weight onto her, wedging a knee between her legs as his hand glided around her body, wrapping her up in his arms. His left hand palmed her head, his right hand cradled her beneath her shirt, his mouth opened to deepen the kiss, to demonstrate his desire.

His desire was long and hard at the juncture of her legs, settled against nerve endings firing on all cylinders. The movement of his lower body was subtle, a slight grind of his hips, but the effect was deliriously sublime. His weight on her was a delicious stabilizing force. Her movements weren't tentative or shy, or even deliberate because her body responded of its own accord, her hips quietly pressing up against him in a slow, languid rhythm.

Jinx didn't know how long they made out, pressed up against one another—moving against one another—but it wasn't long before he growled something in her ear and then pushed up on his hands holding his lower body still and connected. "Unbutton your shirt."

She did as he asked, drawn in by the way his eyes held hers and just as eager for skin-to-skin contact. She let the cotton fabric fall at her sides, granting him a view of her kinda pretty, yet mostly utilitarian bra before she reached down and pulled on the ends of his

T-shirt. She fought to bring it over his head, helping him maneuver out of it one arm at a time.

When he was free and clear, he backed his way down her body, his eyes now locked on the front clasp of her bra. A chin lift was all she needed to have her hands doing his bidding, clumsily unlatching the plastic clasp. She left it open, the cups still in place, covering her breasts. He leaned onto his left forearm and drew an index finger from the center of her collarbone down between her breasts and on further to the waistband of her slacks. He dipped his head and kissed the open space between her breasts and then slid his body down, placing his bare chest against her stomach. He separated the cups of her bra, exposing stiff nipples and round breasts, his hands cupping both. He shoved his nose in between and took in a breath. Then he looked up into her face to tell her she was beautiful.

She shook her head, in her mind insisting he was the beautiful one. His striking features, full masculine symmetry, with his wide mouth and sensuous lips underneath the intoxicating twinkle of his crystal blue eyes. He was glorious. As glorious a man as Jinx had ever met.

And yet he was humble.

And kind.

And *oh* so good with his hands.

And with his lips, which he was now using on her breasts in a way she'd never had the pleasure of experiencing before. His head bent over her, his lips sucking on a nipple while his hands lifted and pressed, playing with the fleshy parts of her breasts while his pelvis kept up a slow, indulgent rhythm. It was the perfect onslaught of sensation. Enough to keep her out of her head and grounded in her body. Grinding against his body. Effortlessly, as if this was a conversation they'd had before and they were eager to have again. Jaxon Wright certainly did have all the right moves, and she was grateful for it. Whether he was what Vance had warned her against, and she would be forever one of his one-and-dones, she promised herself she wouldn't complain. Because right now, what she needed was arms wrapped around her that were sure and strong. Arms that grounded her. That promised not to let her spin frantically.

And everything just *felt … so … good.*

It was way too soon when he pulled his mouth from hers, smiling down into her face, bringing a thumb up to rub against her cheek. "It would be prudent not to be found in Xavier's bed."

"Right." She chuckled nervously, licking her lips, still wanting more of his. "Good word, by the way."

They slowly untangled themselves, Jaxon sneaking in a kiss on her belly before pulling her shirt together and helping her sit. "We need to find my shoes," she said buttoning her shirt. "I don't want to leave any evidence."

He took her hand, pulling her to her feet. She turned to fluff the comforter, plump up the pillows. "You're pretty good at tidying up the scene of a crime, Webster," he joked, bending down and picking up her shoes. He waited until she stood and turned to him. "You done now?"

"We got everything we came in with?" she asked. He nodded, took her by the hand, and led her from the room, pressing her up against the wall outside her bedroom door.

"That was hot," he breathed against her lips, his forehead gently touching hers.

"Mmm," she agreed, knowing full well she had stars in her eyes.

"We can say good night or …" he suggested.

She twisted her lips and gave him a sorrowful smile, knowing it was the *prudent* thing to do. Taking her shoes out of his hand, she turned toward her bedroom. "Good night, Jaxon," she said, looking back over her shoulder.

He'd placed his hands on either side of her door frame, biting his bottom lip as he looked his fill. "Mmm," he hummed. "Can't wait for tomorrow." He pushed himself back into the hall, one hand coming up in a brief wave before he sauntered out of sight.

CHAPTER TWENTY-FIVE

Knock. Knock. Knock.

It wasn't soft—*at all.* The knock was loud and demanding and had Jinx bolting upright in bed from a dead sleep.

"What?" she complained, realizing where she was and therefore could guess who was doing the knocking.

"Bacon," Xavier barked through her door. "Bacon class starts in ten minutes Prom Queen. Don't be late."

"What?" she whispered, wondering what sort of hell she'd fallen into. She flopped backward and heaved a sigh. She'd been having the best dream—not that she had any idea what it had been at this point because Jaxon's bossy big brother thought he was in charge of everyone in the house and apparently, this included her.

KNOCK. KNOCK. "Ten minutes," he shouted.

That was it, she thought, throwing off the covers and putting her feet on the floor. But by the time she yanked open the door, the culprit was nowhere to be found, and she had to lean against the doorjamb because her head was spinning from jumping out of bed before her equilibrium had awakened. Jaxon's brother was a— *Jaxon.* The fallout from having his hands on her last night snapped her into a different thought pattern. She looked right and left and then tiptoed all the way down to Jaxon's room and quietly tapped on his door. She put her ear against it to hear any movement inside.

"Hey."

Jinx startled and spun, clasping her hand to her chest. "Jaxon," she breathed, "you scared me." He stood there, fully dressed, lickable by all accounts, grinning at her while she tried to settle her nerves.

"Sorry, not sorry," he said. "Because ... is this what you wear to bed?" he asked, not being shy about looking her up and down.

She crossed her arms over her chest and stared down at the lacy lavender nightgown McKenna had purchased. It hit her at mid-thigh and was sheer and flouncy. Probably not something she wanted to be found wearing by anyone other than Jaxon. "McKenna brought it."

"Remind me to thank her."

They both stood there, staring at each other.

Okay. Well.

Feeling terribly self-conscious, Jinx ducked her head to scoot by Jaxon, heading to her bedroom.

"Hey. Not so fast." He grabbed her wrist, reeling her back into him, one of his big hands palming the right cheek of her ass. "Good morning," he said as he moved to kiss her.

She pushed a hand between their mouths. "I haven't brushed my teeth."

"Like I care," he said, pulling back, laughing at her. "You gonna answer the ogre's call and come down to learn how to make bacon?"

"*Five minutes,*" Xavier yelled all the way from the kitchen. "*Jinx?*"

"I'm coming," she yelled back. "What time is it?" she asked Jaxon.

"Six forty-five. We're notoriously early risers."

"Obviously," she said, dislodging herself from Jaxon to scurry down the hall. "Go down and placate your brother for me, will you? I'm gonna need fifteen minutes at the very least."

She heard Jaxon snicker as she closed the door.

A half hour later, she was standing over a low-burning flame wrapped in the same apron she'd worn the night before. She'd been getting a very detailed lesson on cooking with gas and how to perfect bacon. Basically, you allow the strips to lie side by side in a wrought iron skillet over a low flame for a very long time.

She could do that.

Next, Xavier had her mixing up a batter for fritters that would need two tablespoons of the bacon grease. *What?* Bunuelos

Mexicanos, Xavier explained right before he reminded her that an oven was the box under the stove that heated things up.

Mrs. Wright came in looking rather chipper and well dressed. Xavier seemed stunned. "Ma," he said, his smile broadening. "You look like a million dollars."

Jinx looked in her direction, offering up a smile as the woman took her seat at the table. "Good morning, Mrs. Wright."

"Good morning, Jinx. Did you sleep well?"

"I did, thank you. How about yourself?"

"I did okay," she said, smiling.

"Xavier is teaching me how to make breakfast," Jinx said.

"Not just any breakfast," Xavier claimed. "*Huevos rancheros* and *bunuelos.*"

"My favorite," his mother announced.

"And bacon," Jaxon added as he brought in the paper from outside, handing it to his mother. "Gotta have bacon."

"Of course," Xavier said. "Prom Queen needs to learn how to cook bacon properly. You can't just crank up the heat and expect things to go well. Cooking is an art."

"Like making love," Jaxon chimed in.

Everybody in the kitchen stilled and looked at Jaxon. "What?" he said. "Same concept, right? You can't just crank up the heat and expect things to go well." He sauntered over past Jinx and took up the tongs she'd left beside the skillet. "You've got to start things slow, on a low flame, and let things sizzle a bit," he said, starting to flip the perfectly cooked bacon.

"You do realize Ma is sitting right here?" Xavier asked.

"You disagree, Ma?" Jaxon asked, looking over at his mother, who smiled into her coffee and waved him off. "What?" he said with his cocky-boy grin.

Jinx turned to continue measuring flour into a bowl, looking over Xavier's recipe and praying no one was going to ask her opinion on cooking or making love. Yet she was completely aware of the joy bubbling up inside her as she continued to listen to the unorthodox conversation being bandied about the kitchen. Being around a family that joked with one another was startling. Hearing Jaxon talk about making love tweaked her girly parts.

This was the type of fun she'd been reading about for months in the *Henderson Happenings*. Funny people, thinking up fun things to do, taunting their friends and neighbors good-naturedly. This morning. Last night. Everything that had happened in this kitchen. *This* was what had reached out to her through that e-newsletter. This is what her spirit craved.

She wasn't going to Brooks's victory party. She didn't want to deal with the Evanses and her mother's secret-life drama. She wasn't ready for her Henderson dream to end by confronting Vance and having him explain why she wasn't getting the position at the library. And out of respect for her father, she wasn't going to let Hale or Emelina pressure her into a paternity test.

No, she wanted to enjoy the fantasy of Henderson she was experiencing here in the Wright household, before the world found out her true connection and a new reality was dealt. There was a bar in this town, right? The Situation? Not everybody would be at the Evans estate, would they?

"I keep tellin' Ma we're all virgins and then you come in here and bust up the illusion." Xavier shook a spatula at Jaxon.

"Like Ma doesn't know you sneak Laidey into your room via the ladder lodged outside your bedroom window."

"What?" his mother exclaimed.

"He's just yanking your chain, Ma. Aren't you, asshole?" Xavier gave Jax the side-eye.

"Been in the backyard lately, Ma?" Jaxon asked, ducking out of the way of the potholder Xavier threw at him. "Probably do you some good to get some fresh air."

"Nothing to see out back," Xavier told her, threatening Jaxon with a look. When Jaxon started to speak, Jinx saw Xavier throw a pointed finger his way. Yeah, that would shut her up too. "Laidey is not going to appreciate you outing her to her future mother-in-law," he angry-whispered at Jaxon.

Jaxon grinned at his brother. "Fine," he said, going back to turn the bacon.

"So what about you, Prom Queen?" Xavier asked. "You enjoy a slow burn?"

"Good morning, Jinx," Mr. Wright's deep voice exclaimed as he entered the kitchen. "I see Xavier has put you to work."

"He's a force of nature." Jinx threw a smile over her shoulder as she mixed the batter. "Does he get that from you or Mrs. Wright?"

"Me," Mr. Wright said proudly. He looked around. "Where's McKenna?"

"McKenna?" Xavier questioned with a hint of disgust. "We don't need McKenna around here getting under my skin on a Tuesday morning, do we?"

"It's a big day. Election Day. She's always here on the big days."

"No," Xavier exclaimed rather forcefully. "You know who should be here though? *Ad-el-aide Bar-tho-lo-mew*," he sung. "That's right. Your future daughter-in-law. She should definitely be here on all the big days," he said, pulling his phone out of his back pocket and bringing it to life.

"I'm counting on McKenna also becoming my daughter-in-law." Mr. Wright sat at the kitchen table. "Soon. Speaking of, has anybody heard from Xander this morning? What time is he arriving?"

"Good morning, Tweets," Xavier said into his phone.

Jinx shot a curious look toward Jaxon.

"It's what he calls Laidey," Jaxon whispered. "Like I call you Webster. It's a term of endearment."

"A term of endearment?" She joked. "You might want to rethink the Webster thing."

Jaxon sidled up close to her as Xavier gave his fiancée hell for already being at the office when it was Election Day and telling her she needed a good breakfast to get the day started right. A breakfast that he cooked. And if she didn't fly her little Tweety-Bird ass over here right away, he was going to be paying her workplace a visit. One that wasn't going to be cordial.

Jinx leaned her face into Jaxon's chest just to stifle her mirth.

"What?" she heard Xavier ask as he hung up his phone. "I'd disappoint my intended if I didn't go off on some crazy rant at least once a day. She expects it." Xavier's eyes twinkled over a lopsided grin. "Kinda why she fell for me."

"So you didn't mean it." Jinx was relieved.

"Oh. No. I meant every word. So when you get around to setting the dining room table, you can add a place for Tweets."

"And McKenna," his father said from behind his paper.

"Pftt. Wishful thinking, Pa," Xavier said. "This is almost as big a day for McKenna as it is for Brooks. I have no doubt pushy McKenna will be all over the place, interviewing everybody, trying to scoop some form of a news story out of what we all know is inevitable."

"Good morning, everyone," McKenna sang as she entered the kitchen kissing Mr. and Mrs. Wright on their cheeks.

"What the hell?" Xavier cried. "Shouldn't you be camped out at one of the damn voting centers?"

"Yes, and I will be as soon as they open," she countered. "But my adrenaline is flowing now that this election is *finally* happening, so I had to come over and—"

"Horn in," Xavier grunted.

"—eat breakfast with the Wrights."

"Happy to have you, honey," Mr. Wright said. "Expected no less."

"That's because she's *always* here," Xavier stressed. "Of course, you expected her."

"Good morning, Jinx. Good morning, Jax." McKenna looked around Xavier, undaunted. "How was your evening?"

"Excellent," Jaxon said.

Jinx gave McKenna a thumbs up.

"Good. Great. I'll set the table and make more coffee."

"Laidey's coming," Xavier told her.

"I know. She told me to text her five minutes before we sit down."

"What?" Xavier asked.

"She's *busy*," McKenna said.

"That's bullshit. It's not even eight o'clock."

"Language," his father barked from behind his paper.

"Doesn't mean she's not busy," McKenna said. "Besides, Crain Carraway's in town, and you *know* how she is about her boss."

Jinx heard Xavier literally *growl*. Like a wolf. One that was really unhappy. Unhappy and guarding its territory. And she was taken aback by how McKenna's gaze changed once *she* heard the growl. She was now looking at Xavier with longing in her eyes.

More secrets?

Shoved unceremoniously out of the way by Xavier, who then seized the wooden spoon out of her hand and took over her job, Jinx thought, *fine*. She wanted to have a word with McKenna anyway, so she followed her from the room, claiming she'd help her set the dining room table.

"What's up?" she asked McKenna quietly, spreading out the placemats. "Which twin are you interested in? For real?"

McKenna sighed in a way Jinx wouldn't have expected. "Xander. Definitely Xander. It's *always* been Xander."

"But the way you were just looking at Xavier."

"Because he's so in love with Laidey that the mention of Crain Carraway sends him into an animalistic rage. I want that from Xander. I want him to love me like that."

"And he doesn't?"

"If he did, he would have broken up with his girlfriend by now, right?"

"Well, you yourself said it was complicated. Maybe he just needs time."

"Yeah. I mean, I get it. I do. He and I sort of stumbled into each other out of the blue and bam—we went off like fireworks—all those old feelings busting loose. There was no denying plenty of heat still burned between us. And he told me so, just as sweet and sexy as could be. And then he *tried* to tell me he was involved with someone else, but at that point I had jumped his bones and just wasn't listening."

"You said he lives out of town."

"Yes. Quite a ways away. So our long-distance relationship doesn't have a lot of teeth yet. He's been back to Henderson five times since we got together, which is five times more than he came home in the past few years, if you don't count major holidays. I've been to Charlotte a few times myself, and things are good with us—they are. He assures me that he and Becca never established exclusivity before I arrived in the picture, but come on. She probably has no idea he's dating me too. And as forthright as I am about most things, for me, Xander's the one who got away. He took my heart right along with him when he left this town. And I really like having him back. So, for the time being, I'm not planning on pushing him too hard."

"Hmm."

"I mean, when we're together, it's good. Just like old times. But for Xander, choosing me would mean moving back to Henderson, changing jobs, and giving up the life he's created in Charlotte."

"So, you're not wrong. It is complicated." Since McKenna appeared to have gone numb, Jinx took the silverware out of her hands. "Maybe tonight, if the time is right, you can simply ask if Becca knows about you. No pressure. Just knowledge."

"Yeah," McKenna sighed. "Or maybe I'll just let things be. If he and I are supposed to be together, it'll work out, right?"

"Are you willing to move? To Charlotte. For him?"

McKenna pursed her lips, thinking. "I might. I mean, I am mad for him, don't doubt that. But my momma's here, and I'm her only kin. And his parents are here, and now Xavier—and they're my second family. I just assumed he'd *want* to move back."

"What's he say about it?"

"That he'd like to, if the right job came along."

"Hmm. Yeah, the right job is important." Jinx finished setting the table, thinking about the right job for her. "I still want the library job."

"Of course, you do. You're like, perfect for it."

"Except for the secret Henderson family connection, I am perfect for it. Talk about complicated."

"Bah. That's what makes you even more perfect for it. You'll be invested. You'll grow roots. You've already got a boyfriend here, and trust me, in Henderson they are not all that easy to come by."

Jinx laughed lightly. "I'm not sure I can consider Jaxon my boyfriend."

"Maybe not yet."

"He's not dating anyone else?" Jinx asked quietly.

"Not that I'm aware of." McKenna quieted her voice. "He's got something going on that he's keeping close to the vest though. I think Xavier's in on it, and another guy, Thurgood Watson. He goes by Thor. He owns a lot of land just outside of town. I've got a feeling the three of them have some ideas brewing."

"Ideas?"

"Maybe something to do with racing," McKenna whispered as they started back toward the kitchen.

"Hmm," Jinx said, raising her brows.

The moment they entered the kitchen, Xavier put everyone to work dishing up their own plates and grabbing various condiments to bring into the dining room. Laidey pushed open the front door after a soft knock just as they were seating themselves.

"Come on, Tweets," Xavier beaconed her in with a grin. "I've got your plate all fixed."

Jinx made a point to observe just how Xavier looked at Laidey. How Laidey looked back at him. How they didn't hug or kiss in front of the crowd, but he touched her subtly on her hip as she laid a hand on his forearm. Intimate.

She agreed with McKenna. She wanted that.

CHAPTER TWENTY-SIX

"Big Day," Harry said to Vance as the two of them worked side by side around the pool early Tuesday morning. There was a team of catering personnel scurrying about here and there, taking orders from Piper as tables, bars, food stations, and a banner that said *Mayor Brooks Bennett* were assembled for the victory party. At the far end of the pool, Pinks and the Outlaw were putting together a stage and setting up their drum set and sound system.

"A long time coming," Vance said, helping Harry lift a table and move it a few feet to the left on Piper's orders. "You don't think we're jinxing things by setting up this early in the day, do you?"

"Nope."

"Really?" Vance asked, because Harry knew stuff. And if Harry thought setting up early was okay, then Vance could feel easy about the election outcome. Not that he didn't truly believe Brooks would win in a fucking landslide because hey, Golden Boy. And thanks to the hard work of Team Henderson, Brooks's reputation over the last sixteen months had just gotten bigger and brighter. No one was stealing this election from them. Not today.

Only ... yesterday, Vance had seen *the Jinx* with his own two eyes, like a black cat crossing his path, and now he wasn't trusting anything to go right.

He'd come home early, shutting himself upstairs, claiming he had serious work that involved a lot of quiet thinking. He didn't join his family for dinner, didn't talk to anyone. He was in full denial and wanted to keep it that way. In his brain, Jinx Davenport didn't exist.

In his brain, the aberration he saw yesterday had gotten in her car, driven out of town, and was now well across the state line.

"We gonna talk about this?" Harry asked quietly once Piper had moved away.

"About Brooks winning, and how this party is going to be epic?" Vance inquired, not looking at Harry as he started unloading liquor bottles off a dolly onto what would become one of three bars. He wasn't an idiot. He knew what Harry wanted to talk about. And not just Harry, but his father, his grandmother, Genevra—he knew what they *all* wanted to talk about.

"Yep," Harry said. "That's exactly what I was referring to. Mr. Bennett winning by a landslide, and everything being right with the world. *Not.*"

Vance ignored him, finishing unpacking the rest of the bottles. Then he started to place the unopened boxes of liquor underneath the table. "You think we've got enough trashcans?" he asked Harry.

"Yes. Trashcans. Very important. I think we're good."

Vance nodded, though his stress level escalated as the dolly emptied of shit to unpack. Finally, he stood, rubbed at his lower back, and said, "I'll run this down to the truck."

"Sure. Sure," Harry said, letting Vance run away from the conversation *everybody* wanted him to have.

He just couldn't do it.

He wasn't ready.

He didn't even know how to describe what he was feeling. None of them had any idea of the shitstorm he was wading through. He'd had his mother's name and all her pertinent contact information in the palm of his hand—buried in his phone—since the day he realized he had a sister, a link to his mother. It had been so easy, he thought with wonder as he trudged down the slope to the garage where trucks of all kinds spilled forth equipment to make this night one of the town's best celebrations ever. So damn easy to find out where his mother had parked herself for the last twenty years.

Three hours away. *Three* hours away.

Three freaking hours, and she'd never come back to see him once.

Never asked for visitation.

Never called.

Never emailed, texted, Skyped, FaceTimed, nothing.

Never.

In *twenty years*.

And yet, he was supposed to believe her offspring had stumbled into him accidentally.

Yeah, right.

He still wasn't buying that bullshit. Too coincidental. "Cal Johnson fan, my ass," Vance choked out to nobody. But apparently Jinx wasn't all that much like her mother because she'd actually found her way *back* to Henderson before the twenty-year mark. It only took her three months to come back, and she'd timed it beautifully too. Just in time to fuck up the one great moment he'd been anticipating for over eighteen months.

Everybody else was free to celebrate Brooks becoming mayor. *He* was going to be stuck feeling edgy as hell, worried Jinx would show up at every turn. Or else he'd be drunk. Neither boded well for the rousing introduction speech he'd planned to deliver as Brooks's campaign manager.

"Stop," he pleaded with himself. *Pull your shit together, dude.* There was no way he was gonna let Jinx Davenport steal this night— this victory—out from under him. He certainly wasn't interested in handing her that kind of power.

Maybe he *should* talk to Harry. It was obvious Harry knew who Jinx was to him and his family. Harry knew everything. He looked up the hill and watched as the guy went about getting things done.

No way, Vance decided. He knew what he'd get out of that conversation. The same thing he'd gotten from his father and Genevra. The same thing he'd get from Piper if he'd allowed her in on the Jinx-is-my-fucking-sister secret. And how he'd managed to keep this Jinx thing from Pinks—how they'd *all* managed to keep it from Piper *and* Pinks—was nothing short of a miracle.

But he hadn't felt like he had a choice. If Piper knew Jinx was his father's daughter, that Jinx was his sister, that Jinx was Piper's very own *sister-in-law,* and that their son had an aunt—he'd never be able to make up his own mind about including Jinx in the family. It would be all over for him. Jinx would be shoved down his throat instead of run out of town.

No, Harry was not the answer. Vance needed to fly solo on this. He needed to confront Jinx on his own terms. And he needed to go ahead and settle this once and for all.

Now.

CHAPTER TWENTY-SEVEN

Jinx's prospects for the day changed the moment Xavier realized schools were closed due to the election. She had planned to head to the library and skulk around quietly to see what was what. She figured Jaxon would have to work, and she'd be left to her own devices. But Xavier put the kibosh on all of it when he declared that Laidey and some kid named Marnie were getting another lesson on riding dirt bikes.

In fact, he made Laidey call her boss right there at the table, while everybody listened, to tell him she was taking the day off. Then he suggested that Jinx should join the all-girl dirt bike team. Told her if she was going to be hanging around an engine specialist, she may as well get to know her way around racetracks.

The idea intrigued Jinx. She'd never been on a dirt bike, and she couldn't imagine Laidey on one. But Laidey didn't seem to be putting up a fight, so heck, why not? "Happy to wait and stage my library coup tomorrow."

When she raced up to grab her phone from the bedside table, she noticed a text had arrived from Vance.

If you're still in town, I'd like a minute of your time.

Her heart sank. He only wants a *minute*? That didn't sound promising for the future of their relationship or her prospects with the library job.

She sat down on the bed and stared at Vance's text, not wanting her foray into Henderson to end so abruptly. Not wanting her stay at the Wrights's to end before she had a chance to ride a dirt bike or party at the local honky-tonk. She wanted to experience the Henderson she'd been reading about, in case Vance insisted she leave and never come back. And ... she thought for the first time, she'd kinda like to meet someone who knew her mother when she'd lived here. Since her mother was obviously not interested in being forthcoming, she needed to do a little investigating of her own.

"You ready to go?" Jaxon asked as he held on to the top of the doorframe, his long body leaning into her room.

Dear Lord, he took her breath away. She waved him in and showed him the text. "Vance says he wants a minute of my time. But honestly, I'm just not ready."

"So, text him back and tell him you've got a full day planned."

Jinx blinked.

"Simple as that," Jax said.

Was it? Was it as simple as that? She nodded, agreeing. "Okay. Yeah. And maybe I'll tell him I am not planning to show up at the victory party. That you're taking me to The Situation instead. Would that be okay with you?"

"Sure," he said. "The Situation is going to be buzzing. Brooks will definitely put in an appearance. Let's go there. No Evanses to deal with."

She kept nodding as she texted.

I'm still in town, but I've got a full day planned. I won't be at the victory party for Brooks, if you're worried about that. And I am not going to mention anything to anybody. So enjoy your day. Okay?

She pressed send.

Before they could get out of the room, another text came in.

I just need a minute. Where are you? I'll come to you.

Jinx held up the text for Jaxon to read. He grabbed her phone from her hands, typed *No,* sent it, and then handed her phone back.

"No? Just, no?" she wondered, panicked.

"Yeah. Here's a lesson, Webster. No is a complete sentence."

"It is?"

"Yep. Just two letters. N-o. Say it. Text it. Leave it. It'll simplify your life."

"But doesn't 'No' require an explanation?" she asked, trailing behind Jaxon as he trotted down the stairs.

"No. See what I just did there?"

"You said no."

"Exactly. Complete sentence."

"Okay."

The idea was so freeing that Jinx jumped down the remaining two steps, landing in the foyer.

CHAPTER TWENTY-EIGHT

"No?" Vance read Jinx's text aloud. "That's it, just no?"

His head popped up, and he looked around the pool area as controlled chaos continued.

He glanced back down and read her text again. She wasn't coming to the party tonight. Told him he didn't have to worry about that. *Clearly she gets I'm not happy with this situation.* Well, it wasn't like he didn't make that perfectly clear when he'd found her in his father's office yesterday. Out of the fucking blue.

Vance rubbed his forehead, feeling at odds with himself. Ever since he found out Jinx and he shared a mother, it was like a solid steel wall had dropped down. Everything that occurred between him and Jinx before that realization was now sealed off from him. Jinx had immediately become the enemy. And he'd circled his wagons fast.

Between Brooks's campaign and breaking ground for the sports academy, he'd been able to—mostly—banish Jinx from existence.

However, the same could not be said about his mother.

He'd thought he'd come to terms with all that. He had Piper and Vance, Jr. now. Lolly and Brooks. His boy Pinks was like his right arm, and hell, he'd even gotten his father back. And with Genevra and his little brother Brody—whom everybody continued to call Beau—his world was a very happy place.

So why the fuck was he still so pissed at his mother?

He shook his head.

He needed professional help. He knew it. When everything else in his life was going so well and he still felt ill at ease? Not that he'd opened up about all of this to Piper … or Pinks … or anyone. And he did his best to shut it all down whenever his father or Genevra had tried to bring it up.

This was not serving him, not serving him at all, and he knew it. He couldn't be an island on this. Now that Jinx was back in town, it had begun to eat him alive.

Still, he was afraid. Because his loved ones would recommend he let Jinx in. They'd all be on her side. They wouldn't understand what recognizing Jinx as part of the family would do to him. That this empty space inside his soul would open up and swallow him whole. He felt it. He felt it happening now. It wasn't logical. It was an emotion so deep and so raw it would absolutely consume him if he let it.

So he couldn't let it.

After careful consideration, he texted Xavier. *Where is your brother hanging out today?* Because if he found Jax, he'd find the Jinx.

Then he headed to the 'Vette, his favorite car to drive when he had to let off steam.

With me. Xavier's reply came in, just as Vance had buckled his seat belt.

Where?

Watson Plantation. Bring Piper. But leave that kid of yours at home. He may have your athletic ability, but six months old is still too young for dirt bikes.

Dirt bikes? What the hell was going on out at Thor's place now? Vance put the car in gear and carefully backed out of the garage, maneuvering around all the trucks and equipment blocking the drive. He had to ease his way onto the grass in order to get around it all. When he finally hit the open road, he asked Siri to call Brooks.

"Fucking-A," Brooks said in greeting.

That put a smile on Vance's face, reminding him of all that was still right with the world and changing his mood immediately. "It's a great day in Henderson."

"Better be. I gotta tell you, I did not expect to feel nervous."

"You're a shoo-in," Vance assured Brooks.

"Not what I'm nervous about."

"What then?"

"I'm actually going to have to do this job."

"Mayor?"

"Yeah, mayor. I'm actually going to have to *be* mayor."

"Fuck, you've been acting like mayor ever since we won the damn championship. Now you're just getting the credentials to go with it. Which means you can finally channel all that Golden Boy bullshit into something useful."

"True that. What's up?"

"Harry's setting up the party. I'm on my way to the polls to cast my vote, and then I'm heading out to Thor's place. You got any idea what his latest project is?"

"The garden club's going organic."

"Nope. He's already got that up and running."

"Oh, yeah. Isn't his Ranger buddy, Bryce, setting something up out there? Something to do with team building?"

"Yeah. Right. I just haven't been paying that much attention. What about dirt bikes?"

"Dirt bikes?"

"Yeah. Xavier texted something about Piper and dirt bikes."

"Piper rides dirt bikes?"

"No. God, no. You think I'm insane?"

"Right. No. I haven't heard a thing about dirt bikes."

"Where's Lolly?"

"Where she always is," Brooks moaned. "At work."

"Trouble in Paradise?"

"Told her if she didn't take time to vote today, we're through."

"Like she's not going to vote."

"Oh, she was concerned about fitting it in, let me tell you. She complained that the polls weren't opening until eight o'clock, when all hard-working people should already be hard at work. I mentioned that most hard-working people took a lunch break, and she scoffed at that. Then she asked me what time the polls closed, and I cannot repeat what I told her."

Vance laughed.

"You think this is funny?"

"I think Lolly's got you by the balls."

"She doesn't cast a vote for me today, I'm cutting her loose."

"With your balls in her hand."

"Ouch."

"Yeah. I'm sure she'll vote. Did you vote?"

"Pinks has me going in at eleven o'clock. Set up a big press event. He's got reporters from Raleigh, Greensboro, Charlotte, and all the other major cities lined up for it. He wants to get us on the news all over the state."

"I assume you're making a statement."

"Pinks wrote something," Brooks said doggedly. "Been rehearsing it all morning."

"Good. Good. He gonna be there?"

"Of course. When is Pinks not under my feet, irritating the skin off me?"

"Once this is over, he'll be out of your hair."

"Doubtful."

"Good luck today, man. Though you're not going to need it."

"Hey! Before you hang up, there's something I want to say."

"Yeah? What's that?" Vance asked.

"Thank you, man. I mean it."

Vance was surprised by the emotion that surged through him hearing Brooks's gratitude. "We've come a long way," he said, his voice sounding hoarse.

"Together. We've come a long way together," Brooks said. "And it is not lost on me that I am the face of this campaign and you are the brains."

"Pinks is the brains," Vance countered.

"You're the brains."

"Yeah, man? Well, you're the heart. And *that's* what is saving Henderson."

"Couldn't do it without you—wouldn't want to—and I know it. So if I get distracted later, I wanted to make sure I said it now. Thank you. For everything."

"The real work starts tomorrow."

Brooks laughed. "I'm taking tomorrow off. Making Lolly take it off too. Hell, E&E should close up for the day."

"Not happening, man. But you take the day. Pinks and I will keep the town afloat. Good luck with the press. I'll try to be there if I can."

"Why are you headed out to Thor's?"

"Personal bullshit."

"Personal? Like what?"

Yeah, he hadn't told Brooks about the Jinx thing either. Vance took a deep breath and blew it out slowly. Life was about to change, that was for sure. Truth was it already had. He was just trying to fend off the fallout until after the election.

"Win the election. Take the day off. Then we'll have lunch."

"That sounds ominous. Everything okay with Piper?"

"Yeah. She's great. Nothing to worry about."

"I hear ya. Okay, man. Gotta go. Love ya, bud."

"Back at ya, Mayor Bennett."

The two of them snickered into the phone before they disconnected.

"Fuck," Vance said with a smile on his lips. It truly was a great day in Henderson.

Once he got to the plantation, it took Vance a good half hour to actually find where the action was happening. Nobody answered the door at Thor's and although a big ass tractor had been left sitting off to the side, Thor's truck, Big Red, was nowhere to be found. Vance had to text Xavier again for his location.

And Xavier had not been lying about dirt bikes. Vance could see the dust rising from where he'd parked the 'Vette alongside Big Red and the Silver Hulk. He stood there, looking down the incline, and tried to make sense out of what he saw.

Thor and Xavier were easy to spot, both standing together with their hands on their hips watching the dirt bikes in action.

Laidey was easy to pick out, although his face twisted up at her pink dress billowing in the breeze as she drove a dirt bike at a conservative pace behind another bike that was moving out like there was a race to be won. The two bikes were making their way around what appeared to be a rudimentary track. Oblong in shape with a few juts and swags here and there.

It had been a long time since he'd been free to ride a dirt bike. All of a sudden, he looked forward to Vance, Jr. and Brody being of an age when they could enjoy something like this.

His eyes locked on the woman tucking her hair up into a helmet as she straddled a bike. Watched as Jaxon Wright helped hook the chinstrap and adjust it for a good fit. Watched as he tapped the top of the helmet and then started showing Jinx—he assumed it was Jinx—how to operate the machine.

Jinx.

His sister.

Fuck.

Vance puffed out his cheeks as he blew a lot of hot air out of his mouth. He couldn't believe Election Day had finally arrived and he was standing here having to deal with this.

Of course, it *was* Election Day, so the only thing he had to do—essentially—was vote. And he'd just taken care of that.

Now, he was going to take care of this.

Except here he stood.

Stuck.

Holding his ground.

CHAPTER TWENTY-NINE

"Got it?"

Jinx smiled that cute little smile of hers. The one that said, she *might* have it. She *hoped* she had it.

"You'll do fine," Jaxon assured her. "Just start off slow. Wait for Marnie-the-Daredevil to pass and then ease out onto the track. As your confidence increases, you can adjust your speed right along with it."

She nodded her head. Grinning. "Okay," she said breathlessly. "This is fun," she told him.

"Just wait until you get moving."

That was the thing about Jinx, he thought as he watched her move out cautiously. Everything seemed to fascinate her. She was curious and enthusiastic about all things Henderson. All things Wright family. All things McKenna, Thor, Marnie—well, just all things. All people.

He walked over to stand with Thor and Xavier. "An all-girls dirt bike team?" he asked. "How'd ya come up with this?"

Xavier raised a shoulder. "Marnie wanted to learn, and I want Laidey to know how to ride. She's good on the back of my bike now, but this is still out of her comfort zone."

"What's up with the new girl?" Thor asked. "She yours?"

"Not mine, *yet*," Jaxon emphasized. "She's from Richmond. Interviewed for the library job a while back."

"Ohhhh."

Jax lifted a brow. "Ohhhh?"

Thor held up his hands. "Missy thinks something suspicious is happening with the library job. Says Vance found a candidate he was all hyped-up on and then nothing. When Missy brings it up to him, she can't get him to talk."

"Missy?" Jaxon asked.

"*My* girl. The CEO of the Henderson rehabilitation program. Got her damn hands and mind in every aspect of what's happening in this town."

"Oh, yeah. What did she say about Jinx?"

"Nothin'. Pretty sure she's never met her because my girl's a talker, and if she had met Jinx, she would have mentioned it, believe me."

"Speaking of Vance," Xavier said, looking back over his shoulder. "He texted me, wanting to know where I was."

Jaxon grunted at the sight of Vance standing up there.

"What's wrong?" Xavier asked him, as Thor waved Vance down.

"He wants a word with Jinx. She was hoping to avoid him until tomorrow."

Xavier squinted at his brother. "What aren't you telling me? She's gonna get the job, right?"

"She *should* get the job. But I'm not exactly sure that's gonna happen."

"Hmm." Xavier looked back and watched Vance approach. "Want me to intervene? Pick a fight? Vance and I have history. He won't know what hit him."

"No," Jaxon said, after truly thinking it over. "As much as Jinx would like to stall what's about to happen, I doubt she'd appreciate your tactics."

"Just sayin'."

Vance joined the three men, eyeing Jaxon pointedly as they exchanged greetings.

"What brings you out here?" Thor asked. "Thought you'd be in town going door-to-door getting everybody out to vote."

"Y'all done that yet?" Vance asked. "Y'all got your vote in for Brooks?"

"Planning to do it on our way back into town," Xavier promised. "Can't have a landslide victory if everyone doesn't vote."

"Don't you forget it," Vance said. "I just need a word with Jinx when she has a minute."

"You giving her the job?" Xavier asked. "I gotta say she looks more like a high school prom queen than she does a librarian. But Jaxon tells me she's highly qualified."

Vance nodded his head, looking at the girls circling the track, not saying anything more on the subject. He pointed. "Thor, what have you got going on out here?"

"Thinking about building a motocross track."

"In conjunction with the Ranger Games team-building stuff?"

"Maybe. Maybe a side item."

"All right. Well"—he looked at Xavier—"what the hell is Laidey doing out there?"

"Getting her out of her comfort zone," Xavier said. "It's good for her."

"Says you." Vance looked at Jaxon next. "What's going on with you and Jinx?"

"Plenty."

"Plenty?" Vance barked out.

"She's a great girl," Jaxon challenged, looking Vance right in the eye. Jeez, if he had a sister like Jinx, he certainly wouldn't have a problem claiming her. He didn't get why Vance was being such a jerk about it, but he sure was done pussyfooting around about what he saw in her. "And she's eager to have that library job you're holding on to so tightly. In spite of *everything else* going on around here."

"That *job* is between me and Jinx. That's why I'm here. I don't want to waste any more of my time or hers."

"You think Jinx is a waste of your time?" That really got Jaxon's back up. "Are you fucking kidding me?"

Thor stepped in front of Jaxon as he threatened to move on Vance. "Hold up there, NASCAR. What's going on here?" Thor looked around at all three men for an explanation.

Xavier held his hands up while lifting his brows. "Jaxon has a thing for Jinx. Beyond that, I have no idea."

"She getting the job?" Thor asked Vance.

"No."

"This is such bullshit," Jax spat. "You can't deny her existence whether you give her the job or not. And none of it has any bearing on her staying in town. This isn't your call."

"It *is* my call. And you don't have any idea what you're talking about."

"Bullshit. I know the whole story. I've been on board since the beginning."

"What story?" Thor asked.

"You don't know *my* story." Vance sneered at Jax, poking himself in the chest.

"Maybe not. But then, neither does Jinx. And you sure as hell don't know hers. I can't understand you, man. If I had a sister dropped on my doorstep, I'd at least have the courtesy to hear her out."

"What?" Xavier choked.

"Sister?" Thor wondered.

Vance was incredulous. "Thanks for that, Jax. You want to throw your girlfriend's secrets around a little louder."

"She's *not* my girlfriend. But I like her. A lot. And so did you, you stupid prick, until you found out you might have to share your father with someone else."

"My father has *nothing* to do with it," Vance declared.

"He doesn't?"

"Hell, no."

"Then what are you so afraid of?"

"What I'm afraid of is none of your goddamn business."

"But it *is* Jinx's business if you plan to keep the library job from her. And it's definitely her business if you're gonna try to keep your father from her, not to mention the Big Em. I can't figure you out, man. Here you have this amazing person fall out of the sky and land in your lap, and you won't even sit down and get to know her."

"I know her."

"Really?" Jaxon challenged, lifting a hand to count off on his fingers. "You know that as a kid she was repeatedly left with the help while the rest of her family ran off to Europe? And that once she reached school age, she was sent to *boarding school*? And while there, she was handed off from teacher to teacher and then grade to grade because she was too smart for anyone to deal with? You're aware that for the majority of her school experience, she was so much younger than the rest of her classmates they treated her like a pariah? You *don't* know her," Jaxon yelled. "You have *no idea* what she's been through. Trust me, you're the one who got off easy. Maybe you ought to think about that."

He saw the change come over Vance's countenance. Saw how he staggered back a step, like he'd been punched. But after that moment of stunned silence, all four men realized no sound was coming from the track. They looked over to find Jinx, Laidey, and Marnie lined up on their bikes, engines cut, listening to every word.

Vance's voice was low and gruff. "Really appreciate that, Jaxon." He took one final glance at Jinx, turned, and marched back up the hill.

CHAPTER THIRTY

Jinx hadn't heard much of what went down between Vance and Jaxon. By the time she joined Laidey at the edge of the track and got her helmet off, the heated discussion had come to an abrupt halt. She'd watched Vance look at her, say something more, and then turn around and walk back up the slope to his 'Vette. When she questioned Jaxon and the other men, they just passed it off as Vance having Election Day jitters.

When she got Jaxon alone, he informed her that Vance had indeed come to see her—had tracked her down by texting an unsuspecting Xavier—but, through a heated debate, Jaxon had managed to convince Vance to leave it until tomorrow. Jinx breathed a sigh of relief hearing that. Reading Vance's stern expression, the writing was on the wall when it came to her job opportunities in Henderson, not to mention her relationship with the Evans family. She certainly didn't need to be told by Vance that he didn't want her here. His actions had made it apparent.

Late that afternoon, after her shower, she sank onto the bed and sat wrapped in a towel, allowing the sorrow of rejection to claim her.

Vance didn't want her here.

She couldn't really blame him. She was an interloper with possible ties to his father. Nothing Vance or anyone in his shoes would want to entertain.

She'd felt rejection before. In fact, rejection was status quo for Jinx. Her meat and potatoes. But, being here in Henderson, she felt this particular rejection deeply. Because she'd come for a job interview hoping to fit in. She'd hoped to find a new home, and finally, finally a sense of belonging. Finally be accepted into a group where she could contribute and feel appreciated.

She'd never had that. Not really. Her family lived their own lives in spite of her. Not that they didn't love her as best they were able, but when it came to the Davenports, she was an afterthought. Something that needed to be handled so her parents could continue to pursue their own agendas.

She'd always just been in their way.

When she'd read about Henderson's library position, she'd had such hope for her future. The town claimed to be eager for newcomers. So much camaraderie seemed to exist here, and being well suited for the job, Henderson seemed the perfect place to try to fit in now that she was ready to strike out on her own.

She knew she could contribute if Vance would just give her the chance. In spite of her age. And personally, she'd started making friends the moment she set foot in town. Jaxon liked her. McKenna liked her. Laidey liked her. And if she remembered correctly, Vance himself had actually liked her.

Why did being Vance's half-sister have to be a deal breaker? Maybe if she promised Vance she'd never reveal their connection. If he didn't want word about their mutual mother getting out, she could live with that. She liked the Wrights far better than she liked the Evanses at the moment. Maybe she could be like McKenna. An honorary member of their family while in town. And it wasn't like she didn't have her own family in Virginia who would welcome her home for the holidays.

Unless they were traveling.

Or something.

Crap.

Jinx flung herself back on the bed, feeling very alone. Very unwanted. Very much back at square one. Because it had never failed. A new school, a new grade, a new college. New hope had always come with new beginnings, but it had ended the same way every time.

She didn't fit in.

She wasn't wanted.

Same old story.

Now there was more family who didn't want her messing up their agenda. Family she didn't even know she had. Family who didn't even know her, yet still didn't want her around.

She wiped tears from her eyes.

Vance Evans liked everything about her until he found out they were siblings. Then she wasn't good enough. For him, for his damn library, for his town.

She flopped over on her side, determined not to give in to the overwhelming sorrow threatening to engulf her. She'd be fine, she told herself. This was a lot to process for sure, but she'd be fine.

Eventually.

She sat up, weighing her options. Trying to figure out the best way to move through this. There appeared to be no reason to speak with Vance tomorrow—or ever, for that matter. His actions had made it clear where that would lead. She didn't need to subject herself to a full-frontal rejection. And she'd already told Hale she wasn't going to have a paternity test, so seeing Hale again wouldn't serve either of them. There was no reason for them to forge a relationship if Vance wasn't on board.

But she did crave one good Henderson memory to take with her, and celebrating with a town that just made their Golden Boy mayor was probably going to deliver. So she wiped at the tears while taking a few deep breaths, grateful for Xavier's voice booming up to her from the first floor.

"Prom Queen. Get your ass down here for cocktails. My ma wants female company, and what my ma wants, she gets. Fast."

At least someone wanted her company.

Smiling through her tear-streaked face, Jinx got up and opened the door. "I'll be down shortly. Thank you."

CHAPTER THIRTY-ONE

"Pipes!" Vance shouted over the throng that filled his father's kitchen. "Christ," he mumbled under his breath, "I've got to get our house built. This place is becoming Grand Central Station."

"It's only Grand Central because your best friend is being elected mayor."

He turned quickly to find his sassy, little blonde smiling up at him holding a wooden spoon covered in Toll House cookie dough. He grabbed it first and then he grabbed her. "You always know just what I need," he whispered over her captivating smile as he began to lick the spoon clean, holding her against him and not letting her go as he did. "Damn, that's good."

"Happy you're happy," she said, taking the spoon and pulling away.

"Truth be told, I'm not all that happy. But I might be able to get there if you can tear yourself away from whatever Big Pie Plate nonsense you've got going on and give me your full attention."

"I gave you my full attention at six thirty this morning."

"Not that kind of attention," he said, reeling her back to him. "Serious attention over a serious matter."

Piper did a double take, meeting his eyes. "What's wrong? Brooks is going to win, right? He has to win. My cake says Congratulations, Mayor Bennett."

"Yeah. Sure. Your cake will be perfect."

"Then what's wrong?"

Vance let out a deep sigh and looked over her blond head around the room, watching the catering staff moving about, circulating with Genevra and the Big Em. "There's somethin' I need to confess," he said quietly. "Something that happened months ago."

Piper blinked at him while taking a step back, horror marring her baby-doll features.

"Stop," he groaned, realizing exactly what conclusion she'd just jumped to. "This isn't about you and me. This isn't about *us*. My God, woman, how could you even think that?"

"Well," she said, licking her lips and wringing her hands, "you sound very serious. And, I know in the past you've had … issues."

"What issues?"

"Women issues."

"I don't have women issues." Although, he thought, Jinx did happen to be a woman. "I have one woman, and that's you. You got any issues?"

"No," she said, stepping back in and putting her hands on his chest. "But for the first time in our married life, I'm scared about whatever this is that happened months ago."

Vance looked into the worried eyes of his beloved and wanted to gnaw on his own fist for having caused her a moment's concern. "Come on," he said, grabbing her hand, pulling her out of the kitchen and toward the staircase. "This won't do. Not at all."

"Please, just tell me," Piper insisted, doing her best to keep up with him as he held on to her, dragging her up the steps behind him.

"First, there are a few things you need to know," he said, moving them quickly down the hallway to their bedroom. "One," he shouted as he whipped her inside their door and then slammed it shut behind them. "I would *never* cheat on you," he said as he whirled on her— angry—because *what the fuck?*

"Vance—"

"Seriously," he interrupted. "You are the thread that I'm hanging on to here. Why in the world would your mind leap to that conclusion?"

"Why? Because you haven't been yourself for the past three months, that's why. You've been avoiding your father, you've been avoiding Genevra and Em, and you are only making love to me two times a week and solely in a *bed*. I've written it off to the last stages of Brooks's campaign and the anticipation of breaking ground on the academy. But when you said there was something you should have told me months ago?" She shook her head, "What else am I supposed to think?"

"Baby doll. Come here." He sat on the end of their bed, pulling her to stand between his spread legs. His hand went to her face, and he spoke calmly but firmly. "I love you, you know this. I can't live without you and Vance, Jr. There's no way I could do what I do, Brooks's campaign or the academy, if you weren't here, constantly filling me back up. You're the reason I wake up happy and look forward to working hard. And I'm sorry if I've allowed myself to get distracted, but please believe me, it has *nothing* to do with us."

"Then what?"

Vance's gaze landed on their feet. "It's about Jinx," he said quietly, his gaze sliding tentatively back to hers.

"Jinx Davenport?"

He nodded and licked his lips, but no words came. Christ, he didn't even know where to start. Of course, Piper—being perfect Piper—saw his distress and eased herself from his grasp and onto the bed behind him. Leaning her weight against him, she kissed the back of his head before she settled herself and began massaging his shoulders. "You told me she decided not to take the library job."

"I lied to you about that."

Her hands stopped, weighing heavy on his shoulders.

He reached up and put his hands on top of hers and squeezed. "I lied to you because I found out Jinx Davenport is my sister, and I was so freaked about it, I just shut it all down."

He had to give it to Piper. After only a slight hesitation, she began massaging his neck, giving him a chance to find the words to explain. "Apparently, when my mother left, she was pregnant with Jinx. Dad didn't know, of course. Didn't have any idea he had a daughter until Jinx showed up in Henderson, applying for the library job, looking exactly like his ex-wife. I had no clue who she was when I met her, but Em sure as hell did. Em took one look at Jinx and started asking all these inappropriate questions. I didn't put the puzzle pieces together until the next day when Pinks mentioned that Jinx and I could be twins."

"She's your *sister*? As in, Hale's daughter?"

"Yeah. Had the DNA to run a paternity test to prove it. Came back positive. Apparently, my mother didn't just abandon me, she stole my baby sister too."

"So Jinx came to Henderson because of you and Hale? To meet you?"

"She *claimed* to have found her way into Henderson because she's a Cal Johnson fan. When I realized who she was, I called bullshit on that. But she never did approach Dad. And she only tried to contact me once to follow up on the library job. I assume she knows something now. I ... ah ... I haven't had the guts to ask Dad since finding her in his office yesterday."

"What does your father think of this?"

"What do you think, he thinks? He wanted to welcome Jinx into the family before he even had proof that she was his daughter."

"Does Genevra know?"

"Yes. Dad told Genevra the moment he met Jinx."

"Of course, he did," Piper whispered.

"Baby doll, please. You know me. I'm not Dad. I don't have his emotional IQ to deal with this. I was the one who insisted he keep Jinx a secret."

"From me?" Her voice shot up high in disbelief.

"Yes, from you. From Pinks. From Brooks and Lolly—from everybody. I did not want Jinx mucking up my amazing life. I wanted to pretend she didn't exist, and I couldn't very well do that if y'all knew about her."

"But you *liked* her? I don't understand why this isn't a good thing."

"Are you kidding me?" Vance took her hands from his shoulders and turned to face her. "Piper, Jinx's *mother* is the woman who left me without explanation or goodbye. She's the woman who never came back, never called, never sent a birthday card, and never wanted *anything* to do with me. Why would I want the child my mother *chose* to raise to move to Henderson and throw all that in my face? Frankly, I just want to forget we ever met."

"Vance, you can't pretend she doesn't exist."

"Yeah, well unfortunately, I'm finding that to be true."

"Vance," she said, shaking her head at the bed beneath her. "This is horrible."

"I know, right." He let out a big, relieved sigh. "I'm so glad you understand."

Piper shook her head, squinting at him. "No. *You're* horrible. She's your *sister*," Piper emphasized. "For a man who is nothing but loyal to his friends and family, to his hometown, and his high school alma mater, how could you not embrace the fact that you have a sister?"

"Because she belongs to my *mother*," he shouted, moving off the bed and pointing a finger in her face. "And you of all people should know what that means to me."

"Are Jinx and her mother close?" Piper asked.

"I don't know."

"What do you mean, you don't know?"

"I haven't spoken to Jinx. At least not about this."

"What?"

"No. No. Do not *what* me on this."

"That's why you didn't tell me. Or Pinks. Or Brooks or Lolly. Because if we knew, we'd make you act like an adult and actually speak to your *sister*."

"Exactly. That's exactly why I didn't tell you. I don't want to be an adult on this issue. I wasn't an adult when my mother left, so I'm entitled to be a selfish ass about this now."

"So then why tell me?" Piper asked, folding her arms over her chest and kneeling up on the bed like she was going to kick his ass.

"Because Jaxon said something today that got me thinking, and I can't in good conscience run Jinx out of town if what he says is true."

"What did he say?"

"He thinks I may have gotten the better end of the deal."

"The better end of what deal? I don't understand."

"He said something about Jinx being left with the help while her parents traveled, and that she was pushed from grade to grade because she was too smart for her teachers and then was too young for her classmates. He said"—Vance stopped and looked up at Piper—"she was lonely."

"Vance," Piper sighed.

"I don't know if any of it's true. And that's why now I need you to know. So you can help me sort all this out before my head explodes."

Piper moved to get off the bed. "We need a family meeting," she said decisively. "How could everyone in this house know about Jinx and let you get away with acting like an ass? How could no one tell me?" she screeched.

"No one told Pinks either," Vance grumbled.

"Not making me feel better. Come on. We're doing this."

"Now?"

"Yes, now," Piper said, flinging her curls out of her face as she turned on Vance. "I have a sister-in-law and Vance, Jr. has an aunt. This Evans family needs a stern talking to," she said, shaking her head as she strode out the door.

CHAPTER THIRTY-TWO

Jinx watched as Laidey grinned into her cocktail while Xavier shouted from the grill about her dragging him all the way to Dallas for their wedding day. When Jinx had asked about their plans, she'd gotten an earful. And although Xavier grinned while he ranted, raved, and shot winks at Laidey, Jinx was amazed at how little Laidey reacted to his boisterous tirade.

"I've heard it all before," Laidey claimed. "He's not getting his way on this."

Apparently, Xavier's twin Xander showed up in town to cast the very last vote before the polls officially closed. He and McKenna were treated like royalty by Mr. and Mrs. Wright when they stepped out into their patio happy hour. That certainly suited Jinx well. She took the opportunity to sip her cocktail and watch the family dynamics as McKenna and Xander regaled everyone with the story about how Xander had to schmooze Zoe Beauchamp to let him in to vote just as she was closing the doors.

"He used his good looks like a weapon, and Zoe was putty in his hands," McKenna stated. "He just sidled up to her, touched her shoulder, dipped himself down to her height, and whispered all of that Wright-brother charm into her ear. Next thing I know, she's giggling up a storm and shooing him inside. When Trace McDaniels tried to do the same thing, he got the door slammed in his face."

"Cutting it close," Mr. Wright scolded.

"I drove from Charlotte, Dad. Had to leave work early to make it," Xander doggedly explained.

"Move back. Simplify your life."

"Sure. Sure," Xander said into his beer.

McKenna dominated the conversation at the dinner table. To be fair, she had the most information about what had happened all over town that day. How big the crowds were at the polling centers, and what rumors were being spread about Brooks and Mayor Stevens having a secret meeting. She talked about the television networks showing up to cover the election and how handsome Brooks appeared as he gave a flawlessly humble, yet inspired speech.

"Humble?" Xavier joked. "Doesn't sound much like Brooks."

"Doesn't sound like *you*," Xander corrected. "It sounds exactly like Brooks."

"Ma, you comin' to The Situation with us tonight?" Xavier asked as if his brother hadn't spoken. "It'd be a good time for you and Daddy to get out and mingle."

"Lord, no." She laughed. "Emelina has invited us to the Evans party, but I've turned her down. With you all out of the house, your father and I are going to enjoy some peace and quiet and watch a movie."

"A movie? You can watch a movie any night. Come on, join us at The Situation."

"I thought y'all would be going to the Evans's," Mr. Wright claimed.

There was a moment of quiet where Jinx felt several pair of eyes land on her. After one strong cocktail and a delicious glass of wine, she felt like she could own this. She set her fork down and wiped her mouth with her napkin before engaging the table.

"It's my fault," she said, addressing Mr. Wright. "I asked Jaxon if we could go to The Situation instead. It's likely my last night in Henderson, and since I've read so much about the epic parties held there, I want to experience one."

"From what I understand, the Evans party is going to be epic as well."

"No doubt," Jinx said. "But …" she took a deep breath, eyed Jaxon, and then let out the truth. "I've recently been made aware I'm related to Vance Evans, and apparently, that doesn't sit well with him. So I told him I'd steer clear of his party."

"Wait. What?" Laidey asked. "You and Vance are related?"

"My mother was Mr. Evans's first wife. I'm Vance's half-sister," she confessed. "Though I imagine he won't want y'all to know that. But you've been wonderful to me—all of you—so I want you to know why I've decided not to pursue the library position. As much as I've sincerely enjoyed my time with the entire Wright family, I need to move on. That library job will never belong to me."

"Jinx. You can't just *leave*," Jaxon said. "Not without a fight. Vance doesn't own the public library."

"I realize that. I do. And I've toyed with the idea of going around Vance, because I really would like that job. But he and I share a mother. And he's done a lot of good for the library and this town. I can't in good conscience mess that up for him or for y'all. Henderson belongs to Vance. It belongs to you. This isn't my hometown, and as much as I'd once hoped to be adopted by it, I've come to terms with that," she said, putting on a cheerful expression as she directed her gaze toward Jaxon. "I'll be fine." Then she turned her attention to the entire table. "My one request is that y'all show me a big time tonight, because this is my one and only chance to be part of the happenings in Henderson."

"The Wright brothers can definitely deliver on a big time," Xavier promised. "Just as long as none of us end up *in* the *Henderson Happenings* come Monday. As much as Ma loves to read about everybody else's children doing dumb shit, I've been warned she's not interested in seeing my name in there ever again."

"Language," Mr. Wright growled as Xavier raised his glass in a toast.

"May all the Wrights *and their guests*"—he acknowledged Jinx— "manage to enjoy what happens in Henderson tonight while avoiding being the lead story in the *Henderson Happenings* tomorrow.

"Here! Here!"

CHAPTER THIRTY-THREE

"If your last name is not Evans, Flores, or Williams, clear out!" Vance's precious Piper had turned full-on Army sergeant the moment she set foot back in the kitchen. Seven hired hands fled to the outdoors.

"What's up?" Pinks asked, looking around like he'd just missed something.

"You," Piper pointed at Pinks. "Trust me. The two of us are going to need a stiff drink."

Pinks looked briefly at Hale, Genevra, and Em's stunned faces before he said cautiously, "Okay. Anybody else?"

Every hand in the kitchen, including Vance's, slowly rose into the air.

"Hmm. All right." Pinks washed his hands and made his way to the bar.

"You people should be ashamed of yourselves," Piper started in, walking slowly around the tall countertop to face them all. "Vance"—she pointed at him accusingly—"has just made me aware that this family has a full-blood relation that you've not only kept as a secret from Pinks and me, but you have refused to embrace."

"Piper," Vance started.

"Not a word out of you," she threatened. "Hale," she snapped. "Does my son have an aunt he hasn't met? Does Beau have a half-sister you're keeping from him?"

Hale looked over at Vance. "Seriously? *I'm* taking the fall for this?"

Vance crossed his arms over his chest and rolled his eyes. "I told her this is all on me."

Piper looked at Hale but shot a finger toward Vance. "How could you possibly let this man-child be any part of a decision when it comes to something this important?"

"Man-child?" Vance protested.

"Piper, take a breath," Pinks said as he brought her a short glass of something that looked suspiciously like Fireball and Ginger Ale. "Now, take a sip."

She knocked that sucker back so fast Vance thought his head would spin. "You remember Jinx Davenport?" she asked Davis, handing him back the glass. "The one you said looked like Vance's twin? The one Vance couldn't stop *raving* about that night after her interview? The one *you and I* couldn't stop raving about after we took her to lunch?" Piper's voice went up so high it squeaked.

"I do," Pinks said cautiously. "She was in the office yesterday. I assumed Vance had finally gotten around to offering her the job."

"Yes, well do yourself a favor and assume *nothing* when it comes to this crowd." She threw out an accusing arm, showcasing the rest of them. "They've been keeping us in the dark. Lying to us through omission. It turns out that Jinx Davenport happens to be Hale's *daughter* and *Vance's* sister."

"Wait. What?" Pinks asked in confusion. "That can't possibly be true."

"Oh, it's true. And they've all known it for *weeks*. All of them. Em. Genevra. Hale. *Vance*." Piper pointed directly at the individual culprit with each declaration.

"Baby doll. Your dramatics are not helping the situation," Vance deadpanned.

"No?" Piper stomped her foot.

"No. Why don't we move this into the study and let the caterers back into the kitchen. In case you forgot, Brooks *is* about to win the election."

Piper looked around her, hands on hips and nodded. "Pinks"— she flailed a hand at him—"call everybody back inside. Then meet me and this riffraff"—she flailed a hand at the rest of them—"in the study."

Once the women were seated and Pinks arrived carrying a tray holding a bottle of wine and some very large cabernet glasses, Hale took the floor.

"Piper, I apologize. I don't blame you for being upset. I let the man-child lead me on this and, in my defense, I will simply say the man-child was my original concern. I'm on his side. Always. But, having said that, since the paternity test revealed Jinx to be my daughter, my heart has been broken, and not a day has gone by that I haven't wanted to reach out to her."

Genevra patted Piper on her leg. "I went and visited Catherine on my own. Not only was Hale concerned about how this was affecting Vance, he wanted Catherine to be the one to tell Jinx. Assuming Jinx didn't already know."

"Which she didn't." Hale's jaw ticked, and his Adam's apple bobbed. "Jinx arrived on our office steps yesterday, frantic. Apparently, Catherine and her husband absconded from the country on a cruise. She'd left a short note for Jinx, informing her that Catherine and I had previously been married and there was a *chance* she could be my daughter."

"What?" Vance spat.

"That's how she found out," Hale informed him. "Yesterday. Via a note."

"A note?" Vance squinted, locking eyes with Hale. For the first time, Vance felt a connection with his father on this subject. "What the fuck?" Vance's frustration reached critical mass. He literally had to sit down, put his aching head in his hands, and breathe. As he felt Piper rub his back, all he could think about was the accusation Jaxon had flung at him that afternoon. That between him and Jinx, he'd been the one who had ended up with the better deal.

He didn't necessarily believe that. Because having your mother never want to see you again was certifiably unbearable. But living with one who'd happily leave you with the household staff and then stuff your ass into a boarding school didn't sound ideal. At least he'd had his grandmother looking out for him. His father around on the weekends. His friends, his teammates, his school.

It was clear what he had to do. He had to shrug off his mantle of man-child and seriously man-the-shit-up. If the same narcissistic mother had fucked up both his and Jinx's childhoods, the least he could do was stop acting like a narcissistic offspring.

"Okay." He lifted his head, glanced at his father and then around the room. "I'll fix it."

CHAPTER THIRTY-FOUR

"She said she's leaving," Jax whispered to Xavier while the two of them cleaned up the kitchen.

"I was sittin' right there when she said it." Xavier kept drying the pots and pans like nothing monumental was happening.

"I don't want her to leave," Jax hissed.

Xavier stopped drying and gave his brother a serious look. "Then tell her to stay."

Jax's mouth hung open a moment. Then he shifted his eyes sideways while he licked his lips before he spoke. "That what you did with Laidey? *Tell* her to stay?"

Xavier shrugged. "Sorta. I decided that she'd stay. To marry me."

"*You* decided? What? You just told her …"

"That I was her last first kiss. She said that was romantic and bossy. And bossy totally gets her off."

"Well, that explains it then. Because if she likes bossy, she's gonna love being married to you."

"Right? You want Prom Queen, you're going to have to figure out what gets her off."

Jax thought back to last night in his brother's bed and smiled. "I do not mind figuring that out."

"I'm guessing not." Xavier looked at his watch. "Last of the polls are due in. Let's gather the troops and head out. We aren't gonna wanna miss Brooks's acceptance speech."

Henderson's local dive bar, The Situation, was jam-packed with Brooks's peers, their parents, and the entire police force from what Jaxon could tell. The mood was jovial, and extra bartenders were on hand to handle the crowd. Xavier started the evening by purchasing six tequila shooters. Jinx, Laidey, and McKenna clinked glasses toasting to Jinx's big Henderson night, while Jax, Xavier, and Xander toasted the new mayor. And as predicted, word came in just a few minutes later that Brooks Bennett had indeed won the election in a landslide.

No surprise.

The mayor-elect himself showed up thirty minutes later and made the rounds, shaking every hand in the room as he dragged Lolly DuVal along with him.

"Speech! Speech! Speech!" the crowd chanted once there was hardly room to move and no one could see anything but the top of his head. Brooks headed toward the makeshift stage and, with Lolly by his side, he expressed his appreciation for everyone there, for everyone who helped with his campaign, for everyone who got out and voted, and for everyone who was not leaving Henderson in their rearview mirror but sticking around to be a part of the new economic plan.

Jax noticed how McKenna jabbed his brother Xander in the shoulder when Brooks mentioned sticking around, right before he himself turned to Jinx, making it clear with a scowl that her intention to leave Henderson did not match up with Brooks's plan. "You need to stay," he whispered. "Be on the leading edge of what's happening here."

Jinx bit the side of her red Solo cup and lifted her brows. "All this excitement? It's tempting." And later, after Brooks's speech, when Jax led her to a quieter corner in the very back room of The Situation, she said, "I mean, it's not like I want to leave. I want to stay," she told him emphatically. "I want to be a part of this. I have no doubt the tide is turning in Henderson. The new sports academy is just the biggest item on a long list of projects. Who wouldn't want to be a part of this?"

"No one." Jax said as he backed her against the wall and placed both his hands on her hips, giving her a squeeze. He leaned in, his mouth just shy of hers, his eyes holding her stare. "Stay. Give it some time. Give *us* some time." He licked his lips as he brought one hand up to caress her soft cheek.

Jinx's eyes closed at his touch. The woman was not immune to him. Not from their first touch and sure as hell not now. He just didn't know if chemical combustion was going to be enough for an out-of-work, genius-librarian to stick around and take a chance on a part-time auto mechanic/part-time construction laborer/NASCAR engine-tech wannabe. So he pulled the family card out of his pocket. "Give Vance a little more time. The two of you hit it off before the shared-mom thing happened. He hasn't given your dream job to anyone else. As much as he's been a pain in the ass about all this, it's very likely he'll come around.

"You think?" She smiled up at him. A way-cute smile, one he hadn't seen before. He leaned down close, tugging on her braid. "Rapunzel. You tipsy?"

She nodded, biting her lower lip, leaning against her hands she'd tucked behind her backside.

"On one shot?"

"Two shots. And a beer."

"Two shots?"

"McKenna."

"McKenna bought you a shot? When?"

"When all you bros were pounding Brooks on the back."

"Hmm. Okay. Well, you good?"

She nodded again. Her smile a little brighter. Her eyes a little drowsy.

"You are twenty-one, right?"

Again, the cute nod. "Mmm-hum."

"You ever drink beer?" he wondered.

She laughed, shaking her pretty head. "Yes. I've had a beer. Though I usually just drink wine. With dinner."

"And tequila shots?" He grinned, because tipsy-as-shit Jinx was fuckin' cute.

"A new passion."

"Passion?" His brows shot up.

"I liked 'em," she confessed while rocking up on her toes so that her chest rubbed up against him before she fell back against the wall.

Man o' man, the way his body reacted to that little rub-up was killer. He shuffled his right foot closer to the wall and dipped his knees. "Babe." He licked his lips. "You wanna get out of here?"

She stared intently at her fingers playing with the button at the center of his chest. "What I want is a big night at The Situation. As promised. *Then*"—she looked him straight in the eye—"I definitely want to *get out of here.*"

"A big night. Right." He snaked an arm around her back and pulled her body up against his, giving her a quick but meaningful kiss. "Time to shake a mean tail-feather then," he said, giving her luscious jean-clad butt a tap as he pushed her toward the dance floor.

The DJ had been hired from a Raleigh nightclub just for the event, so the otherwise lonely Tuesday-night dance floor was crowded. Jax wondered if he'd missed the announcement that tomorrow was a national holiday the way everyone seemed to be throwing 'em back. This included his brother Xander, who was obviously feeling no pain, and had his hands all over McKenna as she ground up against him on the dance floor.

He wondered about those two. He really did. *Something* ... but when Jinx was stolen right out from under him as he was pondering his brother's unlikely romance, he figured he'd better start paying attention.

Yep. There was Jinx, on the damn dance floor, being twirled under the arm of a big, burly dude Jaxon had never seen in his life. "What the?"

Xavier slapped him on the back before handing him another shot. "Army Ranger. Friend of Thurgood Watson. Not a threat."

"Not a threat?" Jax protested. "He literally just stole Jinx out of my arms. And I'd march right fucking out there and get her back except—"

"The dude is four times your size."

"I beg your pardon."

"Okay, twice your size."

"In the bicep department only," Jax stated. He took another look at tipsy Jinx giving her cute smile to the trained-to-kill fucker and drank down the shot in his hand.

Xavier chuckled. "Maybe *he'll* give her a reason to stay."

"Fuck off," Jax warned. "He gets one dance."

Xavier just chuckled before turning and getting himself lost in the crowd.

If Jinx wanted a big night, Henderson was handing it to her on a silver platter. Jaxon considered himself lucky if he got one damn dance out of every three. Not that it mattered all that much because the dance floor was so crowded no one really knew who was dancing with whom. But it was plenty obvious Jinx had been sniffed out as the new blood in this old town, a town that held a whole lot more single men than Jaxon had realized. Where the hell had they all come from?

And then it made sense.

Just like his brother, most of the people partying it up at The Situation had come back to town for one night only. To see Brooks win. To celebrate his victory.

If everyone would just stay, he thought as he felt his phone go off in his pocket at the same time he saw McKenna hand Jinx another shot along with a big beer chaser. Probably a bad idea, he thought as he looked down to see who was calling.

The Prescott Ansil race team.

Well, I gotta take this. He tried to signal Jinx and hoped she'd actually seen him flash her his phone as he quickly dislodged himself from the party on the dance floor and headed outside where he could take the call.

Ten minutes later, he was back inside, looking for Xavier.

"I gotta go," he shouted over the deafening noise.

"What?" Xavier shouted back.

"I gotta go." He held up his phone as Xavier moved closer and the two of them headed toward the front door. "Prescott Ansil called, and I'm on for the trials in Talladega. Need to leave now and drive most of the night to be there in time.

"Why such short notice?"

"Don't know. Said they heard what I did for Rex Ocean, and they want me to do it for them."

Xavier took a step back and said, "This is huge."

Jaxon smiled. "I know. Right?"

"Your reputation is spreading."

"That's a good thing." Really, Jaxon couldn't be more psyched. Maybe he actually could make a name for himself in the industry. "As a consultant, I can make a shit-ton of money."

"You won't be a consultant for long. Some other team is going to snap you up."

"Maybe."

"You don't want that?"

"I don't know. If I were with any one team, I'd be on the road all the time. As a consultant, I can live here. Be a part of the Henderson solution."

"Brooks loves to hear that kind of thinking."

"Listen, I don't wanna bust up Jinx's big Henderson night. So I'm gonna text her and explain. But you gotta promise me you'll keep an eye on her. She's three sheets to the wind in there and the shiny new thing everyone wants to dance with."

"She'll be fine. I'm more worried about you, asshole. You can't drive anywhere in your condition."

"They've sent a car for me. I've just got to get to the house and pack. I've H-Ubered up for that."

"Hubered?"

"Henderson's local Uber service. New start-up, just last week. Then I can sleep the whole way to Talladega. So I'm good. It's Jinx I want you to worry about. Tell her she has to stay the weekend. At least until I get back. Put McKenna and Laidey on it. Tell them they've got to keep her here," he said as he started to back away into the parking lot. "And tell McKenna no more shots. Not sure Jinx has had a lot of drinking experience, being as she's got all those degrees and all."

"She'll be fine, bro. Go tweak the engine and pick up another win."

Jax smiled. "Keep Jinx in town," he ordered. Then he turned to find his ride.

CHAPTER THIRTY-FIVE

Vance stomped around the upstairs hallway of the Evans mansion in front of the guest room where Piper was attending to Jinx.

Jinx. His *sister*.

Jinx. His *drunk-off-her-goddamn-ass* sister.

Jinx. *His sister* who fucking Jaxon Wright had left all alone to vomit her guts out in the parking lot of The Situation.

Vance sucked up a lot of air through his nose and then let it out on a muttered, "I am going to kill that asshole," just as his phone went off. He picked it up and sneered, "Where the fuck is your brother?"

"Have you got Jinx?" Xavier asked, sounding like he really gave a shit.

"Yeah. I have Jinx. No thanks to your no good brother. Asshole left her by herself in the parking lot throwing up. Who the fuck does that?"

"My fault," Xavier said. "Not his."

"Well, it sure is somebody's fault. She was alone, X. Alone and drunk, for Christ sake. Anything could have happened to her."

"I know, man. I'm sorry. Jax got called out on a job. A big break for him. He didn't want to leave her, but he had to go. And I swear to God, I had an eye on her all night. And she was good. Havin' a damn ball. But then I turned around for two minutes, and she was gone. By the time I got out there to scour, the parking lot I heard you'd come and gone. I'm sorry, man. I'll be right over to pick her up."

"Oh, hell no. Don't you come near this place."

"Dude, she's staying at Mom and Dad's. I told Jax I'd look out for her. I'm coming to get her."

"Xavier. Fuck off." Vance ended the call.

"Shh," his wife scolded as she came out of Jinx's room. "You're gonna wake up Vance, Jr., and Jinx already has enough to deal with without you making her any more anxious."

"I have not yet begun to make her anxious," Vance assured his wife. Piper pushed him further down the hall, so he made an effort to lower his voice. "How is she?"

"Sick as a dog."

"Think we should take her to Parham Medical Center? Get her checked out for alcohol poisoning?"

"I think she just got good and drunk and is now paying for it, just like we all did back in our college days."

"Yeah, but she's not in college."

"She's twenty-one. And a scholar, not a partier. From all her apologizing between tossing her cookies, I gather she thought this was her last opportunity for a Henderson adventure."

"Henderson adventure?"

"Yeah. She wanted a night like she's read about in the *Henderson Happenings*. Plans to leave town tomorrow."

Vance's scowl went into shock. "Tomorrow? Why would she leave tomorrow? We haven't even talked."

"She's given up on you." Piper moved in closer, wrapping her arms around his waist. "Not every woman is willing to wait on you forever."

Vance bent his neck and kissed Piper like he meant it. Because his life would suck big turkey dong if she hadn't been willing to wait for him. Always come back for him. "I've messed this up," he admitted over her lips. "But I can fix it. With your help. We can fix this."

"What's going on? I just heard you carried Jinx in through the front door," Hale said as he joined them at the top of the stairs. Brooks's party still raged outside around the pool. Pinks and the Outlaw still played. The party was exactly how Vance had wanted it to be, only he'd been too distracted to enjoy it.

"I felt so bad about Jinx that I wanted to go see her. Talk to her. Tonight. Only when I found her at The Situation, she was puking her guts into the bushes."

Hale's hand flew to his mouth. "Oh, God."

"She's going to be fine," Piper soothed. "Just a little too much of a good time. I've got her in bed down the hall, and I'm happy to sit with her if she'll let me. I doubt she'll want to see either of you in the state she's in, so let's give her a little privacy, huh?"

"Sure. Right. Okay," Hale said. "You good?" he asked his son.

"I'm not good. I'm fucking pissed. At her. At Jax. At myself."

"Come back to the party," Hale insisted, grabbing his son's arm. "This is Brooks's night. Jinx isn't going anywhere."

"Damn right," he said and started shaking his finger at Piper. "If Xavier shows up trying to take Jinx back to the Wrights' you tell him she's not leaving this house, you got me? It's all my fault she was at The Situation in the first place *and* staying with the Wrights. They aren't her family. We are."

"Well, I'm happy you've finally come around to that," Piper said.

He leaned back in and kissed her glumly. "My bad."

"I'll make sure she's okay. Once she's asleep, I'll come down and report in."

"Fine. Just, tell her I'm sorry."

"Nope. You'll get to do that yourself. Tomorrow."

CHAPTER THIRTY-SIX

Jinx woke up with a dry mouth, a sore head, and an off-the-charts level of embarrassment. She rolled over, planting her face into one of the many bed pillows, moaning her exhaustion, her frustration, and her pain from a really, really bad headache into its depths.

This was going to be bad.

She knew exactly where she was. She knew how she'd gotten here. She also knew she spouted a lot of shit at her half-brother as he'd picked up her floppy body and carried her to his truck. She knew that his wife was the one who held her hair back and flushed the toilet over and over and *over* again until she had nothing left but dry-heaves.

It was not her most stellar moment.

And … yeah. She'd probably made the *Henderson Happenings* after all.

Not the impression she wanted to leave behind.

She reached to the bedside table for her phone, which was low on charge and high on texts from Jax.

Rapunzel. You just keep letting your hair down, I gotta go to work. Xavier will explain.

Rapunzel. Xavier says you're having too much fun to bother checking your phone. Sorry I had to leave early, but it's a good gig. Tell you all about it tomorrow.

Holy shit, Webster. I just heard you were dragged away from The Situation by Vance. You okay?

Jinx. WTF? Answer me!

And a new text came in before she finished reading the rest.

That's it. I'm coming back.

She hurriedly pressed the call button to catch him before he did anything stupid. In a breathless voice, he answered, "Jinx? Are you okay?"

"I'm fine," she said and then went into a coughing fit. And then because that hurt her head so bad, she began to cry. "Maybe I'm not fine," she sobbed, "but I'll live. I think. Don't come back. I don't want you to see me like this."

"What the hell happened?"

"Too many shots," she groaned. "Too much McKenna. Not enough ... *you*," she whispered.

"Aww, babe. I thought I left you in good hands."

"Yeah, no. My *brother* was the one who found me praying for death in the parking lot."

"Oh, man. Vance is going to kick my ass."

"Pretty sure he's planning to kick mine first. I heard a lot of shouting outside in the hallway. I need to figure out some kind of escape plan." She moaned as she tried to lift her body and then fell back. "As soon as my brain stops trying to drill through my skull." There was a knock on the door. "Damn," she half whispered, half sobbed. "I think I missed my chance."

Piper's head poked through the door. "Just checking on you. How are you feeling?"

Jinx tried to blink the tears from her eyes. "Rough. And embarrassed. Most especially embarrassed."

Piper waved that away. "I see you're on the phone," she whispered. "Let me just leave a few things for you." Piper hurried in, dropped clothes on the end of the bed, and then put aspirin and a bottle of water on the bedside table. "*Everyone* is moving slowly this morning, but we are gathering for brunch in an hour or so and hope you'll feel well enough to join us."

"Us?"

Piper nodded her head. "The family. Vance and I. Hale and Genevra. Emelina. Pinks. The kids. Brooks and Lolly, probably. Oh, and Scarlett. Mmm, maybe Crain and Tansy."

Jinx couldn't find words. She simply nodded lamely, definitely not feeling up to having brunch with *the family.*

"It's going to be fine," Piper assured her as if she'd read her mind. "And it's long overdue. Whenever you're ready, just come on down. Tell Jaxon hello," she said as she left.

"How did she know you were talking to me?" Jaxon asked.

Jinx thought about it, and when the truth of her situation revealed itself, it actually hurt. So her words were blurted out on a sob. "Who else would I be talking to?"

"Jinx," Jaxon sighed.

Hearing the pity in his voice broke her. "I gotta go," she managed to say just before the waterworks really started to flow.

"Jinx. No. Come on—"

But she hung up on him and let loneliness engulf her.

It was a while later when she heard a soft knock and the door crack open. "Jinx?" Vance called out in a soft voice. "You decent?" She rolled over, struggling for consciousness out of the deep sleep she'd cried herself into.

"Vance?" Her mouth and lips were so dry she pushed herself up and reached for the water Piper had left.

He stuck his head through the crack he'd made with the door, everything from his neck down sheltered from her view. "Yeah. It's me. The jackass. Mind if I come in?" His head darted out of view and then poked through again. "I'd really like a chance to talk with you alone."

This is it, Jinx thought lying back against the myriad of pillows that had been propped behind her last night. She looked down, grateful for the T-shirt Piper had helped her into, and began to tuck the sheet and blanket around her waist, pulling her legs in and crossing them beneath the sheets. She pointed to the end of the bed, offering Vance a seat.

"You okay with this?" he asked as he sat gingerly on the corner. She watched him rub a quick hand over his face and become earnest. "I want to apologize. And explain. If you'll allow me that."

"Apologize and explain?" It came out rather froggy, so she drank some more water and then reached for the aspirin and put them in her mouth.

"Head hurt?" he asked.

She nodded slowly, her mouth still open. "Everything hurts," she mumbled around the pills as she put the water bottle to her lips and drank them down.

Vance gave her a twisted grin. "I'll bet." He scooted closer, helping by taking the water bottle from her hand and placing it on the table beside them. "Looked like you really tied one on."

"McKenna likes tequila shots."

Vance tucked his lips together and nodded. "It's kind of a thing around here."

Jinx let herself lounge back against the pillows and closed her eyes. "I'm sorry I got drunk." She waved a limp hand in front of her face. "I'm sorry I yelled at you." Then emotion welled up inside her chest, and she couldn't stop the tears as she raised her gaze to his face and choked out, "I'm sorry I'm your sister."

"Jinx."

"I didn't know," she wailed, shaking her head. "She didn't tell me." She wiped at her eyes. "Anything," she sobbed and then grabbed at her forehead, because holy shit, did crying ever make it hurt.

"Jinx," Vance whispered, moving closer, taking one of her hands in both of his. "Jinx. Stop. Please," he begged. "Not another word. This is all my fault. None of it yours."

She pulled her hand away and wiped at her eyes, furious. "No. This is *her* fault."

"Well, yeah," he agreed, stunned at her vehemence. "You're damn right it's her fault," he said, getting angry right along with her. "All of this is her fault. Every last bit of it is her fault. I hate her. For leaving me. For leaving my dad. And then I made the mistake of hating you when I realized you were her daughter." His voice lowered. "Right now, I hate her for that most of all. Because I promise you, I'm not the jackass you think I am. I mean, I can be a *total* jackass, but ..." He looked at the bed between them and shook his head. "Christ. I don't know where to begin."

When he glanced up, Jinx shrugged. "Start at the beginning." When he hesitated, she pointed to her puffy eyes and tear-streaked cheeks and said, "I'm not in any shape to get out of this bed and face your family or eat brunch. So please, start at the beginning. You tell me yours, and then I'll tell you mine." She brushed away another tear as the saddest, most empathetic expression appeared on Vance's face. True empathy. The kind that said you'd have to share a mother like theirs to understand.

"I, ah," Vance started. He held up a hand and then let it drop. "She left us when I was ten. For your, ah, father, I guess. We were devastated. Dad and I." He licked his lips and looked away. "Dad spent a lot of years mourning her loss by leaving town to build his business. He didn't say too much when he was home. So, for a while there, I lost him too." His forest-green eyes glanced briefly to her face. "My grandmother moved in and, ah, somehow she and I found a new normal." He started shaking his head, bringing on a cheeky grin. "Over the years, I ... ah ... worked really hard to figure out women. Ah—that is to say I worked really hard at getting physical with any girl who'd let me." He choked out a laugh. "Talk about mommy issues."

Jinx gave him a soft smile. "Under the circumstances, it sounds like you were entitled to a mommy issue or two."

Vance stared straight at her when he said, "She never came back. Never called. Never asked to see me."

Tears stained Jinx's eyes. "Because of me."

Vance shrugged. "That was her choice. Dad never stopped her from seeing me. She never asked. Never came to town. Nothing."

"Because of me. Because she didn't want your father to know that she was pregnant with me."

"Yeah, but Jinx, I'm not blaming you for that. I mean, at least not anymore. And I want to apologize for how I've reacted to all this. Because ..." He looked around, as if he was trying to locate the right words. "Because I really *liked* you. From the moment we met," he said, capturing her gaze in earnest. "And that gets me even more pissed off because I turned into such a selfish ass the moment I realized you were *her* daughter."

"Vance."

"I was an immature idiot, and I can't defend my actions. What I can do is own them and ask for your forgiveness. But"—he held up a finger—"before you decide whether or not to give me that, I will ask you for a favor. Because I very much want to hear your story. The one I should have asked you about the moment Pinks noticed the two of us looked like twins."

"Vance, I don't have a story."

"Of course, you do. And I want to hear it. The good parts. The bad parts. All of the parts up until I decided to pull my head out of my ass—which was yesterday afternoon by the way. So, please. Go on. Tell me the unabridged Jinx Davenport story."

Jinx was speechless. She didn't know what to say. Her mouth opened, but no words came out, because at that moment, sitting in front of a man she shared a mother with—after a night of too many shots—she didn't have the energy or the brainpower to share anything. But she could definitely give him this. "I forgive you. I never thought your actions were out of line, considering." And she meant that. But saying the words caused her to remember how rejected his actions had made her feel and her eyes welled with unbidden tears.

"What?" Vance moved in, wrapped her up in his arms and hugged her to him.

"I'm just …" She hiccupped. "I'm so …" She sniffed. "Lonely."

CHAPTER THIRTY-SEVEN

Lonely.

Probably the saddest word in the human language.

Vance's heart broke hearing Jinx say it, never mind how awful he felt as she sobbed into his chest over it.

Lonely.

He'd been lonely. So damned lonely. For most of his life. And to have this girl, this brilliant, *precious* woman, suffer like he had? Anguish engulfed him, and he broke down, crying into her hair, matching the tears drenching his shirt. Oh, he understood lonely. And how he'd gone ahead and done nothing but add to hers.

"I'm sorry, Jinx," he told her. "I'm so sorry this happened to you."

"To us," she sobbed. "It happened to us."

He nodded, his cheek against her head. Hugging her loosely, even though his instinct was to squeeze her hard enough to banish their collective pain and suffering. "I always wanted a sibling," he told her. "I *always* did." He pulled back and started brushing away her tears, leaving his own eyes wet. "And now I've got Brody *and you.* And you've got me and this tiny, little half-brother who is awesome, believe me. So, between the three of us, we don't ever need to feel lonely again. Fuck our mom. I mean, not Brody's mom, because she's Genevra and practically as perfect as Piper, but you know what I mean."

Jinx laughed through her tears. "Well, *Beau*," she corrected, "may not be *my* brother, but if he's yours I'm happy to claim him. The more the merrier."

"But he *is* your brother. Your half-brother," Vance assured her, eager to share in the bounty that was Beau. "And that "half" stuff is bullshit. I couldn't feel more attached to Brody. *Beau*. He's really Brody. Even though everyone else calls him Beau, he and I know his real name. And now you know it, too. So call him Brody. He'll understand. It'll be our sibling thing."

Vance didn't notice Jinx's distraught expression until he came to the end of his convoluted ramble. "What? What's wrong?"

"You said I'm his sister. But … you can't know that for sure."

"Oh, yeah. No. We're sure," he insisted. "I think that's why Genevra went up to see your mother. To tell her Dad knew, and that he thought it'd be best if she was the one to deliver the news." And then, as he added Jinx's expression to the little bits of information he'd actually paid attention to over the last several months, he immediately realized how badly he'd just fucked up. "Oh, God," he stammered. "You didn't know."

She shook her head, her eyes welling up again.

"Jinx," he breathed into her neck as he attempted to pull her against him. "I'm so sorry. I thought you knew. I mean, maybe I knew you didn't? But then I just got myself all wound up in this conversation about you and me and Brody … and I forgot you didn't know. At least for sure." He pulled back. "And now, oh, God." He felt himself panic, talking in rapid-fire mode, going fully forward since there was no way to backpedal. "Dad's a great guy," he tried to assure her. "A *really* great guy. And since Genevra's come into his life, he's become an amazing father, and—Jinx, listen to me—he *desperately* wants a relationship with you. He's only been holding himself back because *I've* been such a shit about all this. Holy Christ, I have truly screwed up."

Jinx slid down into the covers, rolling to her side wiping away tears as she went. She wasn't looking at him when she asked, "How are you so sure?"

"There was a DNA test."

She shook her head, plucking at the edge of the pillow and sniffing "But I didn't provide a blood sample."

"Jaxon gave Dad some pieces of your hair. Apparently, that was enough to get a positive result."

She turned her head and stared at him. "Jaxon?"

Vance shrugged. "Right after that night he took you to dinner at the club."

She blinked.

Then blinked again.

"Why would he think to do that?" she wondered, sitting up, her face all scrunched up in confusion. "That's the weirdest ..." But then her voice trailed off. "Did he know?" She sat up, her eyes watery, her brow furrowed, but her voice strong. "He did know," she answered her own question aloud. "He told me he thought I was Hale's daughter the moment he saw us together on the road."

"I think, like Dad and my grandmother, Jax suspected you were related right away."

Her head bobbed as she glanced around the room. "Yes, but to orchestrate something like this."

"Orchestrate what?"

"A DNA test," she tossed at him like he was an idiot. "Why would Jax do that? To me?"

"Jinx, he didn't do it to you. My father had questions. Jax helped him find the answers."

"About me," she shouted, clapping a hand against her chest. "Why didn't Jax or your father or your grandmother or even *you* just ask me, 'Jinx, who is your mother?'"

"I didn't ask because considering your age, and your IQ, as soon as Pinks mentioned how much we looked alike, I *knew* who your mother was. And I didn't like it. And don't go blaming Dad, because he took one look at you and he knew it too. Believe me, he *wanted* to ask you, but I forbade him from doing so. I was—" he stopped himself.

"You were what?"

"I was convinced you were a gold digger. I immediately assumed you were here for nefarious reasons." At the panicked expression on Jinx's face, he knew he needed to start talking fast or she was going to bolt. "Jinx, I now know that's not the case. But at the time, it didn't seem probable that you'd stumble into Henderson unaware of your mother's connection to this family." He took her upper arms in his hands to prevent her from fleeing the bed. "That's on me. Please don't blame my father."

"Oh. I don't blame you or your father. I blame Jaxon Wright. Because it seems pretty clear that he took me out solely to fish for personal information. Then he not only passed that personal information on to you and your father, he gave y'all hair samples as well. Who does that?" she yelled.

"He was just trying to help."

"Hale! He was just trying to help Hale. He certainly wasn't trying to help me by not letting me in on the idea that I might be somebody's secret baby. No. He didn't say a word. Oh, my gosh." In that instant, Vance witnessed Jinx's expression drain from heated anger into mournful sorrow. "He didn't really like me at all, did he? He just kissed me because it was all part of the plan."

"Jinx," Vance soothed. "There was no plan."

She looked so grief stricken as she stared into his eyes, her own dark-green irises wet with tears. "I really like him." She tugged at her own fingers. "I really liked him," she said as she doubled over, falling head first into Vance's chest. "And he was just trying to help Hale."

Vance grunted as he fell face-first onto his bed after giving Jinx the space she'd asked for. He rolled over and looked at his wife who sat rocking VJ before he went down for his nap. "Thank God, you're not a crier, Pipes, because I'm no good with weeping women."

"You give me no reason to weep."

He grinned. That was Piper for you. Perfect response. Only …

Vance hadn't thought about it until this moment, but the one time he'd seen his wife cry was when she admitted to him she was pregnant. *Pfft.* As if that was worth crying over. Best damn thing that ever happened to him.

But he bet he'd been the cause of her tears prior to that.

Over the years.

All those times she came back to Henderson to try to connect with him.

Like the time he didn't recognize her and stupidly turned her down when she'd asked him to dance in middle school. And the time in high school when she'd gotten an eyeful of Molly DuVal leaping into his arms, wrapping those long legs around him after the state championship win. And most especially the time he abruptly left her sagging against the back wall of a bar in Raleigh after that kiss to end all kisses.

And yet, now she was his wife.

"Baby doll, how do you think we managed to get here?"

"What do you mean?"

"You and me. After all those misses throughout the years. All the misunderstandings. Basically, all the times I'm guessing I made you cry?"

"I love you."

"You do now. But what about when I disappointed you? Made you cry? How did we survive that crap and come out on the other side?"

"I loved you."

"Always?"

"Always."

He huffed a laugh and then slid a hand over his mouth and mumbled, "I'm damned lucky."

"Why do you ask?"

A big sigh rolled from him as he fell onto his back and stared at the ceiling. "I just fucked up everything between Jinx and Jaxon."

"What?"

At Piper's alarmed wail, he turned his head toward her sharply. "Well, I didn't do it on purpose. She asked why I was so certain Dad was her biological father. When I told her about Jaxon giving Dad her hair samples for a DNA test, she flipped out."

"You told her what?" Piper's eyes were wide in disbelief.

"I'm not going to lie to her."

"But you *told her* Hale is her biological father? When she specifically told him she didn't want to know?"

"Well, I forgot about that in the heat of the moment. We were bonding over the horrible-mother thing, and I was trying to show her that having me and Brody as brothers was a good deal."

"Vance," she breathed.

"It's not like Dad was going to keep this from her forever."

"But did you have to toss her world upside down and throw Jaxon under the bus while you did it?" She stood abruptly with Vance, Jr. in her arms and marched into the adjoining room. VJ's room.

He was *so* not good with women.

Vance wondered if he should try to sneak out and hit the road before Piper had a chance to come back.

Too late.

"I'm going to go talk to Jinx," she said as she returned, closing Vance, Jr.'s door. "You are going to go down and tell your father what you've done."

"All right. Fine. But baby doll, come here a minute, please."

"What?" she snapped, as irritated with him as she ever got.

"I want to fix this. For Jinx. Even for Jaxon."

"What about your father?"

"He's gonna thank me. I'm not worried about him."

Piper's lips twisted, and when she didn't disagree, Vance figured at least he'd gotten that right. He'd done the dirty work. Ripped the Band-Aid off Jinx so his father didn't have to worry any more about how to tell her that she was his daughter.

"Look," he implored. "If the two of us can end up together after all the times I let you down, then I think Jinx and Jaxon can recover from this setback."

"That you created."

"That I created and want to fix. But I can't do that without you. I don't have the skills. But together, the two of us are uniquely qualified to stick our noses into Jinx's business and do what we can for Jax."

Piper sat on the bed, her energy fading. "How do you figure that?"

"She's family."

"She doesn't see herself that way."

"Not yet. But once I make her an offer she can't refuse, she'll stay in Henderson and give the Evans clan a chance to meddle their way into her life. It's a lonely life, Piper. That was abundantly clear. She needs us. She needs Jaxon. At least for as long as she wants him."

"What's your deal with Jaxon?"

Vance lifted a shoulder. "He's good with women. Word has it he's been good with a whole lot of women."

Piper simply raised a brow.

"You know, I do get that I'm insane, right?" He swallowed, feeling a surge of emotion for the handful of women who had entered his life and saved him after the one who mattered most had turned her back. "But I'd be so much worse off if Lolly and Genevra hadn't come into my life. If I hadn't found you again. And now I've got this amazing son, a little brother who I love *so* much, and a *sister* literally dropped into my lap. I want to share all this bounty with her. I need to show her that there is more to life than longing for love from someone who is just not equipped to give it."

"All right," Piper sighed. "When you put it that way."

"You forgive me too fast."

"You're complaining?"

"Nope. Just acknowledging how big my bounty is."

"So how do you propose we get Jinx to forgive Jaxon?"

"Oh—that's your deal. You, Genevra, and Em. And Pinks. Get Pinks in on this. Oh, and you know, Harry. Of course. But no tequila shots. Gotta do this without the magic. I got the sense that Jinx isn't going to be getting up close and personal with Jose Cuervo or any of his ilk for a long time to come."

CHAPTER THIRTY-EIGHT

"You did what?"

Hale listened to his son's explanation—excuse—convoluted thinking—and then took a deep breath and exhaled.

"Okay. How'd she take it?"

He listened on as Vance stumbled, recounted, apologized, and then strategized. Then he did what he'd been longing to do for the past three months. He set off to have a heart-to-heart with his daughter.

His daughter.

Such a gift.

And no matter what happened between them from here on out, that's what he wanted Jinx to know. That to him, she was an unexpected and wonderful gift.

Yet he was greeted by a halting palm as he opened the door and tried to leave his office. "Absolutely not," his mother said.

"Not what?" Hale asked in confusion.

"You're not going to impose yourself on our Jinx after she's been blindsided so indelicately by your eldest offspring." She sent an accusing glance toward Vance.

"*Our* Jinx?" Hale retorted with a dubious look. "Since when has she become *our* Jinx, Mother? Last I recall, you wanted to run her out of town."

"That's before I knew she was yours."

"No, that's when you suspected that she was mine and worried what that would mean to this family."

"Because I didn't want *your ex-wife* mucking up what took me years to straighten out." Em looked emphatically at both Hale and Vance.

"I see Piper's informed you of my faux pas," Vance stated.

"Faux pas? Dear boy"—Em scolded in her lilting Spanish accent—"you've outed the entire family. How are we ever to redeem ourselves if we keep pouncing on her like ill-bred heathens? Let the girl recover from her overindulgence and your oversharing before she has to face the fact that she's one of us."

"You make that sound like it's a bad thing," Hale accused.

"I'm sure at present, being related to this lot doesn't look all that appealing. Give the poor girl some time to digest the news. She's not going anywhere. We're practically holding her captive."

"We aren't holding her captive," Hale insisted.

"We sort of are," Vance said. "I sent Pinks to the Wrights to grab her belongings. Told him to have her car brought here but to tuck it in a garage and hide her keys in the pool house."

"Dear God. We're holding her captive," Hale whispered.

"Just until we have the chance to properly welcome her to the family," his mother insisted.

"And convince her to take the library job and stay in Henderson," Vance added.

"And get her and Jaxon back together," Piper chimed in as she came down the hallway.

CHAPTER THIRTY-NINE

Jinx spent the rest of the day in bed. In her *father's* guest bedroom. Her *biological* father's guest bedroom. Not the father who was going to have the rug ripped out from under him.

Thanks to Jaxon Wright.

Thanks to Jaxon Wright and her mother, her father was going to have to face the facts, just as she had. Of course, he probably wouldn't wallow around in a bed full of self-pity all day when he found out. She may have had one big crying jag over finally knowing that her father wasn't really her father after all, but the rest of them were all about Jax.

Damn him.

It was all so unfair.

She had been drawn to Jaxon Wright the moment she'd met him and had convinced herself that he'd been drawn to her as well. And maybe he had, but that didn't give him the right to swindle information out of her, pluck hair from her head, and hand it all over to the enemy.

Not that Vance and Mr. Evans were the enemy, she mentally corrected her train of thought. But she had been played by literally everyone she knew in this town to one extent or another, and if she had any idea where to actually go now that she knew what she knew, she'd get herself out of bed and go there. But it wasn't like going back to Richmond would bring her any solace. And staying in Henderson, where everyone she knew had gone behind her back ...

She groaned finally throwing off the covers and swinging her legs over the side of the bed. She couldn't go anywhere until she had a shower, so she'd start there and hope inspiration developed as she washed away her tears and the stench of last night's dubious undertaking.

Tequila shots. Whose brilliant idea was that anyway?

McKenna, Jinx thought as she found her footing and wobbled her way into the bathroom. She awkwardly fumbled with the shower faucet, reaching in to monitor the temperature while considering that maybe, just maybe, McKenna could be trusted.

"Oww," she moaned as the shower turned scalding hot. She adjusted it before pulling off the T-shirt and underwear and stepping into the large, luxurious marble shower. "Oh, thank God," she moaned quietly, one hand braced against the wall as she allowed the warmth of the water to ease her tight muscles. She let her head fall back so the water flowed down the back of her head, down her hair. After several minutes of just letting her body find itself again, she picked up the fresh bottle of shampoo and went to work.

With her head wrapped in a towel and her body wrapped in the pink cotton robe Piper had left, Jinx emerged to hear Pinks calling for her from beyond the bedroom door.

"I have your stuff," he said when she opened the door. He held up her satchel and the two shopping bags McKenna had brought.

"Wow," she breathed. She took a step back, delighted at the prospect of having her own clothes and toiletries. "Thank you for doing that."

"No problem," Pinks said as he stepped inside. "Piper said to tell you a hair dryer and most anything you need can be found under the sink."

She nodded, wondering if she'd find an escape ladder under the sink. Then she looked toward the bed. *Maybe under there.*

"You've made quite a splash at the Wrights." Pinks moved past her to place the bags on the end of the bed.

Forgetting her escape plans for the moment, she swung her attention around toward Pinks. "What do you mean?"

"Well, they weren't at all happy Vance snagged you out from under their noses at The Situation last night. Nor were they thrilled when I showed up to collect your things."

"Was Jaxon there?"

"No, and I could tell his brothers are worried about what's gonna happen when he returns on Sunday and finds you missing."

"He's not coming back until Sunday?"

"Something about engine tweaking, Talladega, and Ricky Bobby."

"Ricky Bobby?"

"I don't follow NASCAR, so a Talladega Nights reference is all I got."

Jinx nodded, her mood lightening.

"Listen," he said, standing in front of her, tucking his hands into the pockets of his khaki pants. "Everybody in this household is also freaking out. They know they've mishandled this unexpected turn of events, and not one of them has a clue on how to proceed."

Jinx expelled a breath. "Well, don't look at me. I'm wondering how to react now that I've been outed as Hale's daughter, Vance's sister, and *Brody's* half-sister."

Pinks smirked. "Vance has already gotten to you about the whole Beau-Brody thing, I see."

"Beau-Brody is a good NASCAR name."

"True that." Pinks smiled, standing his ground. Finally, he went on. "You mind if I take a moment and shed a little light on the good people downstairs?"

Jinx motioned an arm in his direction. "Go right ahead. Between too much tequila and allegedly stolen hair follicles, I'm not sure what to think."

Pinks cleared his throat and rocked forward on his feet. "When I first showed up on their doorstep, the Evanses had no idea who I was. I wanted a summer internship with E&E, and they took a chance on me. Eventually, they even housed me. Gave me a room. This room in fact. A year and a half later, I've moved all the way to the pool house, Vance and I are like brothers, and as much as I relish making my own father proud, I work my ass off daily to make Hale Evans proud. Because I respect him, not only as a businessman, but on a personal level as well. He's is not only brilliant, but he embodies kindness and is generous to a fault. His entire family has embraced me, and when I say my life is better off for it, trust me, I don't have the time to list all the ways. Basically, I cannot speak too highly of Hale or Vance.

"Now, Emelina"—Davis went on—"she's a pip. There's no getting around that. She'll keep you on your toes, and she doesn't pull punches. You won't be able to keep anything from her, so don't bother to try.

"Genevra ... well at the risk of sounding like a complete sap, Genevra is the love that holds this entire household together. She's the wellspring of light and joy that gives Hale the strength to be the stable rock for his family and the rest of this town.

"Piper ... you see, Piper is my best friend. She's also what fixed Vance. And from what I understand, Vance definitely needed fixing. And she continues to patch him up when things like the sister-he-didn't-know-he-had shows up in town. Piper's the one who called the family meeting yesterday afternoon when Vance finally told her about you. She's the one who pulled all their heads out of their asses, and I want you to give her and me a chance to mediate this new family dynamic between you and the rest of them. Because trust me, eventually you are gonna want in on this kind of crazy. And Piper ... well, she's been suffering from the loss of her mother a few years back, and she appreciates the women in her life. So I doubt she's going to let a new sister-in-law go. Whether you end up staying in Henderson or move across the globe, Piper will constantly reach out to you, trying to include you in all family holidays and activities. She'll hound your butt. Trust me. I'd just give in now and save yourself the headache."

Jinx's head did ache. And her distress must have shown, because the one they called Pinks stepped forward and wrapped his arms around her, pulling her to him. "Hale isn't going to try to replace your father," he whispered against the side of her head. "He just wants to be added to your life. And Vance is as scared as a grown man can possibly be at the thought of having to confront his mother after twenty-some years. Trust me, that's what's driven his initial reaction. But I truly believe you and Vance would be good for each other. If you can find it in your heart to let him in. Let us all in."

She nodded, feeling the vitality she'd gained from her shower drain out again. "It's a lot," she sniffed.

"It is," Pinks agreed, pulling back to look her in the eye. "So know this. I've declared myself a neutral party. You need me to be a buffer between you and the crazies, I'm in. You need me to get you back to your parents in Richmond, it's done. What I'm going to suggest is that you allow me to escort you downstairs to dinner. Stand by your side as all this all plays out. But, like I said, this is your call."

After a brief hesitation—because really, she had to leave this room and face the Evanses at some point—she nodded her agreement.

"Yes? You'll let me do that?" Pinks inquired.

"What choice do I have?"

"I can deliver dinner to your room and then sit out there and guard the door."

She shook her head. "Come back in forty-five minutes," she said on a breath before she changed her mind. "Let me get my game face on."

Pinks gave her an approving smile. "That's the Evans in you talking. See you shortly."

Prom Queen.

The words accompanied a ping and a number she didn't recognize, but she knew who was texting her. Xavier Wright.

Another ping.

You need me to break you out of there?

Oh, it was tempting. He could do it too, Jinx thought. Xavier would toss that long ladder of his into his huge truck and drive over, shove it underneath her window, and she'd be out of here.

She walked over to the window and looked out, curious. Yep, it would work. Her room looked down on the front circular drive. She was two stories up, but so was the room she and Jaxon had climbed into.

She sat down on the bed, thinking.

Finally she texted Xavier back.

Bring McKenna, a pair of her black heels, and your ladder. I'm in the upper window to the right of the front door.

His response, *Be there in twenty.*

"Here." Jinx handed her satchel and the shopping bag in which she'd consolidated her new clothes through the window to Xavier. She had donned the black dress McKenna had given her and done away with her usual side braid. Instead, she blew-dry her hair and then used the curling iron she'd found under the sink, leaving the thick dark mass hanging to her waist. The bed had been remade and the room straightened, so she stepped carefully onto the bedside table and turned cautiously to back out of the window and onto the ladder in bare feet as night fell around her. Once Jinx had both feet firmly planted on the ground, McKenna pulled her into a hug.

"I'm so sorry I got you kidnapped by Vance during your big Henderson night out."

Xavier pushed the girls toward his truck. "Go on and get," he whispered. "I'll bring down the ladder, and we'll be out of here before they know the barn door's been left open."

"Pack up the ladder, but we're not going anywhere," Jinx announced, grabbing shoes from McKenna and tugging them on her feet. Straightening, she asked, "How do I look?"

"What?"

Jinx fluffed her hair and stood before McKenna. "How do I look?"

"For what?" Xavier whisper-shouted. "Watching me get my ass kicked by the cops when someone spots me stealing you back from the Evanses?"

"Relax. You are here to escort me to dinner. Be my buffer."

"Prom Queen. I came here to break you out. Now get your ass in the Hulk."

"I can't just run away. I mean, I could, but then it would just be all the more embarrassing when I finally did face them. I just wanted to establish some equal footing. Arrive at dinner by the front door, as a normal person, rather than doing the walk of shame down the stairs after hiding in their guest room for an entire day."

Xavier scoffed. "A normal person doesn't sneak out a window and then turn around and knock on the front door."

"These are not normal circumstances," McKenna defended. "And you look beautiful. They'll love you."

"They'll swallow her whole," Xavier countered.

"Shhhhh," Jinx insisted. "You are so loud."

"Oh. You think this is loud?" Xavier argued.

"Come on," McKenna said. "Leave the ladder. If you want the element of surprise, let's ring the bell now before Mr. Boisterous derails your plan."

Jinx took a deep breath. "Okay," she said on its release. "Okay. Yes." She looked at both of them. "You don't have to accompany me, but I wish you would. As far as I can tell, you two are in the minority when it comes to people who have not withheld important information from me. Or worse, gone behind my back and then lied to my face." The last few words were spit out and directed at Xavier.

"Why do I get the feeling my little brother is on your shitlist?" he grumbled.

"Because Jaxon is at the very top of that list," she fumed before leading the way to the door. Xavier and McKenna gave each other a grimace and then followed in her wake. But before they set foot on the first bricked step, the door opened and Pinks flew out.

"Holy …" Pinks skidded to a halt before flying past them into the drive. "Oh, thank God," he said to Jinx, grabbing his chest and trying to catch his breath. "I just went upstairs to get you." He breathed heavily. "Thought you left." Then he looked at all of them and the ladder outside the window. "Wait. Are you leaving?" He threw a quick glance back at the open door. "I mean, I told you I'd make that happen. But I had hoped—"

"I'm not leaving," Jinx broke in to assure him. "But I needed reinforcements."

Pinks looked toward McKenna and then Xavier. "Sure. Sure. Yeah. That works." He dragged his hand through his hair. "Y'all want to come in now, or … should I leave the three of you to strategize and come in when you're comfortable? Xavier, I've got that beer you like stocked in the mini fridge. McKenna, I heard you enjoyed tequila shots last night. I can offer those up or a glass of wine, a cocktail, anything you want. Jinx, I don't know your drink yet, but one of the many hats I wear around here is bartender. Even after the party last night, dinner isn't going to start without a bottle being opened."

"I'll take a Coke," Jinx told him. "Keep the alcohol as far away from me as you can."

Pinks smiled. "Will do."

"What is this?" Hale stood in the open door to his handsome home wearing a welcoming grin.

Jinx felt everyone's eyes land on her. *Again.* In the twenty-one years she'd stood at the edge of a new classroom being singled out for being the oddball, the outcast, and the outsider, the weight of this particular moment felt heaviest of all.

Her father, her biological father, stood before her, holding out a hand. Coming down the steps to bring her into his home, into his family. She willed herself to be up to the task.

Because she knew rejection.

Had lived with its loneliness.

However, what she had little practice with was acceptance. Her mind recalled the feeling she'd had in the Wright's kitchen as Jaxon had shown her how to make mashed potatoes and Xavier had teased her mercilessly. How Mrs. Wright was happy to have another girl in her home and defended her being a librarian, and how McKenna had shared one of her own secrets after keeping Jinx's to herself for months.

She wanted more of that. With the Wrights and with this man in front of her who had done nothing but continually offer his kind smile and gentle words.

"Jinx. You've brought friends. Please, come in. Everyone." Hale's arm motioned toward the inside of his open door.

Pinks darted ahead, busting past Mr. Evans and scrambling up the steps, talking about opening the bar.

McKenna brushed by Jinx, taking Mr. Evans's hand in greeting. Then she felt Xavier at her arm, taking hold of her elbow and ushering her up the last several steps to the porch landing. "Hale," he said, glancing between the two of them. "I don't know for certain, but I'm willing to bet this little prom queen is going to be a soothing balm for a man who had to raise a son like Vance. The good Lord may have taken his sweet time gettin' your daughter to you, but I'm guessing you'll appreciate her all the more for it."

Hale looked from Jinx to Xavier, his eyes getting watery. He patted Xavier's shoulder and said, "I believe you're right," before offering his arm. "May I do the honors?"

"Absolutely." Xavier handed Jinx over to her father and backed out of the way. Hale wrapped Jinx's arm around his and patted her hand. The feel of his sturdy hold comforted her even though her pulse was racing. When she gathered her courage to lift her gaze and look into his eyes, he uttered the most beautiful word her heart had ever heard. "Welcome."

CHAPTER FORTY

It was as if she were meeting everyone for the first time all over again. Only this time, Emelina took her hand in a warm embrace and gifted her an even warmer expression. "We have much to discuss, you and I," she said in her lilting Spanish accent while leading her away from the chaos erupting in the kitchen behind them. "I noticed you staring at my shoes when we happened to meet at the Wrights' the other day."

"Your Roger Viviers? I've admired many a pair but have yet to make a purchase."

"Obviously, you get your good taste from me."

A bark of incredulous indignation came from behind them. "Abuela, you can't hog the new blood, nor claim a damn thing about her yet."

"Of course, I can. The girl has good taste. Who else would she have inherited it from?"

"Oh, and I suppose you'll be asking her to call you Abuela now that there's been a blood test."

"Jinx can call me whatever she chooses," Em said graciously. "And unlike the rest of you, I didn't need a blood test to know this beautiful child was my granddaughter. She has the Evans coloring after all. I took one look at her propensity to put an outfit together and just knew."

"You just knew, huh? Then why did you wrangle poor Jaxon into doing your dirty work for you, sending him to gather all of Jinx's secrets."

"Oh, my dear," she said, dismissing Vance and pulling Jinx down to sit with her on the couch. "Tell me, how is Jaxon? Such a handsome boy. Tall and broad shouldered. He reminds me of your grandfather, Raymond Griffon Evans. Now he was a man among men. My first husband, God rest his soul."

"First of many husbands," Vance mocked.

"And I shall tell you about each of them over lunch. This Friday. We'll go to the club and show you off."

"Madre," Hale warned as he entered the den, three drinks in hand. "Perhaps Jinx isn't interested in being shown off." He walked over to his mother and handed her a drink, nodding in Jinx's direction. "She may not want to claim a-one of us, and who could blame her after all we've put her through." He held a drink out to Jinx. "Davis said you would enjoy a Coca-Cola."

"Yes, thank you." Jinx was trying mightily to get her bearings. This all seemed so surreal. The four of them together. Joking. Being easy. Emelina Flores wasn't asking pointed questions as she had during the interview, Vance was actually smiling in her direction as he had the first time they met, and Hale was ... well frankly, she thought he was beaming. And his beaming warmed the location of her heart, even if her mind was feeling rather loosely tethered and circling somewhere above her body.

Hale took a seat across from her, and when no one else arrived on his heels, Jinx wondered if perhaps the rest of them were giving her time with her newfound blood relations before overwhelming her with all the rest.

Blood relations. She looked at Hale. "So it seems we are indeed related."

Hale leaned forward, a drink in one hand and a hesitant smile on his lips. "I apologize for going about it without your consent. I hope you can forgive me. I wasn't able to sleep much after we met and—"

She held up her hand. "I understand. I do." She looked into her Coke. "I wanted to know. I honestly did. In fact, there's a lot more I want to know. Not now. But soon."

She wanted to know about her mother and Hale's relationship. How it started. How it ended. Catherine Davenport was going to have to get real with her daughter *and son* once she returned to the

States and answer some hard questions. But for now, there were easier things, simpler things she wanted to know.

"What should I call you?" she asked.

"Hale."

"And if people notice a resemblance, what should I tell them?"

"The truth."

She felt her brows lift. "You make it sound so easy."

"Well, the truth is easy. You're the daughter I didn't know I had. The emotions tangled up in our story, maybe not as easy. Jinx, I hate that I've missed out on knowing you all these years."

The mood in the den shifted. Jinx felt Hale's sorrow creeping in over what was lost. Vance probably felt it too, because he rallied and said, "So, in order to balance the scales, Jinx, I think you should live in Henderson, with us, for at least the next twenty-one years. I wanted you for the library three months ago, before nepotism could be considered an issue. The truth is that has never changed. And now, after months of causing our father, our grandmother, myself, and you unnecessary angst, I want to do my part and make it up to all of us. By formally offering you the library job. All of the contractual specifics are negotiable, because in my mind, *my sister* is the only person I plan to entrust the place to."

"Your sister?" she teased, lightening the mood. "What is everyone in Henderson going to say when they find out you have a sister?"

"Well, once they get to know you, I'm sure they'll all say exactly what they said when I married Piper."

"And what was that?"

"That I *really* don't deserve you."

The rest of the evening continued in a blur and, within an hour's time, Jinx noticed—gratefully—that they intentionally helped her step down from the pedestal of Long-Lost Daughter, by allowing the conversation to drift to Brooks's mayoral win and what was next on Team Henderson's agenda.

Vance had called to invite Xavier's fiancée, Laidey Bartholomew to join the group for dinner, bringing more distraction and plenty of amusement because Xavier liked to boss her in front of an audience like it was his job. Jinx had never seen anyone take teasing so well.

She figured Laidey would be a good role model because bossing and teasing seemed to be how Vance related to the women in his life. Piper certainly, but even Genevra and Em too. She wondered how long it would take for her and Vance to establish that kind of relationship. They would have made easy friends, but now they were awkward unintentional siblings.

Although ... she did have an icebreaker up her sleeve. "Vance," she called from across the long dining room table, drawing everyone's attention. "I'm afraid I lied to you during my interview." Everyone stopped moving.

"How?" Vance asked, his hesitation palpable. "Everything on your résumé checked out."

"Yes, but it was something you asked me, off the record. And I didn't tell you the truth."

Vance looked up and down the table. "All right. I'm ... well, I guess we are all, all ears."

"You asked my IQ And at the time, I wanted to impress you."

Vance sat back all smug. "Jinx, it's okay if you're not a certified genius."

"I'm saying I wanted to impress you. And at the same time, I didn't want to ruin my chances for the job by ... overstepping."

"Overstepping?"

"Yes. I didn't want to make you, my potential boss, feel bad."

"How could you possibly make me feel bad?"

"I told you my score was a point less than yours."

"And it's not?"

She shook her head. "Five points more."

"Oh, smack," Pinks said.

"Shove it, Williams," Vance growled as the room broke into laughter.

"I figured since we were siblings now, it would be okay to throw that in your face."

"With all these witnesses?"

"Yes," she laughed. "Especially with all these witnesses."

Vance rolled up his napkin and did a very sibling-like thing. He threw it at her.

When it was time for everyone who didn't reside at the mansion to head home, Jinx found herself in an awkward position. Xavier, being Xavier, was pushing her out the door with him, prepared to take her back to his parents' house.

"Hey. Where do you think you're going?" Vance asked.

"She's coming home with me," Xavier responded.

"Why?" Vance looked crestfallen. "I thought we were good."

"We are," Jinx tried to explain.

"Then why are you leaving? I mean, I know this is new, but you've got your own space here for the time being, and we've still got a lot to talk about."

Jinx looked at Xavier. "I appreciate all you've done for me. I really do. And I want more of your cooking lessons and more cocktail hours with your mother."

"And Jax? How about Jax?" Xavier asked. "You want more of him too? Or are you gonna let your big brother tell you where to stay and who to see?"

"It's not gonna be like that," Vance said.

Xavier took one look at Vance and then slid his gaze to Jinx. "Don't kid yourself. He's going to play the big-brother card whether he has a right to or not."

"I'm an adult. Who could use a big brother," Jinx said with a glance at Vance. "But I'm also in need of friends," she said to Xavier. "Lots and lots of friends who have my back while I figure all this out."

"The entire Wright family has your back, Prom Queen. You know we do. Now are you coming back with me or not?"

She wanted to. The devil you know and all that. But she knew it would hurt Hale and Vance if she didn't take them up on their invitation to stay, and that would just set things back a few paces. She didn't want to hurt the Wrights' feelings either, especially since Xavier had really stepped into Jaxon's shoes for him while he'd been called away.

Jaxon. Another kettle of fish she needed to deal with.

"Please tell your parents thank you. If it would be all right, I'd like to stop by tomorrow and explain everything to them."

Xavier gave a brisk nod. He didn't like it, but he knew he'd pushed as hard as was polite. "They'll look forward to seeing you." Then he leaned down and whispered in her ear, "I'm leaving the ladder underneath your window. Text me if you need a ride."

She nodded, smiling. Then she stood at the Evans front door and waved as McKenna, Laidey, and Xavier pulled out of the drive.

The next three days were unlike anything Jinx could have anticipated. The household she'd been thrust upon was like a beehive from the moment everyone awoke.

And they all woke early.

All except for Em, who managed to somehow sleep in while two babies cried at intervals, the kitchen was overrun by Genevra and Piper cooking and baking, and Pinks and Vance shouted at each other from across rooms about meeting times and which one of them was going out to the house and which was going to the academy today to make sure the contractors showed up and building continued at both sites on schedule. It was usually Pinks who committed to both.

The only one who wasn't in a hurry was Hale, and by accident, it became his and Jinx's custom to take their coffee outdoors and sit by the pool huddled in sweatshirts with a blanket tucked around Jinx's legs.

They didn't talk about anything of importance, but of all manner of subjects as they came up. Jinx learned about the estate grounds and the other businesses Hale owned. About how he met Genevra and how fast he had fallen for her after so many years of nothing but work. About how his son Beau was such an unexpected gift, just as Jinx was, he had said, and then he grew quiet until he was able to speak again and tell Jinx in a low voice how happy he was that she found her way to Henderson.

Hale learned about her schooling, about her love for the library, and inadvertently about his ex-wife's life through the childhood stories Jinx shared. And even though Jinx was prepared to answer honestly any question Hale asked about her mother, he never bothered. She figured Genevra probably gave him an earful after her fateful visit.

Her parents were still on their cruise, and Jinx had decided to let all of that lie for the time being. She didn't try to contact them. Didn't share the paternity test news. Didn't want to think about what faced the entire Davenport family once her parents returned home. Because that felt completely separate from what was happening here.

Where Hale and she enjoyed coffee and their time together every morning before joining Genevra and Piper and the babies for a delicious new Big Pie Plate breakfast recipe, Jinx's time with Vance was almost nonexistent. That was to say the two of them shared meals and entertainment with the rest of the household, but surprisingly, there had been no additional communication on the subject of their mother or the library.

CHAPTER FORTY-ONE

The knocking on the window was loud and angry, startling Jinx out of a sound sleep. With her wits scattered and her heart racing, she looked at the clock and its blue numbers blazing 3:25 A.M.

Then she heard, "Jinx!" from outside the window and another round of bang, bang, bang.

Jaxon.

She scrambled out of bed and around the bedside table, drawing the curtains apart and reaching to unlatch the window, sliding it open. "Shhh," she hissed. "You're gonna wake the entire house."

Uninvited, Jaxon began to crawl through the window into the dark room, tipping a lamp Jinx had to lunge to steady. "Well, if you hadn't blocked my number, I wouldn't have to resort to scaling the wall of a damn castle to have a word with you. You have seriously taken the Rapunzel shit to the next level."

Trying to gain entry and, at the same time, maneuver around a table, Jaxon bounced on one leg, sending a pad of paper, a pen, her phone, and a book careening to the floor, all while he yelled at her. "For crying out loud," he said, finding his footing and finally standing before her on his two feet. "Do you have any idea what hell you've put me through? I'm down in Talladega trying to make a name for myself in my preferred profession, and I can't keep my mind off you! Last we talked, you were trying to escape this place. Next thing I know, my mother calls to tell me that Davis has come to gather your belongings. Then, when Xavier came over to break you out of here, you refused to go. I keep calling you, texting you, but I get no response. Then I see you've blocked my number. What the hell, Webster? I know I left you at The Situation, but duty called. I thought you'd understand. I had to go. I couldn't pass up this opportunity. Instead, you ghost on me?" he shouted.

"Jaxon, keep your voice down, please."

He moved in on a whisper. "Fine," he hissed. But his voice immediately started to escalate. "Put on some clothes, get your ass in my truck, and let's go someplace where I can shout at you until I don't feel like shouting anymore."

Jinx whirled around, desperate to pull on a pair of jeans. Anything to shut him up. "And here I thought your brother was the loud, bossy one."

"It runs in the family, Prom Queen. Grab a sweater, it's cold out."

"It's 3:30 in the morning. Of course, it's cold out," she snipped. "What are you doing here at this hour?"

"You blocked my fucking number! I finished the race—which went really well, no thanks to you—and drove all damn night back from Talladega so I could put a halt to whatever brainwashing is being done here."

"Brainwashing?"

"Keep it moving, Rapunzel." He found a sweatshirt on a chair and threw it at her. "That'll do. Now out the window you go."

"I don't have shoes on."

"Not my problem. Move it."

"Seriously?"

Apparently, Jaxon was done talking. He stormed at her, wrestled her around so her back was pressed up against his chest, and walked the two of them toward the window. "Hit it."

"Wait. We can just walk downstairs and go out the back door. They leave it unlocked for Davis. No alarms."

"Pfft. Like I'm gonna trust the words of a traitor."

She whirled around to face him. "Traitor?"

"When I left here, you wanted nothing to do with the Evans family. I come back to find you literally sleeping with the enemy."

"Sleeping with the enemy? Oh, that's rich, coming from Benedict Arnold."

"Benedict … what the fuck? You're kidding me, right? I've been on your side in all of this."

"Is that so? You were on my side when you stole hairs from my head and gave them to Hale so he could run a paternity test without my knowledge?"

That shut Jaxon up.

"Yeah. I thought so." She turned her back and stepped away, feeling every bit as upset as she had the moment she understood Jaxon's duplicity.

"Out the window and into my truck," he ordered.

"You can't be—oops." She was grabbed from behind and hustled over to the window, where Jaxon lifted her legs like he was ready to shove her through it. "I'll scream," she threatened.

"Go right ahead," he insisted, twisting her around so her feet slid out the window and caught on the rungs of the ladder. "You got it? Now hold on," he said gripping her arms. "Be careful," he ordered. "You're not going to do yourself any favors by falling from a second-floor window."

"You know this is kidnapping," she mumbled halfway down the ladder. Although Jaxon didn't follow her through the window immediately, so he didn't hear her complaint. When she reached the ground, her feet landed on damp grass and the night air stole through her sweatshirt. She turned and hustled on tiptoe over to an old pickup that sat with its engine running and the driver's door open. She hopped in and scooted across the bench seat, happy to find the truck was at least capable of shooting out heat.

Jaxon took his time retracting the ladder and carefully, if not all that quietly, put it in the bed of the truck.

"Where did you get this?" she asked when he finally climbed in and closed the door.

"One of the guys on the race team. He wants to sell it, and I told him I was taking it for a test drive."

"A test drive. From Alabama to North Carolina."

"Yeah, I'll call him in the morning, tell him I'm taking it."

Silence fell between them as they pulled out onto the street. Jaxon was looking straight ahead, and Jinx pretended she was too. But her eyes couldn't help shifting in his direction, stealing glances at his profile. Even now, after this kidnapping and the overwhelming breach of trust, she was still inexplicably drawn to Jaxon Wright.

She asked herself why. Why even now, as he'd just stolen her out of a nice, warm bed, did she feel more comfortable sitting in a crappy pickup, beside a guy who was furious with her than she had in days? It was the middle of the night. On a dark country road. When, by all rights, she should be furious with him. Still, deep inside, there was peace. Like she belonged right where she was.

Belonged?

Yeah. Kinda.

It was a feeling that had swirled and coaxed its way around her insides during their first date. Well, what she had thought of as their first date. She now knew it had been nothing but a calculated fishing expedition for him, but—and she was being as candid as she could with herself—fact-finding mission aside, that night had ended as a date. A sweet date. *A hot date.*

And the feeling resurfaced, fully formed, the next morning when she saw Jaxon standing next to Hale's Rolls Royce, smiling at her in greeting.

And it leapt to life again the moment she heard his voice that fateful day she came back to Henderson feeling so desperate and so confused. That day he took her out on his boat to let her settle her nerves and just be. *Be-long.*

The Wrights had immediately made her feel like she belonged in their midst. They didn't treat her any differently from the rest of the family. They put her to work in the kitchen, started calling her by nicknames, and teased her about kissing Jaxon.

It was easy to become a slave to that feeling. *Belonging.* Too easy. Because it was exactly what she'd craved throughout her entire life.

Her head twisted so she could stare at Jaxon's profile full on.

She belonged with Jaxon Wright.

And if he practically stole a truck to drive all night to get to her, it was safe to assume that he thought he belonged with her too.

She licked her lips to hide her smile as she faced forward and rocked a little in her seat. Jinx Davenport and Jaxon Wright may well belong together, but that didn't mean he wasn't going to have to do a little groveling before she'd admit it to him.

CHAPTER FORTY-TWO

Jaxon didn't know what the hell to do with Jinx now that he had her. It was the wee hours of a Monday morning and as cold as a witch's tit outside. The boat definitely wasn't an option. His back now ached like a son-of-a-bitch from the hours spent driving a piece of shit not worth the gas he'd pumped into it. And, for all his years spent sorting through the idiosyncrasies of women, nothing—absolutely nothing—had prepared him for this one. Jinx Davenport had him completely undone.

"Look," he said gruffly, taking a hard left turn as he made up his mind. "I'm taking you home. To my parents' house. It's too cold to be driving around out here, and I want to be looking you in the eye when I lay into you about blocking my damn number." Realizing his voice had escalated again, he bit out a "Sorry."

When she didn't say anything, he glanced in her direction briefly but thought no response was better than a big, fat fight, which he was sure was on the horizon.

He probably shouldn't have slammed the truck door after they both exited the driver's side, but he was about as tired as a man could get while still being wound tight. Something about Jinx's bare feet and oversized sweatshirt was making him crazier by the minute. Probably that flimsy lavender nightgown sticking out the bottom was the true culprit that kept messing with his mind.

Jaxon yanked the ladder out of the truck and walked it and Jinx around the side of the house. "Won't Xavier be sleeping?" Jinx whispered, bumping up against him in the cold dark night.

"I expect so."

"Then we shouldn't risk climbing into his window. What if he wakes up and thinks we're intruders? Shoves us back out the way we came in?"

"Webster, how is it you've got all those damn degrees and not one lick of common sense?" Jaxon situated the ladder under a window and started tugging on the cord extending it up to the second floor. "Why would we be going in Xavier's window when I have a window of my own?"

"Oh."

"Yeah. Oh," he snapped, making sure the ladder was stable. Then he turned and started shaking his finger under Jinx's nose. "Now look. I'm going up first to make sure the thing's unlocked and to help you climb through. And I swear to God, if you make a run for it, I will track you down and take a switch to your hide."

"I'm not running," she claimed.

He grunted his lack of optimism.

True to her word, Jinx followed him up. Once he had her safely inside, he closed the window, turning to find Jinx rubbing at her arms and shifting on her bare feet. A large part of his irritation melted inside his chest. "Come here." He beckoned, indicating his double bed. "Let's get warm." He pulled back the comforter and then the blanket and sheets, stepping out of his shoes and sliding in completely clothed so Jinx would follow him. He held the covers up invitingly. She didn't give him any grief, but dove for the warmth the bed would provide. "Not the way I intended for the two of us to end up in bed together," he said as he wrapped his arms around her, pulling her close and rubbing his sock-covered feet over her bare ones. But as soon as he let his head collapse into the pillow, exhaustion overtook him. "Jinx," he said into her hair. "I'm really pissed at you. But I've been up for over twenty-four hours, moving nonstop. So if we could put a pin in this blowout we're about to have, I'd appreciate it. I just …" He yawned, closed his eyes, and was out.

Four hours later ...

Jaxon's hand somehow found the hem of that barely-there nightie Jinx was wearing between her sweatshirt and jeans. His fingers and palm caressed bare flesh sleepily, eventually causing Jinx to shift to her side—facing him—the two of them waking up snuggled together, warm and comfortable. The fight they had been leaning into was now all slept out. And *just* as Jax was about to put his lips on Jinx, all hell broke loose.

Pounding, a sharp snap, and then cool air invading the room. For one bloody moment, Jax didn't realize what was happening. And then ...

"Oh, hell no," Vance's voice shouted as he sprung himself through the window and did a super-hero roll across the floor, landing in a wrestling stance. Pinks popped his head through next, took one look at him and Jinx in the bed, rolled his neck, and said, "Told ya."

"This is not happening," Vance seethed, standing upright and tossing a thumb over his shoulder. "Jinx. Out of that bed. Now."

Jinx giggled.

"I'm serious," Vance insisted. "Get up and get out of the way so I can kick Jaxon's ass."

"What?" Jinx said, starting to laugh harder. Apparently, she found this situation funny.

Jaxon wasn't finding Vance Evans cock blocking him in his own bedroom amusing at all. He tossed off the covers and literally stood up, stepped over Jinx and on to the floor, and then got right in the damn guy's face. "You climb uninvited into a man's bedroom and threaten him? That's home invasion. Mayor Bennett's not going to appreciate his right-hand man being held in county jail on criminal charges."

Vance bumped Jaxon's chest with his own. "Like you've got the balls for that. And you're damn lucky the two of you are fully dressed, or I'd totally be busting some whoop over your ass." He looked around Jax. "Come on, Jinx. I'm taking you home."

Jaxon stepped forward, backing Vance up. "Quit the big-brother act, you douchebag. Jinx is here of her own free will. You're not taking her anywhere. I'll bring her back to your place when we've finished our discussion."

"Is that what you kids are calling it these days? A discussion? You've got her trapped in your goddamn bed."

"Fully clothed," Jax shouted, just as his door burst open, and Xavier stumbled into the room wearing a pair of boxers and wielding a golf club.

"What the hell is going on here?" he bellowed.

Behind him, Laidey rushed in, tugging on the ends of an enormous sweatshirt that hung past her knees. Her hair was a bedroom mess, and it was wildly apparent she had little or nothing on underneath that thing. While all the men stopped to stare, Laidey glanced at the bed and said, "Jinx!" She headed straight toward her, where the two of them embraced. "Are you okay?"

"She's *fine*," Jaxon said on an exasperated whine. "Now, please. All of you. Get out!"

Meanwhile, Pinks—whose head was still sticking through the open window—exchanged a wave with Laidey and then began to climb in.

"Jinx, come on," Vance insisted as he stalked around Jaxon. "You come on home with me now. Jax, you can come over later and conduct your *discussion* in the study, with the door open, in full view of the Evans clan."

"Are you serious right now?" Jaxon shouted.

Vance whirled on him, "You do not get to steal a member of my family in the middle of the night and get away with it."

"You stole her?" Xavier asked in awe, a giddy grin on his face. "Awesome, dude." The brothers fist bumped.

What is *wrong* with you," Vance shouted at Xavier. "Jinx is my *sister*. Not some random chick he can go stealing out of her bedroom."

"I didn't *steal* her," Jax insisted.

"Really? Really Jax? Because the front security video shows otherwise," Vance taunted. "It shows you climbing into the window—uninvited—and then *shoving* Jinx out of the window, where she almost fell to her death."

"I didn't shove her," Jax defended. "I would never have shoved her."

"Save it. Or my good friend Mayor Bennett will have the evidence of you not shoving her on his desk before the end of the day."

"Don't worry," Xavier told Jax while rubbing his fist. "I can take Brooks."

Vance pushed Xavier's shoulder. "We've got a truce, remember? Laidey is not going to like you starting that shit up again."

"Did you just shove me?" Xavier was incredulous. "Evans, do you have a death wish?" Now it was Xavier and Vance bumping chests.

"Ladies," Pinks called from the bedroom door. "Shall we leave the Neanderthals to their mating dance? I smell coffee."

"Coffee," Jinx squealed as she hopped out of bed, grabbed Laidey's hand, and rushed after Pinks. "Xavier, when you're done, will you make bacon?" she pleaded. "They don't do bacon over at the Evans's."

"We do so do bacon," Vance shouted after her.

"Do you?" Xavier questioned. "Do you do bacon over at that mansion?"

"Oh my God." Vance was stunned as he realized the truth. "We *don't* do bacon. I haven't had bacon in months."

"Probably why you're always so damn cranky. Come on, then. Let's get you some bacon." Xavier patted Vance's shoulder and led the way out of the room.

Vance turned his attention to Jaxon, who simply shrugged. "Hard to keep fighting once somebody brings up bacon. After you," Jax said.

CHAPTER FORTY-THREE

Jinx and Jax finally did have their discussion. Not in front of the Evans clan as Vance had insisted, but right there in the Wrights' kitchen surrounded by … everyone.

McKenna was the acting barista whose coffee aroma had lured everyone out of Jaxon's room. She was wearing a man's pajama top over bare legs and a pair of men's athletic socks slouched down around her ankles. Xander sported a T-shirt and matching pajama bottoms while lounging with his feet up at the kitchen table. Although it was a Monday morning, he appeared in no hurry to get back to Charlotte and his job. Jinx hoped that boded well for McKenna.

"Well, hello," he said, straightening as he took in the line of non-family members strolling into his kitchen. Although Pinks was completely dressed, Jinx and Laidey sported freshly-rolled-out-of-bed hair and dubious attire. "Was there a slumber party I didn't know about?" Xander asked.

"I just arrived." Pinks headed directly toward McKenna and said, "Keep the coffee coming, there are more on the way."

She gave him a mug and a smile. "Fancy meeting you here."

He looked over her attire. "I could say the same, except at this point, nothing I find in this house will surprise me." He bobbed his head toward Laidey and Jinx and then went to take a seat at the table.

"Oh, Christ," Xavier exclaimed when he stepped into the kitchen wearing sweat pants and a pullover. "You two? Again?" he asked Xander.

"This *is* my home too," Xander responded. "Notwithstanding the fact you refused to let me stay in my own room."

"Can't you stay at her place?" He shoved a thumb over his shoulder at McKenna. "It's bad enough you're dating my ex. You gotta keep rubbing my nose in it?"

Jinx noticed how McKenna and Laidey rolled their eyes at one another. Apparently, Xavier had tried to pull this before.

"You want her back?" Xander offered, which caused McKenna to draw in a deep breath and turn to Xander.

"What?" she snapped.

"Kidding, kidding," Xander soothed.

"No, I don't want her back." Xavier's horrified expression upset McKenna even more. "I want *you* to take *her* far, far away from here. Do you know she eats breakfast in this house more often than I do?"

"That's because she makes the best coffee," Jaxon said as he entered the kitchen with a grim face and Vance Evans right on his heels. "What's breakfast without good coffee? Or bacon?" he asked Xavier. "So quit bitchin' about your twin dating your ex and start cooking, will you? This guy"—he shoved a thumb over his shoulder at Vance—"needs bacon, and I need him off my back."

Xander stood and greeted Vance like they were long-lost buddies. "Good to see you, man," Xander said.

"You too. When ya moving back?"

Jinx had to grin at that. Vance didn't leave the business of Henderson alone for long.

"In due time," Xander said good-naturedly. He pushed out a chair, indicating Vance should sit. With one quick look in Jinx's direction, Vance did just that, getting into a conversation with Xander while Xavier shouted orders. "Laidey, you're on the toaster. We need English muffins for everyone. McKenna, after you start another pot of coffee, butter the toasted muffins and keep them warm in the oven. Jax, you're on bacon duty. Use two pans, we're gonna need a bunch. Prom Queen, good to have you back. You're with me learning to cook eggs for a crowd. Now, grate this cheese," he said, reaching around Jax into the refrigerator and handing her some fancy cheddar. "Then slice these thin"—he handed her stalks of green onions—"and then crack all of these"—he handed her two cartons of eggs—"into a bowl I'll get you in a minute. I'm going to go make sure Ma's up. She's going to want to be a part of this."

He left the kitchen, and Jinx stood there blinking at the ingredients in front of her. Pinks pierced the air with a whistle. "Jaxon," he said, snapping his fingers at Jinx. "Your girlfriend seems overwhelmed." Pinks stood and walked over to the stove and took his place. "I've got the bacon, you help Jinx."

Jinx turned a grateful look to Pinks, and then a sheepish, please-help-me-before-Xavier-gets-back grin to Jaxon. He chuckled, moved in, and kissed her on her forehead.

Her ... *forehead.* WTF?

She turned toward her tasks, mumbling over her shoulder, "You gonna let my recently-acknowledge big brother boss you around?"

"No," Jaxon said, leaning in and helping her peel the white paper from the cheese. "But I wasn't sure tossing his ass back out the window would endear me to you."

She let out a brief laugh. "You just kissed me on my forehead, like I'm *your* sister." She felt him go stiff. Suddenly, she was whirled around and drawn up into his arms. Her hands landed on his chest, her mouth open in surprise, her eyes taking in the white-hot intent in his ice-blue irises.

"I kissed you on the forehead because I didn't know where we stood. Not because of some overbearing big brother." He tucked an arm lower on her back and pulled her up against him, up on her tiptoes, laying a kiss on her like she'd never experienced. It was determined and demanding, and it wasn't missed by anyone in the kitchen because whistles, catcalls, and Vance's protests rang out. But Jaxon wasn't listening, or maybe he just didn't care. He went right on kissing her, and that made her smile against his lips.

He smiled back. "Not afraid of Vance Evans or either of your fathers. Just afraid of you blocking my number. Can we get that settled?" he asked, setting her back to the floor but not releasing her. "That was complete bullshit," he scolded.

"I thought you gave my hair samples to Hale," she argued.

"I did. I did give your hair to Mr. Evans. Why wouldn't I?" he argued back, all eyes in the kitchen fixed on the two of them. "You told me you were lonely. That your family didn't pay attention to you. *You* told me on the night we met that you were looking for a new place to call home. I didn't give Mr. Evans those hairs for him, Jinx. I did that for you."

"What?"

"I did it for you. Because maybe you had more family than you were aware of. And maybe they'd be better *to* you. And because even back then, I wanted Henderson to be your new home. I did it for you, Jinx. Just in case you needed options."

She nodded. Understanding. Only … "You could have told me."

"Really?" Jaxon stepped back. "You just met me, and I should have said, 'Jinx, you look a lot like the richest guy in town. How would you feel about a paternity test to find out?' You would have thought I was out of my mind and run screaming in the opposite direction. Besides, this was between you and Mr. Evans."

"And me," Vance interjected.

That's when the both of them remembered they had an audience. A rather large audience. Jax turned his attention back to Jinx. "I couldn't be the one to tell you, Jinx. Not about my suspicions. Not that first day. But after I found your hair in my watch, and with Mr. Evans so distraught—"

"Wait. My hair was in your watch?"

"Yeah. I guess it got caught when I was"—he glanced briefly at Vance—"kissing you good night."

"Oh." Jinx looked to the floor and shook her head. "So, you didn't, like, pull them out?"

"Why would I pull out your hair?"

"For Hale. For a DNA test."

"No," he said, shaking his head. "Jinx." He stooped down and held her by her forearms, searching her eyes. "Did you think I'd taken you hair premeditatedly? No. No, no, no. In fact, once I realized I had your hair, I thought long and hard about giving it to Mr. Evans. But in the end, what I told you is the truth. If you weren't happy with the family you'd been dealt, I wanted to see if maybe you had another option. I did it for you. I promise."

Vance made a noise like Jaxon was telling one tall tale. But Jinx saw the truth in his eyes, along with how much they belonged together. Jax had seen it from the moment they met.

"I'm glad you did it," she told him. "Now. Now that the shock is behind me, and now that I understand your motivation, even if somebody"—she threw a glare at Vance—"has a problem with it. He's stuck with me. Henderson's stuck with me. And Jax, you're kinda stuck with me too."

Jax sighed. Heavily. It wasn't until she grinned that he followed suit.

"So the prom queen falls for the grease monkey," Xavier's loud voice boomed around the kitchen. "Seen that one a dozen times. You two, back to work," he ordered as Pinks grinned over the two iron skillets of bacon, McKenna and Laidey beamed at one another, and Vance accepted a high-five from Xander.

"We may be family someday," he said to Vance.

Vance nodded and then sipped his coffee, catching Jinx staring over at him.

He winked.

CHAPTER FORTY-FOUR

Over the next two months, Jinx came to a meeting of minds with most of the important people in her life.

Unused to the hover of friends and family, she moved into Brenda and Billy's B&B the week she started her job at the library. She still attended dinners at the Evanses' regularly, only missing their comedic antics for a date with Jaxon, or dinner with the entire Wright family, which curiously included McKenna more often than not. She'd wanted her own space once she started her job, once she and Vance finally sat down to iron out her contract and, more importantly, how the two of them would handle their mother—who they agreed to call Catherine—as they moved forward as siblings.

Vance wanted nothing to do with the woman. He didn't want to see her. He didn't want her coming to Henderson to visit Jinx, which—when mentioned—immediately caused Jinx to belly laugh. The thought of her mother bothering to visit was absurd. But there was just no way she could convince Vance.

"And what if your father wants to visit?" he asked.

"He will," Jinx insisted. "And he'll want to meet you," she said, freaking Vance out, by the look on his face. "He's scared I'm going to cut him out of my life. And where I've definitely considered doing that to my mother, my dad doesn't deserve that, and I want to stay close to my sister Lisette too. Even Andre. If I was the catalyst for their true love, so be it. I've found Jax. I can let that go."

"I was about to say your family is as screwed up as mine"—Vance said on a laugh—"but your family *is* my family. Ahhh, Jinx," he sighed. "We are in this together. For better or worse."

"For better," she told him. "Things for me are getting so much better."

"Me too," he'd said. "Just keep Catherine out of my way, and I'll be fine."

They agreed.

After only two weeks on the job, and when Catherine Davenport had finally had the courage to show her face back in the good ol' U. S. of A, Jinx took time off and headed home to Richmond to give her mother a chance to tell her side of the story.

That had not gone as well as Jinx had hoped.

Her mother insisted her father sit with them while Jinx's paternity was discussed. She claimed she didn't want any more secrets between the three of them, but Jinx knew she was using her poor father as a shield. Jinx respected the man too much to ask the probing, personal questions she wanted answers to about her mother's relationship with Mr. Evans—Hale—while he was in the room. And whenever Jinx cornered her mother in the house alone, she feigned a migraine or told her to wait for her father to get home and then they'd discuss it.

"I don't want to discuss this in front of Daddy. I want to know about your relationship with Hale Evans."

"What!" Her mother spun, lashing out at Jinx. "What do you need to know?" The harshness of her mother's fury set Jinx back on her heels. And in that moment, being the recipient of that cold look on her mother's face, she had her answers. All of them.

She'd texted Vance that very night.

Our parents were mismatched from the beginning. Genevra's a much better fit for Hale. Catherine will never seek you out. And I hope that brings you peace instead of heartache. She isn't good enough for you. For either of us. But she gave us life and each other. Now that I know the truth, I've decided that's enough for me. I hope it's enough for you.

Jinx never got a response to that text. Yet when she made her way back to Henderson, leading a U-Haul truck driven by her father, Vance showed up with Pinks, Jaxon, and Xavier to help them unload it into her tiny, two-bedroom cottage rental. She watched, surprised as Vance graciously shook Daniel Davenport's hand as he introduced himself to her father. She felt a squeeze in her heart as her father accepted and choked up over the greeting.

That was big. For two of the key men in her life.

Now she wanted a Come-to-Jesus moment with the number-one man in her life. *Jaxon.*

Because where she had squared things up with everyone in the Evans family, from Hale down to Beau-Brody, and she and McKenna were as close as friends could get, and as much as she enjoyed his mother and father and crazy band of brothers, Jaxon Wright was holding out on her, and she needed to know why.

Why?

Why had the man of her dreams—the tall, Southern good ol' boy who spiked her pulse every time she saw him—not taken their relationship to the next level?

She didn't know how to go about asking him this. Her sexual experience was limited to one man. One 'meh' of a man. And now she was the recipient of breath-stealing looks, frantically arousing kisses, and exquisitely provocative touches from a *man* among men.

True, Jaxon hadn't been in town all that much, chasing his dream of tweaking NASCAR engines and such. In fact, he'd had to quit his job, leaving Xavier to find new grunt workers for his construction projects. Jaxon's star was rising in the racing world. The occasional week he wasn't hired to consult on race preparations, he made a point to be at the track, giving out cards, promoting his new business. If he wasn't being paid to stay, he'd be back in Henderson by the weekend, and every night he was in town, the two of them were together.

The third time Jaxon walked Jinx to the door of her cozy, little bungalow, she offered him the opportunity to come inside for a brandy. But he only smiled, kissed her like he meant it, and turned, leaving her longing for more.

That first time he'd done it was kinda cute.

The second time was a bit frustrating.

The third time—infuriating.

On top of that, when he was out of town and busy working a job—he was *busy* working a job. If she got one text from him during the day while he took his lunch break and a good night call before she went to bed, she was lucky.

Jinx understood hard work. Even appreciated it. In fact, she was working nights and overtime at the library, trying to clear the clutter of a mess that had accumulated during the three months Vance had stopped the hiring process and apparently refused to acknowledge the library at all. With the hiring up in the air, no forward progress had been made, and all kinds of issues piled up. It was good Jaxon was out of town most weeks, Jinx decided. It gave her a chance to focus on her passion. Indulge her drive.

Only now, what she was feeling passionate about was Jaxon Wright, and he was not indulging her drive. At. All.

This had to end.

Didn't it?

The man was not opposed to heavy petting. Last Saturday night, after getting all hot and bothered on the dance floor, he'd dragged her out of the back of The Situation and pushed her up against the wall and practically had his way with her before they heard the back door open and Vance's voice yelling for Pinks. That broke them apart fast. In fact, it had them running to Jaxon's godawful truck, she giggling the whole way and he trying to shush her up.

The weekend before that, they'd wrapped up in coats and blankets and headed out for an evening cruise on the boat. Things were getting hot. Jaxon had her coat and sweater off, his long body stretched out over hers on the backseat, the two of them underneath a blanket. She thought that was going to be their night because his hand had skirted under her bra just as they heard a lively *toot* echo not far from where they were moored. Turned out it was Brooks and Lolly cruising up on them with Piper and Vance. Even Vance, Jr. was there, all tucked into his baby seat, sleeping away.

That night turned out all right though. They had quite the party with the two boats tied up together. She was learning that wherever Piper was, there was also plenty of food.

Then came that one night Jax seemed determined to make her his. Dragging her from his truck after a serious kissing session they went around to the back of his parents' house, only to find the ladder that had always been lodged under someone's window nowhere to be found. When she suggested they just use a door to get to his room, he grimaced. Inside, they found Red and Pinks, Laidey and Xavier, and Piper and Vance playing charades. Jinx happily jumped into the game, only to watch Jaxon sulk, not helping the boys' team at all.

When the game ended and she tried to head upstairs, he took her hand, led her out the door, and drove her home.

The mystery grated because Jaxon had a very healthy, robust libido. In fact, at times, it was barely contained in public. But then they'd get to her front door and ... zilch.

Her front door.

Her front door?

Stepping out onto her front stoop, Jinx looked around. There was the cute little rocking chair she'd placed to the right of the door, one she'd never actually sat in because who wants to rock alone? Now that she was becoming part of a community, she found she'd much rather be rocking over at Billy and Brenda's where she could hear the latest gossip and check out their weekend guests. Or she'd rather be sitting on a tall stool at the head of Hale's kitchen, getting to know her new family better. Or find a seat at the Wrights' house. Anywhere in the Wrights' house. But her lonely, little porch only had room for one rocking chair. Just looking at the thing now made her feel sad and lonely. She threw her head back in exasperation—because *seriously? This again?*—and caught a glimpse of ... of ... what is that?

Is that a ... security camera?

What would a ...? And then it dawned on her. *Vance.* He'd had that camera installed. After she moved in, he'd sent a crew of electricians over to fix her outdoor lighting and add solar lamps to her front walk. They even lit up the shrubbery and her one tree. It transformed the exterior, making the little bungalow look homey and inviting when she arrived after dark. Like it was waiting for her with open arms.

Only ... why would Vance ...

Her mind recalled Vance's voice echoing from the back door of The Situation.

Vance and his gang showing up on their boat. In the dark.

Vance at the Wrights' playing charades.

Vance sending a crew of electricians.

Maybe Jaxon wasn't the one she needed to talk to after all. Maybe the culprit behind her ever-growing frustration was her newly acquired, overbearing brother.

The perfect retaliation landed in Jinx's hands on a Friday night. Pinks had called and invited her and Jaxon over to enjoy the hot tub with him and Scarlett. She accepted immediately and asked if Vance was going to be there. Pinks gave her a much too drawn out, "Ahhhh," before she told him it didn't matter.

It did.

It would.

She'd see to it.

When she called Jaxon to tell him they'd been invited to a hot tub party at the Evans's he didn't sound thrilled. Which was interesting, since she recalled he'd insisted McKenna buy her a bikini for that specific occasion when she'd first come back to town.

"Are you worried about Vance?" she asked Jaxon over the phone.

"In what way?" he responded cagily.

"You know he's fine with you and me dating, right? That issue has been put to bed." *Unlike* she and Jaxon.

"Webster, you're showing your naiveté if you think Vance is okay with the two of us dating. He is tolerating me. Barely."

"But why?"

"You're his sister."

"Not really. I mean, I am, but it's not like we grew up together. He can't feel that protective of me, trying to scare my boyfriend away."

"Trust me, he can. He tried to scare me away when you were merely his top candidate for the library job. Of course, he's gonna look out for you now."

"Look out for me, yes. Threaten you, no."

"He hasn't threatened me. Much."

"Oh … my … Lord! He's actually threatened you?"

"Not in so many words."

"How many words? What were the words?"

"Jinx, I'm handling it, okay? Vance just needs to get used to seeing us together. He needs to realize I'm for real with you. That I'm not going anywhere."

"Tell him that."

"I did. He doesn't believe me. Apparently, Lolly told him some story about me being a serial dater in high school, so he's put the worst spin on that and decided I'm just like he used to be."

Jinx's curiosity was piqued. "How bad did Vance used to be?"

"When it came to women?" Jax blew out a low whistle. "He's a legend."

"Are you a legend?" Jinx held her breath. She didn't want Jaxon to be a legend.

"No, Jinx. I'm no legend."

"Is that why Vance keeps showing up on our dates at the most inopportune moments?"

"Probably."

"Do you know there is a security camera directed at my front door?"

"Yep."

"Is that why you've never come inside?"

"Yep."

"So that's why you usually kiss me in the truck first. Before you walk me to the door?"

"Pretty much."

"Why? Vance can't possibly be sitting at home monitoring that camera?"

"I wouldn't put it past him having it broadcast directly to his cellphone."

"*Grrrr.* Jaxon! Are you going to let Vance run your life?"

"That depends, Rapunzel."

"On what?"

"Are you going to let him run yours?"

CHAPTER FORTY-FIVE

Jinx found herself in Piper's kitchen. Well, technically, it was Genevra and Hale's kitchen, but Piper ran it.

Hmm. Perhaps Piper wasn't the best one to talk to about Vance's control issues. Jinx shrugged that thought off and got down to spilling the reason she was here.

"Jaxon thinks Vance is running my life."

Piper stopped rolling out dough and looked up with a smile. "He runs everyone's life. Welcome to the club."

Jinx blinked. That wasn't the answer she'd expected to hear. "But how? And why? You let him run your life?"

"Let him?" Piper shrugged. "I wouldn't say I let him. But I understand his need for control, and I have found ways to diffuse it."

"His control?"

"Yes."

"What ways?"

Piper smiled and went back to her rolling. "I give him what he wants most of the time. Which is pretty easy, because generally we want the same thing. But if I want something, like my Big Pie Plate Shop, I sit him down and tell him calmly what I want and why I want it. He will then rant a bit because he's afraid of what he doesn't want and needs to work it out in his head."

"What doesn't he want?"

"For the people he loves to leave him."

Oh.

Piper nodded. "Yeah. To this day, your mother is under every inch of his skin." She moved toward the back of the kitchen, opening up a bowl of some creamy and delicious-looking filling. "So tell me, beloved-sister-in-law, what is it *you* want?"

Jinx cleared her throat and checked the area for others before she stated, "I want to have sex with Jaxon."

Piper broke out with a short laugh. "I'll bet."

"But I think Vance has threatened him."

"I'd be surprised if he hasn't."

"What? Why?"

"He's protective. You're important to him, new to town, and who else is going to warn guys off? I'm guessing he's taking the job very seriously."

"But I don't want him warning guys off. I mean, Jaxon. I don't want him warning Jaxon off. I *like* Jaxon."

"Nothing not to like about Jaxon."

"Right?"

Jinx and her new sister-in-law shared a smile. Piper nodded. "Vance treats his personal relationships like they're his job. Vance, Jr. and Beau are the same age, yet Vance has a completely different relationship with each of them. He's Vance, Jr.'s father and he's Beau's big brother. Even though they are babies, he talks to them differently, he handles them differently. Now you've come along. You're not only his sister, but you're a woman and a business associate. He's probably having trouble holding all that in his brain."

"What do you mean? He's brilliant."

"His emotional IQ is less than stellar. He can only relate to someone as one thing. He's focused on you being his sister. That's how he's chosen to relate to you. Which is a double-edged sword."

"In what way?'

"He'll love you unconditionally and then drive you crazy trying to prove that."

Jinx smiled. "Okay. I understand. I'll do my best to handle it."

"Vance is a handful. But Jaxon doesn't come across as the kind of guy who'd be easily intimidated. I mean, he had the guts to steal you out of a bedroom window because you blocked his number. After he survived that, he's sure to know Vance isn't going to come after him with a gun."

Jinx let Piper's words register and found truth in them. Maybe Vance's intimidation tactics weren't to blame for Jaxon's lack of enthusiasm. Maybe there was something else keeping the two of them apart.

"I had a plan," she confessed to Piper. "We've been invited to your hot tub tonight. I was going to make it uncomfortable for Vance by being overly touchy-feely with Jaxon while wearing a bikini. But that no longer feels like the right way to go. Not very helpful, pushing Vance's buttons like that. And it just might make Jax more uncomfortable." She sighed. "I don't know what to do."

"Talk to Jax. Honestly."

"About sex?"

"Yes, about sex. How else are you going to figure out what's going on?"

"I don't know," she wailed hiding her face in her hands. "Did you know on our first date, I thought Em had sent Jaxon to seduce me? So she could cross my name off the list for the library job citing a lack of moral character?"

"Maybe that's your answer."

"What?"

"Seduce Jaxon."

"Vance has a camera watching my front door. Jax is afraid to be caught going inside."

"Simple," Piper said. "Use the back door."

CHAPTER FORTY-SIX

When Jaxon walked up the front walk to pick Jinx up for their date, his guard was up. Way up. Without a doubt, he anticipated that Vance would show up just as Jinx's lush floral scent, her sexy-as-hell smile, and her slinky, little figure wrapped him up in another one of her spells to soften his defenses while doing the exact opposite to his cock.

Because that's how their dates usually went.

And as exasperated with Vance as his unrequited body was, truth be told, in a lot of ways Vance had been doing him a favor. Because if he and Jinx took it to the next level—if he got a feel for the inside of that warm, sweet woman—*and then* she realized the two of them didn't measure up in the smarts department, he might not survive it. It wasn't a bad idea for Jinx to get to know him—really know him—before the two of them became that kind of intimate.

Because he may *want* Jinx, and he may even *need* her brand of childlike curiosity and pie-in-the-sky optimism in his world, but from what he'd seen over the last couple of months, Jinx Davenport did not need him at all.

She'd already proven she could do just fine on her own, and now that she was living in Henderson, she had a whole new family to feel a part of and to lean on in troubling times. Whatever Jax had once brought to the table was now overshadowed by a whole lot of Evanses. It wasn't going to be long before she realized that she could do better than a guy who was good with his hands.

Still a glutton for punishment he wasn't willing to walk away. Jinx was turning out to be so much more than her pretty face and lonely heart. She was vivacious, especially when she spoke about the library and most things Henderson. She was kind, especially to his mother and pseudo-sister McKenna. And boy, did she have fortitude while facing off with a pack of snarling, snipping, older librarians struggling to accept change. She gifted them with compassion, perspective, and most of all patience while keeping a tight hold on her own enthusiasm, lest it gallop over their resistance.

Yeah, he'd fallen for Jinx fast and hard. But now that he'd witnessed what her heart offered the world, he also understood just how much he stood to lose. He'd felt himself holding back. Hoping that if Jinx were going to come to her senses, it would happen sooner rather than later. But every time he picked her up for a date, the gravel shifted beneath his feet, because the woman was hell-bent on making herself a full-fledged seductress.

She'd gone from expensive working-girl slacks and blouses to silky tops and painted-on jeans. The last time she'd opened her door, she struck a pin-up pose wearing a skin-tight dress and killer red heels, her hair all curled and loose. He wasn't an idiot. He knew women well enough to know when one was trying to seduce him. And back when they first met, that had been *his* MO. But now that his heart was fully invested, he knew if his body got one good fix of Jinx Davenport, he'd be irrevocably addicted. No other woman would do.

So he girded his loins, expecting Jinx to greet him in nothing but that bikini McKenna had purchased months ago. The one he'd fantasized stripping her out of too many times. Worried about keeping his hands to himself, he tucked them into the back pockets of his athletic pants while waiting for her to open the door.

What greeted him was less sultry temptress and more breath of fresh air. Her Rapunzel braid was back in place, her sweatshirt and jeans making him smile.

"I've packed a bag with towels, wine, and a few snacks," she said by way of greeting. "Pinks said not to bring anything, but I've never been to a hot-tub party, and I got excited."

"I'm sure everything will come in handy," he assured her, taking the bag. And being a lovesick sap, he leaned in for a kiss because her pretty pink lips were coated in that shimmery gloss he liked to feel on his mouth. On his cheek. Anywhere she kissed him. It was evidence of her attraction to him, and he couldn't get enough of it.

"Vance will probably make an appearance," she hedged.

"My expectations have been managed."

"You know he's just looking out for me, right?"

"As he should."

She cocked her hip and shot him a saucy look under half-closed eyes. "Are you planning to break my heart?"

Break *her* heart? He was stunned. "God, no," he swore without thinking. "Jinx. Never." The way he said it, the way he felt it, he knew he'd never spoken truer words. And somehow, saying them aloud freed him up, knowing he was fully committed to Jinx Davenport. Whether this ended tonight or sixty years from now, the hurt was gonna hurt but he had no control over loving Jinx.

He just did.

He always would.

And now—he decided—he'd better man-the-hell-up and do it right.

"Because I think I may be in love with you," she told him, bold as ever.

"Is that so?" he said, stepping in, moving her back into her little house, security camera be damned. He let the door slam shut behind him. "A smart girl like you, falling for a grease monkey like me? Vegas has odds against us."

"How could that possibly be?" Her hand landed on his neck, her eyes—the color of spring—laughing at him. "I took one look at you wearing your hat backward and dropped my heart at your feet. You are the finest man I've ever seen."

"Looks are fleeting."

"Not when I can see clear through to your heart. Your character. Your brilliant mind."

Jaxon huffed. "I'm not brilliant, Webster. Not by a long shot."

"You are to me," Jinx insisted. "You talked me into staying. You knew Vance would come around, thought I should give Hale a chance. You *educated* me on how to negotiate family dynamics and held my hand, being my strength, as I've figured it out. But mostly you cared about me enough to want more for me than what I came to town with."

"I didn't want you to be lonely anymore."

"I don't want to be lonely either."

"And you won't be. Not if I have anything to say about it."

She nuzzled into him, her smiling lips pressed up against his chin. "What exactly do you have to say about it?"

"That I'm yours, and you're mine," he said pulling her in against him, kissing her lips. "And if you're game, I'm ready for us to start forming a long-term plan."

"I'd like that."

"Yeah?" He grinned, pulling back so he could see her eyes. "You know if I'm showing up at the library, it's going to be to see you, right? Not to check out a book or study up on somethin'."

"You want to study up on somethin', I'll bring the books home to you."

Jax laughed. "Deal." Then he licked his lips. "I've never considered myself all that intelligent," he confessed. "But I gotta be smarter than I look if I've got a genius, feisty librarian wanting to be mine."

"Jaxon," she breathed, pulling herself up against his chest and holding on tight. "You are my *everything*. Thank you."

He rubbed her back and tucked his nose into her neck, as he teared up. "No, sweet Rapunzel. Thank *you*."

CHAPTER FORTY-SEVEN

As anticipated, Vance and Piper showed up while Jaxon and Jinx were submerged to their chests, enjoying good music, chilled wine, and a whole lot of Pinks versus Red smack talk. The man everyone called Pinks had his hands so full Jaxon felt a little sorry for him. Scarlett Langford was a fierce, headstrong woman who had more ideas than Jax could hold in his brain at one time.

Ideas for Henderson.

Ideas for her new business venture, which Jaxon became confused over, unsure whether it was a wine shop, a restaurant, or a recording label.

"All three," Pinks told him doggedly. "*All. Three.*"

"What?" Scarlett snapped. "It's not like you aren't building an entire academy, a full-fledged stadium, and Lord knows how many athletic fields. Not to mention building Vance's house for him."

"He's not physically building my house brick by brick, Scarlett." Vance said, not only easing himself into the heat of the water but blatantly inserting himself between Jaxon and Jinx. "He's just overseeing the job."

"Just like he does *everything* for you," Scarlett scolded.

"Exactly like he does everything for me," Vance confirmed. "How else would I run my life without actually being present?" Vance's attention immediately shifted to his wife, who had taken off her robe and laid it on a lounge chair. "What the hell?"

The curly-haired blonde's tiny body was outlandishly shown off in a scanty yellow bikini. The top barely covered her full, round breasts, and as she tiptoed to the edge of the pool, it was clear there wasn't much covering her derrière either. Vance dragged a wet hand down his face and grimaced. "Darlin'," he tried to whisper to her. "I thought we discussed that particular suit was not suitable for public display."

"I know." Piper's blue eyes glistened as she daintily stepped into the hot tub, clasping Pink's hand for stability.

"Then *why* are you wearing it?" Vance growled.

"To give you something better to focus on than how much you want to keep Jaxon away from Jinx."

"Jinx is a grown woman. She can date whomever she wants."

"Is that so?" Piper questioned. "Jaxon has your blessing to pursue your sister?"

"Of course, he does," Vance barked.

"I do?" Jaxon inquired, stunned.

"Not really, no," Vance told him. "But this isn't about you, Casanova. Pipes, get the hell out of this pool and go put on that one piece I bought you for these sort of occasions."

"These occasions?" she wondered.

"Occasions where other men are present."

"No."

Vance's brows drew up into his hairline. "No?"

"Yes. No." Piper smiled cheerily. Then she looked at Pinks. "Would you mind pouring me some wine?"

"Absolutl—"

"Do not. Give that woman. A drink," Vance ordered.

Pink's hands stilled on the bottle and a wine glass.

"Not until she changes her bathing suit."

"I'm not changing my suit," Piper said with a wily grin.

"I know what you're trying to do," Vance said as he stood up and headed across the small pool toward Piper.

"What am I trying to do?" she teased.

"You're trying to get a rise out of me."

"Why would I want to do that?"

"So I'll drag you out of this pool, throw you over my shoulder, and carry you back into the house."

"Don't be ridiculous," she scoffed. But her blue eyes were all kinds of playful.

"Everybody, I'm sorry, but Piper and I've got to cut the party short."

"Don't let the screen door hit ya," Jaxon said.

"And you." Vance turned on Jax. Then he eyed Jinx. "Behave," he ordered. "Both of you."

Piper stood up in the water, hands on hips and did a little shimmy.

Vance pointed at his wife. "You are so playin' with fire." He lunged for her. She squealed and scrambled out of the pool. Vance was fast on her heels, wrapping her up in his arms and doing exactly what he said he was going to do. He tossed her over his shoulder and swatted her ass.

"Night y'all," he said as he started toward the house.

Chuckles floated after them.

"She did that for us, you know," Jinx told Jaxon.

He nodded. "I'll swing by and have a talk with Vance tomorrow. A serious conversation so he can stop worrying about you."

She leaned in and kissed his lips. "He'd probably like that."

As the evening wore on, Jaxon's heart grew lighter. Henderson had managed to recapture him, something he hadn't seen coming. His old hometown had brought him a new friend in Pinks (and hopefully, eventually Vance) and a girl so perfect he still didn't know how he'd found her. But here she was, jumping into Henderson's dream. He wasn't exactly sure how he was going to contribute, but contribute he would. Because now he had his own Henderson dream. And as he looked into Jinx's emerald eyes and laughed along with her, he knew it was starting to come true.

CHAPTER FORTY-EIGHT

Jinx didn't know if she'd ever been so happy. Jaxon Wright with his shirt off, his chest all wet and sexy, was a lot for her senses to take in. Mini-tingles like bubbles of champagne drifted throughout her brain making her giddy over the physical yumminess she beheld. She was probably embarrassing herself the way she drooled over his chest all night.

Fortunately, Scarlett and Pinks were kind enough not to mention it. They simply continued to provide ongoing entertainment.

When Jinx announced this was her first ever double date, they all high-fived and declared there would be many more.

She liked Scarlett.

She liked Pinks.

But she *loved* Jaxon.

And Jaxon was finally starting to put some love on her.

It started with little touches. His finger rubbing against her thigh, hidden underneath the bubbling water and steam. He moved in closer by increments, his arm ending up behind her on the pool ledge. He'd tuck his nose into her hair every now and again. Whisper in her ear. Nothing he hadn't necessarily done before, but this seemed different. At first sweeter. Then sultrier. Then downright sexy.

Maybe Pinks was playing the same game with Scarlett. Jinx wouldn't have been able to tell, she was so immersed in her body's response to Jaxon and the physical love notes he was writing.

When the evening ended, and the goodbyes were said, and Pinks and Scarlett walked into the pool house together, Jaxon kissed Jinx's hair and then whispered against her ear. "Invite me in for brandy tonight?"

She smiled, ducking her head, knowing they were finally going to happen.

Not wanting to appear clingy, but definitely not interested in leaving too much space between them either, Jinx moved to the center of the bench seat of Jax's ratty old truck. She was rewarded for her boldness when he tucked his arm around her and pulled her into him. He managed to drive them home one handed and then walked her right up to and inside her front door.

"I'll talk to Vance," he repeated as they entered. "Let him know that we're planning a future together."

"You think it will make him feel better about us?"

"I think it'll make him feel better about me. Whenever we've knocked heads over you, it's been all guns-a-blazin'. I'll make sure this time is different. I don't want you to worry."

"I don't want *you* to worry. Vance might be the brother I didn't know I wanted, but you're definitely the love I've always dreamed of. So ... about that brandy."

The handsome good ol' Southern boy just grinned. Grinned like he wanted to eat her up. "Or ..." he said.

"Yeah," she whispered, agreeing, her heart beating so fast it cost all her energy.

He took her by the hand and walked her slowly across her tiny family room and down the short hall to her bedroom. Jaxon halted just inside the door and wrapped his arms around Jinx, pulling her so that her back landed against his front. She looked at him over her shoulder and watched as he took in her double bed, the glaring overhead light, the small lamp sitting on the dresser.

He reached out and hit the light switch, casting them into darkness. Then he walked to the lamp and turned it on. Still not satisfied, he asked for a light-colored scarf or T-shirt. She found a silky red scarf, which he put over the lampshade, dimming the light and casting the room with a sensuous glow.

He sat on the edge of the bed and drew Jinx to him, situating her between his legs. Both of his hands came up to her face, brushing wisps of hair from her cheeks as his eyes caught hers up in his gentle, blue stare. "This is going to be our first time," he said. She bit her lip and nodded. "You nervous, Jinx Davenport?"

"A little bit. You?"

"Not at all."

"You've done this before."

"No," he whispered. "Never this."

She nodded, understanding. Agreeing.

Never this.

Her hands went to her braid and pulled at the ribbon there, tugging the strands apart, undoing her hair as Jaxon's fingers drifted to the hem of her sweatshirt and pulled it up over her head. Her skin pebbled in the chilly air, her bikini still slightly damp. He leaned in and kissed her belly button as his hands found purchase in the waistband of her jeans. She kicked off her shoes as he unfastened the button and drew down the zipper. She slid them off, shaking her feet loose of the denim, finally standing before him in the bikini McKenna had purchased at his request.

"You are beautiful," he whispered, looking his fill, letting his fingertips drift along the sides of her torso. "Will you …?"

She did. She slowly reached behind her and unhooked the back of her top, pulling that up and over her head, making a show of letting it drop to the floor. She wasn't nervous as much as crazy for the man in front of her. Eager for his touch and kiss. Humbled by the longing she discovered in his eyes.

Smoothing a hand over his jaw and using her fingernails to gently scratch through his sexy stubble, she asked, "Like what you see?"

"So much," he whispered, wrapping an arm around her and whipping her off her feet and onto the bed. She let out a whoop of surprise, landing flat on her back, her hair a tangled mess on the pillow. Jaxon leaned over her, up on all fours, looking his fill as his fingertips leisurely caressed her from collarbone to hip, circling a nipple along the way. He leaned in teasing that nipple with his tongue, glancing up, catching her watching him with fascination.

"I like being able to see you," she panted. He was so gorgeous, and what he was doing to her was thrilling.

"I like being able to lick you," he said in response. And she grinned. His tongue toyed with her nipple before he wet his lips and pulled back, sitting up to take his shirt off. "I'd like to lick you all over."

He would?

Well.

Okay then.

She nodded. Vigorously. But Jax didn't see it because he was busy loosening his sweatpants, stripping them off, along with his swim trunks, in one fell swoop, sending her heart into palpitations and her eyes bugging out of her head.

She wanted to lick him all over too.

He crawled back over her, took one look at her expression and where her focus had landed and stopped. "Jinx? This okay?"

Yeah, yeah, this is okay, she thought. This is better than okay. This … *that* is amazing.

"Jinx?"

She blinked. Rapidly. Bobbing her head in a delirious haze.

"Ah, shit," Jaxon whispered, pulling back and laying his long self against her side.

Shit? What? Jinx pulled her gaze from his beautiful erection up to his face, watching as he rubbed a hand over his mouth before he gave her a short smile. He leaned in to kiss her lips and then pulled back slightly. "There was no professor, was there?"

She shrugged.

"I mean, at least not one you … ah, got with."

She shook her head.

"All right." He held up his hand and let it fall back to slap his hip. "I gotta tell you, I'm a little relieved."

Her brows shot up.

"Yep. I think I've just saved myself jail time. Because now I don't have to beat the shit out of some asshole at the University of Richmond."

She snickered at that, her hands coming up and capturing his face. "I came to my senses about him before it got that far. I'm glad I did. He was nothing, *nothing* compared to you."

He moved back in for a kiss. "I'm glad you came to your senses too."

"But how did you know?"

"Ah, the panic in your eyes was a big clue."

"Panic?" She laughed. "That wasn't panic. That was lust."

"Lust?" His countenance brightened. Then he eyed her sideways. "You sure?"

She nodded vigorously.

His hand glided slowly up the center of her body. "I have to say, in this situation"—he rolled his weight on top of her, his face in line with her breasts—"lust is going to work a whole lot better than panic." His mouth devoured a nipple, sucking in a fair amount of boob as he kneaded her other breast.

Eager to touch him too, Jinx threaded her fingers through his golden hair, massaging his scalp, hoping she was giving him a fraction of the pleasure he was giving her.

She stroked his neck and kneaded his shoulders until his mouth sucked on her flesh in such a way that spirals of longing pinwheeled straight to her groin. And as much as she enjoyed watching Jaxon devour her, the sensations he was creating were so overwhelming her eyes drifted shut, providing less to process. Allowing her to *feel*.

His hands and mouth became bolder, his left hand tucked underneath her, scooting into the back of her bikini bottom and squeezing. Her legs scissored in need, her hips squirmed beneath his weight. "Jaxon," she whispered. And then again. Whenever she said his name, he'd say hers back. Sometimes, he used Webster, which made her smile, and Rapunzel, which made her sigh. In time, both of his hands slid to her hips while his mouth moved up to capture hers, now working at her lips and tongue as expertly as he had her breasts. She sucked his tongue into her mouth, wanting to capture the essence of Jaxon, needing a deeper connection.

Again she was rolled, this time on top of him, his arms tight around her waist as he settled her against him, his erection snuggled into her crotch. Her expression must have amused him because he chuckled softly, his eyes gentle and so full of admiration.

"Do you even know what you like, Jinx?" he asked softly, coaxing her out of her dazzled lust. "Or how you like it?"

"I honestly have no idea. But I've just compiled a list a mile long of things I can't wait for you to do again."

"Again?"

"Yes," she replied with exuberance. "Again."

"Again is a wonderful word, Webster." He kissed her. "Again and again." He kissed her. "And again. What about condoms?"

She cringed. "God, no. I mean … unless we need them."

Jax tilted his head and shot her a squinty-eyed glare.

"I'm on the pill."

"Ahhh," he said, smiling like he'd just won himself a prize. "Rapunzel might have been stuck in a library, but her research has paid off."

"Better than all your bragging about how good you are with your hands?"

"Bragging? Bragging? Them's fightin' words," he told her as he used those strong, wonderful hands of his to cup her ass. He ground his erection up against her, growling. Then he rolled them, landing her on her back and dragging her toward the end of the bed. She was getting the idea that making love with Jaxon Wright was an athletic event sporadically incorporated into his hot, steamy sweet.

Bikini bottoms were whisked down her hips, pushed below her knees, and hauled off just before Jaxon's nose landed at the place where everything had spiraled tight. The two of them groaned together.

"Jaxon," she breathed, raising her hips, nudging his nose with her … her—

"Sweet altar of Venus," he whispered.

Beautiful words, she thought.

Then there were ticklish fingers, a long, slow lick, a grunt of appreciation … and then an endless avalanche of naughty nuzzles, sweet sucks, lavish licks, and sighs—*her sighs*—while Jaxon knelt on the floor at the end of her bed massaging her thighs further and further apart while worshipping at the altar of Venus.

She'd never felt so alive. So turned on. So beautiful. Or so ready.

"Make love to me," she pleaded.

"Soon," he promised. "Soon," he whispered, "Soon," he said before he sent her spiraling into a whole new dimension.

Jaxon was up on the bed kissing her while her higher self was still spinning, still luxuriating in sensation when the most wonderful awareness—the most welcome of all feelings literally penetrated her body. Suddenly aware that her legs were thrown over his thighs and his body was moving into hers, slowly, reverently, filling her easily, little by little, more and more, in and then back out, and then in just a little more.

They fit.

So well.

Together.

A lifelong yearning satisfied on so many levels.

"Jaxon," she whispered.

"Jinx," he answered.

She opened her eyes and stared into the mesmerizing blue gaze of her beloved. "This is so good."

He nodded, his jaw tense, his concentration fierce.

"You love me," she said amazed.

"I do," he told her earnestly.

"Everything is truly going to be all right," she whispered.

"No, Jinx. Everything is going to be *amazing*."

All of my Heroes of Henderson novels and novellas are complete romances in and of themselves and do not need to be read in any particular order. However, it's a little more fun that way.

Heroes of Henderson full-length Novels
Good Cop
Bad Cop
Top Dog
Tempting Vivi
UnderDog
Mr. Wrong
Mr. Wright
Mr. Wright Now

Heroes of Henderson Novellas
Playin' Cop
Taming Molly
Kissing Cooper ~ A Christmas Quickie

Listed in order

Countdown to a Kiss
A New Year's Eve Anthology

Playin' Cop
Heroes of Henderson ~ Prequel
Previously published as
The Keeper of the Debutantes in
Countdown to A Kiss

Good Cop
Heroes of Henderson ~ Book 1

Bad Cop
Heroes of Henderson ~ Book 2

Taming Molly
Heroes of Henderson ~ Book 2.5
A DuVal Cousins Quickie

Top Dog
Heroes of Henderson ~ Book 3

Tempting Vivi
Heroes of Henderson ~ Book 3.5
A DuVal Cousins Novel

Kissing Cooper
Heroes of Henderson ~ A Christmas Quickie

UnderDog
Heroes of Henderson ~ Book 4

Mr. Wrong
Heroes of Henderson ~ Book 5

Mr. Wright
Heroes of Henderson ~ Book 6

Mr. Wright Now
Heroes of Henderson ~ Book 7

Sign up at *www.LizKellyBooks.com*
to be alerted when new books are released.

About the Author

Growing up every summer in a place where *dancing and romancing* are literally part of its theme song, Liz Kelly can't help but be a romantic at heart. And since her favorite author, Kathleen E. Woodiwiss wrote some of the world's greatest romances, she's just trying to give the world a little more of that. (Okay, maybe a little sexier *that*, but we are now in a new millennium after all.)

A graduate of Wake Forest University, where she met her handsome golf-addicted husband (who is now sporting dark glasses everywhere he goes), Liz is a mother of two grown sons (also sporting dark glasses) and a miniature Labradoodle named Annabelle. They split their time between *The Windy City* of Chicago and the *Fountain of Youth,* a.k.a. Naples, Florida, where dancing and romancing continues on ad infinitum.